Talk a Good Game

— *Game Series* —

Sasha Campbell

Angie Daniels

Caramel Kisses
Publishing

ISBN-13: 978-1-941342-03-9

Caramel Kisses
Publishing

Caramel Kisses Publishing
PO Box 2313
Chesterfield, VA 23832
www.caramelkissespublishing.com

Cover Image:
www.Colorful-Covers.com

Talk a Good Game

— Game Series —

Sasha Campbell

Angie Daniels

Caramel Kisses
Publishing

Books you might also like by Sasha Campbell:

Confessions
Suspicions
Scandals
Consequences

Books you might also like by Angie Daniels:

In the Company of My Sistahs
Trouble Loves Company
Careful of the Company You Keep

1

NYREE

I was talking to Veronica when I spotted Janelle Fox strutting her thick ass back to our table.

"What do you have now?" I asked and frowned at the fresh drink in her hand.

"Hell if I know. I just told the bartender to make sure it had vodka in it." Janelle laughed and Veronica and I joined in. Everyone knew my girl can drink you under the table. I've known her long enough to know, she rarely knew when enough was enough.

"Did you get a chance to holla at Chuck?" I asked.

Janelle blew out a heavy breath as she flopped down onto the chair to my right. "Girl, trifling! I tried to ask him how his parents were doing and the second he opened his mouth, I smelled his breath."

"Hell nah!" Our good friend Veronica Houston, tall and attractive, was practically falling out of her chair.

While sipping from the glass in front of me, I looked across the room at Charles. Chuck Beats was who he was known as. He was the radio host of 'After Dark Talk' on 101.2. He had a deep bedroom voice that could make a chick want to drop her panties. Chuck and Janelle used to date back in the day until his ego got in the way of their relationship. I guess he didn't get the memo. When it comes to Janelle Fox it has to be all about her or she's off to the next.

I glanced over at her licking her lips, shamelessly, as she scanned the ballroom for a candidate worthy enough to take home. My eyes traveled from Janelle's designer shoes, up her shapely legs to the red dress that hugged her thick curves. Janelle had the cutest shape with big titties, a small waist, wide hips and ass for days. I'd always admired her dark mahogany skin and big chocolate eyes. Getting a man had never been an issue — keeping one was the problem.

We were all laughing and talking at the same time when the lights dimmed and the MC was once again on the mic.

"Ladies and gentleman, the bride and groom will now have their first dance."

I watched as Gloria stepped out onto the dance floor in a beautiful white floor-length gown that accented her petite frame. We had attended Columbia College together and became good friends. Back then she had been all about getting her education. Now it was quite obvious the only thing on her mind was that fine-ass man dragging her into the circle of his arms.

Their wedding had been held at Second Baptist Church followed by a reception at the Holiday Inn Executive Center with over five hundred guests. Everything had been perfect from the pink roses down to the tender roast beef.

All three of us were quiet as we watched them dance together to Luther Vandross's *'Here and Now'*. The way Gloria's husband was looking at her it was like she was the only person in the entire room. Hell, I'm not going to lie. I was happy but jealous as all get out.

"Damn, I still haven't had a chance to ask Gloria where she met him," Janelle said as if she'd read my mind. She'd never admit it but there was envy in her eyes as well.

"Gloria met Pierre online."

We both turned on our seats and looked at Veronica, my crazy-ass light-skinned friend, who could have been Vanessa Williams's little sister.

"Online?" I repeated.

Smiling, she leaned over the table and nodded. "Uh-huh. Gloria met him on that site they've been advertising on television, www.Blackfolksmeet.com."

"What? I've seen the commercials." I gasped. "Wow! I

didn't know that."

"Neither did I," Janelle said and looked equally surprised. "I can't believe she met someone *that* fine on the Internet."

Veronica nodded. "I know. Right. When she told me that I was shocked."

I was still shaking my head with disbelief. "I thought only busters posted personal ads." I was still trying to process what she had said.

"Exactly," Janelle mumbled.

I turned toward the dance floor, again. Damn, Pierre was fine. When I had first spotted him standing at the altar I was floored. Getting a woman shouldn't have been a problem for him at all. How'd Gloria get to be so lucky? Better yet, when was it going to be my time to shine?

"Here's my take on online dating..." Veronica began as she waved a finger in my direction. "Everyone doesn't have time to be hanging out at the club, so if you're not into that type of thing how else are you going to meet somebody?" she added with a shrug.

Janelle brought the drink to her lips. "I guess you do have a point. But damn! It's like that?"

I laughed. "I know that's right."

Veronica grinned and sat back in her chair, sending her curls bouncing. "Hey, the proof's in the pudding."

"True that," Janelle chimed in as she swayed her head from side to side, showing off her bone-straight weave.

I continued to gaze out onto the dance floor. The way Gloria was staring up at Pierre, grinning from ear to ear, she knew everyone was looking and was enjoying every minute of it. "I think I might have to check out that site." My thoughts were consumed with envy so I wasted no time reaching into my small purse to look for something to write on.

"Hell yeah." Janelle reached over and grabbed a napkin. I settled for a business card some fat dude had given me when we had first arrived at the reception.

Glancing over at Veronica, I asked, "What's that site again?"

"Black folks meet dot com."

I scribbled down the web address, then returned the card and the pen to my Louis Vuitton purse. "The way my luck has been lately. It definitely can't hurt."

Janelle looked at me with a knowing look. "That's for sure."

She's never been married. None of her relationships have lasted for long. But I wasn't one to talk. I married right out of high school to a dude who was a straight joke. Shane was too busy trying to be a rapper that he felt being married would stand in his way. Since then I'd had numerous dead-end relationships and have even been engaged three other times but none ever amounted to anything. It seemed the older you get the harder it is to find someone. I'm thirty with a promising career in the military, my own house, a Lexus and good credit, yet finding a man who was at my level was close to impossible.

I reached for my glass and allowed a peek at a table on the other side of the room. There he was—a man who I thought was my second chance. Rock. He was a recruiter, thirty-five, and fine as hell.

That man was so good in bed, he kept a sistah's toes curled and her kitty wet. And there was nothing he wouldn't do for me except leave his wife.

I gazed over at him, looking fine as hell in a black suit, and then, at the female sitting next to him. A woman hated to admit when another chick was cute, but his wife Regina definitely had that whole Solange Knowles thing going on from the natural hair down to her retro look. She also had his son. Now how in the world could I compete with that? Nope, I needed to stay the hell away and find a man of my own.

"If I wasn't in love with my boo, I would be all over that dating site," Veronica said breaking into my thoughts. I glanced over to see this coy grin on her face then leaned in closer so she could hear me over the beat of the music.

"Hooker, don't be lying. I know your nosy ass better than you know yourself." Veronica and I go way back to Girl Scout days.

Janelle looked her dead in the mouth. "You're lying."

We both stared her down until Veronica finally started laughing. "Y'all think you know me!"

"Because we do," I told her. "Now spill it, Ronnie."

When she finally stopped laughing, she nodded her head. "Yeah, I was on it."

Janelle leaned closer. "And?"

She licked her lips the way she always does when she's about to dish some gossip. "Well... the only way you can see the men on the site you have to set up a trial account. So I entered a phony name and information."

"Did they make you add a picture?" I asked in a rush.

Veronica shook her head. "It's optional so I declined. Although if the two of you are interested I suggest uploading a photo. The last thing you want to do is meet a man if you haven't seen what his body looks like. There are a lot of overweight men on that site," she added with an exaggerated shudder.

"I know that's right," Janelle said and gulped down what was left in her glass.

"Okay, get back to your story," I said, with an impatient wave of the hand.

Veronica smoothed a hand across her curls before continuing. "Anyway, I set up an account and browsed through the men." She paused long enough to lick her lips again. "Girl, once you weed out all the buzzers there are some fine men on the site!"

I fell back against the seat. "Single *and* live in Columbia?" That was hard to believe. In this college town all the good ones have already been snatched up. The only ones left were someone else's leftovers. I looked over at Janelle and both our brows rose at the same time. "I guess I need to check it out."

She was grinning and nodding at the same time. "Hell yeah."

We raised our glasses in time for the toast.

"Just be careful." Veronica looked dead serious. "There's a lotta nuts out there."

I would definitely have to keep that in mind.

2

JANELLE

It was almost ten by the time I pulled in front of my three-bedroom townhouse. As I stepped out of my Honda Accord, my drunk-ass stumbled on the heel of my stiletto. I knew I had no business driving tonight and should have accepted Nyree's offer to take me home. But my ass had always been hardheaded.

I'll give it to her. My girl be watching me like a hawk most of the time and if she knew I had two more drinks while standing at the bar, she would have snatched my keys out of my hand so fast I would have seen stars. I know she worries about me because I do have a habit of getting carried away, especially when I'm old enough to know better.

Nyree and I have known each other for almost fifteen years and been best friends ever since we met in drama club. Over the years we'd gone through everything under the sun and then some. Tall and athletic, tonight she looked posed and sophisticated in a black after-five dress. Just once I would love to see her in something tight and skanky. Hee-Hee! That shit wasn't happening. Nyree had too much class for that. A ho like me didn't give a fuck. Sometimes I wondered how we were even friends and then I remembered opposites attract.

I stepped inside and was greeted at the door by my adorable Pomeranian. "Hey Honey, sweetie," I cooed and scooped my baby in my arms and cuddled him close before stepping back onto the porch and letting him out. Honey was the closest thing I wanted to a child of my own. Kids just weren't my thing.

After Honey got done taking care of his business, we moved upstairs to my master bedroom and I quickly shed my clothes and those damn shoes. Black with rhinestones, they were cute to look at but hell on my feet. I stepped inside my large walk-in closet, glancing at the customs shelves filled with shoes. One hundred pairs to be exact. The rest of the closet was lined with designer clothes, some still with tags on them. I loved my room. When I first bought the house I had taken two of the four bedrooms, had the wall knocked down and converted the space into a master suite that beat any of the shit I saw on HGTV.

I tossed my clothes into the hamper and padded my luscious ass into the ensuite which was my oasis. Heated floors, large jetted tub, Moroccan tile. The beautiful thing about being single and living by myself is that it's all about me. My home was my pride and joy. Eventually I wanted something bigger and grand but this would definitely do for now.

It wasn't until I stepped out of the large glass encased shower and returned to my room that I noticed the phone on my nightstand blinking. I reached over, dialed in my password and listened to the message.

Yo, Janelle… this Al. When you gonna let me kiss that sweet —

I hit Delete and slammed the phone down. Alphonso was a real estate investor who had taken me to dinner last weekend. I thought he had the potential of becoming my newest sponsor until I saw the way he ate his food. It was so disgusting, watching him slurp and slob that I had quickly lost my appetite. After that performance there was no way in hell I could have imagined him kissing my lips or any other parts of my body, and I'd been avoiding his calls ever since.

I slipped into a cute pink nightie I found at *Fredrick's of Hollywood* and then slid my feet into a pair of cute white house slippers. I was just getting ready to head down to the kitchen when I remembered our conversation at the wedding reception.

What do you have to lose?

After my date with Alphonso, not a damn thang. And I have to admit the possibility of meeting someone decent for a change was too tempting to pass up. Face it, at thirty, good dick was almost impossible to find. The good men were either already married or sticking their dicks in something I refused to be sloppy seconds to.

I went back into my bedroom, reached inside my purse for the napkin with the web address on it, and screamed when I couldn't find it. I tried to search my brain and decided I must have used it to spit out that piece of stale gum right before the wedding cake had been served.

I grabbed my cellphone and dialed Nyree's number.

"Hey Jae, you get home okay?"

I blew out a loud breath. Never have I been too drunk to find my way home. Let her tell it, you would think I had a drinking problem. "Please. I've already taken my shower."

"Oh good. *Gurrrl,*" she began, changing the subject. "Rock has been blowing up my phone ever since we left the wedding."

"Really?" He was some square she'd been dating the last few months. "And?"

"And I've been blowing him off. If he was interested in talking to me, he should have done that while we were at the wedding."

"You know why he didn't. His wife was there." I flopped down on the bed.

"Exactly. Rock said he dropped her off at home and wanted to know if he could come by my place and see me." She blew out a breath. "Whateva."

I could hear something in her voice that said she was almost tempted. I don't blame her. Rock was fine. And rumor had it he was slinging dick!

"Girl, forget his trifling ass." Men like him will never know how to truly appreciate a good woman. "Hey, what's the website Ronnie was telling us about?"

"Black folks meet dot com. Why? You about to sign up?"

"Yep. I don't have shit else to do but go to bed, and I'm not sleepy."

Nyree suddenly yawned in the phone. "Well, let me know what you think. I'm about to work-out and then call it a night."

That chick loved working out. The only exercise I got came from fucking. Hell, I've read you can burn over five hundred calories from dickercise.

I promised to holla at her after church tomorrow, then ended the call and tossed my phone onto the bed. I went to the kitchen, grabbed a bottle of water and moved up to the guest room. I flicked on the light then took a seat in front of my desktop computer. The whole time I was setting up my account, I was grinning like a damn fool. I guess I was excited that something new was happening.

I decided to call myself FoxTrot. After putting in the initial information, it was time to talk about me. Something I know all about.

> First off... I like a man who keeps it real. I'm not into the games and pretending you don't have another woman yet you're unavailable every weekend. Come on. Silly rabbit, tricks are for kids. I'm a grown-ass woman who demands to be respected.

By the time I had completed the first paragraph, my fingers were racing across the keyboard. I probably shouldn't have been putting up a personal ad knowing I wasn't in my right state of mind; but to be honest, I really didn't give a fuck. I couldn't wait to see what happened next.

I finally went to bed around midnight and while I was closing my eyes I remembered something my favorite aunt used to say.

Be careful what you wish for because you might end up with more than you can handle.

3

NYREE

After I got off the phone with Janelle, I went into the spare bedroom and decided to do a round of kickboxing. It was probably my favorite workout program. Besides, I needed to sweat off some alcohol. I hadn't drunk much but enough to be considered intoxicated, which always made me nervous. I'm a Master Sergeant in the United States Air Force and getting caught driving drunk is not tolerated. If I lost my security clearance, my career would be ruined.

I slipped on my gloves and put in my workout DVD and went to work pounding on a bag in the spare room. The entire time I was thinking about Gloria and how jealous I felt. Weddings always made me feel that way which is why I didn't want to go in the first place. I wanted a man—my own man. But finding one who had himself at least halfway together seemed to be next to impossible. It didn't make any sense. I was tall with a nutty brown complexion and light brown eyes. I wore a short Rihanna haircut and considered myself pretty. Hell, I was smart and educated, and yet I couldn't find a man worthwhile. I figured at my age I'd have been married with two kids by now. Instead I had neither. Sometimes I think maybe it just wasn't God's plan for me. I don't know.

By the time I had gotten done with the video, I was so fired up I repeated the workout before I finally headed to the kitchen for a bottle of water. One quick glance in my refrigerator and I noticed I needed to take my ass to the grocery store after church tomorrow.

I heard a knock at the door that startled me. Who the hell was over at this time of the night? As soon as I yanked open the door, my heart jumped.

"Rock... what are you doing here?"

He stood there licking those delicious lips of his and I felt my vaginal walls contract. Oh my, who could forget how good they had felt stroking my kitty!

"Hey beautiful. Can I come in?"

Lord knows, I tried to roll my eyes and act like I was angry to see him, but there was something about Rock Curtis I just couldn't resist. But I tried anyway. "I guess," I said and released a long frustrated breath before I stepped aside so he could enter. As he passed I caught a whiff of his cologne. That man always managed to smell so good.

I closed the door, locked it then swung around with my arms crossed below my breasts. I was sweaty as hell and pissed Rock had caught me looking a hot mess. Nothing worse than your ex-boyfriend catching you looking less than perfect.

"What do you want?"

He stood there grinning and still licking his lips. "You. I want you."

I ain't gonna lie. His deep baritone voice had my body quivering. I tried not to fall victim to his voice or the throbbing between my thighs. "And what would your wife have to say about that?"

"I don't care what she thinks." He gave me a serious look, then sighed. "C'mon Nyree. Give me a break." He reached out, took my hand and I let him lead me over to my sofa where we took a seat. He turned so that we were facing each other and I caught myself staring into those chocolate eyes of his that always made me feel like I had been caught under some spell. "I know I lied to you about my relationship with my wife and I'm sorry."

"Sorry isn't going to cut it," I snapped.

He shook his head. "I know that now. When I saw you tonight, I realized I had been wrong. But I had to come and tell you, I don't love my wife, I love you."

I was so sick of hearing his lies. "If that was the case then why were y'all at the wedding together?" My head was rolling around my neck.

He shrugged. "Appearances, that's all. She's still my wife but after I saw you, I realized I can't keep on living a lie."

I held my breath and tried to ignore how good his fingers felt caressing the back of my hand.

"Nyree, I—"

"What Rock? What do you want?" I cut him off with a little attitude. Mostly because I was mad at what I was feeling.

"If you'd let me finish...," he began. "I came over here to tell you, after the wedding, I asked Regina for a divorce."

My breath stalled and I stared him dead in the eye. I couldn't believe I was hearing the words I've been waiting months to hear. I searched his expression trying to see if he was just running game, but his eyes were soft and sincere.

"Say something," he prompted with a small insecure smile. I couldn't believe he was nervous but it was written all over his face.

I gave a soft laugh. "I don't know what to say." And I didn't. Hell, do you know how long I waited to hear those words?

Rock smiled brightly. "I'm hoping you'll say you're willing to take a mothafucka back."

I was ready to jump into his arms, but it was taking everything I had to keep my ass planted on that sofa. "How do I know you ain't lying?" I said taking a deep breath.

I guess he saw the skepticism in my eyes, because Rock brought my hand to his lips and kissed it. "Because if you'll let me, I plan on waking up in your bed in the morning."

Oh snap! I was grinning like a damn fool. Rock never stayed the night. I mean never. He might have stayed until one or two in the morning, but he always went home to Regina.

"I love you and I want to start making it up to you."

"I don't know what to say."

"Say you love me. Tell me it isn't too late for us."

I met his lips halfway and he kissed me like a starving man

and I was prime rib.

"Oooh! Baby, wait a minute."

He pulled back and looked confused. "What's wrong?"

"I'm all sweaty. Let me run and take a shower."

"Babe for what? I'm about to get you all sweaty again." He tried to reach for me, but I pushed hard against his chest. There was no way in hell I was about to let him get some with me smelling like a wild animal. I hadn't had any from him in almost a month and nothing was stopping me tonight from feeling them lips on my clit.

"I'll be right back. I promise," I said, pleading with my eyes for him to hold on. "Watch TV or something." I tossed the remote at him then dashed upstairs into the bathroom and turned on the water. By the time the water was hot, I had peeled off my sweaty clothes and was climbing in the stall. I was cheesing and got a mouthful of water but I didn't care. I was just glad to have my man back. I lathered up, then glanced down at my kitty and noticed I had a bush. There was no way he was going down with my kitty looking like Grizzly Adams. I stepped out, grabbed my razor and gave her a quick haircut, then climbed back in and lathered her. By the time I made it into my bedroom, Rock was already undressed and lying across the bed butt-ass naked, looking delicious.

"Damn baby, get on over here." He swung his legs off the side of the bed and signaled for me to come closer.

I was grinning like an idiot as I sauntered up to him, titties and ass jiggling with every step until I was standing between his legs. "Yes? What do you need?" I joked like I didn't have a clue.

"How about I show you."

My knees practically buckled when he held onto my waist, tugged me close, then took my nipple into in his mouth.

Oh damn, that felt good. Rock sucked deeply, drawing my nipple between his lips. My legs shook and I had to hold on to keep from falling.

"You like that, don't you?" His eyes were dark with lust.

"Yes." I was breathing hard.

Rock finally released me, growled playfully, and then

pulled me laughing, onto the bed with him. I rolled onto my back, my head falling onto the pillow. Rock straddled me with his thighs on either side of my hips. I knew what he was looking at.

"I missed them titties." His hands latched on then he squeezed and rolled my sensitive nipples between his fingers.

"Ooh baby!" I moaned in delight and arched up against him. My kitty was aching to be stroked. I frantically worked at his belt and zipper. "Take these off." We could save the foreplay for another time.

He cocked his head to the side. "Damn, you must really miss this dick." His confident ass was grinning as he rolled over and removed his pants and boxers. As soon as his Johnson sprung free, I released a long slow breath. Long, thick and slightly curved, yet it always hit my spot.

"See how bad I want you," Rock said, climbing on top of me. "When he ran his tongue along my neck and down to my nipples, heat and need throbbed through my body. "Spread your legs for me," he said in that sexy voice of his.

My horny ass did exactly as he asked while he dropped down off the edge of the bed and knelt on the floor. He then grabbed my ankles and dragged me down to meet his tongue. The first long lick had me purring like a kitten and the second nearly sent me through the ceiling.

"Yes, Rock. Just like that," I moaned and grabbed his head, holding him in place. No way was he going anywhere before I came. Sure enough, my hips began to move meeting the rhythm of his mouth. "Ooooh, yesss!" Within minutes a scream ripped from my throat. His tongue continued to stroke me until my legs collapsed on the bed.

"You good?" he asked as if he didn't already know.

I was breathing heavily. "Yeah, now get up here."

I slid up on the bed and waited until Rock removed the plastic foil from his wallet. I loved watching my man roll a condom on his Johnson.

He caught me peeking and grinned "You want this, don't you?"

I nodded, thinking about his crooked dick tickling the roof

of my kitty. "Yes, I do."

"Show me just how much you want me."

No problem. I spread for him, slick and ready, and held my arms open, inviting him to take his rightful place between my thighs. He got into position, then locked his gaze, as he raised my hips toward him. Rock entered me slowly, inch by rigid inch. At first, he kept his strokes slow, pulling almost completely out before burying himself deep within me once again. Rock obviously was trying to draw out the pleasure. But, he didn't have any luck at delaying the inevitable.

"Fuck me, dammit!"

Rock picked up speed, plunging into me, the slap of skin almost as loud as the moans escaping my mouth.

"Nyree!" He cried, thrusting into me over and over with pent up frustration. Waves of pleasure consumed my body again. The exact moment I came, his mouth came down over mine with a hunger that sent me spiraling out of control and crying out his name.

"Rock, yesss!"

When Rock finally collapsed on top of me, I wrapped my arms around him and sighed. While I waited for my breathing to slow, a thought came to mind. Now that I had him—now that Rock was mine—it didn't feel quite as satisfying as I had hoped it would be.

4
JANELLE

"Penny, you put the sign out front?" I asked and waited for an answer.

"Yes. It's out there with today's special."

I nodded and was pleased at how well the morning was going. Damn, I loved my job! I strutted through the restaurant making sure each table had been cleaned and place settings were on point. Everything was fabulous of course.

I owned FoxTrot, a chic restaurant that served southern cuisines without all the saturated fats. Folks traveled for miles to taste my peach cobbler and raved about my chicken and dumplings. Not that I expected any less.

Cooking recipes that have been in my family for generations and opening my own restaurant had always been a dream of mine. Now look at me. I've been nominated for *Restaurant of the Year* and I was confident that award was mine.

I strutted in six-inch heels to the kitchen and immediately the scent of collard greens with smoked turkey legs ruffled my nose. As much as I loved food I don't know how I managed to keep this body looking so good.

"How's things going back here?" I asked Mimi, my head chef.

She was stirring a pot of black-eyed peas when she looked up and smiled. "Everything's fine."

"That's what I like to hear. Jamie, I hope you're not burning the cornbread again."

"No cuz," he said with a groan, then moved over to one of the ovens and removed a beautiful golden brown loaf.

"Now that's what I'm talking 'bout." I winked at my second cousin. He got a felony conviction at eighteen for robbing a convenience store. After serving two years I gave him a chance when no one else would. He's still a knucklehead and I know I'm hard on him, but that's because I want him to want to be better.

"All right y'all. We open in less than an hour." I waved, then left the kitchen and moved down the hall to my office. As soon as I stepped in I grinned. The room was all about me. Pink and cream. From the walls to the pink chaise I kept in the corner near the window. This was my escape when the days got long and the nights even longer.

I moved behind my desk and logged onto my computer. I usually advertised in Wednesday's newspaper and I had yet to send this week's special engagement to the editor. Friday we always featured a live band. And this week was the Hump Band, a local favorite. I logged into my email and I noticed a message from Blackfolksmeet.com. My painted lips curled at the notification that I had three flirts and one personal message in my box. Flirts just means someone likes what they see. As a diva, I didn't expect any less. It also meant they were too damn cheap to subscribe to the site, so they weren't able to send a personal message. Since I had a few minutes before the crowd would start coming through the door, I quickly logged onto the site to take a closer look. Three clicks later, I discovered two of the men flirting were straight up busters. But the third sounded interesting.

> Hey FoxTrot. You're sexy as hell. I'm not into head games either. If you want a real man then hit me back.

I clicked onto his picture and stared at him for several seconds.

"Janelle, we still have that big catering order for Saturday?" My cousin said as she appeared outside my door.

"Yep." I gestured with my hand for April to come here. "What's he look like to you?" I waited while she maneuvered her wide hips around my desk and looked closely at the screen.

"Sexy, but he looks mean."

"That's the same thing I was thinking." Jaguar22 as he called himself was golden-brown, with a close cropped haircut, light brown eyes and a salt-n-pepper goatee. I loved a man with pretty teeth. Yet even smiling he looked mean as hell.

Her chocolate eyes narrowed suspiciously. "Whadda you on? One of them Internet dating sites?"

"Uh-huh. Ronnie hooked me up with it."

April moved in for a closer look. "Hmmm, I don't know about him, cuz. You might wanna pass on that one."

"Yep. That's what I was thinking." Although there was something about him I found intriguing. Lord knows I hated a man who was like an open book.

"Who else they got on that site?"

I clicked the mouse and scrolled through every man who had visited my personal ad. There were a couple that looked good enough to eat and several creature features.

"Hold up!" April shouted just as I was about to click on the last one.

"What?"

One of her brows went up and her mouth kind of hung open. "Hell nah! That's Pat's husband."

I tilted my head and looked up at her. "Pat who?"

She gave me a strange look. "Patricia who works over at Hy-Vee in the deli department."

I clicked through all five photos he had posted. "Oh shit! That *is* him." We started howling with laughter. That fool even had the nerve to upload a photo of himself stunting in her Camry.

"Niggas ain't shit." April shook her microbraids, with disgust. "I'm fina call my girl Shonda and put Pat's man on blast." She hurried out of the office and I was still shaking my head. There was no telling how many of these dudes were married.

I was getting ready to head up front for lunch when an instant message flashed across my screen. It was from Jaguar22.

> **What's up sexy? You get my message?**

I couldn't resist a smile. I turned on the charm and typed away at the keyboard.

> **Me: Yep. I got it.**
>
> **JAGUAR: So? Does that mean you're ready to get to know a real man?**
>
> **ME: I don't know. You look mean.**

I was grinning like crazy.

> **JAGUAR: Yeah, my boy said the same thing when I posted the photo. LOL. My bad. Take the time to get to know me and you'll see I'm definitely worth getting to know.**

He just doesn't know how much grinning he had me doing over here. But there was nothing easy about me.

> **ME: That remains to be seen.**
>
> **JAGUAR: Then let's not waste time. How about we hook up this evening somewhere mutual? You pick the place.**

As intrigued as I was to meet Jaguar, I wasn't sure if that was a good idea.

> **ME: I don't know about all that. You might be some kinda stalker.**
>
> **JAGUAR: And so can you.**

"I don't think so," I murmured under my breath. One thing Janelle doesn't do is sweat a brotha, no matter how fine he is.

JAGUAR: C'mon. Pick a place.

I thought about it all of three seconds, then typed

ME: How about Shakespeare's pizza at 7?

The restaurant was only a few blocks away so that would be perfect. The last thing I wanted was for him to come to my spot and I discover I wasn't feeling him.

JAGUAR: Cool. See you then. And wear something sexy.

ME: One thing about me. I always look sexy.

I quickly logged off and hurried to the front to get ready for the lunch crowd. I was looking forward to meeting Jaguar later today.

* * *

We were so slammed all evening I had to hurry to the pizza joint to meet Jaguar. I strutted out the door and down Ninth Street with my bodacious ass swinging with every step. I knew people were driving by, staring at me, just the way I liked it. I was a dime or better yet, a double deluxe. Haters thought I needed to lose a little weight but I loved my curves and had plenty of brothas on speed-dial who would agree. I glanced down at my skinny jeans that hugged my ass. I was also rocking a black and purple corset with a short-sleeved bolero jacket. On my feet were purple stiletto pumps. If I'd had time I would have run by the house and turned it up a notch. Regardless, I was looking every bit of sexy.

It was one of those perfect evenings when the April sun was shining high, yet there was enough of a breeze to keep a sistah from sweating out her shoulder-length weave.

I was just turning the corner when I spotted a high-end, emerald-green car pulling up in front of the pizza joint. To hell with my date when there was something prime parked ahead. I tilted the Versace glasses away from my eyes and slowed my steps and made sure I gazed inside as I swayed my hips past that beautiful car. Much to my pleasure, what was sitting behind the wheel was even more scrumptious.

"What's up sexy? You wanna go for a ride?"

I did a double-take and then my jaw dropped. "Jaguar?"

He gave one of those laughs that made a woman's pussy meow. "Actually it's Kaleb. Jaguar was just my username."

"Mmmm-Hmmm. I see." I struck a cute pose with one hand resting at my luscious hip and swayed over to the curb. Smiling, I leaned inside the car that just happened to be a Jaguar. Naturally his eyes strayed to my twins that were ripe for the picking. There was nothing mean-looking at all about the man sitting behind that wheel. As a matter of fact, he had a smile with the type of lips that made you want to pop out your titty and stick it inside his mouth.

"You're every bit as sexy as your picture."

At least he appreciated beauty. "Of course… did you expect anything less?"

He chuckled again, revealing perfect white teeth. "You'd be surprised the clowns I've met."

I batted my fake eyelashes. "I aim to please."

"You wanna go for a ride?" he suggested.

I looked around. The sun was out. What were the chances of me coming up missing, although I didn't know shit about this dude. "For all I know you're one of them crazy mofos cutting up women and burying them in your backyard."

He nodded. "You're right. I could be."

I thought about it a moment longer, then reached inside my purse, removed my phone and snapped his picture.

"What's up?" he said and laughed.

"Insurance." I took another picture then backed up, snapped his car and even went as far as the license plate. The whole time he sat behind the driver's seat admiring the view.

"I can see you're going to be a piece of work."

"Absolutely. I'ma game changer." I tagged all the photos then sent a text to April.

Girl, I'm with Kaleb aka Jaguar in his Jaguar. LOL.

I was tapping away at my keyboard as I spoke. "Give me a second to send these pictures to my cousin and I'll be ready to roll."

"Are you serious?" he roared with laughter.

I shrugged. "A diva's gotta be careful."

He rubbed a hand across his nearly trimmed goatee. "I understand. Now will you get in?"

"In a second." I wasn't climbing into that bitch until my phone alerted my message had been sent.

"You like to be in charge." He was observant.

"Of course." Damn, the message was taking forever to send.

"Then we're gonna have a problem."

I looked up from my phone and at him. He appeared to be a few years older than me. "Why's that?"

"Because there can only be one boss in this relationship."

"Who said we're in a relationship?" I said and shuddered with excitement.

"Me. Because I'm not window-shopping. When I like what I see, I grab it and you sweetheart have plenty to hold on to."

Ain't that the truth. The message finally left my phone and I reached for the handle and opened the door. I climbed in and sat down on a butter-soft leather seat and grinned over at him. Kaleb's eyes were all over me.

"You're delicious."

For a chick who loved food that was the ultimate compliment. "Thank you. Now take me for a ride."

He finally pulled away from the curb. The air conditioner was on, blowing in my face. I put my Michael Kors purse on the floor then relaxed on the seat and enjoyed the soft R&B music coming from the speakers.

Kaleb drove through downtown. I saw a few people I knew along the sidewalks. Too bad the windows were tinted. I wanted everyone to see me.

"You gonna tell me your name?"

My headed whipped around to gaze at the curious look on his handsome face. I felt my chocolate face become hot at the way he was licking his bottom lip. Damn that goatee looked good on him. "My bad. It's Janelle but everyone calls me Jae."

"Jae huh? Like in juicy?"

I had to laugh. From anyone else that line would have sounded whack, but he just had this swag about him I was feeling.

As he stopped for a red light, he said, "Tell me, as fine as you are, what made you decide to go on a dating site?"

"Curiosity. More than anything else," I explained as I stared out the window. "I meet a lot of rejects."

"Are you seeing anyone now?"

No one worth talking about. "Nope. Single as it gets." I waved my ring finger just in case he hadn't noticed it was naked. "What about you?"

"No one. I don't settle for anything but the best. If you haven't noticed I'm a first-round draft pick."

I couldn't help but laugh. He was cute, but he wasn't all that. However, what he was lacking in looks, his car definitely made up for.

"Why don't you tell me a little about you?" he asked, making conversation.

"That might take all night." I gave him a saucy grin.

"Babe, for you, I've got nothing but time."

I love when a man knows what he wants, especially when that something was me.

As we rode around town, I talked about my restaurant and growing up in that small-ass town. He was a great listener. He didn't interrupt and that was what I liked most. Like I said, it's all about me! When it was finally Kaleb's time to talk I discovered he was from Atlanta and had been in the area for two years.

He made a right on Nifong into a subdivision surrounding the Columbia Country Club of Missouri. It was one of those status neighborhoods with big-ass houses to die for. Even as hard as I worked at the restaurant I was a long way from living this large.

He turned onto a cul-de-sac and pulled in front of a magnificent brick home.

"Whose house is this?" I asked and looked at him.

"Mine." He reached across the seat and laced my fingers with him. "And it can all be yours, if you play your cards right."

My eyes widened as I stared through the window at the mini-mansion. And when Kaleb reached up, pressed a button and the three garage doors opened, I spotted a Range Rover inside and I knew I had to have him.

Janelle Fox has found a new sponsor!

<u>5</u>

NYREE

"He said that?"

"Yes!" Janelle screeched in my ear. "Kaleb said, 'it can all be yours if you play your cards right.' I couldn't believe it! You shoulda seen his crib! Girl, it was something out of a fucking magazine."

I shifted on the seat, drawing the phone closer to my ear. I could just imagine Janelle sitting in her office, doodling dollar signs on a sheet of paper. She never got this excited about anything other than men and money; and when she could get them both in one shot, she was like a freaking lunatic.

While I scrolled through my emails, Janelle went on and on about her latest catch. Don't get me wrong, it wasn't like what she was saying wasn't entertaining. My best friend was beautiful and men were always falling on their faces to get close to her. It was almost comical to say the least. The problem was I had heard this story so many times before I already knew what questions she was waiting for me to ask.

"Are you listening?" Janelle said, when she finally stopped to take a breath.

"Of course, I'm listening. So what's he do for a living?"

"Nyree, *gurrrrrl*, check this shit out."

What did I tell you?

"You know the Walmart heirs that invested all that money in the new basketball stadium at Mizzou?"

"Yep." Everyone has heard of the local family. They invested in several projects including the University of Missouri-Columbia, and owned a huge mansion south of town. My mother was best friends with one of their housekeepers. "What about them?"

"Well, Kaleb manages their money. Can you believe that shit? My man has his hands on Walmart stocks!"

Oh Lord. "Your man?"

"Hell yeah I'm claiming his ass."

Can you believe this chick? Janelle has always been materialistic. Clothes, cars, men, I could already hear the greed in that chick's voice.

"Money, money, money… MONEY!"

I shook my head. "That's all you care about."

"You'd be surprised, but it ain't just about money with Kaleb. I really like him."

"But having money helps."

"Hell yeah it helps," she laughed.

"Is there anything about the man you don't like?" Because there always has to be something.

"Hmmm. Well, I guess it would be his fucked-up walk."

"What?" I chuckled.

"Girl, he walks like he's broken his ankle or some shit in the past. He waddles like a pregnant woman," she laughed.

"You're wrong for that."

"I'm serious. I told him he reminded me of Fred Sanford the way he walks." She was laughing so hard, I joined in.

"So no swag, huh?'

"Uh-uh, don't get it twisted. Kaleb has plenty of swag."

I sucked my teeth. "You mean money?"

"Yeah, that too!" She howled and had me in tears. The older she got, the crazier Janelle became.

"So what are you going to do about Q? Aren't you supposed to be flying to Vegas at the end of the month?"

"Oh shit." She stopped whatever fantasy was conjuring in her brain and sounded shocked. "I was so caught up with meeting Kaleb I forgot all about Q."

What else was new? Quincy Austin was the spare Janelle

kept in her hip pocket. He used to live in Columbia and moved to Dallas three years ago. Ever since then they'd been traveling every other month to see each other. Q was fine as hell, made decent money, was single and had no kids. The problem is Janelle thinks he's a freaking doormat and according to her, his dick wasn't all that.

"Damn, I forgot all about Q." She had the nerve to sound disappointed.

"I don't know why you keep stringing that man along like that."

"You know why. He's good to me, looks good on my arm, and we have a lot of fun together." The fact that she could laugh at this situation irritated me on so many levels. Mainly because he was the type of man I'd love to meet.

"Yes, but you know Q loves you and wants to spend his life with you."

"True." He really *did* want to spend his life with her. "I'm just not willing to settle just yet," she replied. "Hey, I'm honest with the dude. He just doesn't want to hear it. I'm not ready for a committed relationship."

"Yeah, but Q thinks that when you do, he's gonna be the one."

"Then that's what he gets for thinking. I've got more important things to worry about. I just need to figure out how I'm going to get away for a weekend without Kaleb finding out the truth." It was always about what Janelle wanted, when she wanted it. To her it was that simple.

I blew out a breath. "Why can't you just be honest? After all, this is something you had planned long before this dude came into the picture."

There was silence for a moment. "Yeah, you're right. There's no point in starting off a relationship with a lie. I just liked him so much I don't wanna ruin a chance at being happy with a man who's everything I want in a man."

She meant money. I gave a rude snort. "I guess."

"Anyway… have you set up your personal ad yet?" she asked, totally ignoring my response.

"Yes, and I've received several flirts but nobody I'm

interested in."

"That's because you're too damn picky!"

She thinks she knows me. "I'm not picky. I'm just getting too old for all the games. I want something meaningful."

"Like your relationship with Rock," she said and then had the nerve to laugh.

Leave it to her to go there. Janelle hated the idea of me settling down, and having a family. She wanted me single, partying, and dating a new man every week like her. Part of me thinks she's afraid some man would become more important in my life than her. What she doesn't understand is she was the closest thing I have to a sister.

"Girl, I'm not playing second to nobody. I am a helluva woman and I make sure everyone knows it. You need to do the same. Trust me Ree. Respect is earned and you have to make a man respect you or he'll think he can do whatever he wants to you. And then after a while, you'll stop even respecting yourself."

Janelle was independent and impatient. Love and family weren't her top priority so she would never really understand. "I'm not rushing into anything. Just taking it slow. In fact we're going to St. Louis tomorrow for the weekend."

"Uh-huh. Why is it you have to go outta town to spend time together?" She actually sounded upset.

I didn't know what to say.

"Don't you get tired of being the other woman?"

I looked outside my office door to see if anyone was close enough to overhear before I said, "He left his wife."

She had the audacity to raise her voice. "He's left her before and for how long?" She blew out a breath. "Ree, life is too short. It's about to be summertime. Have some fun. Live a little. We're barely in our thirties so we've got plenty of time for husbands and those got-damn two and a half kids you wanted so badly."

She didn't understand. I was sick of dating and being in dead-end relationships. I wanted something with substance. I was sick of wasting time. And I was crazy about Rock.

"I just care about you, that's all." She almost sounded

sincere. Don't get me wrong. There has never been a time when Janelle hasn't had my back. She was just so self-absorbed that you didn't see it as often as with regular people.

"You heard from Gloria?" I asked changing the subject.

There was a brief pause and I know she was sitting there rolling her eyes. Too bad. I was tired of talking about me. "Yeah girl. She and Pierre are back from the honeymoon. You know he took her to Cabo San Lucas, right? I hate that bitch," she added with a hint of jealousy.

"No you don't." I laughed. "You just hate to see anyone have what you want."

"That's true." She giggled. "But it's now my time to shine. You'll see."

* * *

I left National Guard headquarters and headed out and across the parking lot for a dental appointment, feeling good. I hadn't spoken to Rock all day, however, we were all set to head to St. Louis tomorrow evening for the weekend and I couldn't wait.

It was still hard to believe he was finally mine.

After the night of the wedding, Rock had moved into a hotel. He worked as a recruiter for the School of Engineering and traveled a lot during the week and sometimes over the weekends, but at least I had him at home in my bed several nights this last week. There was nothing like a man who could stimulate your mind and your body. And that man was Rock.

By the time I had gotten done with my six-month dental cleaning, I decided to drop by Rock's office and surprise him. I climbed off the highway at the Stadium exit and made my way across the University of Missouri campus to the School of Engineering.

My mom called as I was turning into the garage.

"Hi Mom," I said as I pulled up the ramp.

"Hello Nyree, I was calling to see if you were coming to dinner this Sunday."

"No Mom." I'm sure I'll never hear the end of it. "I'm

going to St. Louis for the weekend. Why?"

"Because I have someone I want you to meet."

I groaned. There was no way I was going through that matchmaking BS again. "Mom, no."

"Ree, it's just a friend's son."

"Definitely not." I pulled into the garage and cussed under my breath.

"How do you expect to meet anyone if you're not even trying? He's really a nice guy."

Her nice guy meant he was boring as hell. "Mom, I'm seeing someone."

"You are?" There was no mistaking the excitement in her voice.

"Yes. I've been seeing someone for quite a while. He's amazing."

"Really?" Mabeline Dawson didn't sound like she believed me. "When are you bringing him home for your father and I to meet him?"

I blew out another long breath as I pulled into a parking spot. "I'll bring him to dinner on Sunday." We weren't planning on being back until late Sunday evening, but I was sure if I told Rock how important it was, he would agree to dinner.

"Excellent. I'll see you then."

I hit End and climbed out the car and made it almost down to the end of the hall, before I heard someone say, "Thank you for your service."

I smiled at the man with silver hair. "Thank you. I'm proud to be of service." I nodded then continued to walk down the long hall already regretting my decision not stopping long enough to change first. That was the problem with wearing my battle uniform. People always wanted to stop to thank me or shake my hand. I should feel proud but some days it could be quite annoying.

Straight ahead was a pair of double-glass doors, leading to the Dean's office. I walked through and as soon as I turned the corner toward Rock's office I stopped in my tracks. There was no way in hell I was seeing what I thought I saw.

Rock holding hands with his skinny-ass wife.

I stood there witnessing the intimate exchange between them before I decided to make my presence known.

"Hello, may I help you?"

I stopped staring long enough to glance over my shoulder at the young girl sitting behind the reception desk. "No, you may not," I snapped and swung back around to find him staring dead in my face. I walked over to the couple and watched as Rock bit his lip nervously as I approached. "What the—"

"Master Sergeant Dawson," he blurted, cutting me off. "I thought our *meeting* was tomorrow." There was no mistaking the desperation in his voice for me to play along.

"Well, you thought wrong," I said, trying to smile.

Mrs. Size 4 placed a hand to her husband's chest and I noticed the huge diamond sparkling on her ring finger. "Sweetheart, am I interrupting something?" she asked the way women do when we know something smells funny. She was right to be alarmed. She smelled straight bullshit.

Rock stepped back, trying to regain some of his personal space. "No dear. Not at all. Master Sergeant Dawson is coordinating a recruitment fair at the school." No he wasn't trying to play me!

"It's nice to meet you." Regina fake-smiled me. She obviously didn't recognize me from the wedding. The uniform did have a way of making a woman look like a man.

I decided to play dumb. "I'm sorry, Rock. I didn't know you were married."

"Ten years." Regina beamed with pride, then gripped her man's arm possessively. "Actually, we're renewing our vows this weekend in Vegas."

"*You're what?*" I couldn't believe his ass.

Suddenly, Regina was looking at me cross-eyed. "Have we met before?"

I wasted no time busting her bubble. "No, but you've probably tasted my pussy on your husband's lips."

His jaw dropped and her lips began to quiver. *Priceless.*

"What the fuck?" she stared at me for several seconds

before returning her attention to him. "Rock, what is she talking about?"

You should have seen the panic on his face. "Sweetheart, I have no idea." He cleared his throat and tried to act confused.

Couldn't she tell her husband was lying? Apparently not because Regina just stood there like an idiot, nibbling on her bottom lip. Some women are so stupid. Although after this incident, I wasn't one to talk.

"Where did you think your husband's been laying his head this last week?" I asked while staring his lying ass dead in the eyes.

Regina blinked her eyes. "I thought you were away at a conference?"

Rock turned up his nose like I was a stanky diaper. "Regina, can we talk about this at home?" he urged and drew his wife in close, and I noticed the way she melted in his arms.

My neck was rolling now. "Regina, he might wanna talk about this at home, but I think you'd rather hear it coming from me first."

She closed her eyes as if she was afraid of what I was about to say. "Hear what?"

"Regina, honey, your husband talks a good game... I'll give it to him." I was talking with my hands the way I always did when I was pissed. "But I've wasted six months fucking his tired ass. Hell, his dick ain't even circumcised." You shoulda seen her eyes. Now that I've rattled off the appearance of her husband's Johnson there was no way she thought I was lying. "All those months he said he was leaving you was a bunch of bullshit." I quickly pointed my finger in Rock's face. "Don't you ever fucking call my phone again!"

I felt the tears surfacing, but I held them back and headed toward the door. There was no way in hell I was going to let either of them see the tears now streaming down my face.

Damn was I really that desperate to be loved?

6

JANELLE

I made a left onto Banks Road and slowed my car to a crawl. There were no cars parked out front so that was a sign Mommy was home alone. I would have preferred someone else had been there. That way I could have dipped in and out in a matter of minutes.

I parked, turned off the car, but sat there staring at that small ranch style house. Last year I'd had siding installed and had a dude build a brand new porch, hoping the face-lift would bring some life to that house.

Yeah, whatever.

There were so many memories and dark secrets behind that door. Things the neighbors would have found hard to believe because to them the Foxes were the perfect family.

Oh, if those walls could talk.

Shaking the thought from my mind, I climbed out and smoothed down the front of my dress. Trust and believe, there was nothing insecure about me, yet, there was something about the house that no matter how much I tried, I couldn't shake a feeling of uneasiness. Lord knows how many times I have dreamed of that bitch burning to the ground. Hell, I had even tried once or twice back in the day but failed.

"Hey Janelle!" Ms. Gina's voice seemed to come out of nowhere.

I waved at the gray-haired woman sitting on the porch across the street. Her face was hidden by the overgrown bushes. "Hey Ms. Gina!" I sang. For years that nosy heifer spent hours watching the neighborhood so she could be in everyone's business. I found it funny because she had no idea what had gone on right across the street.

As usual, the front door was unlocked. I walked inside and immediately felt like I had stepped through a time warp. Plastic on the furniture, shag carpet, and a big floor model television with a record player on top. I ignored that eerie feeling and headed straight back to the kitchen. My mother was sitting at the kitchen table with a cigarette dangling from her bottom lip.

"Hey, Mommy," I said and forced a smile.

"Hello, Jae," she replied. Her entire face lit up the way it always did when she received visitors. Usually because she was feeling lonely. It also meant it was going to be hard as hell to leave.

She pointed to the chair across from her. "Have a seat."

Obediently, I lowered onto the chair. The pleather seat cushion was cracked and biting my ass. I waited while she puffed away at the cigarette, drawing in a breath so deep her dark cheeks looked sunken in.

"Katherine wants me to go with her to the casino in Boonville on Friday."

"That's good Mommy. You need to get out the house more."

"Yeah, yeah, Katherine said the same thing." She rolled her eyes and tried to act annoyed but Mommy loved the way we all fussed over her.

"I agree so go." I reached inside my purse and peeled off two hundred dollars and set it on the table. "Make sure you enjoy yourself."

"We'll see how I'm feeling tomorrow."

A small television was on the counter and one of those stupid soap operas was playing. Dishes were piled high in the sink and the floor hadn't been swept or mopped in days. I glanced around the tiny room with limited preparation space and remembered when I could barely look over the counter. "Has your housekeeper been by this week?"

She scowled, and waved the cigarette in her hand. "She'll

be here tomorrow."

I nodded and as usual was at a loss for words. "I'll call Brice and have him come over and cut your grass. You need me to pick you up anything from the store?"

"Yeah. Bring me some more cigarettes," She replied and blew a puff of smoke in my face, which pissed me off.

"Mommy, I really wish you'd give up them cigarettes. What did your doctor tell you?"

"What else am I going to do all day?" she argued.

"Where's the crossword puzzles I bought you?"

"On the coffee table. I can only do so many of those."

"Then read a book." I'd brought her over a boxful.

She gave me a knowing look and frowned. "All they talk about is sex!"

I smiled back at her. "Hey, sex sells Mommy."

She wrinkled her nose. "I'm too old for all that. Just get me a good mystery to read."

"I'll bring you one this weekend."

"Has anyone been over today to check on you?"

She nodded. "My nurse was here and then Uncle Todd."

I smiled at the mention of my godfather. "How's he doing?"

"You know him. Always complaining about something," she commented then gave a sad smile. Todd Malcolm had been my father's best friend and like an uncle to me and Brice.

"Have you eaten?"

"Why all the questions?" Mommy snapped, but I didn't take it personal. In the last year she had become increasingly irritated.

I leaned forward before answering, "Because you're my mother and it's my job to make sure you're okay over here by yourself. I don't know why you won't just move in with me." So I could sell this bitch.

She looked frustrated. "I don't know why we keep having this conversation. You know I'm not leaving my house." She took a final draw on the cigarette, then put it out in the ashtray. "My nurse will be back after *Meals on Wheels* delivers my lunch." Avoiding eye contact, she looked over at the television.

"I'll have April bring you over something from the restaurant tonight."

"Have her bring me some of those biscuits. Those are good."

I smirked. "They're rolls not biscuits and that's Granby's recipe."

"It is?" she said and her expression softened. "No wonder they tasted so good. My mama sho did know how to throw down in the kitchen. "

I nodded. "Yes, she did."

I felt myself looking down at my manicured hands. Uh-uh. I wasn't about to started tearing up.

My grandmother had meant the world to me. Growing up she only lived a few blocks away, so I was always able to go over and spend hours watching her cook in the kitchen. When she passed away my entire world crumbled.

I glanced down impatiently, at my watch. The sooner I got out of there the better. "I better get going," I said and rose.

"Before you leave can you go in my room and get that big blue picture album off the shelf in my closet?"

I was slow to answer. "What for?"

There was that frustrated look again. "Because I can't reach it, that's why."

I looked down at her small frail body in the chair, with the blanket draped over the stump that was once her left leg. Diabetes. Years of not listening to her doctor had cost her half her leg.

I hated seeing her that way—incapable of taking care of herself and needing the help of others. Judith Fox had always been quiet and weak with self-esteem issues, now she was subjected to a life at the mercy of others.

I walked back through the living room and down the short narrow hall. The closer I got to her bedroom the harder my heart thumped. The old peeling wallpaper, and the squeaky wood floors didn't help the situation none.

It took everything not to look at the closed door to my right. The room had once been my own personal hell.

I pushed open my parent's bedroom door--because there was no doorknob. There never was any privacy. Not even the bathroom. The only lock had been on the basement door.

I brushed an eerie feeling aside and moved around my mother's unmade bed toward the closet. The sooner I got the album the sooner I could get the fuck out of there.

I opened the closet door and fumbled around on the top shelf and somehow the old wood shelving collapsed and everything came tumbling down.

"Jae! You okay?" my mother cried from the kitchen.

"Yes Mommy! I'm fine." The last thing I wanted was to worry her.

Irritated, I popped the shelf back in place then looked to see what had fallen onto the floor. I reached for a blanket and jumped at what I found underneath.

My father's hat.

The Columbia Police Department. Even after all these years the big brass CPD emblem on front still shined like a new quarter.

I remembered Pops coming through the front door with that hat on his head and the gun holster around his waist.

That had been worse than any nightmare.

Quickly I tossed everything back onto the shelf, then grabbed the album, closed the closet, and hurried into the kitchen.

"Here you go." I was out of breath as I put the book on the table.

Mommy looked pleased. "Thanks. Felicia wants some baby pictures of Brice."

I nodded. My brother's wife had been talking about putting together a collage for their wall.

"Mama, I gotta go." Leaning over, I kissed her cheek and moved toward the door.

"Jae?" she called after me and I stopped in the doorway, and turned around. "Thanks for everything."

I nodded and without another word, rushed out the door and down the sidewalk to the car. Ms. Gina was saying something, but I ignored her nosy ass. All I wanted to do was get inside my car before I fell apart. I climbed in, shut the door and realized my hands were shaking and my heart was beating fast. All because of that damn hat. "You bastard!" I screamed and punched the dashboard.

I will no longer allow you to control me!

I sat there for the longest time, fighting back tears when my cellphone started ringing. Oh shit! I had to take this call. No time for crying. It was Kaleb.

"Hey you," I purred.

"What's going on beautiful?" There was that deep mesmerizing voice of his.

I wiped my eyes and gazed in the rearview mirror as I spoke. "Nothing much. What are you doing?"

"Thinking about you." His words were just what I needed to hear. "My son and I are heading to Applebee's near the mall. You wanna join us?"

I tilted the rearview mirror, took in my appearance while hesitating like I was giving his question some thought. "Sure. I can stop through." Lord knows I needed something else to be thinking about.

I pulled into the parking lot, and made sure my face and hair were perfect. They were. I then climbed out my car, gracefully, and sauntered through the door of the restaurant. I spotted Kaleb immediately, over in the corner, but I played dumb until he started waving to get my attention.

I can be such a bitch.

Smiling, I strutted over to the table where he was sitting across from a lanky kid with glasses.

"You made it." Kaleb rose and planted a kiss to my cheek then whispered, "You look sexy."

Of course I do.

"Jae, this is my son, Christopher John Kerrington, but we call him CJ."

As I sat down next to Kaleb onto the bench, I grinned at the kid who looked really uncomfortable. "Hi CJ."

"Hi," he said and pushed his glasses up onto his face.

I liked kids, just as long as they weren't my own.

Kaleb shifted on the bench. "We just ordered. You want

something?"

I turned up my nose. "No, the food here is horrible."

He shrugged. "True, but it's CJ's favorite."

I could tell the kid had self-esteem issues. His shoulders were hunched and he was staring down at his napkin. Goodness, this was why I didn't want kids.

He was dark chocolate unlike his father, with a round face dotted with acne. His hair was cut too low for the fine grade, so you could practically see his scalp, and the long sleeve t-shirt he was wearing had seen better days. For someone with money, Kaleb definitely wasn't spending it on his son's appearance.

I decided to order a diet soda and some potato twisters. They were hell on my hips, but I planned on burning them off soon and I didn't mean in the damn gym. Kaleb was rubbing my knee under the table, and I was caressing the part of him I had yet to be introduced. After three dates, numerous kisses, and me rubbing on his dick, I was certain Kaleb was probably getting tired of me teasing him. Personally I didn't see it as playing hard to get. A man needed to earn the right to fuck me. Pussy this good didn't come cheap.

Besides it served him right for trying to play me all day. He wanted to play games. Then bring it out. I was the queen of bullshit.

CJ was tapping his finger, annoyingly, on the table. I had to grit my teeth to keep from demanding he stop. "So how's school?" I asked.

"It's good." *Tap. Tap. Tap.*

Okay, so much for a conversation.

"He's a straight A student," Kaleb offered and was grinning like a proud father.

"Really?" I was impressed. Since he was intelligent maybe being his stepmother wouldn't be *that* bad. "That's excellent. What's your favorite subject?"

"Science."

"That's impressive. You ever attend any science fairs?"

He shook his head.

"We'll have to look into that." I nodded my head. "As a

matter of fact, I have a friend who runs a summer minority enrichment program and if you have good math and science I might be able to get you in this summer."

While I talked to him about living in a dorm on the university campus, his eyes grew big. He kept looking over at his dad, who was leaned back on the seat still grinning. Other than their round faces the two didn't look anything alike. And if CJ looked like his mom then it was no wonder Kaleb thought he had won the lottery with me.

The waitress returned with my diet soda.

"What have you been doing today?" Kaleb asked as she moved to the next table.

I took a sip then looked in those big pretty eyes of his. "I just left from visiting my mother."

Intrigue was written all over his face. "Both your parents still around?"

It took everything I had to keep a straight face as I said softly even though I was certain CJ was listening, "My father passed away."

"What happened?"

As far as I knew the man had gone straight to hell. "He was a cop. He died while investigating a burglary." Remembering his hat falling onto the floor flooded my mind and actually gave me goose bumps. "What about you?"

Kaleb took a sip from his straw as he spoke. "My parents live in Houston. Them, my sister... we all have our own lives so we don't really talk much."

I wondered which was worse, his family or mine?

"It's just me and my son. Right CJ?"

His eyes shifted to the table before he nodded. "Yes sir."

"He's quiet, isn't he?" Except for that damn tapping. I don't know why the sound didn't bother his father because it sure annoyed the hell out of me.

"Dad, may I be excused to the restroom?"

Kaleb nodded, and he sprang from the seat, hitting his knee on the table.

"Slow down!" he scolded a little too loudly. I noticed the couple at the next table looking at us.

CJ looked so embarrassed I almost felt sorry for him. "Yes sir," he mumbled then hurried off toward the restroom.

When I turned on the seat, I could tell Kaleb was waiting for me to say something about his kid. "How old is he?" That was the best I could come up with.

"Going on thirteen."

"Goodness, he's tall!" CJ had to be about six feet.

Kaleb gave me a sexy smirk. And to think I thought he looked mean. "Yeah, I guess he takes that after my side of the family."

I shifted on the seat to make sure he saw my good side. Oh hell, either one was my good side. "Where's his mother?"

His face suddenly became very serious. "Dead."

"Dead," I mocked. "I'm sorry. What happened?"

"She was shot." Kaleb leaned in close and lowered his voice so no one else would overhear us. "She had dropped by the grocery store on her way home from work. Someone shot her in the parking lot and took her purse." He shook his head and there was no mistaking the despair. "My wife never carried more than twenty bucks."

"I'm sorry to hear that. Did they ever catch the person who did it?"

"Hell no." He shifted on the seat and I could tell this was hard for him to talk about. "The camera in the parking lot was a piece of shit. No leads. Nothing."

I raised an eyebrow. "How old was CJ at that time?"

"He was three. He doesn't even remember his mother. Sometimes I wonder if that's a good or a bad thing."

I placed a hand on his forearm. "It's up to you to keep the memories alive."

"Anyway, that was almost ten years ago." He reached down and squeezed my knee again. "I have finally come to terms with what happened and let go because I know her memory will always be with me. But right now I want to focus on this beautiful... sexy woman sitting beside me."

I was cheesing. So much for playing it cool. "I have no problem with that."

CJ returned around the same time the food arrived. We

joined hands and while their heads were bowed I peeked out the slits of my eyes and glanced at them. Kaleb was praying while CJ was fidgeting on the seat. Dammit. I needed to pray for patience. Something I've never had.

7

NYREE

I glanced down at my phone. Rock's lying ass had been calling me for the past week trying to get me to listen to him. The last thing I wanted was to hear his excuses.

I tried watching the basketball game. The Oklahoma Thunders was my team and they were beating the Boston Celtics, but I just wasn't hyped like I was used to. I decided to call Janelle. She answered but I could barely hear her.

"Why are you whispering?" Damn, now she had me doing it.

"Because I'm in the bathroom taking a bath, tryna get this kitty-kat smelling fresh to death and nothing less."

"I was calling to see if you wanted to go and see a movie this evening."

"Nah, I'm hoping to have my legs up in the air," she said and I giggled loudly. Janelle had the nerve to start hushing me like that dude could really hear me. "Rock still blowing up your phone?" she asked, suspiciously.

I sucked my teeth for great measure. "You know he is."

She tsked in the phone. "I told you that man wasn't leaving his wife."

"Yeah, yeah." I don't know why I had even told her except I needed to talk to someone. Veronica was out of town and Gloria was too busy with her new husband, besides I had to admit Janelle really is a good listener. I just wished I hadn't told my mother about having a new man in my life. I'll never hear the end of it.

"Listen Ree, I gotta go. But, I'll call you later."

I hung up feeling a little disappointed. Ever since she started dating Kaleb, Janelle barely had time for me. Not that I was hating. I was happy she had found someone she really liked. I just wished it was me.

I was watching the second quarter when I logged onto Blackfolksmeet.com, and scanned my Flirts then decided to upload a photo to my profile during the half-time show. I then answered a few random questions that were pretty standard, and when it came to what I was looking for in a man, I decided to change it up and just keep it real.

> I'm looking for a Christian man who will keep it 100
> with me. No head games. No married men. Serious
> inquiries only.

I hoped that would help to weed out the ones who were strictly window-shopping. I had heard the rumor about men joining these sites just for something to do because they were unhappy with their marriages. I wasn't going there. Not anymore. Rock made me feel like a fool and I couldn't blame anyone but myself.

I posted two of my favorite photos, one I had taken at Gloria's wedding and one while clowning with some girls in my unit, then republished my profile.

Feeling slightly hopeful, I sprung from the couch and grabbed some snacks. I was munching on cheese puffs and watching the second half of the game while I surfed Blackfolksmeet.com for a potential match. Veronica wasn't lying. There were some fine men on there, which made me wonder if they're really single or just running game. Like Rock's tired ass.

Derek Fisher had landed a three pointer when I noticed an instant message on my screen from a BOO-MAN29.

> How are you doing?

Before responding, I clicked on his photo to get a closer

look and frowned. He wasn't bad looking although his bald head was like a honeydew melon. But I had to admit as I scrolled through all his photos, he wasn't half bad. Dark skin, big eyes, and there was a cute, boyish look about him.

> Me: Hey. You watching the game?

I figured that would be a good way to get the conversation going. I hadn't met a man yet who didn't like sports.

> BOO-MAN: Most definitely. Let me guess, you're a Celtic fan?

> Me: Nope. OKC all day long.

We went back and forth and in the meantime I received a few messages and Flirts from some other members, but nobody worth striking up a conversation. I had just returned from a bathroom break when I noticed another message from BOO-MAN.

> BOO-MAN: I read your profile. Are you bitter?

Bitter? I guess I never thought about it like that.

> ME: No. I'm not bitter. Just wiser. I deserve nothing less than love and respect.

Both were things that bastard, Rock, didn't know the first thing about.

> BOO-MAN: Just make sure you don't take your anger out on every man you meet. You might miss out on your soul-mate.

I had to smile at his comment. He was right. I couldn't blame everyone else for Rock taking my kindness for weakness.

> ME: Thanks for the advice.

He immediately messaged me back.

BOO-MAN: If you feel like it, give me a call

I waited until after I made dinner and then I called the number he had messaged me. I couldn't believe the way my hands were shaking. He answered after the first ring.

"Hello."

I turned up my nose. Eww! I didn't like his voice. It was all squeaky and soft like a little boy.

"Hey this is Nyree."

"Hi Nyree. My name is Jeremy Anthony Lee Samuels, Jr."

"Damn, you have a long name!" I said, trying to break the ice and expected him to laugh but I guess he didn't think it was funny. "What should I call you?"

"My friends call me Jeremy."

"Hmmm, maybe I can call you Tony."

There was a slight pause. "I don't know if my father will like that."

"Why?"

"He's never liked that name. He's Jeremy Lee Samuels, Sr," he said by way of an explanation.

He was so damn serious. "Okay then how about I call you Jeremy?"

"Okay."

After a long pause, I was so through with this conversation. "Well, it was nice talking to you."

"Same here."

Goodness talking to him was like pulling teeth. I hung up and went back to surf the website. So far I was striking out.

8

JANELLE

I was strapping my stilettos when I heard Kaleb pulling into my driveway. I moved over to my bedroom window, peeked outside and smiled with satisfaction when I spotted a charcoal gray Range Rover with that fine-ass mothafucka sitting behind the wheel.

"Cha-ching bitches," I murmured under my breath. Kaleb was everything I had ever wanted and thought I'd never find and I planned to have him and every perk that came with being his woman. We'd been dating for almost three weeks and I still hadn't given him my goodies. There's power in pussy and Kaleb had been working so hard to romance me, I was almost ready to at least give the brotha a sniff of my vajay-jay.

I grabbed my purse and hurried down the stairs and out onto the porch just as Kaleb came up the walkway with swag that was all his own. Honey followed at my feet.

"Hey," I said and grinned as I took in his relaxed blue jeans, the gray running shoes on his feet and a blue Michigan jersey. My man was so sexy.

"Whassup beautiful?"

Tilting my head, I stared up into Kaleb's eyes as he leaned down to kiss my lips. "Who do we have here?"

I stepped away and beamed down at my baby. "This is Honey."

"Hey Honey! C'mere boy."

Honey started jumping up and down. Kaleb smiled while he rubbed him behind his ears. "He's a cute little dog."

"Thanks. He's my baby." You can tell a lot about a man when it comes to your dog. Like I had placed in my personal ad, Honey and I were a package deal.

"Where are you taking me?" I asked for the thousandth time, and hated he still hadn't told me where we were going.

"Damn, you don't believe in surprises, do you?" he teased.

"I just like to know." Kaleb said clear my schedule for the entire afternoon. Hell, I don't do that for just anybody.

"We aren't going anywhere."

I frowned. "What do you mean, we aren't going anywhere?" Hell, I didn't spend all morning getting ready for nothing.

"We're not going anywhere until you go back upstairs and put on something comfortable."

I glanced down at the blue sundress and four inch sandals. "This *is* comfortable."

"No it isn't. I said wear jeans and tennis shoes. Now get back inside and change." He swatted me playfully on the butt then pointed toward the door.

It sounded like a command and after a controlling father, I normally didn't take too well to a man telling me what to do. But for some reason, I actually enjoyed it when Kaleb did it.

I invited him inside and he played with Honey, while I disappeared upstairs and frantically searched my closet for my favorite skinny jeans. I slipped on a fitted Mizzou t-shirt and a brand new pair of white Nike sneakers. "How is this?" I said as I stepped back into my living room to find Kaleb looking at the photographs I had displayed on my book shelves.

He swung around, and his approval shone in his eyes. "Good job."

I don't know why his approval was so important. I guess I just didn't want to miss out on what could possibly be my life.

"Who is this?"

I looked over to see which photograph he was referring to. "That's my brother Brice."

He glanced at me skeptically. "You sure he isn't one of your men?"

It took everything I had not to roll my eyes. Men can be so damn territorial. "No, that's my younger brother. And I don't have a man."

"Really? Then what am I? Chopped liver?" He stood there with this serious look waiting for a response.

Grinning, I stepped over to the bookshelf. "I don't remember you saying anything about being exclusive." Trust me. I wouldn't forget something like that.

Kaleb returned the picture frame to the shelf, then faced me as he said, "Does it have to be spelled out? I could be out there spending my time with someone else. Instead, I'm here with you. I'm crazy about you. You can't tell?"

His declaration was like music to my ears. I had to do everything I could not to jump for joy. "And I'm crazy about you."

Kaleb dragged me into his arms and kissed me hard. Lips, tongue, deep moans. I got it all.

"C'mon. Let's get out of here before we miss our balloon."

I couldn't possibly have heard him right. "Balloon?"

Kaleb just winked and headed out the door.

We arrived at a small field south of town and within minutes we were boarding a large red hot air balloon.

"I'm so excited! I've never had a man do anything like this for me."

"Hopefully this will be the first of several new experiences."

My cellphone vibrated in my pocket and I reached inside then glanced down at the screen. It was Q. He'd been texting all morning about our weekend and I had yet to respond. Of course he would pick now to decide to call. I quickly swiped Decline on my phone.

"Is that your man calling you?"

I groaned then pressed the button silencing my ringer. "Nope, just my girl Janelle checking to see what I got planned."

"Then why don't you answer it?" Something in his eyes

said he didn't believe me.

I forced a smile. "Because I'm with you and I don't want any distraction. When I call her later I'll have something to talk about." It was obvious, Kaleb was no fool. I was used to dudes taking what I said at face value but, Kaleb was definitely different from the others I've dated. I'd be lying if I didn't say I was intrigued.

We were hundreds of feet in the air when Kaleb came up behind me and wrapped his arms around my middle section. "What are you thinking about?"

I leaned into his embrace. Man I could get used to this. "I'm thinking this is one of the most rewarding experiences of my life. When I was younger, I used to sit on my grandmother's front porch and watch all the balloons go by. I always wondered what it would feel like to be up this high in the air looking down on the entire city."

"Now you know longer have to wonder."

I shook my head as I continued to gaze down at my city. "No, I don't."

We stood there, with his arms wrapped around me, until I felt Kaleb reach down for my hand. "C'mon."

I swung around and followed Kaleb to the other side of the balloon where I noticed for the first time a large wicker picnic basket. "What's this?"

"Lunch."

He reached inside and removed a large blue blanket and spread it onto the floor and took a seat. I lowered beside him and watched as he removed subs, potato salad, and sodas. The whole time I was grinning. This man was impressing me more and more by the second.

"You are full of surprises."

He winked. "Baby, this is only the beginning."

That's exactly what a sistah wanted to hear.

We were almost to my house, when I pulled out my cell phone and turned it back on. I quickly scrolled through my voicemail messages. Q had called twice and so had Janelle. I caught Kaleb giving me a strange look. That dude seriously

believed in having your full attention. I put the phone back in
my purse.

"You're sure you don't have a man in your life?" he asked
impatiently.

My head whipped around. "Why you say that?"

"Because you spend a lotta time checking your phone."

He was right. I do, but so what? I liked staying connected.
Besides, I paid the bill not him.

"I've had a wonderful last few weeks. I'm really looking
forward to getting to know you better but like I said before I
don't believe in sharing."

I had never been one for playing games or putting all my
cards on the table but there was something about Kaleb. I
guess I just really liked him or maybe it was knowing he was
seasoned that made me want to go about this relationship
differently from all the others in the past. Really, it wasn't just
about the money. Despite being a ready-made family, this
man had almost every quality I wanted in a man and because
of that I didn't want to bullshit him.

"Look, I gotta be honest with you," I said and he nodded
and waited.

"I'm listening."

I couldn't believe I was about to say this. "I've been seeing
someone."

Kaleb gave me this look like he had known all along I had
been lying. "Where is he?"

"He moved to Dallas. We fly and see each other once a
month."

There was no mistaking the disappointment on his face. "I
appreciate you being honest but I don't believe in stepping on
another brotha's toes." He held up his hands in surrender. "So
I'm gonna tap out."

"Tap out? I don't want you to do that. I like you and I just
felt like I needed to be honest."

"How long y'all been together?"

"Off and on, for about three years."

"So if you gotta man then what were you doing on the
dating site?"

I took a deep breath. "What's the best way to explain it? He is a good guy. What you see is what you get. I never felt compelled to be exclusive with him because I've always believed there was something missing in our relationship."

"Sounds to me like you need to be making a choice because I'm a first round draft pick. I don't play second to nobody."

I nodded, because he was right. And for once in my life, a man had made it clear I couldn't have it both ways. And I had mad respect for that.

"You figure out what you want then, you let me know. Unlike you, I'm not window-shopping. I'm dating to find someone."

I nodded and leaned over for him to kiss me. I caught him looking at my DD-cups but apparently that wasn't enough.

Kaleb walked me to the door and the whole time I was thinking about how wonderful a day I'd had. After the balloon ride we had gone to explore the caves in Rockbridge State Park then we went to listen to jazz and have dinner at Murray's restaurant. Kaleb was romantic, spontaneous and rich. Everything I wanted in a man and I'd be a fool to let such a good man go.

He was backing out of the driveway when I cried, "Wait!" and rushed over to his Range Rover. Kaleb put his foot on the brake and rolled down the window. I wasted no time. "I wanna be with you."

"I hope you mean it," he said and looked serious.

I was more sure than I've been about anything in my life. "I am. Just give me a chance to talk to him next weekend."

Kaleb looked pleased. "One week. After that, you belong to me."

Once we were inside, I led him up to my bedroom, where he dragged me into his arms and kissed me. This time it was more powerful than before and had my breasts swelling and my nipples hardening.

I lifted the shirt over my head then unclasped and tossed my bra away. Just as I hoped a low growl rumbled in his chest and then he shocked me and dropped to his knees and kissed the skin at my belly. "You're so beautiful."

Tension coiled inside me while he kissed and nibbled, swirling his tongue along my navel. It honestly felt better than I had imagined.

Reaching down I unsnapped my jeans, followed by the zipper and lowered it along with my panties down to my ankles and kicked them away.

"Damn!" was all he could say and yet I felt so excited when his eyes settled over me. "You want some of my cupcake, don't you?"

He laughed. "Cupcake?"

"Hell yeah, my cupcake. It's sweet and if you lick just right you'll find my creamy center." He was staring at me so hard, my legs started to quiver with anticipation.

His hand moved slowly up my leg, until his thumb stroked the lips of my sex before he parted my swollen lips. "I hope it taste like chocolate," he murmured then he leaned in close. I shuddered the second his tongue dipped inside me and then slid along the length of my slit.

"Oh my God!" I gasped. His tongue was on point. I'm serious.

Nothing could have prepared me for this. Not the books or the number of men I have brought to my bedroom over the years. I mean nothing could touch what Kaleb was doing with his tongue. The brotha had skills and confidence and definitely experience. I actually felt some type of way at just thinking about him eating someone else's pussy. He flicked the tip of his tongue over my clit, then sucked it gently between his lips causing my hips to jerk toward him.

"Hmmm. Chocolate, just the way I like it," he murmured.

"And you're tasting me just the way I like it," I managed between moans. "Oh yeah, just like that... yes," I raised up and just had to witness him in action. I watched Kaleb's tongue darting in and out. His eyes were opened and he didn't even blink as he stared up at me. God, it was such a turn on! I licked my lips and breathed deeply.

"Feel good to you?" he asked, his voice deep and arousing.

"Hell yeah," I hissed between my teeth. He parted my

folds with his fingers and slipped one through my folds. All I could do was moan in response. "Oh." I rocked my hips forward. As he added another finger I cried out. *Ohmygoodness!* I was so close to coming my knees shook. His technique was on point. Kaleb was sucking my clit and doing some swirling motion with his tongue that made it hard to stay still.

"Yesss... oh yesss," I moaned while he thrust his fingers in a slow in-and-out motion that kept me gasping for each breath yet I became quickly addicted that instead of demanding he stop, I ground against his mouth, riding his hand until he increased his strokes. His lips pulled at my clit and then his fingers drove deeper and he crooked that one finger until he found my g-spot.

"Yesss, yesss!" I came apart in a hot rush of release that had me singing.

While I laid there gasping, Kaleb rose and removed his clothes. Naked, he wasn't nothing you'd find in a calendar, but he was tight in all the right places. And his dick was just the way I liked it.

"You like what you see?" It was odd—the look he gave me. He was almost insecure waiting for my approval.

"Yes daddy," I whispered.

Pleased, Kaleb resembled my Pomeranian after I rubbed him behind the ear.

He slipped under the covers and dragged me into his arms. "You're so beautiful," he whispered as he caressed my hip and leaned in to lick at my throat. "I can get used to this."

"Keep doing what you're doing and I'll be packing my bags."

There was this pause and he gave me a serious look. "I hope you mean that. I don't think I could handle it if you're playing. CJ and I are really starting to get attached."

I ran the flat of my palm down along his chest to that beautiful piece of equipment swinging between his thighs and squeezed while he sucked in a harsh breath.

"Don't."

I started stroking him. "Why not?"

"Because I said so." He rolled me onto my back and his mouth closed around my nipple. Moans slipped from my mouth as his wet lips met my skin. His tongue circled my nipples while his hands kneaded my breasts.

"I see you like being in charge," I moaned.

"Exactly. I like my women submissive."

Yeah, okay, whatever. Right now I would say yes to just about anything. I was horny and my body aroused. Kaleb ran his hand over my hip and then dipped his fingers into the slick moisture between my legs.

"Tell me you belong to me," he commanded. I felt his warm breath at my neck while his thumb teased my kitty. Desire surged through my veins. "Tell me."

"Yes," I managed between gasps. "I belong to you."

He positioned himself between my legs. The head of his dick teased. He was grinding and rubbing up through my folds to my clit and then back down to the doors to my kitty.

"Kaleb, quit teasing!" I cried and arched against him, desperate to feel him inside me, and then finally pushed inside me.

I wrapped my legs tightly around his waist and grabbed onto his ass to pull him deeper. I lifted my pelvis, moving my hips in slow circles, and smirked with satisfaction when I heard him draw in a long breath.

"I can see I'm gonna have to show you who's boss." He said then raised my legs to his shoulders and gave me two sharp thrusts.

I couldn't speak. He started pumping hard. Oh, it was too much and not enough all at the same time.

"*Yesss,*" I cried. He pulled out, the head of his dick hovering at my entrance and I started whimpering with need, "please!"

Kaleb plunged deep, filling me with long hard pumps that sent me over the edge and into a place I hadn't been in months.

He was breathing softly, but not a word was coming from his lips. I sneaked a peek and he had this weird smile on his face. OMG! He was lost in his own personal ecstasy. Most men were tryna tear it up and talking shit but Kaleb was quiet almost to the point it made a woman wonder if he was aroused or not but then I tightened my vaginal walls and within minutes I felt Kaleb shudder.

"I'm coming baby," I whispered and then he stiffened against me as his own orgasm took him. Well... it was definitely a start.

As his heart slowed, he drew me tight in his arms and kissed my neck. "You're mine."

I lay there long after he was sleep thinking about Kaleb and our relationship. I wondered exactly what I'd agreed to and how much of a price I'd have to pay for the most intense relationship of my life.

9

NYREE

"Master Sergeant Dawson, do you have a requisition for a Supply Technician?"

I looked up to see Sergeant Jenna Carter, one of the personnel specialists on my team, standing in my doorway. "Yep, I was just getting ready to bring it out to you." I stopped typing and reached over into my inbox and handed her the blue requisition. "Make sure this isn't a union position and if not post it internally."

"No problem." Jenna nodded as she took the sheet of paper from my hand. "What time are you going to lunch?" she asked as she pushed the bangs of that horrible brown wig from in front of her eyes. Somebody needed to tell her to throw that damn thing away. I've tried talking to that girl about her outrageous hairstyles but it's never does any good. All she does is get rid of one and buy another.

Jenna and I coordinated our lunches so there was always coverage in our section. I glanced down at the watch on my wrist. "I have an appointment at twelve." I actually had a lunch date with a guy I had met on Blackfolksmeet.com. Alan's pictures were handsome and the phone conversations we'd had the last two evenings had been quite interesting. In fact, last night he had me fantasizing about a lot more than just talking.

"Appointment?" Jenna brought a hand to her narrow hip

and stared like she was trying to figure something out. "Uh-uh, something on your face says this is a *special* kinda appointment."

I couldn't resist a smile. "Maybe. It depends on how the date goes."

"Oh so now it's a date!" Jenna was smiling and shaking her head at the same time. "Is this a blind date?"

I leaned back on my chair, nodding and tried to keep the excitement out of my voice. "You could say that."

Her nutty brown face lit up. I think she was just as excited as I was. "Oh you know I'm gonna want all the details!"

She was a few years younger than me and had a lot of relationship drama with her no good baby daddy. After working together for over six years she and I shared a lot of tears and heavy conversations.

"Girl, his voice is so sexy over the phone, and he can sing!"

"What? He sang to you?"

I was laughing and nodding at the same time. "Jenna girl…" I leaned on the desk and lowered my voice to make sure no one outside my office could hear us. You know the walls are paper-thin. "You would have thought he was Tyrese somebody the way he was going *whoo-whoo* all up in my ears!" I started telling her everything I knew about him so far. Thirty, divorced, no kids, educated and seemed so intelligent. I couldn't wait to finally meet him. By the time she left my office we were both certain Alan just might be the one.

I made it to El Jimador's Mexican restaurant with ten minutes to spare. I looked in my rearview mirror to make sure my hair and face looked perfect. I loved my new hairstyle. I was rocking a short Rihanna cut with cinnamon highlights.

I stepped out and started across the lots. I felt myself looking all around because there was no telling if he was already in the parking lot watching me walk inside. All I knew was Alan was a lobbyist at the state capitol. Tall, educated, and his voice—sexy as hell. I couldn't wait to finally see him in person.

A quick sweep of the dining room, I didn't see anyone trying to get my attention. I told Alan I would be in uniform which made me easy to identify. Since no one was waving his hands in the air, I decided to wait before being seated. I flopped down on the bench near the hostess station. I was looking down at my nails when I felt someone staring at me.

"Nyree?"

My head snapped up to see eyes that were familiar. "Yeah?"

He grinned and then stuck out his hand. "Hello, I'm Alan."

What the fuck! When I rose to my feet, he barely reached to my nose. "Wow!"

He folded his arms. "Wow, is right! You're beautiful."

His face was decent, but I wished I could find something else attractive about him. He was shorter than the six feet he'd indicated in his profile, with little arms, and not to mention he was suffering from Dunlap Disease—his belly dun lapped over.

We followed the hostess to a booth near the window. He waited until I was seated before he slid onto the seat across from me. "You want to order something?"

Hell no. "I'm not really hungry so maybe just an ice tea and an appetizer." I figured I'd order and get the hell outta there. I was studying the menu when I spotted him staring at me.

"What?" I asked suspiciously.

He was grinning. "You look just like your profile picture."

"And you look nothing like yours."

Alan hesitated, avoiding eyes contact. "I took that photo about ten years ago."

"Then why did you post it?"

"Because I wanted women to see the real me."

"The real me?" I repeated. Then who the fuck was that sitting across the table?

"Yes, right now I got on my winter coat. Like a bear, I shed this weight every spring." He was chuckling like what he said was funny. But it was already late April.

"And I thought you were six-five?"

He looked confused then had the nerve to start laughing. "Six-five? No, I'm five-six."

And I'm five-nine. "Then why did your profile say you were over six feet?"

I swear he gave me the most sincere look, which pissed me off even more. "I just wanted a fair shot."

Talk about desperation. "Are you serious?" I put my menu down. This conversation was just going around in a circle, always coming back to the fact he had lied. "That's misleading."

He shrugged the way a person does when they realized they've been busted. "Maybe. But there was no way I would have had a chance to meet you."

I stared at him in silence. I know I should have felt flattered but I didn't. Instead I felt like I had been played. I had spent hours fantasizing about a tall, dark and handsome man. Instead I was sitting across from someone who looked like he was related to Cee Lo Green.

Our drinks arrived and I gulped down my iced tea wishing it was something stronger. While he ordered tacos, I stared at his little hands and shivered. There was no way in hell this relationship was going any further than lunch.

Thirty minutes later, I was peeling out the parking lot when I called Janelle.

"Hey girl. What's up?"

"What's up is that short mothafucka I just met at El Jimador's!"

"*What?*" she said with a laugh.

"Jae, he was cut off at the knees talking about he was six feet. Chile, he was barely five-three and losing his hair. That picture he had posted was more than ten years old."

"Girl, you ain't right!" She was cracking up. And before I knew it I had started laughing with her.

"I don't know why I let you convince me to join that damn site," I said, sucking my teeth for good measure. Men were all the same. Full of shit. It didn't matter who they hurt or that they were running game.

"Everybody can't be lucky like me." Leave it to Janelle to rub it in.

"Whatever. I was so disgusted I barely ate my food." I

shook my head, trying to rid myself of the image of his small hands and hairy knuckles.

By the time she got done laughing and trying to encourage me give the site one last try, I hung up and realized I was still hungry. I decided to stop at McDonald's and grab a burger. It would probably have me shitting the rest of the evening but right now I was too hungry to care.

I ordered a Big Kid's Meal then moved to the side for a woman with two children to order when I spotted someone who looked familiar standing in line. I think I recognized him at the exact moment he noticed me staring at him.

He walked over. "Excuse me. Are you Nyree?"

"Yep. And you're Jeremy Anthony Lee Samuels, Jr." Now that I had a face to match the squeaky voice, it didn't sound so bad.

He smiled and I noticed he had thick eyebrows and large brown eyes that were both beautiful and sincere. He had a big swollen head but it actually worked for his face. Up close and personal I realized he had an amazing dark chocolate complexion. Jeremy had to be about five-eleven with a medium build. And he had this boyish grin that lit up his entire face.

"I can't believe I ran into you," he said with a nervous laugh that I found cute.

"Me either."

They called my number for my food. I grabbed my bag then turned and looked over at him.

His face suddenly became very serious. "You have time to sit and eat?" he asked and was staring at me like he was star stuck.

Damn. I hated to respond, "No, I have a meeting."

Jeremy gave a look like he wasn't surprised. I didn't want him to think I was blowing him off because I wasn't. He was far better than that reject I had just left.

"Maybe some other time?" he said but it sounded more like a question.

I nodded. "I'd like that. Really... just call me," I said and noticed I was sounding nervous. He gave me a goofy smile and I felt the space between my thighs becoming moist. I know I was grinning like a fool. I had just said all those negative things about meeting nothing but rejects on the Internet but now that I had a chance to meet Jeremy in person, things were starting to look up.

By the time I had pulled back into the parking lot at the unit, my phone vibrated in my purse. I reached for it and read the text on the screen and my heart skipped a beat. It was from Jeremy. I quickly typed in my passcode and clicked on my messages.

Look forward to seeing you again.

So am I, I thought with a smile. So am I.

<u>10</u>

JANELLE

"Jae, baby. You wanna go and have dinner before the show?"

I was lounging across the bed in our suite at the Mandalay Bay Resort and Casino in Las Vegas. Quincy and I had spent most of the day shopping and walking along the strip. With the heat beaming down on me, I made it back to the hotel two shades darker and dead on my feet. We took a shower, made love and I fell asleep. Q slapped me playfully across my ass.

"Janelle, you hear me talking to you?"

I moaned and rolled my naked body over to my side. I hated to be disturbed when I'm sleep. "Yeah yeah just give me a second to get up."

Leaning in close, Q pressed his lips to my cheek. "No rush. As good as you're looking I'd rather get some more of that."

I was smirking too hard to object to him rolling me onto my back. I opened my eyes and stared up at him. Q was so fine with his cocoa-brown skin. He had a beautiful chest from hours of pumping weights in the gym and his salt and pepper beard was definitely on point. He buried his face between my breasts. I was lying there moaning while Q sucked at my nipples like a hungry man. Reaching down between us I stroked on his penis though there was no need. He was already brick hard.

"Mmmm babe," he moaned. "That's it. Play with your

dick."

Mine? I rolled my eyes toward the ceiling and told myself to focus on how good he made my breasts feel. Q had skills and knew exactly how much pressure to apply to my nipples before releasing and suckling on the other. Just the way I liked it. Then he replaced his lips with his talented hands, taking my nipples between his fingers and caressing them to the point of pure torture. I was moaning and wetness slid between my legs. He always had this way of getting me so aroused, I was ready to lose my mind.

"Please," I moaned, spreading my legs. "Fuck the foreplay, I need to feel that dick inside me."

He wasted no time positioning himself and in one push he was buried deep. He started stroking long and I had to force myself not to groan. All that teasing and for what? Disappointment. His skinny ass dick wasn't hitting nothing. And it was a shame because Q was truly putting his back into it.

"Huh? Did you say something?"

Whatever. "No."

"Does it feel good to you?"

The way he was moaning there was no doubt how good it felt to him. "Ooh yeah! That feels good." Actually, I was thinking about what I was going to wear to the Michael Jackson show tonight. Ever since I heard they were putting together a cirque du soleil of all the King of Pop's number one hits, I knew I had to see it, and Q was the sponsor to make that shit happen. Speaking of Q... he was pumping away like a lunatic while I moaned on cue and rocked my hips. I really care about this dude, but there was no way in hell I could spend the rest of my life with his little curved dick. And it was a damn shame because he really did look good on my arm.

"Roll over."

Smiling, I did as he said. Doggy-style meant it was my turn and I was about to feel more than my pussy being tickled. I rolled onto my back then folded a pillow in half and slipped it under my stomach like the wedge I kept in my bedroom closet, and lifted my ass up high off the bed. Q grabbed onto my hips and pushed inside.

"Awww!" I cried the second I felt him moving. There was something about a man with a crooked dick pounding me from behind. If it was angled just right, it hit your g-spot each and every time, no matter how skinny his thing was. "Yesss."

"Did you say something?"

"Oooh! I said that dick feels good." If it could feel like this all the time, maybe I might have considered marrying him.

I rocked my hips back, pounding my wide ass against his stomach. I loved that sound and the feel of his dick scratching my itch. "Oh... Q... just like that!"

He was pumping so hard it only took a matter of minutes before I was crying out his name and collapsing on the bed. "I missed you," Q managed between kisses to my back.

"Me too," I whispered. And really I did. Spending time with Q was fun because when we were together, it was all about me. I know that may sound selfish but it was his choice, not mine. But we truly had fun together.

I heard my ringtone, Beyoncé's *Drunk in Love* and I knew it was Kaleb. He'd been on my ass all afternoon. I don't understand why he was sweating me. He knew I was in Las Vegas with Q.

Once Q had fallen asleep, I slipped out from beneath him, grabbed my cellphone from my purse and disappeared into the bathroom. As soon as the door was locked, I looked down at all the missed phone calls and then there were the text messages.

Answer the phone!

Please, answer the damn phone!

Seriously? I was a little turned off but then I thought maybe something might have happened and he needed to speak to me. I turned on the faucet so the water was running and Q couldn't hear me through the wall then dialed Kaleb's number. He answered on the first ring.

"Why aren't you answering the damn phone?"

I had to take the phone away from my ear and look around to see if there was someone else in the bathroom he was talking to. Unfortunately the only one in here was me. Now I had a slight attitude. "I *told* you I'm with Q."

"I thought you were ending it?" He had the nerve to sound like he was my damn daddy. Last I checked that crazy mothafucka was dead.

"Kaleb, I'm gonna end it, but on *my* terms."

"What's that supposed to mean?"

"It means I don't need you micromanaging my actions. I got this! We're here until tomorrow, so I'm not breaking his heart until the end of the weekend."

"Jae—"

"Uh-uh! I'm not doing that to him! Q hasn't done anything to me. I'm the one ending it with him."

There was a long pause. "Do you wanna be with me?"

"Of course I do," I whispered into the phone.

"Then tell me! Tell me you want to be with big daddy!"

Goodness, he sounded crazed and yet my nipples beaded. What was it about this controlling man that turned me on? "I wanna be with you, big daddy."

He chuckled. "That's more like it."

I heard the television click on which meant Q was up from his nap. "Look, I gotta go. I'll call you tomorrow."

"Wait!" he yelled before I could end the call. "Answer one question."

"Yes?"

"Are you fucking him?" he demanded.

No he didn't just ask me that. "Excuse me?" I needed him to repeat that.

"You heard me. Are you fucking him?" Kaleb was practically screaming so I had to take the phone from my ear. "Janelle, answer the damn question!"

Anyone else I would have cussed out but Kaleb had something I craved. What that was I wasn't quite sure. All I know is I liked it. "No boo, I'm not fucking him. I'm on my period."

He was quiet like he was thinking about my answer, before he finally said. "Good, because you need to bring that pussy back home to me."

"Of course I will," I cooed in the phone. "As soon as my period is over, it's on." I giggled a little so he'd know I was truly feeling him. It's crazy, but I felt this high that was better than any rush I had gotten from smoking weed.

We talked a few more minutes before Kaleb said, "What time you landing tomorrow?"

"Seven."

"I'll be at the airport waiting." He hung up and I took a deep breath. Kaleb was really getting possessive. I know this sounds crazy, but my heart was pounding so hard because I had never had a man who felt so strongly about me and was that determined to make me his own. Of course being rich was an incentive as well.

I heard Q calling me from the other room. "Baby, what's taking so long?"

"Here I come!" I flushed the toilet and then turned off the water. As unpredictable as Kaleb is, it would probably be a good idea to leave my phone off until I left for the airport tomorrow.

11

NYREE

I gave the delivery guy a five-dollar tip then carried the two pizzas and wings to the kitchen.

Jeremy was coming over to watch the game and I was nervous. We've been texting and talking on the phone since we had run into each other at McDonald's last week and tonight would be our first official date.

I put the food on the counter, then rushed into the half-bath to check and make sure there were no boogers hanging from my nose. I turned from side to side in front of the mirror and was pleased at how I looked in a pair of skinny Levi's and an Oklahoma City Thunder's t-shirt, both accented my curves.

I was ready to run up to my bathroom to gargle with mouthwash for the third time when the doorbell rang, and I jumped. "C'mon Nyree. Get it together," I murmured under my breath then made myself take a few deep breaths before I went to the door. I don't know why I was so nervous. I mean, unlike that phony Alan who I had to block from calling me, I already knew what Jeremy looked like. Yet even still, my heart raced and my hands sweated. "It's now or never," I mumbled then headed toward the living room. I unlocked the door and swung it open, and there Jeremy was wearing a Washington Redskins jersey and loose-fitting jeans. There was even a matching fitted cap covering his big head.

I raised an eyebrow. "You do realize we're gonna be

watching *basketball*," I greeted him playfully.

"I do, but I'm a diehard football fan," he said with a chuckle.

"And let me guess who your favorite team is," I teased.

"How'd you guess?" All of a sudden, he busted out laughing and there was that squeaky sound again.

Smiling, I stepped aside so he could enter my house. I shut the door and turned around to find him admiring my living room that I had decorated the contemporary-styled room in vibrant shades of blue and yellow.

"You have a nice place."

"Thank you." I was beaming. "Please go ahead, have a seat and make yourself comfortable."

He nodded. "Yes, ma'am."

Ma'am? Jeremy was way too mannerable, but cute, nonetheless. I could eat his mama boy ass up.

He took a seat on the couch. I reached for the remote, and turned to the game on the fifty-five inch screen. "Hold up. Let me grab our food."

"You want some help?" He was halfway off the couch when I held up a hand and stopped him.

"No, please, relax. I got it."

"Yes, ma'am." He winked then lowered onto the cushions again.

Smiling, I hurried toward the kitchen and rushed into the bathroom just to make sure everything was still intact and was pleased that it was. As soon as I grabbed the boxes from the counter and two Sprite cans, I brought them back to the coffee table. "I ordered you the pepperoni and I got veggie. But you're welcome to have some if you want."

Just like a man, he turned up his nose. "Veggies? No way. I gotta have my meat."

"Yeah, yeah. I figured as much." I was smiling so hard my face hurt. I took a seat at the other end of the couch and we got into the basketball game while we ate. Conversation wasn't needed, although I didn't have an idea what to talk about during the commercials. Jeremy looked uncomfortable and I couldn't believe that little ole me was at a loss for words. Then my cellphone started vibrating like crazy. It was Janelle texting me.

Is he there?

Is he cuter this time?

I just giggled and texted yes and yes, then went back to eating my pizza. At the end of the second quarter I noticed Jeremy was falling asleep. Oh my goodness! Was I really that boring?

"Hey, can you explain to me the whole 'in the paint' crap." I asked and realized I startled him when he jerked upright on the couch. "Sorry."

"No problem."

"I was saying, I don't understand how a player can just stand there and if another player runs into him it's considered a foul."

Jeremy grinned then was suddenly wide awake. He rose from the couch and demonstrated while he explained. I was pleased I could think so fast on my feet. While demonstrating the cap fell onto the carpet, and even though he had that big ass head, Jeremy really was cute. I know I keep saying that but there was really something wholesome about him. Like he just wanted to make sure he was saying and doing the right thing.

We settled down and spent the last quarter of the game cheering for OKC who ended up winning 103-98.

As soon as Charles Barkley started analyzing the game, I noticed Jeremy looking down at his watch and knew it was time for our date to end.

"Well, thanks for inviting me over." He rose and did a full body stretch.

"I appreciate you coming." Now I was nervous all over again. "I'll walk out with you. I need to put my trash on the curb." I rose then flicked on the light and we stepped out onto the porch together.

"I'll drag it out for you," Jeremy offered and grabbed the large trash container that was against the side of the house. "I've never watched basketball with a female before," he suddenly said out of the blue.

"Really? Then I guess you've been dating the wrong women," I teased and I was pleased when he looked back and grinned at me.

"You're right. I have." We walked down my driveway together and he pulled the trash can to the left of my mailbox and then headed toward his Tahoe. He was almost to his door before he turned around again. "I have tickets to see Lavell Crawford at Déjà Vu Comedy Club on Thursday. You wanna come?"

"I'd love too." I was screaming "Yes" inside. For a moment there I really thought the date had been a flop and Jeremy wasn't going to call me again.

"Good deal," he said with another boyish grin. He then took my hand and stared down at me for so long I thought he was going to kiss me before he asked, "You have time for a walk?"

"Sure, let me lock up." Grinning, I scurried back into the house, grabbed my spare key on a keychain I kept on a hook in the kitchen and slipped it in my pocket. Janelle was texting me again.

So how was the date?

I quickly texted back.

It ain't over. Now leave me alone.

I hit Send then left my phone on the coffee table and locked up the door. I was practically skipping as I moved to join Jeremy at the curb where he was waiting patiently. He extended his hand and I accepted it. We started walking up my block and then over to the next. It was nice. Maybe because I never met a man who wanted to take walks.

"Tell me what you're thinking about?" he said breaking the silence.

I also haven't ever dated a man who had been interested in what I was feeling let along thinking. "I'm thinking… this is *really* nice."

"Good stuff." He stared down at the street like he was trying to wrap his mind around what I had just said. "Taking walks is the way I like ending a long week."

"I'll have to try this more often," I said and he looked over at me and smiled.

"I'd love to do it with you." Again it was as if he was asking a question then he squeezed my hand. "I think walking's a good way for couples to talk and share their day. What about you?"

"Couples, huh?" I teased.

He grinned and tightened his hold. The evening had started out a little awkward but the more we walked and talked, the easier the conversation became.

"What are you looking for?" he asked.

That's a good question. "I'm not sure what I want. I just have a feeling I'll know what it is when I find it." I just know I wanted it to feel like this.

Jeremy continued to probe. "Why didn't your last relationship work?"

I paused. "I wanted a commitment and he did not. I'm starting to think I'm asking too much."

He shook his head. "You're not. You were hoping for a future with the wrong men."

"Hmmm. Maybe you're right." Especially since the last one had been married but I wasn't going there. "I want a man who has my back and I have his. Someone who loves my dirty draws." I laughed because I was sure that sounded ridiculous. Apparently Jeremy didn't think so.

"I want the same thing." The look in his eyes said he wanted it with me. Damn! Was this man too good to be true? I tried to contain my excitement. "I learned communication is one of the most important things in a relationship."

My head whipped around. "I agree."

He looked pleased. "Do you go to church?"

I nodded. "Yes, Sugar Grove Baptist Church almost every Sunday. I've been going to the same church since I was a little girl."

"I really wanna find a home church. I've visited a lot since I've moved here from Chicago but nothing that I've walked in and wanted to make my home."

"You should come and visit mine. Reverend Williams is

really powerful."

"Is that an invite?"

I smiled over at him. "Any time you want. I usually sit with my parents but I go all by myself."

"I'd like that. I believe every serious relationship should have a spiritual foundation." Damn, he had me feeling all giddy inside. "Do you fellowship?" he asked.

I nodded. "Every morning I pray and read *Our Daily Bread*. The chaplain hands them out at the unit."

Jeremy suddenly stopped walking and turned to look at me. "I don't want to come off as some religious freak because I'm not but I do believe in Jesus Christ. I've always desired a woman who believes as well."

I was staring up at him. My heart was pounding so hard. This man was everything I wanted on so many levels. "I want the same." I could just see the two of us going to church together on Sunday. *Wait until my mother meets him.*

We started walking again. "Do you have any kids?" The last thing I wanted was baby mama drama.

He nodded and pulled me to the side protectively as a car came by. "I have three children with my ex-wife and my little adopted daughter."

My head whipped around curiously. "Adopted?"

He shrugged then blew out a long breath. "I used to date her mother and grew attached to Jasmine."

As I listened, I fell into step beside him. "And how's your relationship with your ex-wife?"

There was a long exaggerated sigh. "We get along for the sake of the kids. She's a good mother so I can't complain." He gave me another uncertain smile. "Do you ever want children?"

"I like kids. I hope to have one or two before it's too late. Do you think you'll ever want more?" It's crazy but I was dreaming about having this man's baby.

"If God blesses me with another wife, then yes. How do you feel about dating a man with kids?"

"It's not a problem." Although my personal profile had said I wasn't interested in dating a man with small children, I knew the chance of meeting a man without any was next to impossible. "I think if they lived with you it would be something I'd need to seriously think about." Again he looked pleased by my answer. "How old are they?"

"Eighteen, sixteen and fourteen."

Perfect. They were all self-sufficient. If we were to ever have a child, I wanted our child to be the only baby in the family.

"How long you been in the military?"

He asked a lot of questions but I didn't see him as being nosy. I loved a man who was interested in learning about me. "Twelve years."

"What do you plan to do when you get out?"

"Wow! I don't know. I hope to retire in eight years. I have a degree in business administration and a master's in Public Administration so I guess I'll find a personnel position in the civilian world."

"That's good stuff. I have a bachelor's in sociology and a master's in Criminology."

Educated. Yes! "That's cool. Are you working in law enforcement?"

"No, nothing like that." He shook his head. "I'm working as a program manager for the department of transportation."

We continued to walk and talk and by the time we had circled back to my house I was feeling real good about him.

"Thanks for inviting me over." We were standing next to his Tahoe grinning like two nuts.

"Thanks for coming over. I wanted to spend some time together before I leave for Salt Lake City on Sunday."

"What are you doing there?"

"Training," I murmured.

Jeremy nodded. "Thank you for letting me put in my application. I am very interested in the job." He then held out his hand and struggled to keep a straight face. I'm a little slow so it took me a few minutes to figure out what he was talking about. And then I was laughing like crazy and shook his hand.

"I'll be making my decision in a few days," I joked and then suddenly the laughing stopped and we were staring at each other. It was something like out of a movie. Jeremy dragged me closer then waited for some type of cue. I finally gave up and leaned in and kissed him. Any other dude would have swooped in for the score. He was so damn mannerable. I was going to have to work on that.

"And I'll be here to pick you up on Friday for the comedy club." Jeremy finally wrapped his arms around my waist and pulled me tightly in his arms. His tongue entered my mouth and this warm feeling spread through my body. It was like I was melting or something. I'd never felt like that before and it was so overwhelming I didn't know how to handle it. Trust me, I've been kissed by more men than I could count but it was just something about the way he made me feel like I was the luckiest woman in the world. And I couldn't help wondering if maybe I had finally met the one.

12

JANELLE

Friday night, I left my cousin April in charge of the restaurant, rushed home to let Honey out for the evening, and then headed over to Kaleb's place. Ever since I had gotten back from Las Vegas we had been spending so much time together I practically lived at his house. Not that I was complaining. His house was amazing with wood flooring, custom molding, and five thousand square feet of living space. Kaleb had sent me a text an hour ago that he had the wine chilling. Someone please pinch my ass! Hee-Hee! I still couldn't believe how lucky I was to meet a man like him, who showered and treated me the way a man was supposed to treat a woman—like a queen.

When I had landed at the St. Louis International Airport, I spotted Kaleb waiting and holding a sign that said, "I'm Janelle's Man." That man instantly stole a piece of my heart. We went back to his place and five days later, I was still spending every second I could with him. Last night he had hinted at me moving in with him but I wasn't sure yet if he was serious. I would do anything to make this house my permanent address. But I wasn't accepting anything short of a ring. Sorry, boo-boo, but this pussy ain't for free.

I pulled into the circular drive, parked my Honda in front of the garage door and stepped out. I glanced down at my ankle length strapless sundress and simple tan BCBG sandals and grinned. I made even the simplest outfit look good.

"What took your sexy ass so long," Kaleb said with a playful smile as he opened the front door.

"I had to get some orders ready for tomorrow." I leaned over and kissed his lips and the second I stepped into the house, I gasped. You would have thought Kaleb owned a candle factory at all of the scented candles that were flickering along the long foyer. I looked over at him puzzled. "Kaleb, what's going on?" I asked, afraid that maybe I had missed an important event.

Kaleb smirked. "Nothing's going on other than I wanna treat my baby to a special night. C'mon."

I was smiling and laughing at the same time as he extended his hand and I accept it. I followed him across the beautiful bamboo flooring his housekeeper kept shiny like a new penny. There was high ceilings and wainscoting along the walls. The house reeked of money but the cheap furnishings were another story all together. I looked into the living room where the stereo was playing soft soothing jazz music. I couldn't have planned a more relaxing evening.

We were walking into his dream kitchen when CJ came barreling down the back staircase followed by this big-ass wolf.

"*Oh my God!* What the hell is that?" I shrieked, and jumped behind Kaleb for protection.

"That's Midnight. He won't hurt you." CJ then tried to show me how gentle his dog was but I wasn't buying it. I usually came over when CJ was sleep, so the dog must have been in his room because this was the first time I'd ever seen that monster. He was nothing like my precious Honey.

"Dad I'm getting ready to head over to Jordan's."

I noticed the backpack on his back. We were going to have the house to ourselves. I was jumping for joy, knowing I'd have my man to myself.

"Okay but son before you leave I'd like to say something to you." Reaching over Kaleb took my hand and then looked so serious I held my breathing as I waited to hear what he was about to say. "Ms. Jae is really special to me." Pausing he brought my hand to his mouth and kissed it. "What do you think about her moving in with us?"

"No!" he yelled. "It's too soon!"

What the fuck!

I kid you not, CJ was stomping his feet like a child. "Dad, it's too soon! Why you always rushing?"

"CJ, get the fuck outta my face!" Kaleb suddenly exploded and even I flinched.

The kid looked crushed as he wailed, "Why you getting mad? You asked me!"

I started popping my gum as I nodded my head and agreed, "Yeah, you did ask."

"Dad's always doing that!"

"CJ go!" he ordered.

His son was muttering under his breath as he moved around the center island. "You're always rushing and then you'll break up and be back on Blackfolksmeet.com looking for another woman."

No he didn't just say that! This was better than Maury.

"I said shut the fuck up," Kaleb said in this eerie low voice that caused his son to tense. "Get outta here *NOW!*"

CJ sulked out the room and was heading toward the stairs. Wait a minute! The front door's that way.

"How you gonna ask him a question and then get mad when you don't like the answer?" I'm just keeping it real. Besides, I wanted our romantic evening *alone* dammit.

Kaleb's face cracked, and went from anger to remorse in a matter of seconds. "You're right. Hey, son!" he called after him. "Go to Jordan's. I'll see you in the morning."

"Okay," he said in this baby voice that sounded odd coming from him. In fact there was something about him that reminded me of my brother Brice and that really bothered me.

"I'll be home in the morning, by ten," he said and I could tell that was his designated time to return.

"I'm sorry, son," Kaleb said and looked so pathetic. Ewww! I hope I'm not going to see that look too often.

CJ then gave his dad a kiss, which I thought was weird for a boy who was almost six feet but then he came over and kissed my cheek as well. I guess it bothered me, because my father never showed affection and the only time my mother ever dared to tell us she loved us was when he wasn't around.

"See you later CJ," I replied and tried to hide my excitement that he wasn't going to be at home and in the way. The only problem was he was leaving behind that big horse he called a dog.

After he left, Kaleb took my hand. I walked around Midnight, who was now lying on the floor in the kitchen. He was cute—just too damn big.

I followed him back to the family room where there were more candles, strawberries, and a bottle of wine chilling in an ice bucket. I allowed my eyes to travel around what was so far my favorite room. He had every electronic gadget imaginable and an old comfortable leather sectional sofa.

"This is so romantic," I cooed.

Kaleb grinned and looked pleased by my response, then his expression became somber. "Jae… thanks so much for stepping in. You're right. I was wrong for getting mad at CJ for expressing how he felt."

"You're welcome," I tilted my chin and met his delicious lips in a kiss. One minute he was crazy, the next minute he was the gentlest man. Damn, there was that rush again.

"Take a seat and relax." He tapped one of the large body-sized pillows on the floor. I flopped down, then Kaleb lowered and took my shoes off my feet. He was so gentle he brought tears to my eyes.

My man had gone to a lot of trouble to plan the perfect night. "You're something else."

He chuckled. "I told you I believe in treating a woman the way she deserved to be treated. Mom raised me to be a gentleman."

"I'll have to remember to thank your mother," I said lounging back against the pillow.

He rose and moved over to the table, poured me a glass of wine and handed it to me. "Here you go, babe."

I just loved the way he called me, babe. "Thank you."

"How about a toast?" he suggested then lifted his glass. I

nodded and kept my eyes locked on his as I raised mine.

"Here's to black folks meet dot com because if it wasn't for them I never would have found you."

"*Awww!*" I was blushing now. "To black folks meet dot com," I repeated, clicked my glass against his then brought it to my lips. "Mmmm, this tastes good." It was a moscato that wasn't overly sweet.

"I had the guy at the wine store recommended a brand."

It was so good or maybe I was just so caught up in our romantic evening.

I took mine to the head, and then handed him my empty glass. "Baby while you refill my glass, let me run to the bathroom real quick."

He winked at me. "As soon as you get back, I'm ready to go upstairs and run a bath for two."

I jumped up from the floor and headed through the kitchen to the half bath. I was so excited I almost peed on myself. Life with Kaleb was so good and he was good to me. I washed my hands and was heading back through the kitchen when I noticed the horse's water bowl was empty. I stopped, rolled my eyes and reached down for it. He was lying on the floor near the back stairs and the second he saw me carry his bowl over to the sink his tail started wagging. I may not care for big dogs but one thing I'd never do is mistreat an animal. I put the bowl back onto floor and he immediately rushed over and started slurping, sending water all over my bare feet.

I jumped back. "Stupid dog," I mumbled under my breath then hurried back to the family room. When I spotted Kaleb holding my phone in his hand I came to a screeching halt.

"Why is dude still calling you?"

"What?" I was trying to stall. Damn, talk about bad timing!

"Don't play dumb. Your phone rang twice while you were in the bathroom so I looked down and saw that dude's name flash across your screen."

"How did you know who was calling if my phone was in my purse?"

"It wasn't in your purse. It must have been in your pocket because you left it on the pillow."

I frowned. I was almost certain my phone had been in my purse.

"Answer the question! I thought it was over between you and Q?" He was definitely pissed off.

I shrugged. "It is."

"Then why the hell is he calling you?"

I shrugged and stepped into the room. "He's just having a hard time accepting that it's over."

Kaleb paused, met my eyes then handed back my phone. "I can't blame him. I would hate to lose you myself. But you need to handle that."

"What's there to handle?"

"Oh, I get it! You're trying to keep him around so you can have a spare."

"*A spare?* Are you serious?" I cried.

"Yes, a spare." He held up his hand. "Look I already told you I'm not gonna share my woman with anyone."

I was quite certain he was getting tired of this and if the roles were reversed I guess I would be too. "Okay, I'll handle it." Oh well, so much for a romantic evening.

"You need to handle it now! I'm trying to make you my wife and you're still hanging on to your exe."

His words went straight to my head. "Make me your wife?"

That smirk of his suddenly turned into a piercing smile. "You heard me. I want to marry you and share *all* this with you." He emphasized with a sweep of his hand. "But like I said from the word go, I'm not into games. You want a good man then you got one standing right here. But I don't have time for window shopping. Claim it and let's build a life together."

Kaleb's words were everything I had wanted to hear and more. "Yes, baby! I want that too," I said and grinned wickedly. I practically leaped into his arms and wrapped my legs around his waist.

My future was definitely looking up.

13

NYREE

"Master Sergeant."

I felt someone kick my boot under the table and my eyes popped open to find Timmy staring at me.

"Wake up," he mouthed with this amused look on his face. I grinned then shifted on the seat.

We had been in a training class for the last two days, learning how to properly use the new defense personnel database. It was an interesting class. I was just tired as hell. Last night Timmy and I went down to the bar in our hotel and sat up drinking until we had reached our limit. I went back to my room, crashed, and slept through my alarm. Timmy and I had been carpooling since Monday. If he hadn't called my cellphone I probably would still be laid across the bed passed out.

I sat up straight and took a drink of the diet Coke that was now lukewarm but it still felt good going down my throat. I listened as Maria demonstrated how to generated reports using the self-service center. I scribbled notes in my binder then heard my cellphone vibrating in my purse. I reached down and discreetly noticed I had a text from Jeremy.

> Hey beautiful. Hope you're having a blessed day. I'm thinking ahead to when u come back. What days can I plan some things with u? It could be hourly. I just want some time.

Wow. He was already planning ahead. I smiled because it was obvious that he liked me, which was a good thing since I felt the same way about him.

>Any day you want next week. You just tell me. I'll be working on a training class but ur worth making time for.

I hit Send then glanced up at the projector to see if Maria noticed I was not paying attention. She hadn't. Good, because my phone vibrated again.

>Wow! I appreciate that. I believe I am also. Lol.

I grinned as another text came in.

>Hope you're smiling. It's pretty.

I was really grinning now.

>I'm giving you permission to. LOL

I texted back.

>Yes, I'm smiling.

Timmy kicked my boot again. "Ouch!" My head whipped around and I glared at him.

"Yo, pay attention," he whispered. I was ready to kick him back because that shit hurt but he was so cute with those deep dimples of his.

Timmy was a senior master sergeant so he outranked me and was assigned to the 192nd Fighter Wing in Hampton, VA. We had met years ago at the senior NCO academy and ended up sleeping together on more than one occasion. We tried the long distance thing for a while, but eventually I met Rock and the relationship tapered off. Last night we had laughed and talked for so long that it felt like old times yet instead of thinking about kicking it again with Timmy, I found myself looking forward to Jeremy's phone calls and text messages.

I made myself focus on class. And when it was time to break for lunch I rose and reached for my purse under the seat.

"You wanna go and get something to eat?" Timmy

suggested.

I'm not going to lie. The brotha was gorgeous. He stood to his full six-five stance and I tilted my head and looked up into his beautiful chocolate eyes. Timmy made a military uniform look good. "Sure, what you got a taste for today?" I followed him out the room and down the hall along, with the other twenty airmen in our class.

"I figure Wendy's would be quick."

I nodded and put my hat on my head just as we stepped out the building. Tim was quiet. I could tell there was something on his mind. He waited until we got into the rental car before he said something.

"Look, after we went back to our rooms last night I spent a lot of time thinking about us and what coulda been."

I looked at the glove compartment and blushed. "I was thinking the same thing."

His eyes lit up and he reached over for my hand and squeezed it. "I've missed you, Nyree. I wanna see if we can get this relationship back where it used to be."

If he had asked me weeks ago I would have jumped at the chance. Hell as desperate as I was after the situation with Rock, I would have taken anything I could get. But now that I had met someone that lived close enough I could see him as often as I wanted I wasn't sure if a long distance relationship was where I wanted to be.

I shrugged. "I don't know.. Maybe."

"Damn, baby, you make it sound like I'm putting a gun to your head." Timmy even had the nerve to try and look hurt.

"Nah, I didn't mean it like that."

We got to Wendy's and I felt my phone ringing in my purse. "I gotta pee. Order me a strawberry salad," I said and dashed into the stall. By then the phone had stopped ringing but I noticed Jeremy had sent me another text.

> J: Whatcha doing? Thinking about me? Notice I
> didn't put a LOL

I'm a big believer of multitasking so I decided to text and pee.

Me: Actually I am.

J: I knew it. Care to share??

Me: I was thinking about the comedy show last Friday. You were laughing, joking and so relaxed. I'd like to see more of that side of you.

J: I told you I am a clown. I enjoyed u also.

I sat there on the toilet, sighing. This was like one of those romance novels or something. Jeremy was sweet and respectable and I kept wondering how in the world was this amazing man single?

* * *

"What the hell is he waiting for?" Timmy screamed.

We were in my hotel room watching the Lakers play Portland, and Kobe Bryant was looking sad out on the court.

"I don't know what's wrong with them?" All I could do was shake my head. I was a diehard basketball fan and the Lakers used to be my team before I fell in love with Kevin Durant. "Kobe ain't been the same since Shaq left."

Timmy looked at me with that beautiful grin of his. "You're something else."

I was sitting beside him on the bed with a bowl of popcorn between us. It was nice being here with him again. As soon as I first found out I was attending the training class I was wondering if Timmy was going. And then, when I saw the list of people planning to attend I had gotten excited and started thinking about the way things used to be and what if we could hook up while we were here. But like I said, that was before I met Jeremy.

Speaking of him, I'd been ignoring his calls all evening. If fact, I had to turn off my ringer.

"I've been thinking about applying for a position at Whiteman AFB."

"Really?" That was less than two hours away from Columbia.

"Yeah, the superintendent is retiring."

I snapped my fingers. "I think I heard something about that."

"I was thinking about applying. I would be closer to my dad." His father lived in Des Moines, Iowa. "And this sexy woman sitting beside me."

I was grinning like a damn fool when he leaned over and pressed his lips against mine.

"So tell me what's going through your head. What do you think about all this?"

I'm thinking weeks ago I would have been all for it. "Well…" I didn't know where to begin. "Look… I've gotta be honest." *I can't believe I'm doing this.* "I'm sorta seeing someone."

"And what does that mean for us?"

I have this fine man sitting beside me, single, with no kids, who's willing to relocate so he can be closer to me so we can finally have a relationship and yet my dumb ass was hesitating. I can't explain it but I guess it's something about what coulda-shoulda been and trying to rekindle a flame that had burned out years ago. I don't know. When I wanted him he wasn't available but now that he's ready, well, just like a brotha, they expect you to drop everything and be on board. I just wasn't with that.

Images of a life with Jeremy had been dancing in my head. "I'm seeing someone I really like. I don't know where it's headed but I'm interested in finding out. I'm not saying you and I don't have a chance. I'm just saying someone has jumped ahead of you in line."

His eyes started to twinkle and there was that smirk on those pretty lips of his. "Well since he's not here and I am, then I guess I need to give you a reason to put me ahead of the rest."

Timmy started kissing me and I rolled onto my back and allowed him to draw me close in his arms. The kiss was nice and when his tongue slipped into my mouth, I was all about meeting his strokes, yet the entire time I caught myself thinking about what was waiting for me at home.

14

JANELLE

I had just finished checking on how dinner was going when I stepped out of the kitchen and spotted Kaleb standing up front looking scrumptious in gray slack, a white dress shirt and Ferragamo loafers. Trust me, I know my designers. The second Kaleb spotted me he grinned. I sauntered over to him and watched as his eyes took in everything from the blue Manolos on my feet to the black wrap dress that tied at my small waist. Yesterday I had made a trip to the mall so my new push-up bra had my girls covered in satin and looking ripe for the picking.

"You made it," I purred and tilted my head for a brief succulent kiss.

As he pulled away, Kaleb had a sexy smirk on his face. "I wouldn't have missed it."

"Then come on and follow me. I have a table reserved." I signaled for him to follow my lead as we weaved through the small intimate tables covered with fine linen. Closer to a long bar were a couple of oversized love seats. Of course several customers stopped me along the way, wanting to comment on how good the food tasted. I smiled, sucked it all up, and kept it moving.

"You're popular," I heard Kaleb say.

I shrugged and glanced briefly over my shoulder. "I'm the owner and everyone knows how hands-on I am with my restaurant."

"I can't wait for you to show me a little hands-on experience," he teased.

I giggled and pointed for him to take a seat at the best table in the house.

He did that sexy one eyebrow thing. "You joining me, right?"

"Absolutely. Tonight's my night off." Or at least it officially started the moment he stepped into the restaurant.

"You got a nice place here." He glanced around and looked clearly impressed. He should. I spent a lot of money designing a place with class. Thanks to my cousin Toby who was a hell of a contractor I was able to get most of the renovations for dirt cheap.

"Thanks. This is my pride and joy." I was probably glowing.

Kaleb leaned back on the bench. Damn, the dude had swag. "As I was coming in, I noticed the space next door is for sale."

He was observant. I'm impressed. "Yes, that was a bridal shop that went out of business."

"You ever think about knocking out that wall and expanding your restaurant?"

I gave a rude grunt. "All the damn time but I know I need to crawl before I walk. My restaurant is just starting to turn a profit so I don't have the money to expand just yet."

He brought a hand to his chin and gave me a calculated look. "Well, we'll have to see about that."

See, that what I'm talking about! Kaleb went out of his way to make me feel special by doing things for me that showed he was interested in more than just dating. I didn't want to get ahead of myself but if he was saying what I thought he was saying, I was going to be doing a lot of slobbering on that beautiful penis of his.

He reached for a menu and opened it in front of him. "So what do you suggest I order?" he asked with a curious look.

"Everything's good on my menu." I wasn't trying to boast but it is what it is. I personally selected every item on that menu.

"Oxtails and rice?" His brow rose. "I gotta see this. Nobody makes them like my Big Mama."

I pointed a finger at him. "That's because you haven't tasted mine."

"So what you saying? They're better than Big Mama's?"

Uh-huh. I wasn't even about to get between a man and his grandmother. "I'm saying they're probably the next best thang." He looked pleased by my answer. The last thing I was going to do was offend this man especially when I was dying for him to make me a permanent part of his life.

"How about we place a bet?" I said.

"What kind of bet?" Men never could resist a challenge.

I crossed my legs. "If you don't like them then I'll make it up to you with a little hands-on experience."

"And if I do like them?"

"Then by midnight I expect to feel your hands all over me." I licked my lips and leaned in close so the twins were resting on the table. His eyes dropped to my cleavage and lingered there long enough for me to know he had accepted my challenge. Not that I had expected any less.

"You're on." He accepted with the cutest little smirk.

To moved my menu to the side. "And when you finish my oxtails you'll have to top that off with peach cobbler and ice cream."

"Damn babe. You're tryna reel a nigga in."

I winked. "That's the plan."

My cousin Charmaine came over and took our drink orders. Kaleb moved his chair over next to mine and we held hands and listened while the band did their thang. Folks were still coming through the door and several recognized Kaleb and came over to speak briefly. I felt special being with him and I held his hand proudly. I could get used to being with this rich and powerful man.

"That band's good."

I nodded in agreement. "Fluidity be jamming. I heard them one weekend while I was in St. Louis at this joint on the north side and I invited them to drop through whenever they were in the area." We chatted some more and placed our dinner order then I excused myself long enough to run to the kitchen and threaten Mimi that Kaleb's oxtails had better be on point. When I finally made it back to our table he was checking messages on his phone. I took my seat. We chatted and listened to the band while they sung Atlantic Starr's "Secret Lovers."

I was humming and sipping an Apple Martini when I caught him looking at me. "What?"

"You sure you're single?" he asked with a piercing stare.

"Why you ask that?"

"Because you got every brotha in here staring at you."

I did a quick sweep of the restaurant. There were a few. Most of them were dudes I knew from the neighborhood, but I didn't bother correcting him. A man loves having a woman everyone wants. And I was definitely worth having. Kaleb needed to know he wasn't the only man yanking my chain even though right at the moment he was the only one who mattered.

I gave a shrug like it was no big deal. "No one I'm interested in."

He grinned and brought my hands to his lips and kissed it.

A couple of friends stopped by my table to say hello and I introduced them to Kaleb. Shortly after our food arrived. I had ordered the oxtails as well and waited for him to dive in first. The second he put the fork in his mouth and his eyelids lowered I knew I had him.

"*Daaayum* this is good!" He moaned and shook his head as he took another bite.

"I'm sorry… I don't think I heard you." I cupped my ear with my hand.

He laughed. "Babe, you heard me. This food is off the chain!"

I waved a fork in the air. "Does that mean it's as good as Big Mama's?"

He gave me that cute smirk again. "Nah babe. It's better. Just don't tell Big Mama I said that." He laughed and I joined in. Kaleb planned to introduce me to his grandmother. That meant I was in there.

Around nine the lights dimmed dramatically. I looked over and said, "C'mon. Let's dance."

He took my hand and led me out onto the floor. It was a fast number and now that I had a slight buzz I was ready to wiggle my hips and show him what this diva was all about. Kaleb had some moves and I ain't mad at the way he was dancing to the music. Damn that brotha had so much swag and he moved with enough confidence he had me getting moist between the thighs.

We were doing our thing when I spotted Alphonso's redbone ass stepping out onto the dance floor. *What the hell did he want?* I've been avoiding his calls ever since our dinner when he was eating like a puppy dog. What was it going to take for that idiot to get the hint? We made eye contact, and I just gave him a quick nod then returned my attention to Kaleb.

"Who's that?"

Kaleb didn't miss a beat. I noticed the way he was watching me waiting for my reaction. "Just someone who comes into the restaurant a lot." I tried to say it like it was no big deal because in actuality it wasn't a big deal. I went back to dancing and tried to ignore Alphonso even if it wasn't easy. He was standing off near the bar staring at me.

The band performed a Kool and the Gang hit and I started gyrating me hips, ignoring him. The only man on my mind was that sexy mutha in front of me. I was laughing and having such a good time I didn't spot Al until he was walking across the dance floor again. This time, he had the nerve to brush past us.

"Are you sure there isn't anything going on between the two of you?"

"I said there isn't!" I didn't mean to shout, but it was the only way he could hear me over the beat of the music.

"That's funny, because I swore that mothafucka just bumped up against me."

"What? Why would he do that?"

He glared at me. "I don't know, you tell me."

I tried to play it off. But trust me, my insides were churning. "It ain't shit going on between us. Now quit tripping off that dude and dance."

"I'm not tripping. But I'm not stupid. I know what I saw."

I blew out a breath. "I barely even know his name."

We were dancing when I saw Alphonso coming around again. The second he came up behind me, and I felt his hand grope my ass. It took everything I had not to swing around and cuss his ass out. If I did then Kaleb would know I had been lying.

I went back to dancing and was glad when the song was finally over so that we could return to our seat. Kaleb seemed agitated.

"You okay?"

He shook his head. "I don't appreciate that nigga bumping all up against me. If there's something I need to know then you need to tell me so I'll know how to handle the situation."

For a weak moment I almost blurted out about Alphonso groping my ass. But I knew better than that. Instead, I placed a hand on Kaleb's arm trying to reassure him. "There is nothing to tell you. I don't know. Maybe the dude is crazy."

"And you're sure there is nothing going on between the two of you?"

"No." I was really starting to get worried with all of the questions. I really like Kaleb and I didn't want anyone especially not lame-ass Al blowing this chance for me. "Sweetheart, the only man I want is you."

He grinned, and I released a sigh of relief, but then I spotted Alphonso coming passed our table. Quickly I draped an arm around Kaleb's neck and pulled him in for a long kiss. If Al didn't know, he knew now. This was my man. I'd be damned before I let someone stand in the way of my future. After that Kaleb seemed to relax a bit.

Our dessert arrived and we dug in and he commented on how much he enjoyed the peach cobbler. The whole time I kept my eyes on Alphonso. The second I got home I planned to call and lay his ass out.

He moved past the table again and I dropped my eyes to the table making sure Kaleb didn't see me and him make eye contact. Apparently Kaleb was watching him as well. "If that dude looks over here at my woman one more time you might as well alert security."

I grinned. "Your woman, huh? I'm not thinking about that dude and neither should you." We ordered another round of drinks and danced two slow dances. We were heading back to our table when I said, "Hey, babe. I'm going to the ladies room real quick. I'll be right back."

I turned and hurried to the restroom. Those drinks were running right through me. I moved into the only empty stall, peed then washed my hands and slipped down the hall to my office. As soon as I was seated behind my desk, I removed my phone from my purse and sent Alphonso a text.

What the hell are you doing???

That was the reason why I didn't let men I was dating know where I worked. They just couldn't resist stalking me.

I grabbed my purse then hurried back into the main room and over to my hostess.

"Get Al's ass out of my restaurant now!" I hissed loud enough for Penny's ears only.

There was no need to explain. "Sure, Jae. I'll handle it."

I was confident she'd get security right on it. The place was packed. I waved at a few customers then moved back to the table where Kaleb was leaving a nice fat tip.

"Baby you didn't have to do that. Although Charmaine will be real happy to get it."

"That's what a gentleman does." He put his wallet back in his pocket then swung around on the seat. "So what did you go back there to do… meet that mothafucka in the kitchen?"

It took a moment for his words to register. Even then my eyes grew large and my jaw dropped. I was so stung by his comment that it took me a second to find my voice. "Excuse me? I went to the bathroom."

"No the fuck you didn't. You met that mothafucka!" He was practically yelling. Thank goodness the music was too loud for anyone else to hear.

"What?"

"You heard me. You went in the bathroom, called him on

the phone and told him to meet you in the kitchen. I watched him walked that way right after you did."

I couldn't believe what I was hearing. "You're crazy."

He held out his hand. "Then show me your phone."

It took everything I had not to flinch. The last thing I was going to do was give him my phone so he could see that text message I sent. He would swear up and down I'd been lying all the time.

"I'm not going to ask you again. Show me your got-damn phone!" His eyes were large and his chest was heaving. Who the hell was this psycho mothafucka? He had this scared crazy kinda look that I didn't know how to begin to explain.

"You're tripping. Sorry but you got the wrong bitch. I don't do jealous or crazy." With that I rolled my eyes and stormed back to my office. I still couldn't believe what had just happened. How dare he accuse me of meeting another mothafucka around the corner? Back in the day, maybe, but the new me was all about him.

I had just turned on the light and flopped down onto my chair when I glanced up to see Kaleb standing in my doorway.

"The exit is that way." I pointed toward the front of the restaurant.

"Look... I'm sorry."

Seriously? Did he think it would be that easy? "Whatever." I mumbled under my breath.

"I'm serious. I guess I got carried away. I saw the dude looking at my woman all night and I didn't know what to think. For all I knew he could have tried to bust me upside my head."

"Puhleeze. That's what I got security for." I turned on the seat and rolled my eyes. It was going to take a lot more than that before I forgave him.

"I'm sorry. I saw that dude and I just went crazy thinking about someone else being with you."

Anyone else I would have sent packing but Kaleb just intrigued me too much that I felt myself being drawn in again by his charm.

"Babe, I apologize for going crazy like that. Can you please find it in your heart to forgive your man?" He was shaking his head and looked so full of remorse as he stepped into my office. "Baby, we've got so many plans. A life together. A restaurant to expand that we can't let some fool come between what we're tryna build here."

Did he say expand my restaurant? Cha-ching bitch! I was about to cash in. I acted like I was still considering his apology even though I had already made up my mind. I pretended I was looking through a file. Hopefully he wouldn't notice it was upside down.

"I've got so much going on in my life and I need a good woman but it has really been hard for me to be able to trust anyone. I have females running game and trying to get their hands on my money. If you haven't noticed, well, I'm pretty wealthy and I just need someone in my life who's ready for some next-level-type shit. Can you understand where I'm coming from?"

All I heard was wealthy. I could already see us getting married and he buying the vacant space next door, eliminating my student loans and everything else I wanted and needed. That was reason enough to keep hanging in there with his jealous ass. I just had to remember that nothing got past Kaleb and what worked with the other dudes wasn't going to work with him.

But it wasn't anything I couldn't handle.

"Okay," I said like it had been a difficult decision. He just didn't know how easy it had been. "But don't you ever try to embarrass me again!"

"Thank you, babe." By the time he leaned down my head was tilted waiting for his kiss. "I love you," he said between kisses.

"I love you too." I heard myself say and I wasn't sure if I meant it but I knew in my heart that was what I was feeling at this time. He was gorgeous and the sex was decent so what more did I need?

When he finally broke the kiss, I gazed up into his eyes and there it was, love, uncertainty, and swag, all rolled up in one. And let's not forget he was rich. A girl couldn't possibly ask for more.

"Since we're alone, how about I give you a little of my hands-on experience?" I purred then reached down for his zipper.

15

NYREE

Why when you're in a rush everyone wants to move so damn slow? I just don't get it.

We had just landed at St. Louis International Airport and the door was open yet everyone was moving like they had all the time in the world. I didn't want to push my way down the aisle but I was eager to see Jeremy.

I finally got off the plane dragging my rolling suitcase behind me. I decided to dip into a restroom and freshen my make-up. The whole time I was putting on my mascara my hand was shaking. I couldn't believe how nervous I was to see him. I was wearing Rocawear jeans, a form fitting chocolate blouse that dipped low in the front and brown pumps. I looked good. Hell, I looked better than good. I looked fierce! I popped a few breath mints in my mouth then hurried toward the exit.

And there he was.

Jeremy was standing right at the end of the exit holding a bouquet of flowers and looking nervous, with that boyish grin of his that I liked so much. His melon shaped head was even starting to grow on me.

"Hey, beautiful," he greeted, and stared at me as if I was Mariah Carey or somebody.

I blushed and moved toward him, swaying my hips, hoping he hadn't missed all these curves. "Hey, Jeremy." When I was close enough, he wrapped me in his strong arms and squeezed me tightly. I wasted no time tilting my head, and then our lips met. It was like the Fourth of July. I got these sparks that shot through my entire body. I'm serious, warmth flooded through me and when his tongue touched mine I had to fight back a moan. I loved the way Jeremy kissed. He had this way of making me feel beautiful and wanted. Something that Rock had never been able to do for me no matter how much I tried to convince myself otherwise. This man made me feel like the luckiest woman in Missouri.

When we finally broke off the kiss, Jeremy handed me my flowers. "These are for you," he said.

I looked briefly down at the beautiful spring bouquet then back up into his eyes that were waiting for affirmation. "Thank you. It's beautiful."

He sighed and I noticed how his shoulders sagged with relief. There was just this innocence about this man that intrigued me. I hadn't quite put my finger on what it was but it was almost as if he was unsure what to do or say at the risk of making a mistake. I wasn't sure if it was because his marriage of ten years had ended badly or that he really wanted things between us to work.

"We better get outta here," he said and took my rolling bag and my hand in the other. We walked down to the lower level, bumping playfully into each other while grinning like school kids.

"I missed you." He was honest like that.

"I missed you, too," I replied.

"After I had made it clear to Timmy I wasn't interested in rekindling, Jeremy and I spent the rest of the week talking on the phone getting to know each other and there were so many things about this man I admired. He was interested in being a student of my past and I never thought about relationships that way. Nevertheless, the fact that he was interested in learning everything he could made me feel important.

"So where do you want to eat?" he asked once we had my bags and were in his Tahoe, heading away from the airport. He was holding my hand and looking at me with so much adoration I felt like I was floating.

"Anywhere is fine with me." My mind was already on the

days ahead. I know I was probably moving fast, especially since I've been burned before but I couldn't help it.

He pulled into Olive Garden's parking lot. I hated their food but since I had already said it didn't matter, I decided to keep my mouth shut for now. The man was nervous enough as it was.

Ten minutes after our orders had been taken, Jeremy reached across the table for my hands. "Hey beautiful," he teased.

"Hey handsome." Jeremy was getting cuter with every passing minute. I think with him his inner beautiful was starting to outshine everything else.

"What are you feeling right now?"

I drew in a shaky breath. "Excited... scared."

He nodded. "I feel the same way. What are you most afraid of?"

"How much I really like you," I said, in a rush of words.

Jeremy looked confused. "What do you mean?"

I squeezed his hand. "I mean how quickly you have become such an important part of my life. It's like I've known you for a long time."

Jeremy nodded. "I feel the same way. I had a long talk with my dad yesterday and I was telling him about you. He said, "Son, this is the first woman I've heard you talk about like this.""

Of course I was grinning.

He squeezed my hand. "I don't know why God brought you in my life, but I do know it was for a reason. I'm looking forward to finding out what that reason is."

Our food arrived and he took my hands again and we said grace. I had always believed in God but there was something about Jeremy that made me want to dig deeper and develop a stronger relationship. I truly had a lot in my life to be thankful for.

"...And Lord, thank you so much for bringing my Angel back home safely to me. In your precious son's name I pray, Amen." Before he released my hand, Jeremy brought it to his lips and kissed it. "You don't mind me calling you Angel, do you?" he asked and he released his hold.

"No, not at all." Hopefully I could live up to the name.

I reached for my fork. I was so excited just being here with him I didn't have much of an appetite, which was crazy since I hadn't eaten anything since lunch and it was already after seven.

"What you got planned for the rest of the night?" he asked.

I didn't even hesitate. "Spending it with you."

Jeremy nodded. "I like the sound of that."

Leaning closer, I whispered, "I even have a clean change of clothes in my suitcase."

He stared across the table at me then down at his plate, as if gathering the guts to say whatever was coming next. "I can't promise you I'm going to behave with you lying in the bed beside me."

"I would be disappointed if you were," I said and Jeremy nodded in response.

We talked and flirted the entire ride to his apartment. We stepped inside and I barely had time to look around his place when Jeremy pressed his mouth to mine. Nothing rough or persuasive. Just a few nervous pecks. *Really?* I had never been considered the aggressor but with this dude I could tell I was going to have to jump into the driver's seat.

I parted my lips and pushed between his with my tongue and slipped inside. Within seconds I had him eagerly following my lead. Despite his insecurity, Jeremy was really an amazing kisser. He just needed a little push, that's all. He wrapped his arms around me and I tilted my head back slightly and stepped out of my heels so I had a better angle. He was so gentle and his strokes so fluid and slow I might come on myself by the time he figured out I was tryna give him my kitty-kat on a silver platter. Hell, I gave up sex with Timmy because I wanted to make sure I was good and horny the next time I got some.

"I want you to make love to me," I whispered.

He drew back, appeared surprised and finally nodded.

I was amazed when he reached for my zipper, dropped to his knees, and pulled my jeans down over my hips. I knew what was coming next. Jeremy brought his lips to the side of my stomach and around to my hip. Oh my! His lips were so soft, he was driving crazy and I could already imagine how his tongue would feel lapping at my clit. Only he didn't pull my jeans down quickly. Instead, he lowered it inch by inch, the slow motion caressing my pussy. Damn, he was torturing me.

Once my jeans fell to the floor, I thought he would have ripped my panties off. Instead he sat back on the carpet and leaned against the couch as he stared at me.

"I can't believe how beautiful you are."

There I was standing in low rise panties, acting shy. It's crazy but I wanted him to like me. I needed him to want me to be in his life.

He smiled. "C'mere."

I lowered and straddled his waist and he wasted no time lifting my shirt over my head then reaching behind me and fumbling with my bra.

"Let me help you with that," I offered and unclasped it and tossed it to the side. The way he was looking at me made me feel so beautiful. Jeremy finally reached out and stroked my breasts. When he grazed his thumb over a nipple, I gasped. I didn't know if it was the anticipation or the gentle way he teased the tip. Whatever it was, I moaned and closed my eyes while I enjoyed. I couldn't believe he was playing with my breasts.

Oh, this little choir boy had skills.

Jeremy finally leaned forward and sucked a nipple into his mouth. Need ricocheted through my body. I caught myself leaning in close to his lips while he sucked and teased with his tongue. I had to grab onto his shoulders to keep from falling over.

I think what I liked most was that he was gentle. Rock had always been rough like he had to prove a point but Jeremy performed as if we had all the time in the world. And I guess we did. There was no one waiting at home for me. In fact, everything I wanted, everything I needed for the moment was right here in front of me, although this foreplay was starting to go into overkill.

While he feasted at my nipples, I ran my hands down his back and tugged at his shirt. "Take this off."

He lifted his arms and I dragged it up over his head and tossed it away. I wish I could say his body was all that but at least he didn't have a gut or anything. I was hoping his chest had been cut up the way Timmy's was, but I guess you can't have everything.

I rose from his lap and slowly lowered my panties like I was doing a striptease.

"You like what you see?" I asked with a saucy grin.

"Wow!" was all he said but that one word spoke volumes.

I lowered my panties to my feet and was pleased I had remembered to trim my girl up this morning in the shower. Reaching forward he slid his hand between my thighs.

He caught me off guard so I stumbled and fell across his lap. Wow was right! His touch was amazing. It has been a long time since a man has finger fucked me and even longer since a man knew what he was doing.

Maybe I had underestimated him. Jeremy's fingers were long and calloused as they stroked and penetrated me.

"Open your legs," he whispered against my cheek. I was draped across his lap, so I rolled off his legs, resting my weight onto my elbows and parted my thighs.

"Come and get it," I cooed.

"Yes, ma'am," he said playfully. He was grinning and I liked that. And then he was licking me. I hadn't even noticed he had shifted until he was practically lying across the floor on his stomach, and his tongue was right where I needed it. All warm and wet, I was moaning and in a matter of minutes I was crying out his name

"Jeremy, yes!" The orgasm was mind-boggling. As I regained my breathing, I gazed at his smiling face.

"Satisfied?" he asked.

"Yes, but what else you got?" I said still sounding breathless.

He rose and lowered his jeans and his drawers. He had nice legs and a decent size dick. I definitely liked what I saw.

The only complaint was he was hairless. Armpits, chest and pubic were all smooth like a baby's ass.

"What's wrong?"

"Oh, nothing," I lied. "Nothing at all." I spread my legs and waited while he settled between my thighs.

"Shit," I heard him mutter under his breath.

I raised my gaze and looked at him. "What's wrong?" Jeremy lowered his eyelids. "Just give me a moment."

He started slapping the head of his dick along my kitty and I immediately knew what the problem was. Jeremy couldn't get it up.

I then tried to give him a hand job and even tried slobbering on his knob, but it was useless.

"Wow! I'm sorry," he said and was clearly embarrassed. Jeremy rolled over onto his back and was gazing up at the ceiling.

"Hey, I've been known to have that effect on men," I joked hoping he would relax only it seemed to make matter worse.

"I never have this problem."

I knew he was probably lying but honestly it didn't matter. His tongue skills had been on point and he looked so cute lying there beside me. "There will be plenty of time for sex. Right now I'm happy just to be with you."

Jeremy scowled with disbelief. "Yeah right."

"I'm serious." I moved closer so I could look down into his eyes. "You might not believe this but I really like what we have. And sex, whenever it happens, will just be an added bonus," I commented with a wink.

Finally smiling, he dragged me into his arms and kissed me.

16

JANELLE

"Oh hell nah!" I gasped as I pulled into an empty parking space and brought the car to a quick stop.

Please tell me it's not too late!

I climbed out and stepped into the street without even bothering to look both ways. Of course some fool in a Fiat slammed on his brakes to avoid hitting me. My heart was racing out of control. He gave me the evil eye then zoomed by. Okay, so maybe I did step out into the middle of a busy street, but I was under the impression the pedestrian always had the right-of-way.

After looking both ways, I dashed across Broadway in mustard-yellow pumps and a slamming chocolate suit I had found at Macy's. As soon as I reached the sidewalk I hurried over to the space next to my restaurant and stepped inside.

"Excuse me," I said and the two men inside turned and both greeted me with a smile. Naturally, they were captivated by my beauty.

"I noticed the sign was gone from the window. Did someone buy this space?" I asked.

The carpenter in white bib overalls nodded. "Yep, some management company took it off the market yesterday."

"Damn," I scowled. That was truly disappointing.

"Hey, haven't I seen you in the restaurant next door?" asked the one with a hammer in his hand.

I nodded. "Yes, and this space would have been perfect for expanding." I turned and was heading toward the door when he called after me, and I paused.

"Hey, I have a contact name if you want it." Before I could respond, he reached inside his pocket. "He dropped by this morning and left his card." I took the black business card from his hand and gazed down at the name on the card.

"*Alphonso Rucker?*" I looked up. "He owns this space?"

He nodded. And I felt like someone had just punched me in the stomach. "Yes. He's planning on opening a store."

"Yeah, a tacky store," I mumbled under my breath. "Thank you."

I stormed out the door. How dare that bastard buy the space next door to me! His hip-hop gear and hoodlum clientele would be bad for business. Sure he was the top real estate developer in the city, but his name was also linked to several crack houses and juke joints, not to mention his little tacky clothing shops.

I unlocked the door and stepped into the restaurant. We didn't open for two more hours and that was a good thing. I was pissed off!

The lights were still dim up front but the kitchen was in full swing. I heard music and laughter. I stormed toward the back. "What are y'all so damn happy about?" I didn't mean to snap but I wasn't in the best of mood.

Mimi was beaming with pride. "Jamie got accepted into barber school."

I put my feelings aside and smiled over at my cousin. "Good for you!" I said. "You decided to follow after Brice?"

With his head lowered, he nodded. "Yep."

"Well I would have rather you worked for me but I'm sure my knucklehead brother will be glad to have you working at his shop." Brice owned a large barbershop off Providence Road. Everybody went there to get their hair cut.

"No doubt he will." April then clapped her hands. "A'ight everybody. We need to get back to work. I need to smell cornbread and black-eyed peas."

I patted Jamie on the back so he'd know just how proud I

was of him then moved out the kitchen and down the hall to my office. April followed.

"You look pissed."

She never did miss much.

I flopped down in my chair. "I am. Guess who got the space next door?"

Her brow quirked as she lowered onto one of the chairs across from my desk. "Who?"

It pained me to say it. "Alphonso."

"What!" she screamed.

"Exactly." I was so mad I couldn't do anything but shake my head. That man was determined to get my attention. "He's probably still pissed I kicked him out my restaurant." After Kaleb got done acting a damn fool in the restaurant that evening, Al started blowing up my phone most of the night. Luckily, Kaleb hadn't noticed.

April gave me a curious look. "So what are you going to do?"

"I'm going to his job to see him," I announced with a stubborn tilt of my chin. Trust and believe nothing was stopping me from getting what I wanted.

"You know that's what he wants you to do."

I swung a jeweled wrist in the air. "Yeah, I know, but he also knows how badly I wanted that space to expand my restaurant."

She shook her head. "All this just to get your attention? Your coochie must be dipped in gold or some shit," she added with a laugh and despite feeling some type of way about the situation, I joined in.

"Yeah girl. It's all about the power of the pussy. Unfortunately, I'm gonna have to use her to get what I want from Al."

After April left my office to check on lunch, I sent Alphonso a quick text and invited him to the restaurant for lunch. He texted back.

I'll meet you at your house instead.

I thought about it for all of thirty seconds before I replied then I grabbed my purse and headed home to set the stage.

* * *

Will I ever learn that some men are not to be played with?

Two hours later I was trying to remain calm when what I wanted to do was crack that fool over his head. It's not often that a woman finds herself in a compromising position when another man shows up. Why the hell didn't I stick with my original plan and have Alphonso meet me at the restaurant? If I had then I would be surrounded by witnesses instead of hiding in the bathroom of my townhouse.

After Alphonso had texted he would meet me at my house, I hurried home and decided to create a scene of seduction.

As soon as I arrived, I lit several candles, turned on some soft music and then searched my clothes for something slutty to wear. I settled on a tight red number with no bra or panties and had just lubed my pussy with oil when I heard the doorbell.

I swung it opened and screamed when I realized who was standing on my front porch. "Kaleb!"

"Why you look so surprised?" he said suspiciously as he pushed past and stepped inside my living room.

"Be… because I was just getting ready to call and tell you to come over," I said. Damn, I was quick.

"No you weren't," he said like he knew what I had really been up to.

"Yes, I was. I wanted to surprise you. I decided to take the day off and was going to see if you could come and spend the afternoon in bed with me."

Honey came in the room sniffing around his feet. "Hey Honey," he cooed and his face softened for a few moments while he rubbed him behind the ear, but it didn't last. "Where you get that outfit?" he asked as he suddenly realized what I was wearing was hot. *Really?*

I struck a pose. "I bought it at a lingerie party a while back and have been waiting for the perfect opportunity to wear it."

I gave a coy smile. "I thought today was perfect, don't you think?" I sashayed over to him and started loosening his tie. "I'm horny. For once I'd like my man to fuck me and be able to scream as loud as I'd like."

"You *know* I have a son."

Goodness, don't remind me. "Yes, I know but sometimes I want my man all to myself."

I guess I must have said the right thing because he started grinning and unbuttoning his jacket. "Hold up. Let me go take a leak."

I nodded and started backing up toward the stairs. "Okay, I'll be upstairs waiting."

He was already walking in the direction of the half-bath near the kitchen when he suddenly stopped and swung around. "I'll just use the bathroom upstairs."

Damn.

I struggled to keep a straight face and took his hand and led him up to my bedroom. We stepped inside and I felt nervous sweat start beading along, my forehead. My cellphone was on the side of my bed, and I just prayed it didn't ring before I had a chance to shut that damn thing off.

As soon as Kaleb shut the bathroom door behind him, I dived onto the bed and grabbed my phone. My fingers were shaking so hard it took three tries before I was able to unlock the screen. By then I heard water running on the other side of the door.

Don't come. My man's here.

I quickly hit Send, turned off the ringer and tossed the phone back onto the nightstand just as Kaleb yanked open the door, like he was expecting to catch me.

"What are you doing?"

"Nothing," I said and hoped Alphonso received my text in time.

He walked over to the nightstand and glanced down at my phone. Sorry Charlie, I stop receiving text notifications the last time I caught that fool holding my phone.

"What were you doing, texting your man telling him not

to come over?" It was more a statement than a question. You could see the distrust in his eyes. What the hell happened to him that he was so insecure when it came to women and relationships?

"Now why would I do that when my man is right here?" I stood my ground.

"Jae... who were you texting?"

"Okay, whatever." I rolled my eyes because his jealousy was really starting to get on my nerves. I rolled off the bed and gazed out the window in time to see Alphonso driving slowly past my house. *What the fuck?*

"Babe?"

I whipped around and stepped over to Kaleb before he even had a chance to look out the window. If he saw a car out front I would never hear the end of it. "Sweetheart, let's quit wasting time. I want to show my man how much I care about him." I took his hand and led him over to the chair to the right of the room. "Have a seat." The further he was from that window, the better. I just prayed Alphonso kept right on going.

I then moved over to my iPad on the dresser, searched through the music until I found what I was looking for then turned it on and watched as Kaleb's mouth dropped.

A couple of months ago I had decided to dance for this dude I was dating and had choreographed a striptease to Ciara's *Body Party*. I dumped his ass long before I got to perform it so what better time to showcase my skills than now.

I was gyrating my hips and licking my lips and Kaleb was so caught up in watching, he forgot all about my cellphone and instead was watching as I lowered my panties to my ankles.

"Damn, babe." His eyes were ready to pop out of his head.

"You see something you like," I purred and tossed my panties at him. I was so bad. I removed the outfit and approached him wearing nothing.

By the end of the song Kaleb exploded from the chair and backed me over onto the bed. As soon as I fell onto the mattress, he lowered onto his knees. "How about a little afternoon snack?" he said.

"Mmmm, lunch is my favorite meal of the day," I cooed.

While he feasted between my legs, I laid there with my eyes closed, knees spread, moaning on cue. My mind was elsewhere. I still needed to see Alphonso and get that space back.

"Babe?"

"Hmmm," I mumbled.

"Who's that knocking at the door?"

My eyelids flew open and I jerked upright on the bed sending Kaleb crashing to the floor. "Oh, sweetheart... I'm so sorry!" I said, while I was scrambling to my feet.

Kaleb rose with that suspicious look in his eyes. "Who's at the door Jae?"

I was already heading to the closet for my silk robe, avoiding eye contact. "How the hell should I know?" I swung my arms inside and was tying the belt as I said, "But let me go down and see."

"Uh-uh. Hell no! My girl's not going to the door, dressed like that. I'll get it."

I was so busted I couldn't do anything but nod. As soon as he walked out the room my heart went into overdrive. I moved over to the window to see if I saw Alphonso's car and spotted it parked at the corner.

Stupid! Stupid!

I raced into the bathroom and locked the door behind me. There was no telling what Kaleb was going to do when he saw Alphonso standing on the other side of the door.

It wasn't long before I heard heavy footsteps coming up the stairs. "Babe!"

Oh shit!

I flushed the toilet and pretended I didn't hear Kaleb. I had no idea where Alphonso was. Probably laid the fuck out on my living room floor.

"Jae, where you at?" he called from on the other side of the door.

"I-I'll be out in a moment."

Frantically I looked through my bathroom drawers for

something sharp just in case that crazy mothafucka tried to lay me out as well. Damn! The only thing I could find was a nail file.

"Hurry your ass up!" Kaleb was practically screaming.

Damn I shoulda brought my phone with me so I could have called 911 for an ambulance, possibly two.

There was no way I could stay in the bathroom all day. I stuck the file in my sleeve and slowly turned the knob. I expected to find Kaleb waiting on the other side of the door.

"Babe!" he called.

"Yeah?" I said, cautiously, then stuck my head out.

"Bring yo ass over here!"

Kaleb was lying across the bed, butt-naked with his dick standing straight up. *What the fuck?*

I crept out the room and glanced out into the hallway. "Sweetheart, who was at the door?" I questioned and searched his face for some kind of reaction.

He waved his hand. "Those damn Jehovah Witnesses! I gave 'em a five dollar donation and sent her on her way."

Her?

"C'mon babe. I'm horny as hell!" He started shaking his dick at me.

I started chuckling and shrugged out of the robe, dropping the file to the floor then climbed on for a French kiss and a nice long ride. I'll worry about Alphonso later. Right now I had to take care of my man.

17

NYREE

I heard a horn blow. I reached for my purse and stepped out onto the porch.

"Hooker, hurry up!"

I tossed a dismissive wave in the air. Janelle can be such a drama whore. I don't know what the rush was but I didn't have anything else to do on a Saturday afternoon. Jeremy was at choir rehearsal.

"So you went and got yourself a church boy," Janelle teased as she pulled out the driveway.

"Girl, whatever," I said. "I got myself a good man."

She looked away from the road long enough to give me a weird look. "Aren't they all in the beginning?"

I leaned back on the seat and changed the subject. "So what do you need me for?"

"Alphonso snatched the space beside Foxtrot."

My head whipped around. "Really? For what?"

Janelle frowned. "To open one of those tacky clothing stores of his."

She forgot about the hot royal blue pantsuit she had bought at that tacky shop. In fact while they were dating she had been raving about his inventory.

"Anyway," she began dismissively. "I want you to go with me to his real estate office and convince him to give me the space."

My head whipped around. *"What?* He's not gonna listen to me!"

Her eyes were all but studying me. "Why not? You used to date him." She was trying to sound as convincing as possible.

"You're right. I *used* to date him."

What gets me is, as friends we're supposed to have an unspoken rule — don't date your best friend's ex-boyfriend. I mean sure, Alphonso and I had dated for a brief time in high school and never had sex but still dating is dating. Janelle thinks since it's been a decade the statute of limitations is over. *Wow! Really?* At first I had been pissed but then I decided, who cares? The three weeks Alphonso and I were together was barely a memory.

"But he respects you as a friend," she stated firmly.

"And he doesn't respect you?"

I caught her eyebrow inching up before saying, "Hell no. Ever since I saw him lapping his soup like a puppy dog and dumped him, he's been on some psycho bullshit."

"I'm not getting involved in your crap!"

Janelle sucked her teeth. "Okay, whatever. Then stay in the car as a witness. If I don't come out in fifteen minutes then you need to call the police."

Like I said, she's a drama queen. She pulled onto Ash Street into a small strip mall and climbed out then sauntered inside with her wide hips swinging in a short yellow dress that was perfect for her curves and lime green pumps. One thing she knew was fashion.

I watched as she swung open the glass door to his office and went inside.

I leaned back onto the seat, sulking. I could be at Sam's Club doing some bulk shopping. Instead I was about to be an accessory to who knows what. Since I've been ignoring my mother all morning I decided to give her a call. She too could be a drama queen.

"Hey Mom."

"About time you call me back. For all you know I could have fallen and can't get up."

I laughed. "Mama, I've seen the commercial. How are you

this afternoon?"

"Blessed. I just left church. Everyone is talking about that wonderful new man of yours."

I shifted on the seat and brought the phone closer to my ear. "What are they saying?"

"That Jeremy is truly a child of God! I was happy to see him at choir rehearsal. Why weren't you there?"

"Because I can't sing." Although neither could Jeremy, but that didn't stop him. With that squeaky voice of his, hopefully the choir director had stuck him way in the back. I was crazy about him but I was gonna keep it real.

"Whether you can sing or not doesn't matter. Chile, you're singing for the Lord."

"Trust me, Mama. The Lord doesn't want to hear me."

She released a long sigh of disappointment. "I don't know what I'm going to do with you."

I couldn't help but smile. Mabeline Dawson was something else. "Just keep loving me Mama. That's all I ask." That's all I've ever wanted. Being the middle child was tough.

"Your father and I would love to have you both for Sunday dinner tomorrow."

I groaned. An afternoon with my family grilling him, I wasn't sure if Jeremy was up for the task. He always seemed to get nervous when there were a lot of people around. For such a good looking man, he sure had insecurity issues but it wasn't anything I didn't think I could work with. I don't know what it was but I always liked a challenge. Not like that bullshit Janelle get off on but the challenge that came with being with a good man with a great deal of potential. I always believed that behind every great man was a woman pushing him to be the best he could be.

"Sure Mama. We'll be there." I glanced up to see Janelle storming out of the office. Oh shit, she was mad! "Mama, I'll see you in the morning." I hung up just as she hopped into the car. "What's wrong?" I asked even though I already knew. Janelle didn't get her way.

"The bastard. No problem. I have something for that ass!" She hissed then threw the car in reverse and peeled around to the side of the parking lot, where she brought the car to a screeching halt.

"Why're you stopping?" This whole situation just spelled trouble in too many ways.

She didn't bother to answer me as she reached into the glove box, and what I saw her pull out made me gasp, "Janelle, where the hell are you going with that switchblade?"

"Watch," was all she said before she rushed out of the car.

"What is that crazy chick about to do?" I mumbled under my breath as I watched her walk over to a black Lexus and stab the rear tires with the blades. Laughing, she hurried back over to the car and jumped in.

"*Are you crazy?*" I squealed.

She put her Honda into Drive and hurried out the parking lot then headed down Ash Street. "That's what he gets!" she screamed with laughter.

I tightened my seatbelt and shook my head. "You have lost your mind."

"Nope. Not yet but if he moves in next to me you're going to see just how crazy I can get." She held up her finger to emphasize her position.

I couldn't believe this shit. Not only did she vandalize his car but she took me along as an accomplice. "What if he calls the police?"

Janelle shrugged and didn't bother to look away from the road as she said, "Call them for what? I'm with you shopping at the mall. Besides, the plates are illegal on that vehicle so he ain't calling nobody."

"Illegal? I don't want to know." Her cellphone started buzzing.

"No, you don't." She was laughing like a crazy woman now. "Speaking of shopping... let's go to Macy's right quick. They have this new UGGS purse I want you to see."

Her phone was ringing again. "Aren't you going to answer your phone?"

"Nope. It's just Kaleb's needy ass trying to keep track of me. I'm playing possum for the next hour."

See, I told you she's crazy.

Sometimes I think my life must really be boring because I keep hanging and living vicariously through Janelle. Seriously. I'm in the military so there is no way in hell I'm risking my security clearance smoking weed or dating shady dudes like Janelle. Instead I get to listen to her stories and watch the crazy stuff that she does. It's the next best thing to real life.

* * *

I had made it back home and was lying on the couch watching reruns of Martin when Jeremy called. "Hey Angel, whadda you want for dinner?"

He was so thoughtful. "How about Tony's Pizza?"

"No problem. Text me what you want on it and I'll go get it."

I hung up and sat there half watching the sitcom while I was thinking about this wonderful new man in my life. He was definitely something special. And my parents liked him which made it even better because Deacon Charles Dawson was a hard man to please.

My daddy was retired military. We traveled around most of my life before he finally returned to his roots in Missouri. He was actually from Sedalia but we moved to Columbia. Thank goodness he didn't return to that little-ass town. My parents met in grammar school and have been together ever since. Growing up I've always wanted what they have, commitment, dedication, something I never had with my ex-husband Shane.

Sometimes I think I move too fast thinking every man was that special guy in my life. I get so caught up in the moment that all I can see is right now. I'll admit that I'm flawed. I wanted so desperately to stop meeting Mr. Right Now and finally find my Mr. Right.

With Jeremy I was already imagining a long relationship. I just had to keep reminding myself to take it one day at a time and not rush this time. I already had a feeling that wasn't going to be easy.

By the time I went and got sodas and plates from the

kitchen, Jeremy was knocking at my door. It was crazy how excited I was to see him, especially since we've been together almost every day since we'd met.

"Hey sweetheart," I said as I opened the door and met his smile. He leaned in and kissed me soundly on the lips before stepping into the living room.

"What are you watching?" he asked.

"Nothing really. Just waiting for the game to come on."

I took a seat on the couch beside him and took in his faded jeans and button up shirt he was wearing. It looked like another one of those George brand shirts he bought at Walmart. I really was going to have to start shopping for him.

"I brought over something I want to show you after we get done eating," he said with the nervous smile of his again.

I smiled and reached for his hand as we prepared to say grace. "Okay."

We bowed our head and I listened as he blessed our food. "...And Lord thank you for bringing this beautiful Angel into my life. Amen." Before releasing my hand he kissed it then let it go. I felt special. This was our thing—his and mine. And I enjoyed every second of it.

We ate pizza and I told him about my shopping trip with Janelle, minus the detour to Alphonso's job.

"Mama invited us to dinner tomorrow," I managed between chews.

He nodded. "Good stuff. I like your parents."

I playfully rolled my eyes. "And they like you."

"I really want you to meet my parents. I know they'll like you." He reached for his soda.

"I would like that."

"We usually have a big family get together for the Fourth of July weekend so maybe you can go with me?"

There was that look of insecurity again. "Sure. I would love to go with you to Memphis."

He was grinning like a little boy again. Why did I have this strong urge to pat his head?

"I was talking to my daughter on the way over here."

"She's the senior, right?"

He nodded and swallowed before saying, "Yes, she's graduating next month and wanted to know how many tickets I needed. I told her two." He was looking at me staring, waiting for my reaction. "I was wondering if you would drive to Chicago with me for her graduation?"

My eyes snapped to his. This man was ready to introduce me to his kids. I can't even begin to tell you how good that made me feel!

"I would love to go with you," I said between bites. "Now which one is this?"

"This is my oldest Tiffany. Caleb graduates next year and Jose is fourteen."

I nodded. He always sounded so proud when he talked about his kids.

"I'll warn you. Their mother is ignorant."

"Delaney, right?" A man loves when he knows a woman has been paying attention.

"Right. She is a bitter woman and probably won't say two words to you the entire graduation luncheon."

I wasn't the least bit worried. It was her loss, not mine.

"Graduation is at nine o'clock on Saturday, so I was hoping we could go down on Friday, right after work."

Nodding, I replied, "No problem." I was already looking forward to taking the six-hour drive together.

He reached for a napkin, wiped his hands then reached for a bag and pulled out a book. "Have you ever read this before?"

I took it from his hands. "*The Five Love Languages*." I flipped it over, then shook my head. "No, I never heard of it."

"It's a powerful book."

"What's it about?"

His face lit up at my interest. "It talks about speaking your mate's love language. It really reveals how people express love in different way."

"Love huh?"

He looked down at his feet. "Yeah there are five languages, quality time, words of affirmation, gifts, acts of service and physical touch."

"So what are you?"

"That's the fun part," he laughed nervously as he spoke. "We take the test and learn how to communicate to each other."

I nodded. "So are you trying to tell me something?"

He grinned. "Yeah, actually, I am."

"And?"

He sighed then put the book on the table beside the pizza, reached for the remote and turned off the television before he swung around to face me on the couch. Whatever he was about to say had to be serious. "C'mere." I didn't even have a chance before he dragged me into his arms and held me close. His lips were only inches away. "Nyree... I have prayed for years for God to bring someone like you in my life. I have desired a wife and a second chance and I feel in my heart that woman is you."

My heart was pounding as if a car had pulled out in front of me.

"If this isn't what you want please tell me now." He studied my face trying to figure out if I was serious.

"You're everything I've always wanted and more." And I was about to find out in the next few seconds.

His lips came crashing into my mine and I wasted no time tangling my tongue with his. Like I've said before I loved kissing my man. I moaned and he leaned forward and lowered me onto the couch with him on top of me.

"I missed you today," he murmured.

"And I missed you," I whispered. His hand went underneath my t-shirt and wasted no time at finding my breasts. "Yes," I moaned hoping if I continued to encourage him we might for once finish what he was starting. But after a few more minutes of fondling I was growing increasingly irritated. "Are you planning to fuck me, or what?"

First he looked offended then he suddenly got all nervous again.

What the fuck? I could see I was going to have to run things in the bedroom because this dude was just too naïve, insecure or something. What, I didn't have a clue. All I knew was I was going to have to show him what I liked.

I rolled out from underneath him and then removed my clothes while he just sat there on the couch, staring at me. "On the floor," I ordered and like an obedient puppy, he scrambled onto the thick rug in front of the television. "Now get undressed."

"You must think you're the man," he joked.

Somebody's gotta be.

Jeremy did as he was told and tossed his clothes aside, revealing his throbbing erection. Deep down, I think my being in charge, turned him on.

I lowered to my knees and took hold of his Johnson. Of course he bucked beneath my touch.

"I think you like that," I teased then went to work licking the length of him, tasting precum at the tip.

"I do… oh yeah," he moaned.

I straddled him, brushing my vagina against his thigh then leaned forward and allowed my tongue to trace the head before taking him into my mouth again.

"Oh babe!" he moaned softly.

My head game was on point. I took my time learning my man, squeezing his balls, sucking his Johnson, drawing him deeper into my mouth. The entire time he was watching me. I didn't dare look at him because he was sure to get nervous all over again so I just continued putting on one hell of a show.

"That's it, baby," he groaned appreciatively. "Suck my dick."

I froze, completely caught off guard to hear something like that coming out Jeremy's mouth. "What did you just say?" I giggled with his dick still between my lips.

"You heard me," he whispered, "suck my dick."

Yeah baby. I heard you. There might be some hope for you after all.

The harder I sucked, the louder he panted. His hips were rocking and his hands were now at the back of my head guiding my motion.

"No more, please!" he insisted hoarsely. "Ride me."

No point in the party ending before it really got started.

I watched Jeremy's face as I eased down onto his length until he was completely inside. Oh snap! He felt *sooo* good. I had to take a moment and pause just to adjust to the way he felt.

I started to ride him. Slow at first then I began to pick up speed but not too fast because I wanted this moment to last. Placing his hands at my hips, Jeremy slowly began to move up and down while using my hips as leverage to glide in and out of me.

"Sssssh, *ooooh, yesss,*" I moaned.

I moved his hands to my breasts and his thumb teased my nipples. "Look at me," I commanded. "Look at me and don't you dare move."

As soon as our eyes locked, I began rocking my hips again.

This control thing was arousing. I kept staring at him and wouldn't allow him to guide our rhythm. It was fucking incredible. I wasn't sure how much longer he could hold on. His face look strained and his dick was so damn hard, I was ready to explode.

I reached down between us and stroked my clit then slid up and down his Johnson like crazy. Forget lovemaking. Sometimes a woman needed to be fucked, hard and rough. Finding a rhythm, I pumped away, moaning with delight. Jeremy had me feeling so good. He panted beneath me as I slammed down on his dick.

"I'm getting ready to come," he said on a harsh breath.

His words were all I needed to hear. My body shook, and then I exploded with pleasure. "Oh God! Oh God, Jeremy!"

Jeremy suddenly flipped me over onto my back and pumped hard and fast while I cried out his name some more.

"That's it, Angel," he groaned as he continued his deep thrusts. My release went on and on until a climax rocked Jeremy's body as well.

I was breathless as I gazed up at his face and saw everything he was feeling. "There's hope for you yet."

His eyes widened like he didn't understand. "Is that a good thing?" he asked.

"Yes." Because he wasn't the only one falling in love.

18

JANELLE

It was almost ten o'clock when I pulled my car onto the circular driveway and killed the engine. *I love my new life,* I thought as I gazed at the grand house. I was practically living at Kaleb's. The house was dark, no lights were coming from his bedroom window, which was disappointing because I was hoping Kaleb was still up waiting for me.

I sighed then grabbed my purse and climbed out the car. It was such a beautiful night. If I wasn't so tired I would have sat out on the porch with a glass of wine and meditated. Instead all I wanted was a hot shower and the bed. Brice and I had spent the evening clearing out my mother's storage shed for Goodwill tomorrow. Seeing all that stuff had brought back way too many memories of a time in my life I'd just rather forget.

I moved up the stairs and typed the four-digit passcode into the keypad and stepped inside. No one came down and greeted me. Not even Honey. I slipped off my heels and padded into the kitchen barefoot where I retrieved a bottle of water. It was then I noticed the red rose petals on the floor. I followed the trailed up the back stairs and when I reached the landing I saw roses scattered all down the hall. I couldn't contain my excitement as I moved toward his bedroom. But as I passed CJ's door, it swung open. His big horse and Honey came dashing out the room. For some odd reason the two of them were thick as thieves.

"Ms. Jae, can I talk to you for a moment?" CJ asked and looked so freaked out about something.

Damn, talk about bad timing. "What is it CJ?" I said and followed him into his funky bedroom.

CJ swung around and it was then that I noticed he was holding a small box. Is that what I think—

"Ms. Jae, will you marry me *and* my dad?"

At that very moment I heard movement behind me and I swung around to find Kaleb standing behind me with a single white rose in his hand. I smiled then looked over at the ring again. Hot damn! That rock was huge!

"Well babe, you heard the boy... will you marry us?"

I looked from the pitiful look on CJ's face to the solemn one on his father's face. They both looked like they were preparing for me to say no. Sure, I wanted to marry Kaleb but I was thinking months from now after he started spending some of his money on me. If Kaleb had proposed in private maybe I could have convinced him it was a little soon but there was that sad look in CJ' eyes that said these two mothafuckas desperately needed me.

I paused briefly, glancing up at the ceiling as if considering my answer and then I answered. "Yes... I'll marry you."

CJ's shoulders sagged with relief and he looked to his father and grinned.

"You made us so happy." Kaleb stepped inside the room and I wrapped my arms around both of them. We were now a family. Apparently, Honey liked the idea, because my little Pomeranian was out in the hall dry humping Midnight.

19

NYREE

It's been weeks since we had all gotten together so I was actually smiling as I climbed out of my Lexus and moved up the long driveway to Gloria's new house. I passed Veronica's Audi. Of course she was already there.

Jeremy was at some Kingdom Man religious conference in Bloomington, IL for the weekend so I was free for some girl's time.

I rang the doorbell and Gloria came to the door looking like she had just won the lottery.

"Hey girl!" she cried.

I threw my arms around Gloria's neck and hugged her. She kissed me on the cheek. "How are you Mrs. Married Woman?" I said as I released her.

"I couldn't be happier. Come on in and make yourself at home." She was grinning from ear to ear.

The moment I stepped into the foyer my eyes shot open wide with surprise. "Girl, your house is beautiful!" I squealed. There was no mistaking the pride on her face. And I don't blame her. Talk about something out of a magazine. I walked around, admiring the expensive décor. High ceilings. Mahogany flooring. Beautiful furnishing. "I'm so jealous." Hey, might as well keep it real. Her house was something I hoped to someday have with Jeremy. My house was only fifteen-hundred square feet. That little apartment where Jeremy lived was embarrassing. But *this* was exactly what I wanted us to have.

"Gloria, you've been holding out on me! You and Pierre pick this house out together?"

Her face was absolutely beaming. "We closed on it right before the wedding."

"Damn, I hate you," I said playfully before she signaled for me to follow her down the hall to a large family room in back where Veronica and Janelle were already sitting on the couch with a glass in their hands.

"Hey girl!" Veronica waved.

"Hey, Ronnie," I said then looked over at Janelle with my brow raised. "Where's your car?"

She gave me a saucy grin. "My man dropped me off."

"What? He still tryna to keep tabs on you?" I said like it was a joke but I was serious.

She waved her hand as if she was dismissing me. "You know how men are, they wanna make sure ain't nobody else sniffing their pussy."

Veronica was practically falling off the couch. She was definitely a clown.

"Nyree you want something to drink?"

I swung around and walked over to the bar where Gloria was standing pouring herself a glass of wine. "Yes, I'll have one of those, as well."

"Hey, you like my shoes?"

Veronica stuck out her bare leg and showed off a slamming pair of purple and gold pumps. "Ooh, I love those! Where'd you find them?"

"I found this online shoe club y'all gonna have to join." She started talking about the website while Gloria filled my flute. As soon as I had a glass in my hand I moved over to a lovely leather sectional and took a seat.

"Are those the honeymoon pictures?" I asked, pointing to the two large albums sitting on the coffee table.

"Ooh! Girl, check these out." Janelle handed me both the books. "We need to plan us a trip to Cabo."

Veronica nodded. "Hell yeah! Let's go."

"I'm so glad y'all came over. It feels like it's been forever since we've gotten together." Gloria was still smiling.

I wonder if I looked like that when I'm with Jeremy? I sure hope so. The whole *Five Love Languages* book and even a daily one-minute guide had really made a difference in our relationship. We talked, fellowship, and even prayed together. With each day Jeremy seemed more sure about himself and where he stood in our relationship, and I knew it could only get better.

Gloria came around, long dark ponytail bouncing, and took a seat on the ottoman, stretching her long legs out in front of her. Her skin was a banana yellow with a tinge of honey and after two months of marriage, she was still glowing. "So what have you two been up to?" Gloria asked between sips.

I looked over at Janelle and she looked at me. We were both grinning.

"Y'all want me to tell her," Veronica said looking from her to me.

I nodded my head, too excited to say anything.

"What's going on?" Gloria had no idea.

Veronica pointed her finger at us. "Gloria these two have been on Black folks meet dot com."

"What?" she leaned forward on the ottoman. "And? Did y'all meet anyone?"

I was nodding. "Yes, I've met a wonderful man, spiritual, gentle, loving and most importantly, single."

"I know that's right!" Veronica gave me a high five.

Gloria's eyes were wide. "Oh that's wonderful! I'm so happy for you."

"Thanks, Jeremy is really special."

"Jeremy, huh?" She was nodding her head and was clearly happy for me. "And what about you Janelle, you meet someone too?"

"Ladies, I've done more than met someone."

There was that wide smirk on her face, but it was the way she was waving her hand that finally drew my attention to her finger.

"What the hell?" I screamed and dropped the albums onto the floor as I moved over to the sofa to get a closer look. "*You got engaged?*" I couldn't believe it.

"*Whaaat?*" the other two echoed, then moved to get a closer look.

Janelle held her hand out and gladly gave us a view of the beautiful platinum band with three perfectly cut diamonds.

"Get the fuck outta here! You're engaged?" Veronica asked. I'm like her. I needed to hear it.

Janelle nodded. "Yes, I'm engaged."

Gloria got all close and personal. "It's so pretty. How many carats is it?"

"Four," she said and I could tell she was proud that her ring was bigger than the one Gloria was wearing.

I sat back in my chair, stunned.

"Damn! Who did you meet? Some millionaire?" Veronica said with a chuckle.

Her smile gave way to a chuckle. "You could say that. He works for some of the biggest alumnus at the university."

Veronica's brow drew down. "What's his name?"

"Kaleb Kerrington."

The look she gave said she knew him. "Oh yeah. I've heard of him. Drives an emerald green Jaguar?"

"That would be him," she beamed. Janelle was so materialistic.

It was Gloria's turn to frown. "Does he have custody of his son?"

"Yeah, his mom died when he was young."

She suddenly looked as if she'd been sucking on a lemon. "Uh-huh. Laquita used to go out with him. She said he was too damn controlling for her."

"That's because she wasn't the right woman. Kaleb knows I'm one woman he can't control," Janelle testified with a wicked smile.

"Uh-huh... ain't that the truth," Veronica added with an exaggerated nod.

Gloria laughed. "If anyone can handle him, it's Janelle."

I crossed my arms in front of me. "So when did this happen?" There was attitude in my voice, but Janelle didn't seem to notice.

She reached for her glass avoiding eye contact as she took

a sip of wine. "Two days ago. Sorry boo. I wanted to wait until today to share it with all of you."

She also knew I probably would have tried to talk her out of it if I had gotten her all by myself. Don't get me wrong I'm not one to judge especially since I hadn't had a chance to meet the dude, but I know Janelle and Janelle doesn't do needy. And the way Kaleb blows up her phone when they aren't together, trust me, that shit was going to get old fast.

"When's the wedding?" Gloria asked her.

Janelle immediately frowned. "Not so fast. I want this to be the wedding of the year so I'm thinking next spring."

Now *that's* the Janelle I know and love. She's going to put that shit off for as long as she can.

Don't get me wrong, the thing about Janelle I admire the most is she always knows what she wants and she doesn't let anything stop her from getting it.

All my life I had tried to please my parents. Saving my virginity for marriage only turned me into a freak after Shane deserted me. I ended up screwing anyone who looked interesting. I grew up in the church and that meant four days a week plus any other time my parents could suck out of me. Don't get me wrong. I loved the Lord but I didn't believe he expects every second of my day to be dedicated to him.

I just couldn't get my parents to understand that. Especially since my brother followed in my father's footsteps and joined the military right after college, while my younger sister's engaged to a theology major.

I was the middle child and just once in my life, I wanted to find favor in my parent's eyes. For once, I wanted to get something right and I was certain Jeremy was everything I had ever wanted and needed.

"It's your turn Nyree. Tell us about your man."

Veronica broke into my thoughts. I put my phone away and found that I was smiling. I couldn't wait to share the details.

"Well… what do you want to hear? We have a lot in common. Basketball, church —"

Janelle's eyes rolled up into her head. "Basketball and

church, sounds like you found a winner."

Veronica punched her in the arm, and I had to laugh at them.

"I'm not paying Jae no mind. I did find a winner and that's all that matters."

"Good for you," Veronica said.

While I finished my wine, I gave them the details of my relationship. Gloria was hanging on every word.

"*Ohmygoodness!* Look at your face. You're in love!" Gloria clapped her hands.

"Hell nah!" Janelle was laughing her ass off. "And you didn't even want to meet a man online."

"Hey... be nice," Veronica warned.

"Jae's just being a hater," I said rolling my neck.

She threw her hands up innocently. "Nyree knows I'm just playing."

Gloria leaned forward, swinging her leg. "So does he work, have kids, etcetera...?"

"He works in Jeff City... has three kids," I finally managed.

"Three kids? What the fuck?" Ronnie gasped.

I felt the need to defend him. "He was married for ten years."

"Damn but three!" Janelle sneered. "How old is the youngest?"

"Fourteen."

Janelle was shaking her head. "Girl, join the damn club."

Gloria focused her green eyes in her direction. "How old's Kaleb's son?"

She rolled her eyes. "Thirteen and since he's a boy I don't have to worry about raising him. That's his daddy's job."

That was probably a good thing because she had never been any good with kids.

Gloria rose and moved over to refill our glasses. "I'm just so happy for both of you."

"Me too," Veronica chimed in then held up her glass. "We might have another wedding before the year's over."

I know it was soon, but I sure hoped that person was me.

20

JANELLE

I always spend Saturday morning's shopping and cleaning up my house. But ever since Kaleb and I started dating, finding time for myself had been few and far between. Not that I'm complaining. I have a good man and life couldn't get any better than it was right now. I was practically living with him, and now that we were engaged I was planning to put my townhouse on the market. I glanced down at the rock on my finger and giggled. Hee-Hee! I was so happy.

Kaleb was getting my oil changed so I was rolling in his Range Rover. I parked it near the front of Walmart then grabbed my purse and moved inside. As usual it was packed with people. The whole reason for shopping before ten was to beat the crowd but I guess I didn't get the memo this morning.

"Jae!"

I turned around and this tall, peanut-butter-brown brotha was walking toward me. There was something familiar about his walk, but I couldn't quite place him with the baseball cap tilted low on his face.

"Don't act like you don't know me," he said like I had a lot of nerve forgetting who he was. He then removed the cap and I gasped.

"Frankie? Oh my God! When did you get back?"

I was talking and hugging him all at the same time.

"I got home last week."

I shook my head and smiled. It was so good to see him. "Mommy didn't tell me you were back."

"That's because I've been chilling trying to get a few days in by myself before I started hollering at my crew."

I was standing in front of one of the most handsome men I knew. Frankie Simmons and I went way back. He grew up next door to me and we hung out and had been friends up until I started getting attention from other teenage boys and realized how gorgeous I was. I then didn't have time to hang out with a nerd who was two years younger than me. I was too busy dating boys with cars and college guys. I went off to college and Frankie had joined the army. I remembered running into Ms. Lorraine a couple of months ago and she mentioned Frankie had busted up his ankle and was being medically discharged.

"So you're back for good?"

"Yep. I'm planning to open a carwash."

I was impressed. Back then he was tall and lanky. Now he was sexy as all get out. "Look at you."

He was grinning showing off a set of beautiful white teeth. "So whadda you been up to?"

"I opened a restaurant."

"Yeah I remember hearing something about that." He nodded and looked clearly impressed. "So you finally did it?"

I was grinning too hard to do anything but nod.

"I remember you used to spend hours in the kitchen dirtying up Granby's kitchen."

I playfully punched him in the chest. "Yeah, but you enjoyed everything I made."

"Hell yeah! You could slam in the kitchen." He rubbed his stomach and lifted his shirt slightly and I noticed how flat his stomach was. I was standing there staring at him and heard the *Drunk In Love* ringtone in my purse. "I'ma have to drop by your restaurant for some vittles."

"Yes, you should. I'm right at seventh and Broadway up from CJ's Wings." I decided to ignore Kaleb and call him back in a few minutes.

"Damn, remember how we used to tear up them wings?"

I nodded. "Yep and they're still good."

"I'ma have to check you out." He was then looking at me as if he had just noticed me standing there. And I couldn't believe it. I suddenly lost my composure and swallowed nervously as he took his time checking me out.

"Damn, Janelle. I always knew you were fine, but baby, you're thick as hell!"

"Thanks, you don't look bad yourself."

He looked so tasty I was tempted to take a lick just to see if he tasted like peanut butter.

"So what's been up with you? Kids? Married?"

"No kids. And never been married. At least not yet." I heard my phone chirping again in my purse, reminding me I was engaged but yet I couldn't find it in me to share that bit of information. In fact, I noticed I was keeping my left hand down to my side so he wouldn't catch the gleam of the diamond on my ring finger.

"What about you?" I asked.

"I was married for about five years then my wife was killed in a car crash."

"Oh no. I'm sorry to hear that." There was pain in his eyes so it was easy to see that he had really loved her.

"Hey, if you're not busy, how about we hurry up in here and head to Bandana's for some ribs?"

I was staring up at him watching his beautiful lips as he spoke, and found myself wondering what they would feel like licking away at my throbbing kitty. Frankie looked like he knew how to eat pussy. I was so caught up in my fantasy that it took me a few seconds to realize my phone was vibrating. I didn't have to look to know it was Kaleb trying to reach me, but for the life of me I didn't want to talk to him. My mind raced with possibilities. I was enjoying Frankie's company way too much.

"Hey, Janelle, did you hear me? How about lunch?"

How in the world could I say no when I wanted so badly to say yes? "I've got an appointment in an hour. Sorry." Why did I feel more compelled to lie than tell Frankie the truth?

"Okay, well then how about dinner? I found this little spot

downtown Jeff City I know you would love."

My phone was ringing again. Irritated, I reached inside my purse and silenced it. How in the world could I think with Kaleb blowing up my phone? "How do you like being back home?"

"It's cool being back here. When I left I knew there was no way in hell I was ever coming back to the Midwest, but after being gone for so long nothing else has ever come close to feeling like home."

"I know that's right." I nodded knowingly. I knew exactly how he felt. I couldn't imagine living anywhere else. Don't get me wrong, in a little college town there wasn't much to do, but they had great schools, a close knit community of people, and everything you needed was within a short drive, not to mention the cost of living was perfect.

"So what's up with dinner?" Frankie was standing there with a relaxed stance that I found so sexy, while he waited for an answer. What was wrong with two friends eating dinner and catching up? A far as Kaleb was concerned, everything.

Frankie kept staring at me with those light brown eyes and his sexy mouth and I caught myself licking my lips. Damn, for the first time in weeks, I hated being committed to one man.

"Today really isn't a good day at all. We're busy at the restaurant. Hey, how about you drop through this evening and I give you the royal treatment?"

"The royal treatment, huh? That's what's up!"

I breathed a sigh of relief. "Just come around seven." Kaleb was calling again and I figured I had ignored him long enough. We exchanged numbers and Frankie promised to drop by later. I hurried and moved toward the register. I had been in the store long enough. It wasn't until I had the groceries loaded in the Range Rover that I finally answered.

"Where the hell have you been?" he barked.

Sometimes Kaleb acted like he was my damn daddy. "I told you. I was going shopping."

He sucked his teeth. "You must think I'm stupid. There ain't no way you've been shopping for almost two hours."

"I'm a woman. That's what we do." And I wasn't about to

apologize for it.

"You didn't get my messages?" he probed.

"Which, the phone or the text messages?" I said calmly.

"Okay, so if you got them, why didn't you call me back?" Kaleb's voice was getting real loud now.

"There's a bad reception in Walmart. I was planning to call you back as soon as I got outside. Quit tripping."

"You must have been with some nigga."

I rolled my eyes. Why is it I had to be messing around? Sure. I was beautiful and getting a man wasn't a problem but I didn't want just any man. I wanted Kaleb.

"I wasn't with nobody. I'm on my way home to you, big daddy." Any time I used the pet name it always seemed to calm his jealous outburst.

"Well hurry the fuck up! I got something I wanna show you."

"What?" I asked suspiciously.

"You'll see when you get here."

I hung up and blew out a heavy breath. The last thing I was in the mood for was another argument.

I pulled onto his street and as I grew closer to the house, I spotted a red 435i BMW in the driveway with a big white bow on top.

"Oh shit!" I almost ran into a parked SUV staring at the beautiful car. I turned into the driveway, jumped out, then quickly hopped back in.

I had forgotten to put the car in Park.

Kaleb came walking down the front steps, grinning.

"Baby, what is this?" I was hoping it was what I thought it was but I didn't dare get ahead of myself.

"If you had answered the phone you would have found out."

"Oh baby!" I wrapped my arms around him and kissed him hard on the mouth. "I've got a trunkful of groceries. There ain't nobody I want but you." I gave him another big sloppy kiss.

Smiling, Kaleb reached inside his pocket and pulled out a BMW keychain and waved it over his head.

I jumped up and down trying to get it. "Baby, quit playing!"

"Do you love me?" he asked and he was so serious, a chill snaked my spine.

"Yes baby, you know I love you!"

He finally handed the key to me. "Go ahead and get in."

"Who's car is it?" I just had to know.

"It's yours."

I was screaming and laughing all at the same time. I slipped in behind the wheel and turned the key. *Ohmygoodness!* She purred just like my pussy did when I was turned on.

While Kaleb carried the groceries inside, I played with all of the buttons and adjusted the mirrors and seat. When he finally came back outside I waved over at him. "Baby, get in so we can go for a ride," I urged. He smiled and walked around my ride with that cripple walk of his that made me smile. I loved his broken-down ass!

As soon as the door was shut, I backed slowly out the driveway and then took off down the road.

"Oh shit! Baby, hurry... Open the sunroof!" I screamed. This was so unreal.

"Alright," he chuckled and reached up and pressed a button and the glass rolled back.

I can't believe it! I had a hot new ride, sunroof, five disc changer, heated seats—you name it. I clicked on the music and realized I had Sirius satellite radio. As I zoomed up one street after another, I reached over and squeezed my man's hand.

"You like it?" he asked as if he didn't already know.

"Oh baby, I love it so much. Thank you, thank you!"

Kaleb looked genuinely pleased. "I'm glad you like it."

It was almost an hour later before I pulled back onto the driveway and killed the engine. "That was fun!" I couldn't stop grinning but when I looked over at Kaleb he looked so serious.

"Babe... I wasn't going to mention this until after we were married, but," he paused and drew a breath and the look on his face made me sit up on the soft black leather.

"Oh my God!" I whispered. "What's wrong?" He looked like he wanted to cry. And there was nothing sexy about that.

"A couple of years ago I received two million dollars."

Did I hear him right? "Two million?"

"My father worked for years at this meat packing plant, and lost his arm a few years back in a meat grinder." He sat up on the bed and I waited for him to continue. "Something was wrong with the switch. He tried to cut off the blade and it sliced into his arms. He had to have it amputated."

"Oh no!" I shifted on the seat so I could see him better and waited for him to get to the money. It was then I noticed CJ standing out on the porch, probably wondering what was taking us so long to come inside. "And then what happened?" I urged. I wanted to hear the good part before his pesky son came over and put his dirty fingers all over my car.

"He settled in court and got millions. Instead of moving out of Sugar Land, my mom and him stayed in that little-ass town and built a house on a hill looking down on the city."

"That sounds pretty."

He gave me a look that said, "whatever". "It's okay, but they act like it's a museum. They want their grandkids to visit, and when they come down they bitch and complain if they touch anything." He shook his head. "Anyway, my father set it up so me and my sisters each receive ten million."

"Ten million?" I choked out.

"Two in the beginning, three in December, and another in five years."

"Wow! Your dad doesn't sound like a bad guy. It sounds to me like he loves you." That was more than I could say about my father.

"I don't know why my father did it," he replied with a scowl. "I guess that's why he had his lawyer draw it up so he couldn't change his mind. I think he was drunk when he did it." He winked and started chuckling and I giggled along with him. I was laughing because I was tickled and so damn happy. I was going to marry a fucking millionaire! I knew Kaleb had money. I just didn't know he had that much. And even better he had more to come.

"Anyway... I'm telling you this to explain why I act so paranoid. My ex-girlfriend was only interested in getting her hands on my money. I had no problem sharing because I believe in spoiling my woman, but she just wanted the money. I don't even think she really wanted to be bothered with my son. I remember she used to tell me CJ acted retarded."

It took everything I had not to laugh because she was right. CJ *did* act retarded.

He squeezed my hand. "What I'm saying is, I need a woman who's gonna have my back... CJ's back. Someone we can trust."

"You can trust me."

"I hope so." He brought his lips to my forehead, then gave me a hard look. "We have a promising future and I want to share that life with you."

And so do I.

CJ came racing over to the car and slammed the palm of his grimy hands onto the glass. "Dad, what are you doing?" he whined.

It took everything I had not to put my new vehicle in Reverse and roll over his big ass feet. Instead, I focused on the money.

Cha-ching bitches!

<u>21</u>

NYREE

"There she is."

I swung around, searched the crowd of high school graduates and their family and watched as Jeremy's daughter raced toward us. She was followed by her brothers Chad and Jose, and the fat woman behind them had to be their mother and her twin sister.

"Daddy, I'm so glad you made it!" Tiffany practically fell into his arms while the other two circled and hugged him as well.

It was good to see he had a great relationship with his children. While they talked, I stood back feeling like an outcast while his ex-wife tried to avoid eye contact. She was a chunky Latina with short-cropped black hair and a round face. I bet it was killing her to see her ex-husband with a woman as beautiful as me. I was rocking a black pencil skirt and a white ruffle blouse with stilettos that showed off my legs. She had on some frumpy, red dress that showed every roll on her round body. I had to resist the urge to laugh.

"Babe, let me introduce you to my kids. This is Tiffany… Jose… and Chad."

They each gave me a warm smile and a hello. I grinned at all of them. So far they seemed like they were receptive to their father dating.

His ex-wife and her sister stood off to the side and exchanged looks.

"Congratulations," I said to Tiffany, and handed her a card.

Just as I thought, her eyes lit up with surprise. I guess she wasn't used to her father's girlfriends buying her gifts. We talked and chatted for a few minutes before everyone agreed to go to some popular soul food restaurant a couple miles away to eat.

"Dad, I'm going to ride with you," Jose said and followed us back to his Tahoe.

I found myself imagining what it would be like to be his wife and these kids being my stepchildren. It wasn't so bad. In time I'm sure I could learn to love them as well. Jeremy took my hand and led me to his SUV where he opened the door.

"Everything okay?" he asked searching my eyes.

I nodded. "Everything is great."

We've been dating for over two months now and each day our relationship grew stronger.

Last week, I finished *The Five Love Languages* and had called my mother raving about that book.

"Chile, me and your dad discovered that book years ago."

"Really? What's your love languages?" I asked, drawing the phone closer to my lips.

"Well your father is acts of service, which I should have known the way I'm always running around taking his clothes to the cleaners." She giggled. "And I'm quality time."

"Ooh, so am I! Jeremy's words of affirmation." Not that I was surprised. As insecure as he was, I should have already guessed his love language. Which meant it was my job to make sure my man felt good about himself with positive and supportive words. What could be hard about that?

We had a great lunch with his children. Despite their mother sitting at the end of the table sneering her nose at me, I felt relaxed and at ease. Jeremy squeezed my hand under the table, and I knew he was feeling what I was feeling—family.

We made plans for them to come down in July and spend some time with us. The entire time I was thinking, *Nyree, girl you can do this! You'll be a great stepmother!* I know I was getting ahead of myself again but Jeremy had already been hinting about a future together so I knew it was just a matter of time.

After the luncheon, Jeremy kissed his kids goodbye and I was shocked when they each came up and gave me a hug.

"Ms. Nyree, it's so nice to meet you," Jose said. I was amazed at how much he favored his father. He had the same big melon head and goofy smile. I could have hugged him all evening he was just that cute.

"Nice meeting you Delaney," I said with a two finger wave. And since I did it in front of her kids, she was left with no choice but to respond.

"Nice to meet you, too," she muttered under her breath and then quickly climbed into her car.

We waved again and waited until she peeled her Sonata out the lot before we moved to his Tahoe.

"What do you think?" Jeremy reached over and took my hand.

"I like them."

He nodded, pleased. "They like you too."

That definitely made me feel good because I really wanted his children to like me.

Jeremy helped me into the car and I sat there feeling like I was on top of the world.

Was I dreaming?

I must have been because I finally came down off the cloud and realized Jeremy was driving in the wrong direction. "Where are we going?"

"I want to take you to meet my adopted daughter, Jasmine."

My excitement suddenly came crashing down. *Talk about sticking me with a pin.* "Oh, okay."

I wasn't sure how I felt about meeting the child of a woman he used to date but I didn't see the point in making a big deal about it.

He pulled into a parking lot in front of a south side Chicago daycare center. I gave him a curious look but Jeremy's eyes were everywhere but on me.

I had a hundred questions and he knew it, which is probably why he was still avoiding eye contact. I decided to just see how things played out. Jeremy held the door open and I stepped inside. Kids could be heard laughing and playing in the playground in back.

A childcare worker came over to greet us. "May I help you?" she said with a curious look.

Jeremy cleared his throat. "Yes, I'm here to see Jasmine."

"Oh, right! Hold on." She had that familiar look in her eyes as she turned and moved to the back door and called for the little girl. I just looked at Jeremy out the corner of my eyes. He was fidgeting nervously and still avoiding eye contact, but I didn't say anything. Like I said I wanted to see how this played out.

Within minutes a little girl came around the corner and screamed, "Daddy!" and then I watched as she raced into his arms.

Daddy? Why in the world was her mother confusing that child like that? I watched the way she was hugging his neck and grinning down at his face. It was obvious how much she missed him.

He finally turned to me. "Jazzy, this here is Ms. Nyree."

She waved. "Hi Ms. Nyree."

"Hi, sweetie." She really was cute with a smooth dark complexion and two long pigtails. Gold studs were in her earlobes. She was wearing jeans and a pink t-shirt. On her feet were Nike tennis shoes. Somebody was taking good care of her.

I stood by and listened as Jeremy told Jasmine we had just attended Tiffany's graduation.

"Daddy, can I go home with you? Please," she pleaded and looked so pitiful I almost felt sorry for her.

"I can't Jazz, but maybe next time," he said. She whined a little more then finally he kissed her a couple of times, lowered her to the floor and she hurried back outside.

"Thanks for coming by." The childcare worker said, then she went back to writing something on a clipboard.

We waved and headed out to his Tahoe. Jeremy pulled

onto the street and I just sat there waiting.

I caught him looking at me. "What's wrong?"

"*Really*? What do you think?"

"I told you about her," he said and had the nerve to sound defensive.

Oh no he didn't. "You told me you had an "adopted" daughter." I tossed quotation marks in the air. "I was thinking a *fake* daughter. I wasn't expecting her to call you Daddy."

He had the nerve to look dumbfounded. "Why wouldn't she? I *am* her father."

I crossed my arms beneath my breasts and shook my head. There was no way this was happening. "You knew I wasn't interested in dating a man with little kids."

He blew out a long breath. "So I guess now you're ready to break up with me?" He looked frantic but I didn't care or at least I pretended I didn't care.

Jeremy pulled into the gas station and instead of answering him I got out the SUV and went inside the store. I wasn't even sure if I wanted to hear his explanation. I could deal with the teenagers, but a four-year-old... I just wasn't feeling that idea at all. I was already thirty. I wanted children of our own. Hell, how in the world could we afford that with him making child support for the next fifteen years? I know it sounded crazy. It wasn't like he had asked me to be his wife. At least not yet, but I was expecting it soon. Well, a girl can only hope. But he wasn't going to play games with me. I needed a man to be on the up and up. And what he had done was sneaky.

I grabbed a Pepsi and was reaching for a bag of hot cheese puffs when Jeremy stepped inside the convenience store. I rolled my eyes and pretend I didn't see him.

"Hey," he came up from behind and wrapped his arms around me.

"What?" I said but not with as much attitude as before. It was something about the way his arms felt wrapped around my body that always seemed to make it hard to stay angry at him.

"Baby, I'm sorry I threw that at you like that. On the ride

home I'll tell you about it."

I pouted and decided to act stubborn because that's what a woman has to do sometimes to make sure her man knows she wasn't going to put up with his shit.

"Hey," he swung me around and I tilted my head and stared up into his eyes.

"Angel, I'm sorry." He lowered his head and pressed his lips to mine and it was a wrap. There was no way I was leaving this wonderful man.

I took his hand and followed him up to the register and waited while he paid for our things. We went back to the SUV and headed for the highway before he began talking.

"When I first started dating her mother, I had no idea she had Jasmine."

I glanced over at him. "What do you mean?"

"I mean... Mia and I had been dating for two weeks and she had practically moved in. I came home from work one day to see this baby in her arms."

"*What*? Where was the baby?"

He was shaking his head, like he was embarrassed by the whole story. "Mia said her mother had been keeping her. She was afraid if I had known she had a daughter, I wouldn't have dated her."

Yeah, I know exactly how she felt. But I'm sure he was already in love with her and she could have said she had HIV, and it probably wouldn't have mattered at that point.

"So what did you do?" I said, giving him a little nudge.

"They moved in, and we talked about getting married. In the meantime I fell in love with Jasmine, and I decided to adopt her."

"Where was her father?"

He hesitated. "He was standing trial for sodomy and rape."

I raised an eyebrow and muttered, "Damn."

"Exactly." He waited until he had pulled onto Interstate 55 before he continued. "Mia had ended the relationship with him long before she had Jasmine."

"So ol' boy gave you permission to adopt his daughter?"

He shook his head. "Nah, his name was never on the birth certificate. So I signed it and she became mine."

Okay, so now my neck was rolling. "So then call it what it is. You didn't *adopt* Jazz. By you signing the document she became your daughter."

"Yeah, pretty much." There were those puppy dog eyes again.

"Did you and her mother get married?"

Jeremy shook his head. "Nah, something just wasn't ever right about our relationship and when I found out she was messing around with a friend of mine I ended it."

Damn, he went through some shit. "But by then you had already adopted her child." I concluded. "I guess you're paying child support too, right?"

He looked nervous by my question before he finally answered. "Yep."

I shook my head. I tried to keep my anger to myself. Some men are so stupid when it comes to getting with a woman. "Tell me, what was it about Mia that had you adopting her child before you even married her?"

I could tell Jeremy didn't even want to answer my question. Well, too bad.

"I don't know, she was on the bowling team and one of my boys said she was interested in me. I guess I was so flattered this young, beautiful woman wanted me."

"How young?"

"Fifteen years."

What did I tell you? He met a beautiful woman and lost his damn mind. Did anybody teach him that what looks good isn't always good for you? But instead of saying it, I just kept my comments to myself and turned and looked out the window.

"So what? You mad at me now?"

Goodness, he needed me to pat his head and tell him it was okay. Not this time.

"Well say something." He reached across the seat and squeezed my hand. "Just tell me what you're thinking or feeling."

I wanted to say I felt like I had been played. Nowhere in that damn online profile of his did he say anything about having a four-year-old daughter. She wasn't adopted. She was his, dammit.

I sat there staring out the window and pouting for what felt like forever. The fantasy of this wonderful life with just Jeremy and I was starting to have a few flaws.

Nobody's perfect.

I released a long sigh and closed my eyes and said a silent prayer. *Lord please guide my actions and my heart.*

With my eyes still closed, I suddenly remembered *The Five Love Languages* and the secrets to a love that lasted. Christ, commitment and consistency were important. I had a good man whose life had been filled with so many disappointments. And I didn't want to be one of them.

I reached over and laced my fingers with his.

"You still mad?"

I shook my head. "What can I say? I'm in love with a man who has four kids."

There was that goofy smile. "Is that a bad thing?"

I wanted to scream, hell yeah, but in all honestly I couldn't say that. I loved Jeremy. Despite all the kids and the fact there was one he would be paying child support to for the next fifteen years, for some reason, nothing else seemed to matter except how crazy I was about this fool. He was almost everything I wanted in a man and I learned years ago you can't get everything you want. You just have to figure out what you can and can't live without. Since the kids were only coming down for brief visits I could deal with them, but Jeremy, his love, faith, and magic tongue, I just couldn't live without.

He squeezed my hand. "Nyree... You know I love you, right?"

Jeremy glanced at me with those big eyes of his looking all serious. I hated when he did that. My heart had a mind of its own when it came to him. I tried to shake the feeling off and tossed Jeremy a look that said, "don't try that shit again". I yanked my hand free and stared out the window again.

"I really am sorry. I know what you're thinking and you're right. I shoulda been honest about Jasmine from the beginning. But I swear to you Angel, I promise it won't ever happen again." He took my hand and brought it to my lips.

As crazy as it sounded, it didn't matter to me if that man had twelve kids and lived in a shoe. I still would have loved him. Jeremy pulled off to the side of the road.

"Why are we stopping?"

He put his SUV in park then took my hand again and closed his eyes. "Lord, please help me to shake my insecurities so I can be everything I need to be for this woman. I know I'm a work in progress..."

By the time he had finished, there were tears in both our eyes and I knew without a shadow of a doubt this was where God wanted me to be.

22

JANELLE

You ever feel like throwing your phone across the room?

Well, that's exactly how I felt when I heard Kaleb's personal ringtone, signaling that he was calling me once again. I was three seconds away from turning the phone off all together, but I was expecting a call from Mimi about a liquor order I needed for the restaurant this weekend.

Asshole!

He could call all he wanted because after his latest stunt I decided it was time for the two of us to slow it down a bit.

Kaleb had taken me to St. Louis for the weekend. As usual he spoiled me with an afternoon of shopping at Nordstrom's. At this point in our relationship, he knew my weakness was purses and he bought me three new designer bags in pink, red and blue then we had dinner at the Cheesecake Factory. We finally made it back to our suite at the Marriott Hotel and burned up the sheets.

That evening, Kaleb took me to this new thirty and over club. I was having such a good time, laughing, holding hands, and dancing that when Kaleb suddenly went off on me. I was caught completely off guard.

"What are you talking about?"

"You heard me. I see you staring at the ugly mothafucka at the bar! You want him that bad, then take your ass over there!" he screamed.

My mouth was wide open while he stormed away leaving me standing there on the middle of the floor looking like a damn fool. A couple of people were looking over at me with curious looks. Apparently, they had overheard everything.

By the time I had made it back to the table, Kaleb was asking for the bill. He gave me the evil eye. "You always doing that secret squirrel shit? You must think I'm fucking stupid!"

"I don't know what the fuck you're taking about!" I wasn't about to waste my time arguing when I had no idea what he was pissed off about, and I stormed out of the club. It wasn't until I was outside I remembered we had driven down to St. Louis in his Jaguar. I paced across the parking lot, and by the time Kaleb had come out the club, I was calling my cousin Christina who had a loft downtown. As soon as she confirmed she was coming to pick me up, I told Kaleb to "go fuck himself" and then watched as he angrily peeled out the parking lot. It took Christina's slow ass thirty minutes to arrive and not once did Kaleb call or come back to check on me. If fact, I didn't hear from him until the following morning. By then I had already rented a car and rolled back to Columbia on my own.

I loved a jealous man, but Kaleb's behavior was beyond ridiculous. All the needy shit, checking my cellphone, and accusing me of messing around on him was crazy as hell. He acted like a real life Dr. Jekyll and Mr. Hyde.

I would never tell Nyree this but I was starting to feel smothered with all that "we, we, we." Lord forbid, if I said anything about me doing something that didn't include him and his son. I know Kaleb was trying to get me in the mindset of being a wife and a mother but damn did it have to happen overnight?

My phone started ringing again and I ignored it and moved into the bathroom to shower and get ready to meet Frankie at Macy's. It was his mother's birthday and he wanted some help picking her out a nice dress. He appreciated my taste. Ever since we ran into each other at Walmart, he's been coming by the restaurant hanging out in the kitchen. It was like old times.

It was close to five by the time I had pulled into the parking lot. I removed my designer glasses, took one look in the rearview mirror and was pleased at what I saw. A true diva. I was rocking red shorts, a white spaghetti strap shirt and white sandals. I don't know why, but I looked around to make sure no one was looking, then I discreetly slipped off my engagement ring and stuck it in the glove box.

I was climbing out the car as my phone was ringing. This time I answered.

"Yo, where you at?"

I laughed as I strutted toward the door. "I'm getting ready to walk into the store now. Where you at?"

"Right behind you."

I swung around and as soon as I spotted Frankie jumping out his Sequoia, I ended the call and smiled. He was wearing blue jeans and a crisp white t-shirt. That brotha was fine as he wanted to be.

"Damn girl, yo man let you come out looking like that?" he joked although I noticed his eyes were traveling over every last one of my curves.

I brought my hands to my hips, making sure he didn't miss anything. "Whatever. No man tells me how to dress."

"I see that."

I winked and fell into step beside him but noticed I was looking over my shoulder making sure Kaleb wasn't somewhere lurking around. As jealous as he was I didn't put anything past him.

We stepped into Macy's together and I caught our reflection in the glass and was stunned at how good the two of us looked together. Too bad I was already in a relationship.

We walked over to the women's department and I headed straight for the dresses. "What occasion are we shopping for?"

"She's has a woman's day conference next month and she likes to dress to impress." He walked over to the rack beside me as he explained. "I need a hat, shoes, and all the accessories."

"You're such a good son," I teased. "I got my mom some roses for her birthday to brighten up that dreary house."

Although nothing could do that other than gutting it and starting over.

"How's your mom doing?"

I glanced over at him and shrugged. "Uh... I guess she's okay. Losing her leg last year has been pretty hard for her."

He nodded. "No doubt. Nam told me she had to have one amputated. I'm gonna have to get by there to see her."

"She'd like that." Mommy had always been fond of Frankie. It had been my father who'd had the problem with him or any other boy for that matter.

I never forget that afternoon when he had caught me and Frankie in his treehouse. Dad tried to beat the black off of me. And that's hard to do considering how dark I am. The worst part, he scared Frankie so bad, he never came over to my house again.

My father had always been controlling and crazy.

Just like Kaleb.

I brushed that ridiculous thoughts aside and went back to looking through the racks. My cellphone started chirping again. I retrieved my phone and noticed I had a text message from CJ.

Ms. Jae, are you coming back tonight?

Goodness, the kid was starting to get attached already.

ME: No, your dad and I are having problems.

I hit Send and he immediately hit me right back.

CJ: I don't want anyone else to be my stepmother but you.

I wasn't sure why he liked me but then I was lovable even to the kids.

ME: Don't worry I'm going to be your stepmother.

CJ: I hope so. I love you

There was something about this kid telling me he loved me that messed with me.

ME: Luv u 2

I put my phone away. The last thing I wanted was to start getting attached to some needy kid but I guess if I planned to eventually marry his father, I had to maintain some type of relationship.

"How you doing over there?" Frankie asked.

"How about this one?" I held up a black dress that gathered at the waist and had a white lapel. It screamed Lorraine Simmons.

Frankie came over, took it from my hand and started grinning. "Oh yeah, I could see her wearing this."

"Of course you could. You know I know fashion."

"And that's why I asked for your help."

Smiling, I signaled for him to follow. "Come on. Let's go find her some shoes."

I managed to find myself a slamming pair as well and then we went over to G&D Steakhouse and had dinner. I was really enjoying myself. I mean really enjoying myself for the first time in months. Sometimes it takes being with friends to feel relaxed.

"Have you seen Connie's crazy ass since you been back?" I asked as I bit into my Texas toast.

"Hell no," he managed between chews. "But she knows I'm here. Mom's says she's been calling the house looking for me."

I gave a rude snort. "You know how this place is. It doesn't take long for the word to get out."

Frankie poured A-1 on his steak while he shook his head. "That relationship is in the past. I'm ready for a real woman who's gonna hold a nigga down. Not that crap."

I laughed. "I was hoping you weren't planning on hooking up with her ratchet-ass again."

He pointed his fork at me. "So who's the lucky dude?"

While we ate I told him about Kaleb Kerrington.

"Sounds to me life you hit the lottery."

"I'm not one to brag," I said with a saucy grin.

"But are you happy?"

Did he hear a word I said? I'm marrying a millionaire. "Whadda you mean? Of course I'm happy."

While stroking his chin, Frankie explained. "What I mean is you got the nice new ride, you telling me about all the things dude's doing for you, but does he make you happy?"

I took a sip of my diet Pepsi because I wasn't sure how to answer that. "Yeah, I guess he does."

Frankie stared at me. "So you're saying you love him?"

Where was he going with this? "Yes, I love him."

He shook his head. "Uh-huh, your mouth says one thing but your eyes are saying another."

"What are you getting at?" I didn't like where this conversation was going.

Frankie cut his steak as he replied, "See the problem with you is that you've always been in love with the idea of being in love."

My brow went up. "That's not true."

He pointed his knife at me. "Yes, it is. We used to spend hours in my treehouse. All you talked about was falling in love with a man who was so rich you never had to come back home."

I just chewed my steak and waited for him to continue.

"See you forget I grew up right next door to you. I heard what went on in your house, even witnessed it a few occasions."

"You did?" My hand was trembling as I lowered the fork to the table.

He nodded and then reached for my hand. "I know your old man used to beat the shit outta you. We all did. But Pops used to say it was none of our business."

So the neighborhood had known what had gone on in our house. Yet no one did anything to stop him.

I snatched my hand away. "My dad was an ass," I said and tried to act like it was old news.

"Hell yeah. He had the whole neighborhood shook. But he was a cop, so what could anyone do?"

"Nothing. The same thing my mom used to say after he got done knocking her head into a wall." Mommy had been a scared, weak woman. Anybody who let a man beat her children was a coward. As much as I loved her she had always represented everything I didn't want to be.

I pushed my plate aside. Suddenly, I lost my appetite.

Frankie leaned over the table, staring at me. "Hey, I understand what you went through."

I gave a rude snort. "What... your dad used to beat you too?"

He hesitated. "No but I felt your pain. Every time I saw the bruises you tried to hide, I felt it. I just wished you had talked to me about it."

"What good would that have done? My own mother couldn't protect me. The only peace I had was going to my grandmother's house." After Granby had passed away no one had been there to protect us. "Remember that was the only way we could be friends?"

He swallowed and there was this faraway look in his eyes. "I remember."

My phone chirped and I sighed and tossed the napkin onto the table. "My dad is dead now so enough of the depressing shit. I heard your father bought a brand new Caddy."

For a moment it looked like Frankie wanted to say something to me, but then thought better of it and reached for his iced tea. "Yeah, Ol' Man is profiling in his new whip!"

I smiled. "I definitely have to get by and see him."

After we got done eating, I went by Tropical Liqueurs for the best frozen Long Island iced tea and sipped it all the way home.

I showered, put on my favorite pajamas—boy shorts and a sports bra—then went downstairs and got comfortable on my new sofa. Last fall I decided to give my living room a new look and had the room painted a yellow and bought a white couch and accessorized the entire room in dramatic shades of blue. The room was definitely making a statement.

A quick glance at the clock and I realized Scandal was getting ready to come on in ten minutes. I sprang from the sofa and went into the kitchen. There was no way I could watch without my own glass of red wine. I removed a brand new bottle from the frig, popped the cork and poured a small glass. I made it back to my spot with just a minute before the drama began to unfold.

Knock! Knock!

"Damn," I scowled and hurried to the door before I missed much. I should have known it was Kaleb. He was standing there with his hands in the pockets of a pair of stone-washed jeans. The red Sean John t-shirt he was wearing looked so good on him.

I rolled my eyes. "What do you want?"

"Can we talk?"

He didn't even wait for me to invite him inside. He brushed past and waddled in. I rolled my eyes, shut the door then swung around with straight attitude. "What do you wanna talk about?"

He held his hands up in surrender. "Babe... listen to me."

"I really don't want to hear anything you have to say." I walked over to the television and hit Record on the DVR. Damn, why couldn't he have waited another hour?

"Babe... I just want five minutes of your time." There was that rejected look about him—shoulders slouched, pitiful look on his face.

I folded my arms across my chest. "What do you want?" Damn, Scandal is on!

"Babe... I'm stupid. I do dumb stuff."

Okay, tell me something I don't know.

"I was worried. I didn't know if you had made it back or what? Did you get my messages?"

"Yep, all five hundred calls and text messages," I said icily.

"You could have at least let me know you were okay." He had the nerve to have an attitude!

"As you can see I am fine. Now leave." I didn't really want him to go but it was part of the performance. I headed toward the door.

"Babe... Please. Just hear me out."

I made sure the smirk was gone before I swung around. "I'm listening, but I don't hear anything coming out of your mouth."

A brief look of panic crossed his face. "Babe, I'm telling you I'm stupid! I do and say stupid stuff. I don't know why.

All I know is I love you more than life itself."

I sucked my teeth and tried to curb my attitude. "You sure gotta helluva way of showing it."

"I know and I'm sorry. I just go crazy when I think of some other man being with you."

He took a step forward and as he closed in I knew I was going to forgive him. Kaleb took my hands in his and gazed down into my eyes. There it was—jealousy, uncertainty and something else.

"Come home, babe. I miss you. CJ misses you like crazy. He told me I better go and get you back." He pulled me toward him until our foreheads were touching.

I was hoping to give the impression that I was having a hard time deciding, but my mind was already made up. There was no way I was walking away from all that money. "I'm not gonna keep dealing with your jealous bullshit," I warned.

"I understand. You're right. And I'm sorry." He brought his arms around and held me tight. "Just come back home to me. We want you there with us."

That was the extent of our conversation.

Kaleb brought his lips down on mine in a kiss so hot and delicious, I ended it just long enough to take his hand and lead him up to my bedroom.

Sorry Shonda Rhimes.

But I'm about to do something scandalous of my own.

23

NYREE

There was a soft knock at my door. I looked up and there was Timmy standing in my doorway.

"Hey Nyree," he said with that gorgeous smile of his. That man was too fine for his own good. Tall, handsome and a body that made a sistah want to lick him up and down like he was a fudge pop.

I sprung out my chair like a jack-n-a-box and walked around the desk and hugged him. As soon as I felt that solid body against mine, I closed my eyes. He felt good. So good I knew I needed to put some distance between us fast. Besides public displays of affection was frowned on while in uniform.

"What are you doing here?" I asked as I moved back over to my chair.

He grinned in my direction as he straddled the chair across from my desk. "I flew down to interview for the superintendent spot."

"Oh snap! I forgot you had applied for the position."

"Damn! You forgot about a brotha already?" Timmy tried to look hurt but I've known him long enough to know he was flirting with me.

"Whatever," I said with a dismissive wave and tried to ignore the affect his deep voice was having on my nipples. Thank goodness for uniforms.

"How did the interview go?"

"It went really good," he said with that cocky look that was so Timmy. He leaned forward on the chair with his large arms resting on my desk. "I think I gotta good chance at getting it."

"So do I." Since I worked in personnel it wasn't hard to find out how many other candidates were being considered for the position. And trust me the second he left I was going to Janet's desk to find out. She was a civilian, so she wasn't there, but I knew where she kept the active job postings.

"You got time to go grab a bite to eat?" he asked and there was the wolf gleam in his eyes that screamed, "Beware!"

"I-I don't know," I stuttered.

"You know you want to," he began with a cocky smirk. "We can just run and get a sandwich." He rose from the chair like it was no longer up for discussion. "C'mon I haven't eaten all day." His voice had dropped to a low tone that I felt clear down in my belly. Moving toward the door, Timmy waved his hand and signaled for me to follow.

There was something about the way he was always sure about himself that was such a turn-on about him. I tried to tell myself going out to lunch with an ex-boyfriend wasn't a good idea but deep down I knew I wanted to go and spend some time with him. I grabbed my purse from the bottom drawer and followed him out to his rental car. We chatted nonstop until Timmy pulled into one of the drive-up stations at Sonic's. The second the car was in Park, Timmy swung around on the seat.

"So what's the deal? You in love with dude?" he asked.

Goodness, he was so sexy. I nodded. "Yes, I'm in love."

He kept staring at me and licking his lips at the same time. I started to squirm. Timmy knew he was working on me. "But is he the right man?"

Timmy has always been one to get straight to it. I looked down briefly at my hand then back up to him again. "Yes, I believe he is. I'm at a point in my life I am tired of the games. I want something real... something solid."

"So do I." he dragged a hand down along his face. "I was hoping if I got this position you and I would have a chance to finish where we left off. We're good together, Nyree. Remember?"

How could I forget with him sitting over there licking those juicy lips of his? But I had to remind myself with Jeremy it wasn't about sex. We had something that connected our souls.

"Yeah, we *were* good, but Jeremy and I are better. For someone who's supposed to be starving you sure are taking all doggone day to order." I tried to add a little attitude to my voice.

"Yeah, okay." Timmy started laughing then pressed the button and we ordered our food. After he paid with a credit card, we waited and I should have known he wasn't ready to put our conversation to rest.

"I bet that Jeremy dude can't suck that pussy like I do."

"What?" I yelled trying to sound offended when in actuality I was squeezing my thighs together fighting the memories. Like I said, Timmy had some juicy lips and they were made for sucking Ms. Kitty. "Timmy shut the hell up."

He shifted on the seat, so he could look me dead in the eye. "Why? Because you hate hearing the truth?"

"No because you're being ridiculous," I spat and looked everywhere but at him because if I did he would have seen the truth. Nobody ate pussy like Timmy. But sex ain't everything. "I love Jeremy. We're practically living together."

That knocked that cocky grin off his face. "Damn, you really are serious, aren't you?"

"I told you I am. With Jeremy I've learned there's a lot more to a relationship than just sex, especially when you meet the right person."

There was no disguising the disappointment on his face. "I guess you're serious about dude."

"I'm dead serious." I released a long breath and was proud I was able to resist temptation. Our food arrived and he handed me my drink and burger.

"Yo, Nyree. Listen, I'm sorry for disrespecting you. I'm not gonna lie. I'm jealous as hell. But it's my loss. I had a chance to get with you and I fucked that up. Now another mothafucka slipped in and snatched yo ass up. I hate to lose but I'm happy for you."

"Thank you."

Suddenly, Timmy leaned in close enough so his lips were touching my ear and whispered, "But I'm gonna try every chance I get to steal yo fine ass away."

As we sat and ate our lunch I had a sinking feeling resisting Timmy wasn't going to be easy.

* * *

By the time five o'clock rolled around, I was worn out. I made it back to Columbia, ready for a night with my feet up on the couch. But the second I pulled into my driveway and raised my garage, I was suddenly full of energy when I saw Jeremy's car parked inside.

I had given him a key over a week ago and he hadn't used it until today. Part of me wondered if the reason he was here was because he knew I had been out to lunch with another man.

I stepped into the house and drew in a long slow breath. The scent of my favorite margarita scented candle was in the air. Soft music was playing in the background and Jeremy knew how much I loved me some Ne-Yo. I stepped into the living room and left my purse and keys on the coffee table.

"Welcome home, Angel." I looked over to see Jeremy coming down the stairs in a white beater and a pair of Redskins shorts. Did I mention how much I loved this man?

"What's going on?" I said and shook my head. He was carrying flowers in his hand. I couldn't believe how romantic this was.

"I just wanted to come over and show my Angel how special she is to me." I tilted my head and met his warm, sweet kiss then drew back and stared up into his eyes.

"I know you had a long day and I wanted to do something to make your evening nice."

"This is so nice." I took the bouquet from him into the kitchen and went in search of a vase.

"Babe, let me take care of that. Why don't you go and get undressed. I just filled your tub. I thought maybe we'd get in, kick back and relax together."

I was smiling like a nut because no man had ever been that thoughtful before. "That sounds so romantic," I cooed and leaned over and pressed my lips against his again.

"Go on and take your sexy behind on upstairs." I squealed when he swatted me playfully on my butt then hurried up to strip out of my uniform. By the time Jeremy came up, I was standing in nothing but my birthday suit.

"You're so beautiful," he said and quickly pulled off his t-shirt and shorts.

"Go on. I'll join you in a second." He ushered me into the bathroom and what I saw brought tears to my eyes. The large garden tub was filled with my favorite stress relief scent that I got from Bath and Body Works. There was a bottle of red wine chilling in a bucket on the side of the tub as well as candles flickering around the room.

"You like?" Jeremy asked coming up from behind and wrapping his arms around my waist.

I was so choked up I couldn't even speak so I nodded. If I didn't know it before I definitely knew it then. How much I loved that man.

My bottom lip began to quiver. That man had transformed my bathroom into something you would have seen in the movies. It was beyond romantic.

"Angel, say something," Jeremy urged with that squeaky voice that suddenly gave me goose bumps.

"I can't believe you did all this." I was shaking my head and looking around the room all at the same time.

"You're my queen. I plan on showing you every day how truly special you are."

I closed my eyes and thanked the Lord for bringing this amazing man into my life, and suddenly felt guilty for spending lunch with Timmy. Not that I had done anything inappropriate but it still felt like I had been cheating, so apparently something had been wrong about the entire situation.

"Thank you so much," I murmured then tilted my head back and met his lips in a kiss that I felt clear down to my toes.

"Whadda you waiting on? Go ahead and get on in." Jeremy released me and I started giggling as I stepped over to the tub and climbed inside.

"I hope you're planning on joining me?" He was standing over the tub grinning

"I will in a minute." Jeremy reached for one of the flutes and filled it with wine. I took the glass from his proffered hand then brought it to my lips and moaned. It was so smooth. He then poured himself a glass.

"Are we celebrating something?" I asked and gave him a curious look.

He hesitated long enough that I had this feeling at the pit of my stomach.

"Baby… what's wrong?"

He took a sip then took a seat on the end of the tub and looked in my direction. "I got a job promotion."

I breathed a sigh of relief. "Jeremy, oh that's wonderful news! Congratulations!" I expected him to look happy but instead he had this painful look in his eyes. "What's wrong?"

"The job is in Hawaii."

I sprung up from the pillow. "Hawaii?" There is no way I had heard him correctly.

He nodded. "I'm afraid so. I interviewed for a GS-12 position long before we'd started dating. I just figured they had given the job to someone else, but I found out this morning I had been selected."

I was stunned. That was the last thing I had expected to hear was that my man had gotten a job in a state that was probably several thousand miles away.

"What did you tell them?" I said in this far off voice.

Jeremy paused then said the words I wasn't prepared to hear. "I accepted the position. I report November first."

"I'm excited for you. Really I am." I tried to act happy for him but it was hard, considering my heart was hurting. Here it was—I had met the man of my dreams and now he was leaving. The story of my life. I guess some people just weren't meant to have a man for any length of time.

"Excited?" he mocked. "No you're not, so quit lying."

His comment made me angry. "What the hell you expect me to say? No baby, please don't leave!" I mocked.

"Yeah, something like that would be nice. At least then I would know that you cared." A half-smile curled at the corners of his lips.

"You know I care about you. I love you and you know that!"

"And I love you." His eyes locked with mine.

"Well if you love me then I can't understand how you would accept a job without consulting me first!" I protested.

He looked glum. "Because I was hoping you'd go with me."

"What?" I searched his eyes. Was he serious? Me go to Hawaii with him?

"You heard me. I want you to come to Hawaii with me."

Oh my God! Jeremy was dead serious. "Uh... well... maybe. There *is* the Hawaii National Guard."

"Yep. I already checked. Their headquarters is a twenty minute drive from my job."

I had to grin. He had put his work in. "That's something to think about."

"I want you to do more than think about it." He rose, then slipped off his boxers and I gazed down at his beautiful erection. My man might not have the same equipment as Timmy, but he knew how to work with what he had. Again I felt guilty about my lunch date but I brushed it aside and slid over in the tub and made room for two.

"C'mere," Jeremy commanded.

I moved between his legs then leaned back against his chest.

"Finish your wine," he said and then reached for his own.

Silence fell between us. We sat there together, sipping and listening to music. I know it was wrong but with him leaving in a few months I suddenly thought about Timmy. Thinking now that Jeremy was leaving maybe we could have a chance to see if there was anything left between us. But instead of being hopeful about the idea, I felt sad. I knew there was no way I could live without this. Now that I had Jeremy in my life, I didn't want to be without him.

"Angel, I love you and I wanna spend my life with you. But if you don't want to move to Hawaii then I'll call them tomorrow and decline the position."

"Hell no. I would never make you do that. You've been looking for a supervisory position and who am I to stand in your way."

He brought his lips close to my ear. "What you think matters. After all, I plan on you being my wife."

I gazed up at him. "You do?"

"Of course I do. Look," he said and then pointed to my glass.

I stared at it, with no idea what he was pointing at. "What?"

He chuckled. "Angel, look inside the glass."

I tilted the glass and stared into the wine and gasped. At the bottom of the flute was a sparkling diamond ring. I gulped down the rest of the contents then turned it upside down so that the ring fell into my hands.

"Oh my God!" I cried.

Jeremy took it from my hand and slipped it onto my finger. "Nyree Gail Dawson, will you marry me?"

It was white gold with a diamond surrounding by baguette. It wasn't all that big but it was beautiful just the same. "I had no idea!" I said and started crying.

"Angel, what's the matter?" he asked then turned me around and cradled me in his arms.

"When you said you wanted me to go with you to Hawaii, I had no idea you meant as your wife."

He dropped his lips to my forehead and cheek. "Sweetheart I would never ask you to uproot your life for me unless I was offering to spend the rest of my life with you." He put his hand to my chin and tilted my head for another kiss. "Now answer the question… will you marry me?"

I was laughing and crying at the same time. "Yes, I'll marry you."

We kissed and laughed and hurried into my bedroom and then made love. I didn't think life could be any more perfect.

He was holding me in his arms, waiting for our heart rates to slow when I said, "I don't have much time to plan a wedding."

Jeremy smoothed my hair away from my face. "All I care about is you and I being there. I don't even care if my family can't make it."

"Well, I can't get married without my parents." I was pouting, but I couldn't help it.

"Invite the whole world. All I know is I'm marrying you and the sooner the better, hopefully, before my orders are cut. The agency is paying relocation expenses."

"I'll need to put my house on the market."

He grinned. "So, the sooner we're married the better."

"I agree."

He had the nerve to suggest, "How about we just go to the justice of the peace?"

I swung around in his arms and faced him. "Hell no! You're not cheating me out of my special day."

"Okay, then something small." He dragged a hand across his face. "I promise I'll make it up to you later. But right now pick a date. Then we need to move you into my place and make this happen. It's already the end of June."

I felt a shiver. I was finally going to be someone's wife again. But this time I was going to make it work.

24

JANELLE

It was slow at the restaurant, so I decided to head home with dinner for the men in my life.

I stepped out the restaurant and walked passed Al's tacky clothing store. A mannequin with some tight-ass zebra leggings was on display in the window. Every morning when I walked past, I was tempted to sling a big brick through that damn window but I talked myself out of it.

As I walked over toward my BMW, I forgot all about Alphonso Rucker and couldn't resist a grin. That little beauty was all mine. I pulled off down the road, and noticed the people looking at my car, staring with envy. *I truly love my life.*

Things were starting to settle in pretty nicely. I never thought of myself as being a wife and a mother at the same time, but, like I said before, CJ was relatively a good kid so he made motherhood pretty easy. They were both needy as hell and wanted all my attention the second I stepped into the door but I was learning to adjust to the demand. Hell, for all them millions, I could even consider having that man's baby.

I climbed out of my car and reached for the two aluminum pans on the back seat and stepped inside. Immediately, Midnight came trotting into the kitchen sending dog hair flying everywhere. Ugh! I backed up just before he could brush against my Antonio Melani dress.

"Midnight, get down!" I cried as CJ came stomping into the kitchen with his big heavy feet.

"Midnight no!" he said with an apologetic smile. "Sorry,

Ms. Jae."

I smiled and carried the food over to the counter and heard his father pounding down the stairs, as well and Honey's collar jingling.

"How's mama's baby?" I cooed, as Honey bounced around trying to get my attention. "You missed me?" Of course he did. As usual Midnight was stepping all over my dog trying to get closer.

"What did you bring?" CJ asked.

"I brought home some food from the restaurant. Ribs, corn on the cob, and macaroni and cheese."

"Oooh, ribs!" Immediately he reached for a plate from the cabinet.

"Go wash your hands." I tried to say it as nice as I could but I saw the way his face dropped at being scolded. Damn, did his father teach him anything? "And not dish soap. Go in the bathroom." We went through this almost every day. I didn't even want to think what he was doing when I wasn't around.

"Hey babe."

I turned and grinned at my man walking into the room while CJ moved into the powder room sulking. I wrapped my arms around Kaleb's neck and leaned in for a kiss.

"What's wrong with him?" he asked with a frown.

"I told him to wash his hands before eating."

"CJ, what the fuck you upset about! Just wash your got-damn hands so we can eat!" he shouted, and had me even flinching.

"Yes, sir. I *am* washing my hands."

I smiled, glad my man had my back.

"What you got in those pans?"

I pulled back the aluminum foil so Kaleb could see inside. "Hell yeah! That looks good." He pulled me into his arms again.

"How was work?" I asked because Mama taught me to always ask about your man. It made him feel important.

"Bullshit like always," he said with a scowl.

We washed our hands, said grace then all dug in. CJ went

up to his room with his plate and his big ass dog. Honey was under the table beneath my chair waiting for something to fall on the floor.

"Babe, I have a game tonight."

I frowned. "What? I was hoping we could spend the evening together."

"Me too but I forgot I agreed to referee a basketball tournament at Hickman High School tonight."

Well, at least when Kaleb was refereeing he was too busy to blow up my phone. "Okay. I'll just go back to the restaurant later and lock up."

After dinner I put the food away and Kaleb came down shortly after in his black and white referee gear.

"Babe, I'll call you between games." He walked over and gave me a sweet kiss then swung a large duffel bag onto his shoulder.

I nodded and walked over to wipe down the island. "What's that?" I said, pointing to some small green army men.

Kaleb looked almost embarrassed as he scooped them off the counter. "Those are CJ's little men he carries around in his pocket."

I tried to keep a straight face. That kid got weirder by the second.

"If he asks I'm sticking them in the drawer in the living room." I nodded and leaned in for another long wet kiss. "Love you babe. I'll see you later."

He went back upstairs to grab his whistle and by the time I was finished with the kitchen he was pulling out of the driveway.

I went up to the third bedroom that Kaleb had given me to set up as a home office. It was his way of getting me to spend more time at his place than at mine. I padded into the room with Honey under my feet and took a seat behind a glass desk. I made it clear if he wanted me here, then I needed space that was conducive to working. Last weekend we also moved my red love seat from my bedroom to his house so I could feel more at home.

I spent the next hour working on an advertisement for Fourth of July weekend. The holiday was always a big draw for the restaurant and I was planning on having a buffet style dinner that would top any other restaurant in the area.

By the time I had a draft ready to be sent off to the printers, Frankie was calling. Since Kaleb was nowhere around, I answered.

"Guess what?"

I smiled. "What?"

"I found a gas station I want to buy."

I could hear the excitement in his voice. "Good for you."

"But I want you to come down and look at it."

I looked over at the clock. It was six thirty. Kaleb wasn't due home until around eight. I had planned on dropping by the restaurant anyway, so I could do both. "Where you at?" I was already heading to the bedroom to change.

"I'm at the corner of Providence and Texas."

I slipped into a pair of skinny jeans and a blue blouse and grabbed a pair of yellow pumps.

I knocked once at CJ's door and then opened it. He was sitting on the end of his bed playing his video game. Midnight was on his bed and the room stunk like wet dog. "I'm running over to the restaurant."

"Okay." He didn't even bother to look away from the video game. He spent so much time in front of that television, one of these days I would have to bring him down to the restaurant and put him to work.

Honey was whining and wanting to go with me."No Honey. I'll be back." I rubbed his head then hurried out the house and climbed into my BMW, before Kaleb decided to come home early.

I opened the sunroof. It was just one of those June nights when the weather was just perfect.

I spotted Frankie's SUV as I pulled into the abandoned gas station. As soon as he saw my car, he trotted over and opened the door for me.

"Hey you," he said with that sexy ass smile of his. I climbed out and gave him a hug.

"C'mon, let me show you around."

My eyes swept the area. "Remember when we were teenagers and after we got done with those teen center parties we all hung out in this parking lot?"

He laughed. "You remember that?"

I nodded. "Hell yeah! Them were the days."

This gas station used to be the place to be. I remember all of us with a driver's license, filling up the parking lot. Music thumping, folks dancing, and acting a fool. The only reason why the store manager didn't complain was because we were all inside buying up the stores, especially the slushies. We were good for business. Every now and again, a fight would pop off and the police would come and run us all off but for the most part we just weren't ready to go home and were hanging out.

The place hadn't been open in years. The gas price still displayed one-ninety-eight a gallon. Something we haven't seen in years.

"I'm planning to take this garage and install a carwash. And then right on this side we'll have hand-washing and detailing."

"You gonna sell gas?"

Frankie smirked. "Hell yeah and run a convenience store just like back in the day."

I nodded and visualized his dream, while I walked around the lot. The windows were busted on the front of the store and the inside was a janitorial mess, but it wasn't anything sweat and hard work couldn't fix.

"I think this will be a great location."

He looked down at me and grinned. "Me too. I'm going to have the pumps inspected for contamination but other than that I'm already sold on this place."

"Why would they be contaminated?"

"Sometimes tanks leak underneath. And that's a bitch to clean up. Besides, the bank will never approve the loan until it's inspected." He looked around and grinned. "But this is my dream."

"It's better to have some kinda dream than none at all." I

looked around and smiled. "I remember when I first told everyone I wanted to open a restaurant downtown."

"I remember that. And I said there was no way in hell folks are gonna come downtown for soul food. But you proved us all wrong."

"Yes I did."

Frankie gave me a fist bump and we stood there like two fools staring at each other. I starting thinking about when we were in high school. I had been so young and confused back then. Now he was simply delicious and looked so good in blue jeans and a fresh white t-shirt.

My cellphone rang, breaking the spell. I reached inside my purse and look down at the screen.

"Hey CJ. What's up?"

"Have you seen my men?"

It took me a second to figure out what he was talking about. "Your little army men?"

"Yes, my men." He sounded impatient.

"Yeah you left them on the counter so your dad stuck them in the drawer in the living room."

I could hear him moving through the house.

"Where in the drawer?"

"I don't know. He said he was putting them in the living room."

"There not in here!" He sounded frantic.

Oh my God! He was such a pussy. "I don't know CJ. You'll have to text him."

"Why did he move them?" he whined.

What's the big fucking deal about those men? "I don't know. Look, I'll try and reach your dad for you."

"Okay." He hung up, and probably went back to looking for those men.

"Is everything okay?" Frankie asked.

I nodded. "Yeah, let me try texting Kaleb. He moved his son's toys and now he's freaking out."

He scratched his chin. "How old is the boy?"

I rolled my eyes while I texted. "Thirteen. He carries these little men around in his pocket and now he can't find them."

Frankie gave me this look and I held up a hand. "Let me stop you before you even ask. I can't even begin to explain it."

I hit Send then put my phone away. "I better get over to the restaurant before Kaleb starts blowing up my phone."

There was that look again. I decided to ignore it. "I think this place is great. What are you planning on calling it?"

"Frankie's."

I grinned. "Of course."

He shrugged. "Like you always say, 'It's all about me.'"

We laughed and then he took my hand and got all serious. "So how are you doing?"

Didn't he just ask me the same thing two weeks ago? "I'm doing good."

"I mean really. You just don't seem yourself."

"What does that mean?" I didn't mean to get defensive but I did.

"I mean you're usually really talkative, laughing. I don't know, you just seem different."

I shrugged. "Maybe it's called maturity."

"Or it could be stress."

I blew out a breath. You never could hide much from him. "Yeah, that's true. I just gotta lot going on right now."

"You've always been able to juggle a lot of things but that man and his son they're so needy. I thought you didn't like needy men?"

"I don't and he isn't." This was one conversation I just didn't want to have. My phone started vibrating in my purse. I didn't even have to look down to know who it was. "Look, I better get to the restaurant so I can go home and help CJ find his men." I tried to laugh it off like it was a joke but Frankie barely broke a smile. "Let me know what you find out about the gas tanks. Otherwise, I think you better snatch this place up." I moved over and gave him a quick hug then hurried off to my car just as my phone started vibrating again.

I waited until I had started the car to answer.

"Where you at?" Kaleb barked.

"Heading to the restaurant. What did you do with CJ's men?"

He laughed. "Oh I have them in my pocket."

"*In your pocket?* You told me you were putting them in the drawer. That boy is practically in tears over those men!" I didn't mean to snap but I didn't like the way he was behaving.

"Sorry. I was just playing with him." He had the nerve to sound defensive.

"Then keep that shit between the two of you! He's calling all frantic over his men while you're at a basketball game."

"How long you gonna be at the restaurant?"

"For a slit second then I'll go back to the house with CJ. You got him all upset."

Kaleb blew out a long breath. "I'll call him."

I ended the call and went to the restaurant. CJ and his dad were both blowing up my phone, but I left it in the car and went inside. It was definitely slow for a Wednesday night.

When I finally made it back to the house I noticed the entire place was lit up with lights. Honey was on the porch waiting for me. CJ had obviously let him out and forgot to bring him back in.

"CJ!" I called as I stepped inside the house.

"Yes ma'am."

I moved into the living room where he was sitting on the couch rocking back and forth hugging the pillow to his chest. Cartoons were on.

"Why are all the lights on?"

"I'm sorry. I was looking for my men." He got up from the couch and started turning out lights. I saw the dried tears on his face and the sad look on his face.

"Did you speak to your dad?"

He nodded. "He says he has my men." His bottom lip quivered. Ugh! I was so tired of feeling sorry for him.

"He'll be home I'm sure in the next hour."

"An hour?" His eyes widened.

"How about some ice cream with chocolate syrup?" I suggested.

He nodded. "Yeah, yeah, yeah!" I knew he loved chocolate syrup. I just hid it at the back of the closet because he liked to drink chocolate milk with a spoon and all that damn slurping got on my last nerve.

I put the syrup on the counter along with the ice cream and suddenly felt compelled to strike up a conversation. "I hear you're an honor roll student."

"We don't get mid-grades until next week." He mumbled without looking at me.

"So do you think you made it?"

He nodded. "Yes ma'am. But math has been tough."

"I'm sure you'll do fine. If you need some help just let me know."

"Okay," he said in that annoying babyfied voice. I left him eating ice cream in front of the television and went upstairs to put on something comfortable. By the time I was coming back down, Kaleb was coming through the front door. CJ practically knocked me over.

"Dad, where are my men?" he said in a frenzy.

"They're in my bag," Kaleb said like it was no big deal.

"W-why'd you move them?" he stuttered.

"Quit whining like a fucking baby!" It was clear he was now annoyed.

CJ stood there rocking side to side. "I just wanted to know why you moved them." I couldn't believe his little ass was demanding answers.

"CJ, get your men and go to your room!" Kaleb snapped and there was that crazed look again. I was starting to think something was wrong with both of them.

I waited until he was up in his room before I turned to Kaleb, completely puzzled by the entire situation and said, "What's up with him and those men?"

Again he shrugged like it was no big deal. "He's had them since he was a little kid and I can't get him to part with them."

"So they're like his security blanket."

"Yeah, pretty much. He carries them around in his pocket all the time."

I looked over at the staircase. Something about this boy gave me this sick eerie feeling like there was so much more to this story. I just couldn't put my finger on it.

<u>25</u>

NYREE

Ever since the proposal I haven't been able to sleep a wink. Instead my mind has been racing with thoughts and so many emotions I'm ready to go find a psychiatrist and ask him to prescribe me something. My feelings were torn. Should I follow my heart or use common sense? I love my man and wanted to follow him to the ends of the Earth. But at the same time, I'm giving up my job, my home, and friends to travel across the world with a man I have known for three months.

Trust me, I was eager to walk down the aisle and be Mrs. Samuels but I had gone down this path so many times before that for once I was scared. I'm serious. I was afraid that maybe I really was moving too fast and I needed to pull on the reins and say, "Whoa!" and slow it down. However, if I did, I ran the risk of losing my man, and I simply couldn't imagine living without him.

I didn't know who to turn to for advice. If I even dared to call my mother and mention marriage, she would be contacting Reverend Williams and booking the church, so I decided to ask Janelle to meet me for lunch. Normally she can be a male basher but ever since she started dating Kaleb she seemed happier and more positive about men.

I called and asked her to drive down to Jefferson City and meet me for lunch at this little bistro downtown. I was feeling a little better knowing Janelle was coming, because if I didn't tell someone soon, I was going to go crazy. To be honest I wasn't sure why I was losing my mind over the proposal. Jeremy and I were in love. He got a job offer on the most romantic island and asked me to go with him as his wife. End of story.

If things were that simple why have you been second guessing your decision to marry him for almost two weeks?

All I know is I needed to talk to my girl and hear her advice.

I had just ordered two waters with lemon when I looked out the window and spotted Janelle sauntering cross the street. She was wearing a smoking red dress that hit every curve on her thick body and with the small black clutch purse in her hand I didn't have to guess she was strutting in black five-inch stilettos. That chick could dress. And as always she made me feel self-conscious in my military uniform.

"Hey girl!" she squealed as soon as she spotted me sitting at a booth in the corner. I waved and signaled for her to come and join me.

Janelle slid onto the sit across from me batting her fake eyelash extensions like a little kid with a secret.

"Now you know my restaurant is busy as hell during lunch time," she scolded as she put the Chanel bag on the seat beside her. "You better be glad I love you."

I smiled. "I know and I appreciate you driving down."

She settled on the seat, reached for a menu and I noticed her perfectly sculptured nails. I needed to remember to make an appointment myself.

"So what did you want to talk to me about?" she asked and brushed her shoulder-length hair away from her chocolate face.

I still had my hand hidden underneath the table. I swallowed and was getting ready to tell her when her cellphone ringtone chimed that new Beyoncé song. Janelle frowned.

"What's wrong?"

"Nothing... just Kaleb checking up on me."

"Checking up on you? He's still sweating you like that?" I

said but she simply waved her hand like it was no big deal.

"Girl, once I let him taste my goodies, the fool lost his damn mind." She made a joke out of the situation, but I was starting to worry because the laughter didn't quite reach her eyes. Janelle went back to looking over the menu. "I swore I wouldn't move in with him until after I was married but... I'm now planning to move in with him next weekend."

"*Really*?" I couldn't believe it. The way she liked her space?

Janelle was grinning and nodding at the same time. "Yep. I can rent out my townhouse and put that eleven hundred dollars a month right back in my pocket. You know Mama loves to shop!" she chuckled.

"We know."

Our waitress arrived and took our orders.

"Okay, so you had me meet you for lunch for a reason, so what is it?" Janelle asked like she was in a hurry.

I stared directly at Janelle, while I removed my hand from underneath the table and wiggled my ring finger.

"Oh shit! You're engaged?" She snatched my hand and brought it to her eyes so she could get a closer look. Damn, I know the diamond was small but it wasn't *that* bad.

"Jeremy proposed two weeks ago."

"Damn bitch and you're just telling me now!" She pushed my hand away.

"You got a lotta nerve!" I was talking with my hand now. "At least I'm telling you in private. I wasn't ready to say anything until I had a chance to get used to the idea."

"Uh-huh." Her eyes traveled over to my ring finger again. "He works for the federal government and that's the best he could do?"

"Whatever," I said but couldn't resist a laugh because I had been thinking the same thing. "That man is paying child support for three kids. He doesn't have it like Kaleb."

I noticed the way she rolled her eyes at the mention of her man, but I decided to leave it alone, and focus on my own issues.

"I haven't even told my mother I was engaged."

"Hell naw!" Janelle fell back against the bench. "Why

not?"

Leaning forward, I rested my elbows on the table. "I can't help wondering if I'm moving too fast."

She gave a rude snort. "You always do, so what's the difference?"

"See," I pointed to her. "That's what I'm talking about. I've been married and engaged more times than I care to admit and you see where that has gotten me."

Janelle looked at me then nodded. "True."

I shrugged. "For once I want to get it right."

"Now you know I'm the last person you should be talking to about getting all serious and shit," she pointed out impatiently. "What does your heart say?"

I grinned. "It says, marry my man."

"Well? Then I guess you need to marry him." Janelle said it like the decision was that easy. And maybe it was.

"Jeremy wants to get married next month."

She choked on her water. "Next month? Don't you think that's a little soon?"

I took a deep breath. "Yes and no. Like you said, follow my heart. For the first time in my life I know what love is."

She snorted. "You said the same thing about Rock."

I shook my head. "That wasn't love. That was lust and a bit of a challenge. But what I feel for Jeremy, I have never felt before in my life. All I care about is hearing his scratchy voice and feeling his arms wrapped around me. He has this way of making me feel like nothing else matters. I thank God every night for bringing him in my life and I pray the same thing in the morning."

Janelle's mouth fell open. "Damn, you got it bad."

"I know, right?" I replied, and started playing with the condensation running off the glass. "That's why I can't imagine spending my life without him."

"Yeah, but what's the rush? I'm engaged, but I plan on milking this shit for as long as I can."

I rolled my eyes. She's a mess! "Jeremy accepted a job in Hawaii and is supposed to report by the end of October. He wants me to go with him."

Her large, brown eyes widened. "Damn! Hawaii? Okay, *now* I understand. I wouldn't pass up an opportunity like that either."

Shaking my head, I replied, "It wouldn't matter to me if we were moving to Alaska. All that really matters is that I get to be with him."

Janell leaned across the table and gave me this weird look. "You really are in love this time."

"What did you think I was doing..., lying like you?"

"*Lying*? I'm not lying. I do love Kaleb, but his money does help." She took a sip from her straw and I noticed she was staring at me.

"What?" I don't know why I felt so self-conscious.

"You *do* seem different." I didn't like the way she was looking at me.

"What do you mean?"

Janelle looked a moment longer then gazed up toward the ceiling, like she was careful choosing her words. "I mean there's a sort of calm about you that I've never seen in you."

I shrugged. "Is that a bad thing?"

She hesitated, searching my eyes then shook her head, sending her curls swinging around her shoulders. "No, it's great. You just seem... I wanna say happy but it's more than that."

I swallowed dry at the truth of her words. "That's because it is. I can't even begin to describe it. It's like I'm walking on a cloud. It's a wonderful feeling I can't even begin to bring to words. But I love it."

"Oh my God! You're shaking. I can hear it in your voice. Damn girl... you *are* in love!"

"I know, right." I nodded and couldn't stop the tears gathering at the corners. "I've always read those romance novels wondering about that amazing feeling the heroine was experiencing and now I know." Tears started running down my cheeks.

"Dammit Nyree! You're gonna ruin your make up," Janelle scolded and leaned over with her napkin and dabbed at my eyes.

"Sorry," I muttered.

"You don't have to apologize but you do have to keep it cute, girl. I can't send you back to work looking a hot mess." She did this crazy eye-roll thing that caused me to start laughing. "I am so happy for you. Really I am. If you love 'em, then I like 'em. Y'all know how I do."

"Thank you, Jae," I said between sniffles. "I was starting to think maybe I was crazy for feeling this way."

"Only you know what you feel. Hell, I'm going through the same damn thing with that crazy mothafucka I'm with." She shook her head with this far-off look. "I can't believe I've changed for him."

"I can't believe it either. You sure you're being faithful?"

While laughing Janelle waved a hand in the air. "Girl as God is my witness, I ain't thought about another man since I've been with Kaleb. I'm dick-notized."

"Dick-notized!" I roared with laughter.

Giggling, she replied, "I'm serious. I told all my exes to stop calling and I meant it. I don't even look at another man because I know that crazy mothafucka will clown if he caught me."

"He ain't no punk." Just the way Jae liked them.

"No, but he's crazy."

My brow rose. "Sounds like that's what you need."

I noticed she frowned, but our waitress returned with our food before I could ask her about it. By the time I said grace, Janelle was already digging into her salad.

"So seriously, when is the big day?" she asked.

Wiping my mouth with a napkin, I replied, "I told you. In the next three to four weeks."

She shook her head. "How can we plan a wedding that quickly?"

I shrugged because now that Janelle had given me her stamp of approval, time was the last thing on my mind. All I cared about was being with Jeremy. "We're just doing something small at church."

"Small?" Janelle turned up her nose. "You're supposed to do it up right this time, remember?"

"I want to be married in a church. That's more than I can say for the last relationship."

She blew out a long breath like I was being ridiculous.

"At least my parents will be happy."

"This isn't about your parents," she snapped and stabbed a tomato with her fork. "You gotta live with the man, not them." Leave it to her to correct me.

"I know but the good thing is my parents already like him," I pointed out with a grin.

Janelle rolled her eyes. "If I did everything to try and please everyone else I would lose my mind."

Maybe that's what my problem is.

"Are you going to at least have a maid of honor?"

I nodded. "Yes, Jeremy's planning on having a best man. But other than that we are keeping it small and simple. I was thinking of buying this white dress I saw at Dillard's that would be cute as hell. I could wear it again."

"A Dillard's wedding dress?" Janelle scrunched up her nose at that idea. "Are you having food and cake?"

I bit into the dinner roll and chewed before replying, "Yep, but like I said it's gonna be small, no more than a hundred people."

Silence fell over the table. While I dug into my chef salad, Janelle searched through her emails on her phone. "Is his family coming?" she asked, out of the blue.

I didn't even want to tell her I hadn't met anyone, but his children. "He invited his sister and his parents. But he doesn't think they will come."

"Why?" Damn, she was all up in my business.

I shrugged because I didn't know the answer to that. I was still trying to figure out his relationship with his family, but it didn't seem like they were close at all.

"What about his kids?" she asked between chews.

"It's too much trouble to get them here then we want to honeymoon right after. How can we do that if we have four kids on our hip?"

Her eyes snapped to mine. "Four? Whoa, wait a minute! I thought he had three?"

Damn, me and my big mouth. "Well he did, but then I realized when he said an adopted daughter, he didn't mean like a play-daughter he meant a little girl he adopted."

"How little?"

I was almost embarrassed to say. "Four."

Janelle fell back against her chair. "Damn, that's little! You gonna have to deal with baby-mama drama!"

"They'll be none of that." I shrugged. "At least they're all in Chicago."

"And at least you like kids," Janelle mentioned with an exaggerated eye-roll.

"I do, but I couldn't deal with someone being dropped off at the house every weekend. The middle child is already talking about moving in with us after graduation."

Janelle was shaking her head with disbelief. "Nyree, you better think about it. What if something happened to their Mama then you'd be stuck raising them."

"Are you tryna make me choke on my food!" I rolled my eyes. "Girl, don't even play like that."

She pointed her fork at me. "Hey, it's something you need to think about."

I gave a rude snort. "The only thing I want to think about is spending the rest of my life with Jeremy."

Janelle shook her head again. "Sounds like your man has a lotta baggage."

Yep, but I had no idea just how much.

26

JANELLE

I had just come upstairs holding my morning coffee when Kaleb said, "Babe, can you take CJ to the dentist for me?"

It took everything I had not to cringe. Me? Alone in the car with his son all the way to the dentist office? Hell no! Now that I was officially living with them it was hard enough just being across the hall.

Lord forgive me, but there's something about that kid irritates me.

I had to think fast. "Uh, I've got a meeting at ten-thirty."

Kaleb was buttoning a white dress shirt as he said, "That's cool. His appointment is at eight-thirty. I would do it but I got a conference call at nine that I can't miss."

I was ready to say no when I made myself take a deep breath. *Janelle you gotta be willing to change. That man is a package deal just like you and that damn dog.*

I stifled a groan and replied, "Sure babe. I'll be glad to."

"Thanks." He kissed my lips then stepped out the bedroom and down the hall to knock on CJ's door. "Son, get dressed! Ms. Jae is gonna take you to your appointment."

"Yes, sir." He called from the other side of the door.

While Kaleb finished getting ready for work, I jumped into the large walk-in shower and took a deep breath. Damn. I hated being alone with his son. I know that may sound crazy but the kid was weird and so fucking needy. I feel sorry he didn't have a mother and maybe that's why he was growing attached to me. I don't know. All I know is I didn't have kids for a reason—I don't want any. Yet, somehow I had fooled myself into thinking being a stepmother of a teenage boy would be easy, but it wasn't. It was nerve-racking. That kid was like a pesky fly.

I had to keep reminding myself we were a family and this was my home. My townhouse had been rented so there was no turning back. I still had a hard time believing I was doing this "*we*" shit. But I was. All because I had fallen in love.

Even now my feelings for Kaleb took me by surprise. I always knew he would be different and there had to be some reason why I was drawn to him. I tried to fight it, I even tried to deny it and convinced myself it was all about the money, but I was just fooling myself. What I felt was much deeper than that. I was in love with that complex man of mine. And it scared the hell outta me. Although lately things have been good between us. He started taking me on business trips with him to Kansas City, where we stayed at five-star hotels and ate in only the best restaurants. Last weekend we had even gone down to the Lake of the Ozarks and spent the day shopping at the outlets. I had everything I could possible want, so why was I complaining about having to spend a few hours with his wimpy kid?

I pushed the thought aside, got ready and took one final look in the mirror. I made sure my hair and makeup was looking fabulous then I grabbed my purse and headed toward the stairs. "CJ, I'll meet you in the car!"

"Yes, ma'am." He called from inside his room. I don't understand why the only person who smells that stench seeping from beneath his door was me.

The minute I hit the bottom step CJ's big-ass dog came racing down the stairs. I had to grab onto the handrail to keep from falling. Damn, I hated that big horse. Honey was at the bottom of the wooden stairs and had quickly moved out the way. I guess he was tired of getting his little ass ran over.

I climbed into my car and waited in the driveway. By the time I got done checking my emails CJ was climbing in. Just like his daddy he looked at me crazy for being on my phone. I sighed and put it away.

"You lock the front door?"

He nodded. "Yes ma'am."

"Well, then let's get this journey underway." The sooner I took him to the dentist, the sooner I could drop him back off at home. Like most teenagers, he was spending his summer eating up all the food and playing his video games. When I was growing up, as soon as our chores were done, we had to take our asses outside. Swimming at the community center, hanging with my girls, fucking some little boy in his mama's house while she was at work, you name it, Janelle Fox was doing it, but I definitely didn't spend my summer vacation sitting in the house.

As I backed out the driveway, I reached down and turned on the Tom Joyner Show.

"Can we ride in silence?"

I swung around and stared at CJ like he was crazy. "Why?"

There was that far off look in his eyes like his father. "Because I like it quiet."

Hell no, then I would have to strike up a conversation with him.

I pointed a finger in his direction. "You just sit over there and relax. I'm running this." Gotta let him know who's in control.

I pulled off and after minutes had passed, I felt compelled to say something. He was sitting over there quiet and looking so out of place.

Damn you Kaleb Kerrington!

"How's summer break going?" I asked.

"Good."

Okay, so much for that conversation.

I went back to listening to the talk show but then CJ started rocking. The way nervous people do, back and forth, banging the back of his big round head against the headrest. This wasn't the first time I'd seen him rocking. I'd seen him doing it on the living room couch. I never said anything before but enough was enough.

"CJ, quit rocking."

"I can't help it," he said defensively.

"Yes, you can, now stop it." He better realize I'm not to be messed with. Of course he obeyed but now he looked like he wanted to cry.

See, this is why Janelle doesn't do kids.

"See, I told ya, you'd stop."

"But I'll just start again!" He wailed.

I looked at him cockeyed. "Then you need to start training yourself. I promise you, people are gonna pick on you in high school if you don't stop."

"I can't help it!" CJ whined.

Oh my goodness, he was a big-ass baby! In my honest opinion this boy needed some professional help. "CJ, you can't go through life like that. If you're rocking at home and in the car then I bet you're rocking at school."

His silence was all the confirmation I needed.

"And while we're at it how long have you had those little men?"

He cringed and I could tell the question made him uncomfortable. "Since I was a little kid," he said in that babyfied voice.

The last thing I wanted to do was make him feel self-conscious. "You like those men?"

He nodded. "My mom gave them to me."

I was speechless but quickly found my voice. "You remember your mom?"

He gave me a weird look and nodded. "Yes, ma'am. I think about her all the time."

"What do you remember about her?" I didn't mean to ask but CJ had this sad look in his eyes and I felt this need to comfort him. Ugh, what the hell was wrong with me?

CJ sneaked a peek in my direction. "I remember her singing to me and reading me bedtime stories."

"Really? You remember all that?" Wasn't he three at the time?

"Yes ma'am." He nodded then looked sad. "Did you know she died?"

I nodded. "Yes, your dad told me."

"I miss her." His lower lip quivered and this time when he started rocking I didn't even bother telling him to stop. That kid needed some help that he wasn't going to get from his father. Hell, Kaleb had enough problems of his own.

I put my foot on the brake at the next light then reached over and turned down the radio. "My father died when I was young." Where the hell did that come from?

CJ turned on the seat. "He did? What happened?"

I kept my gaze on the traffic light as I said, "My father was a cop. One night he was called to check out a burglary and was shot. He died on the way to the hospital."

"Do you miss him?"

Every damn day. "Sometimes, but I don't know why," I replied and felt the need to explain as I put my foot on the gas again. "My dad was mean. He used to beat my brother and I all the time."

He gave me a knowing look. "Like my dad."

I slammed on the brake and swung around on the seat. "Your dad doesn't hit you!" I didn't mean to snap but I wasn't about to have him telling lies about Kaleb. What if someone found out the way someone did with my dad?

I moved into the flow of traffic again. To this day I still blamed myself for his death which was crazy since I wasn't the one who shot the bullet, yet I spent years wishing I had a gun so I could have shot him myself.

"Dad yells all the time and blames me for stuff I didn't even do!"

Nodding, I muttered, "Yeah, that's what dad's do." That's why it's a mother's job to protect her children. Only mine had been weak. For years, I had wished my mother had been strong enough to protect us. I guess that's hard to do when you're being beaten as well.

27

NYREE

"Let me get an amen!"

"AMEN!"

I shouted along with the rest of the congregation then glanced over to my right as Jeremy squeezed my hand. We were attending my family church and every time we sat on the same pew with my parents, I had this warm feeling inside. I was a firm believer that a family that prays together, stays together.

I crossed my legs and sat there smiling as I listened to the minister talk about faith and believing. That was me on so many levels. I truly believed the Lord had put this together and spirituality was important for any relationship to succeed.

"How are you feeling?" he asked with that goofy grin of his. Service was over and we were going out to lunch.

"I'm feeling good," I said and was swinging my arms then we started skipping, like kids, all the way to his Tahoe.

Laughing, I waited for him to open the door then I leaned in and kissed him. The way his eyes lit up was something else. I loved making him happy. And it didn't take much. A few hugs, kisses, and words of affirmation—his primary love language.

Jeremy climbed in, put the key in the ignition but before he pulled off he turned and looked at me.

"Angel…, I love you with my every breath. You just don't know how many times I prayed for a woman to fellowship with me, and make God the foundation of our relationship."

I stared in his eyes. I was bubbling with so much joy I felt tears burning the corners of my eyes. "That's exactly how I feel. I knew something was missing from my past relationships, but I never knew what those qualities were until I met you." Overwhelmed by emotion, I paused long enough to push back tears. "Now that I know, I will never accept anything less."

Jeremy nodded, and looked pleased by my answer. "You don't have to because you now have me."

After lunch at Denny's we went back to his place and kicked off our shoes at the door.

"What do you wanna do for the rest of the afternoon?" he asked.

I flopped down on the sofa and rubbed my stomach. "Right now, I think I'm gonna take a nap," I laughed.

He sat beside me and wrapped his arms around my middle. "Poor baby. Why don't you go on up and get comfortable?"

Jeremy didn't have to tell me twice. I went up to the room and clicked on the television then laid across the bed. Jeremy cleaned up the breakfast dishes, and came up just as I was dozing off.

"Hey Angel, if you don't mind, I'm gonna go run off some of this food while you're relaxing."

I yawned. "Run? How can you run with all that food on your stomach?"

"That's why I'm running. I never lie down after eating all those carbs."

"Now you're making me feel guilty," I said around another yawn.

Leaning forward, Jeremy kissed my lips. "Nah, you look good just the way you are."

I watched as he changed into a pair of shorts, t-shirt, and running shoes. *All that soft smooth skin.* Jeremy told me he shaved because he hated to sweat, but damn. I didn't know too many men who shaved not only their pubic but also the hair from their armpits.

"I'll be right back," he said then leaned over the bed and kissed me.

I laid there for a while dozing and watching *Everybody Hates Chris* when I heard something vibrating. I sat up on the bed and slid over to the edge and looked down. Jeremy had left his pants on the floor near his dresser. I reached inside his pocket and looked down at the screen.

Alexis Samuels.

My eyes were nearly popped out of my head.

Alexis Samuels? Who the hell was that?

I sat there staring at his phone trying to talk myself out of doing what I was about to do, but oh well. Sue me. I typed in the passcode I had seen him use to unlock his screen, and on the first try, it unlocked.

My hand was shaking as I took a seat on the end of the bed and scrolled through his phone history. Alexis Samuels had left a voice message. Lord knows I shouldn't, but I did. I listened to it.

"This is the last time I'm calling your sorry ass. Send me my damn child support or I'm calling my lawyer."

What the fuck? I sat there dumbfounded and clearly confused. His ex-wife's name was Delaney. Not Alexis. My mind started working overtime, and no matter how I tried to spin it, I still came up with the same conclusion.

Jeremy had another child by a woman named Alexis.

I was so angry I scrolled through his text messages and started reading them. There were several with his children in Chicago and I saw one Jeremy had sent to his sister telling her how much he loved me and my heart flipped. But then I saw a series of text messages that made me gasp.

J: Tracy I need my ring back.

T: I'll be in town next week.

J: Call me and I'll meet you at our spot.

I gazed down at the date of the text messages. It was less than a month ago. Around the same time he had proposed.

By the time Jeremy had returned from jogging, I was packing my stuff.

"I had a good run." Jeremy stopped when he saw my duffel bag. "Where you going?"

"Home. You are a damn liar!" I hissed as I tossed my things inside.

He grabbed my arm, and swung me around. "What? What are you talking about?" He took on a serious tone.

I snatched my arm away then reached over and grabbed his phone and handed it to him. "Alexis called." The horror on his face was all the answer I needed. I shook my head in disgust then reached for my bag and pushed past him.

"Angel, let me explain."

I glared at him through narrowed eyes. "Explain what? Another 'adopted' daughter!" I yelled. "Oh and by the way, who the fuck is Tracy, and is this her recycled engagement ring?" I held up my hand. While he played dumb, I slipped off the ring and tossed it onto the bed. I was so tired of this mess. I swung the bag onto my shoulder and kept on walking until I was out the house and heading toward my Lexus. I should have known things were too good to be true.

"Nyree, wait. Can you please give me a chance to explain?"

I shook my head. "No dammit! Not now. I just need to go home and just clear my head."

Jeremy hesitated then finally nodded his head and got the fuck out of my way. I finished loading my car and wasted no time driving off.

I was barely down the road before I called Janelle.

"What's up girl?" she sounded too damned giddy.

"You will not believe what just happened?" I was too stunned to know what to feel.

"What?" Of course she was all ears.

"That bastard has another child!" I said bluntly.

"What?" Janelle sputtered and then started laughing. Sometimes I hated her ass. "Hell nah! He's got more kids. What's this make it, five?"

I sighed as I turned the corner. "Yeah."

"Damn girl! So how did you find out?"

I told her about finding his cellphone.

"Hell nah! That mothafucka is fertile! You better start using protection before your ass ends up pregnant."

I know this sounded crazy but I felt this tingling at my stomach at the thought of carrying Jeremy's baby. I didn't want to lose my fiancé. I had hoped he would be the father of my children. Now I just didn't know anymore.

"That's not all," I began and paused for dramatic effect because I knew Janelle was going to have a field day with this one.

"What?"

"Jeremy was engaged with someone else. He…" Goodness this was painful. "He gave me the same ring he gave that chick!"

"*What the fuck?*" Janelle howled then was laughing so hard I had to drag the phone away from my ear. "How the hell you find that shit out?"

"I don't know for sure. I saw some text messages so I just *assumed* the rest."

"What did he think you were, stuck on stupid? Niggas ain't shit!" she snorted. "Hey, meet me at the mall. We can talk there."

"Okay." I hung up and hopped on Interstate 70 for three exits then pulled into the Columbia Mall parking lot. We always parked near JCPenney's.

There was no missing the red BMW as it pulled into the lot or Janelle as she climbed out. I came around my car as she wiggled her hips in my direction in black leggings and a blouse that was so tight her titties looked ready to pop out. "What are you buying today?"

"My stepson needs some new clothes." She rolled her eyes but she wasn't fooling me.

I couldn't resist a grin. "He's starting to wear on you, huh?"

She shrugged and then smoothly changed the subject. "You okay?"

I kept walking toward the door, glancing around to see if anyone noticed how miserable I was. "I don't know how I feel."

"What did Jeremy have to say when you confronted him?"

"I didn't give him a chance to say anything. I just left and told him I needed some space."

"Space is probably a good thing." Janelle reached for the door and searched my face. The last thing I wanted was pity." Damn girl, five step-kids?"

"Don't remind me," I mumbled under my breath as I walked into the department store. Five definitely sounded like a lot, and maybe that was because I didn't have any. When Jeremy told me he had a big family, I had no idea he was talking about his own.

I followed Janelle over to the boy's department.

"You know his size?"

Her brow rose. "I know everything."

It was strange watching her shop for someone other than herself. "How are you and Kaleb doing?" I'd rather talk about anything other than me.

"Apparently better than you and Jeremy," she said with a wink and without the sarcasm. "And that ain't saying much." She moved over to the next rack. "Look over there for a pair of Levi's in size twenty-eight."

"Goodness, that kid's big!"

"And tall too." She smirked and I saw something in her eyes she would deny. Janelle was starting to get attached.

"Listen boo, it's gonna all work out. Anybody can see that Jeremy makes you happy."

My mouth dropped. Who was this person and where the hell was Janelle? "I am happy or at least I was until… today." A sob caught in my throat and Janelle swiveled over to where I was standing and rubbed my back gently as she said, "It's gonna be okay."

I nodded and tried to pull myself together. "I know. I just can't understand why he lied?" Suddenly right there in the store I was crying real tears. Janelle pulled me into her arms and held me close.

"Shhh! Before they call security," she whispered.

"I can't believe this is happening to me!"

"Girl, when are you going to realize all men are alike? They don't know any better. That's why they need good women to whip their asses in shape." She was stroking my hair trying to make me feel better. "Maybe he was tryna impress you."

"Yeah... maybe." I wiped my eyes and pulled away from her embrace. "I'm okay. I just need some time to think." I was certain all I needed was just a little time to sort out my feeling.

Janelle took my hands and looked me dead in the eyes. I'd never seen her look that serious before as she said, "Listen, girl. I'll never tell you to leave your man, trust me, if I wasn't in love, I would have left Kaleb's psycho-ass a long time ago. But if you decide to stay then think about what's gonna make you happy." She paused and struck a dramatic pose. "For me it's all about the money."

Now *that's* the Janelle I know.

* * *

I was sleeping when I heard the doorbell. I thought I was dreaming so I ignored it. But then I heard knocking and my cellphone was ringing. I rolled over and reached for my phone and looked at the clock. It was three in the morning. I tried to remain calm.

"Hello?"

"Angel?"

I blew out a breath. "What Jeremy?"

"Open the door before the neighbors call the police."

Goodness, the liar was at my door. I ended the call and slipped into my house slippers. I grabbed a few breath mints from the glass dish I kept on the end of my dresser and popped one in my mouth as I went downstairs. I swung the door open and glared at him. Anyone driving down the street would have seen me in my Victoria's Secret pajamas but I was too angry to care. It was too early in the morning for this crap.

"Jeremy, what do you want?" So much for keeping calm.

He looked so pitiful standing there with his hands stuffed in his pockets. "I came to bring my angel home."

I gave a rude snort. "Home? I *am* home."

"Home is where the heart is and it's with me." I just looked at him with one eye open but I'd be lying if I wasn't impressed he was here fighting for his woman. When was the last time I had a man do that?

"Can I please come in?"

I blew out a long breath because I was really sleepy and needed to get up in three hours and get ready for work. But I stepped aside and moved over to the sofa and took a seat. Jeremy sat beside me and took my hand in his. "Angel, I'm sorry."

"Sorry for what?" I wanted to shout, "Sorry for lying?" but I contained myself.

"For not telling you about Alexis."

I cut my eyes in his direction and waited.

If the look on his face wasn't a sign of a guilty conscience I don't know what was. "Alexis isn't my wife, she's my daughter. That was her phone her mother called me on."

"I'm listening," I replied suspiciously.

"I met Gwen in high school. We were only sixteen and dated off and on and then she found out she was pregnant. I don't even know if Alexis is really mine, but I've been raising her anyway."

"And paying child support," I added with sarcasm.

Jeremy looked down at the floor as he nodded. "Yes, until she turns twenty-one. She's a freshman in college."

Well, at least she was doing something with her life.

I guess the silence got to be too much for him. "So now what? You're breaking off our engagement?"

I just stared off at the wall. I was in no rush to answer. All the lying. He had five kids. Dammit! Did I really want a man with *that* much responsibility?

I shook my head. No way was I making this easy for him. "I don't know. I just need time to think."

"Angel, look at me." I tilted my head and gazed into his big brown eyes that were full of remorse. "Do you love me?" he asked.

God, why do I love this man so much? He was so insecure but it was clear to see he had so much love in his heart.

"Yes, I love you."

"Then if you love me, why does it matter?"

No he didn't. "It matters because you lied!" My neck was rolling with attitude.

"I didn't lie," he said.

"Yes, you did!" I snapped. "You told me you had three kids, then I found out you have an 'adopted' daughter, and now I discover your oldest daughter is in college. All you had to do was just be honest in the first damn place!"

"You're right." I thought he was going to confess everything—right then and there. So imagine my disappointment, when Jeremy lowered his head like a little boy being scolded by his mama, and it made me feel bad. Damn, why does he do that?

His eyes finally met mine and he simply said, "I understand if you don't want to be with me anymore. You're beautiful, educated, and you have no kids. That's why I didn't tell you because I figured if you knew the truth you never woulda gone out with me in the first place."

His explanation didn't prove a damn thing as far as I was concerned. "Okay..., but correct me if I'm wrong. Wouldn't you rather a woman be with you because of *who* you are not *who* you pretend to be?"

Jeremy was quiet again and looked so pathetic I was the one squeezing his hand. After a long silence, I leaned back on the couch and closed my eyes. This was some soap opera shit.

"Angel." I opened my eyes and my heart warmed at the seriousness of his expression. "I know I was wrong, but I'm a good man. I just made a stupid mistake. Give me another chance and I promise from this point on I'll be honest." He was down on his knee, pleading with me to forgive him. "But I can't lose my rib."

Rib? This was some ridiculous Adam and Eve crap. "What about Tracy? What ring were you talking about?"

He shook his head. "She's my ex-girlfriend. While we were dating she was wearing my fraternity ring. I asked her for it back."

I stared into his eyes, trying to read him. After a long moment, I replied, "Why do I believe you?"

He smirked. "Because Angel, you know I'm telling you the

truth."

No. I didn't know because part of me didn't want to know. It was crazy and insane.

"Angel, please forgive me?" Jeremy looked at me, studying my facial expressions then leaned forward until I was lying flat on my back. "I can't lose my angel."

I should have told him to kiss my ass and get out of my house, but I couldn't. "I don't know why I'm even considering forgiving you."

"Maybe because you know I'm a good man with good intentions. And I promise you no man will ever love you like I do."

His lips brushed against mine and one of us—maybe it was me—leaned forward and captured his lips in a kiss. My kitty cat started purring and I was spreading my legs and wrapping them around his waist. "Don't you ever keep anything that important from me again," I scolded between kisses.

"I promise," he said and I felt his lip quiver and thought he was about to cry, but then he slid his tongue inside my mouth.

God had truly put this together.

28

JANELLE

"What's that—?"

I had just stepped out the shower onto the heated ceramic flooring when I heard a bed squeaking like someone was fucking. I wrapped a thick robe around my body then slowly opened the door, expecting to see my man jacking off or something.

Imagine my relief to see Kaleb sitting on my chaise lounge watching television. "What wrong?" he asked.

I listened again and sure enough there was that sound again. "What's that squeaking?"

Kaleb said like it was no big deal, "Oh, that's CJ rocking."

"Rocking? Like he does in his chair?"

What the fuck? I tied the robe tightly around my waist, then stepped out the room. I moved down the hall and stood outside CJ's room with my ear to the door. Sure enough the sound was coming from inside.

I hurried back to the master suite. "It sounds like he's fucking."

Kaleb didn't even bother to look up from the television screen. "Nah, that's how he goes to sleep. It's soothing."

Really? "No, it's crazy! That boy is thirteen and he still needs to be rocked to sleep."

Of course that pissed him off. "You always got something slick to say."

Ignoring him, I hurried back down the hall and flung CJ's

door open and stared in horror. The television was on so I could clearly see him up on all four, rocking back and forth, with his head on the pillow and his eyes closed.

"CJ!"

Kaleb stormed down the hall. "Jae, leave that boy alone."

"Nobody wants to listen to that shit. Christopher John, quit rocking!" I cried. He moved around on the bed, mumbled something that sounded like, "yes ma'am" then went back to sleep. Cussing under my breath, I shut his door and padded past Kaleb and went back to our bedroom.

"I guess now you're gonna make fun of him."

"Make fun? Whatever," I mumbled, under my breath.

Kaleb glared at me itching for a fight, but I just ignored him and reached for my lotion and spread it on my body, seductively of course. One thing about me, I know how to defuse a bomb.

"You want me to oil your back?"

Bingo! I grinned. "Sure."

Kaleb walked over and took a seat on the bed beside me then reached for the bottle of spearmint scented lotion and started spreading it on my back. "Look… I know you act like that, because you care about CJ and me."

Actually the thought of a thirteen-year- old dry humping his mattress gave me the creeps, but I wasn't going to say that out loud.

He kissed my back, shoulder, and breasts then lifted one leg and nudged at my opening. I rested my hands at his waist and thrust my hips forward, causing his length to slip inside.

By morning I was hearing that damn rocking again. I waited until we were down at the table eating breakfast before I brought it up. Nothing worse than bitching on an empty stomach.

"Kaleb, the boy needs help," I insisted.

"What the fuck you mean my son needs help?"

"I tossed my arm in the air. "I mean… all that rocking. He can't go through life like that."

"Ask my parents." He waved his hand blowing me off. "I

used to do the same thing when I was a kid. He'll grow out of it."

That was hard to do, since I had yet to speak to his parents. Kaleb and CJ had been by to see my mom several times.

I couldn't believe the way he was blowing it off like it wasn't a big deal. I hated to ask the next question but I did it anyway. "Was he abused as a child?"

His fork stopped midair. "What?"

"I mean he acts like he's either been abused or just slow."

"Fuck no!" Kaleb shoveled eggs in his mouth and scowled. "I only beat his ass when he needs it, but other than that you know I punish him by taking away his video games."

I can't understand why he gets so defensive when I question the way he raises his son. "Then maybe he has some other issues."

"You sound just like my ex-girlfriend. She was always trying to say CJ acts like he's retarded."

That's because he does.

I shrugged and said innocently, "Maybe he's slow."

Kaleb slammed his hand on the table. "My son is an honor roll student!"

"Okay and so was Rain Man."

He looked at me with fury in his eyes. "Don't you ever get tired of talking about folks? You ain't all that."

I had no problem pointing a finger at him. "You might not believe this but I care about CJ. He's a good kid and I hate to see him get teased. He's at that age."

He reached for his toast and took a bite. "You're right."

I looked at him and shrugged. "We just need to get him to recognize when he's doing it and get him to stop."

Again, he nodded in agreement.

I decided to slide in one other idea. "I also think he needs to see a therapist."

Kaleb shook his head. "No therapist."

I blew out a long breath and reached for a slice of bacon. "Let him make that decision. Ask him if he wants to see someone. You have no idea what he's gone through or what he might be hiding. Can you honestly say if something has happened CJ would come and tell you?" I added between chews.

A muscle ticked at his cheek. "CJ! Come down here!"

Oh Lord, no wonder the boy is a bundle of nerves.

He came racing down the stairs like he was falling. "Yes sir?"

Kaleb looked over at me.

I turned around and took his hand. "Um... CJ... I was talking to your dad about your rocking..." I immediately noticed how he tensed up. "I suggested you see a therapist. Someone you can talk to about anything that's bothering you."

He flinched slightly. "Do I have to?" He had this blank look on his face while he rocked side to side. Damn, I was getting dizzy.

"No son. You don't have to." His father gave me this I-told-you-so look.

I rose from my chair put my plate in the sink, then moved over to CJ and draped an arm across his shoulders as I said softly, "There is nothing wrong with seeing someone just to talk to. Hell, I saw a psychologist when I was a child."

"You did?" he asked. "When?"

I nodded. "Yep. When I was fifteen. I was going through some things after my father was killed. Mama was ready to put me in juvie."

His face relaxed somewhat. "What did y'all talk about?"

"Anything I wanted to talk about." I then leaned in close and said, "And anything you say is confidential. Your counselor can't tell your dad anything unless you give permission."

CJ's eyes lit up. "Really?"

I nodded. "Really? That way you can feel comfortable to say whatever is on your mind."

CJ seemed nervous and hesitated for a moment before he looked at this dad then back to me. "Okay, I wanna see a counselor."

Checkmate. There might be hope for this kid after all.

<u>29</u>

NYREE

"Ooh, I like this one!"

I looked over at Janelle, who was standing at the end of the rack holding up a long wedding dress with way too much lace and I frowned, "Uh-uh. That dress will makes me itch."

She blew out a breath and returned it to the rack.

We had been at David's Bridal for over two hours and I still hadn't found the perfect dress. Short, long, I just wasn't sure what I wanted. I was certain Janelle was getting sick of me but I didn't care. I could have settled for a simple white dress I had spotted at Dillard's, but she insisted on buying me a wedding gown as a gift. So in other words, this was my time.

I walked over to another rack of dresses that were strapless and more of my style and rummaged through the selections.

"Does Jeremy know when you'll be leaving for Hawaii?"

I looked away from a possible contender to grin at her. "He's supposed to report the end of October." I just loved rubbing it in her face. For once something good was happening to me. Janelle had the chance to meet Jeremy at lunch last week.

"You know I hate you, right?"

I laughed at that. "Why you say that?"

Jae didn't even try to hide the jealousy. "Because you're getting everything you want."

"Yes I am, aren't I?" I laughed and I'm not going to lie. It felt good. "Ooh! I like this one!" I pulled the gown from the rack so Janelle could see it.

Janelle nodded in agreement. "That one would look good on you."

"Would you like me to start a dressing room?"

I swung around with my hand at my chest. Damn where did she come from?

"Yes, that would be great." I handed over the dress to the perky blonde sales assistant and went back to looking.

"What about this one?" Janelle held up a dress with a plunging neckline.

"I like that too," I said and then my phone started ringing. I didn't even bother to see who it was.

"Is that Jeremy calling you again?" Janelle asked with a rude snort.

I shrugged. "Probably. I'll call him later."

Janelle shook her head. "Damn, that's the fourth call. His ass sure is needy."

"You're one to talk." I gave her a hard look, because she knew I knew better. "He's just excited about the wedding. That's all."

She didn't look convinced but like I said before Janelle can be such a hater. "How's everything going with the whole *kid* situation?" She tossed quotation marks in the air.

"Better. We were supposed to get the three teenagers last week, but they're coming down for the wedding instead. And his oldest, Alexis, is hoping to attend as well," I explained.

Janelle narrowed her brow at me. "What about that little one?"

I shook my head. "Jeremy is still tryna work that one out. He and her mother don't get along too well." I told her about how their relationship had ended when Jeremy discovered she had been screwing one of his good friends on the bowling team.

"Girl, that's too much playing!"

"I know, right." I pulled another dress from the rack and looked at all the beading at the bodice. But as soon as I saw the six hundred dollar price tag, I put it back. Sorry, but I just couldn't justify anyone spending that much money for one day.

"Have you told your job you're moving?"

I shook my head. "Nope. I thought I'd wait until after we're married before I do all that."

She nodded and sucked her teeth. "I don't blame you. Just in case you change your mind. Hopefully you can find a job when you get there."

I looked at Janelle. "I don't know. I'm planning to transfer to the Hawaii Air National Guard and do my one weekend a month, but other than that, I might just enjoy being a wife for a little while."

"I guess," she mumbled although she didn't look the least bit convinced. I should have known she wouldn't understand. One thing Janelle didn't believe in was depending on a man to put food on her table. To me, marriage was totally different. There was nothing wrong with depending on my husband, at least, for a little while.

"Here, try this one on."

I glanced at the dress Janelle was holding in her hands, and my eyes lit up. "Ooh, I like that!"

"I think it's perfect. Go try them all on, but I guarantee this one's gonna look the best." She dismissed me with an impatient fanning of her hand, then moved over to take a seat.

"You need to be finding a purple dress if you're going to be my maid of honor." I stared over at her. As usual Janelle was looking fierce in a pair of skinny jeans, rhinestone stilettos, and a red blouse that hung off her shoulders.

Her phone vibrated, and she reached down inside a cute red hobo purse and mumbled something under her breath when she realized who was calling.

She didn't even bother to look up as she replied, "I got this under control. You just go try on that dress."

I carried the gowns to the dressing room the sales assistant had started for me, and as I peeled off my clothes, I felt myself shaking. I still couldn't believe this day was almost here. I was getting remarried.

I love that man. I can't explain why or how it happened, and I questioned it almost every day. Jeremy had so much baggage, yet somehow he touched something in my soul that I just never felt with any other man before. And for the last week, since we kissed and made up, he has been doing everything in his power to show me just how much he truly loves me.

"You need some help?" I heard the sales assistant. She was standing on the other side of the door.

Hell no. I didn't want her to see me in my Spanx. "No, I think I got it." I wiggled the dress Janelle picked out over my hips and gasped at my reflection in the mirror. Janelle was right. It was perfect. I turned the knob and stepped out of the dressing room.

"Oh, you look sooo beautiful!"

My eyes widened. "Mama! You made it." I hurried over and hugged her round body.

She wrapped me in her arms, then drew back and gave me a gappy-tooth smile. "I wouldna missed this for the world." There were tears in her hazel eyes as she shook her head and said, "Your father will be so proud."

"I told you I had good taste," Janelle said with her leg swinging, and that big I-told-you-so grin on her face. "My work here is done."

I spun around and gazed in the mirror that was the length of the entire platform and just stared in awe. I was wearing a strapless mid length gown with beautiful beading at the bodice and a satin waist that flattered my curves. Looking at my reflection in the small dressing room was one thing but seeing myself from several different angles, I couldn't believe how beautiful I looked.

"Ree... it's a beautiful gown but I thought we were planning a small wedding?"

I looked at my mother's worried expression through the mirror. "Mama, it's gonna be small, but I still want to look fabulous."

"Mrs. Dawson, I don't have any problem helping you plan a bigger wedding." Janelle offered.

I shook my head at her. "Uh-uh, I told you we don't want anything big. That's just a waste of money."

My mother waved her hand dismissively. "You let me worry about how I spend my money. It isn't often when my daughter gets married."

"Mom, I've been married before."

She gave a rude snort. "Oh please! You went to the courthouse. I knew it was doomed from the beginning."

I saw Janelle was trying not to laugh. Neither one of them had cared much for Shane.

"Mrs. Dawson, what do you think of Jeremy?" she asked.

I rolled my eyes and noticed Janelle was trying not to laugh again. She was such a shit starter.

Mommy had a dreamy smile on her face. "He seems like a really nice guy. Mannerable, so sweet, and God-fearing. I think Ree's really done good this time."

I stuck my tongue out at Janelle. It meant a lot that my mother approved of the man I was getting ready to spend the rest of my life with.

"I agree. Jeremy does seem nice..." Janelle began slowly. "But I just feel like he's hiding something." I wanted to smack the black off her, but I forced a smile instead.

"No, you're just too nosy. He doesn't have to tell you all his business." I said struggling to keep the sarcasm from my voice.

"I didn't say he did but even when I asked him simple stuff he didn't want to tell the truth. What's up with that?"

My mom's brow rose with curiosity.

"Mama, that's because he was tired of Janelle giving him the third degree." Leave it to Janelle to try and stir up some trouble. "All that matters is that I know he's the man for me. What he shares or doesn't want to share with others doesn't matter just as long as I know the truth."

Crossing her arms, Janelle leaned forward and said, "And? Do you know the truth?"

The sales assistant came over, saving me from having to answer. "This dress was made for your body! You barely need *any* alterations." She knew exactly what to say to guarantee a sale.

I nodded in agreement. "I don't need to try on the other

gowns. I want this one."

She clapped her hands gleefully. "Wonderful! Let me go and get some pins for the hem." While she scurried off, I looked in the mirror again and could already see myself walking down the aisle in this gown. I was going to be the talk of the town for sure.

Mama moved over and took a seat beside Janelle.

"Mrs. Dawson I hear you're finally going to have plenty of grandchildren to spoil."

My heart nearly stopped. Oh no she didn't.

Mama had a proud smile on her lips. "Yes, I'm looking forward to meeting his three. They'll be down for a week, right Ree?"

Janelle's brow rose. "Three chil—?"

"Yes, Mama. They'll be down for a whole week." I said cutting Janelle off and then gave her the stink eye. I hadn't had a chance to tell my mother there were five kids, instead of three. And I was planning on doing that on my terms not Janelle's.

"I'm looking forward to it." Mama then pursed her lips. "I'll have one foot in the grave by the time Nyree has a baby."

Janelle snickered and went back to texting on her phone, while I ignored the comment and focused on how good I looked in the dress.

"And what about you Jae?" I heard Mama say. "I hear congratulations are in order for your engagement. When are you planning on making it official?"

"Yeah Jae, when's your big day?" I instigated.

Janelle blew out a long breath. "That's a good question, Mrs. Dawson. I'm in no rush. I figure we'll focus on Ree's wedding first. I definitely don't want to steal the spotlight from her," she added with a saucy grin.

The sales assistant signaled for me to follow her in back. "Whateva," I mumbled under my breath and stepped off the platform.

"You know you love me!" Janelle yelled after me.

Yep, and that's the only reason why I tolerated her crazy ass.

30

JANELLE

I could tell as soon as I padded into the kitchen for breakfast that something was on Kaleb's mind. In the months we'd been together I'd started to read him like a book. "What's wrong, baby?" I asked.

He looked over at me, then shrugged and said. "Nothing."

"Yeah, it's *something*. You've been quiet all morning. Something is bothering you." I took a moment to see if I had remembered to wipe down the bathroom after getting out of the shower, or if I had left my clothes on the floor. I was certain that I had done neither. Kaleb might have been tripping because he had caught me texting or surfing the web this morning. Either of those things was subject to tick him off.

"Nothing. Just got a lot on my plate today."

"Anything you want to talk about?" I asked between chews because I was taught that a good woman is always there to listen to her man even if she didn't fucking feel like it.

He sighed then shook his head as if he was annoyed. By this point I rolled my eyes and mumbled, "Whateva," under my breath. I wasn't about to beg this man to tell me what was bothering him. I tell you. Sometimes he acted like a woman on her damn period.

After another long moment of silence, I decided to try a different approach. "What time's your first game tonight?"

Kaleb looked surprised by my question. I don't know why. Unlike him I listen to what he tells me. A few weeks ago, he had joined a softball team with some of his colleagues. I put the first game on my calendar and received an alert this morning.

"Uh... it's tonight at six or seven."

And when were you planning to tell me? I was more than a little annoyed. "Oh, okay. What position are you playing?"

I noticed he was glancing down at his plate as he spoke. "Second base. You know I wasn't planning on playing but since they're short one player, I guess I will."

Yeah, I just bet.

CJ came racing down the wooden stairs as if he was falling and once again it took everything I had not to scream at him. Why can't he walk like normal people?

Kaleb looked at him over the rim of his coffee cup and said, "Son, you ready for camp?"

"Yes, sir." He walked over, wrapped his arms around his shoulders and kissed his cheek. "Love you," he said then walked around the table and leaned in so I could kiss him.

"Love you," I said and gave him a loud smack on the cheek. He really was a good kid.

I watched him grab his backpack and head out the door to catch the bus that stopped at the corner, to summer camp.

Camp had been my idea. I had gotten sick of watching that kid spending the summer doing nothing but playing video games so I had signed him up for three weeks of camp. Something was better than wasting his whole summer doing nothing constructive. As promised, I tried to get him in a summer minority program but those programs started receiving applicants way back in January, so I insisted on summer camp instead. CJ was resistant at first but once I had gotten his father in agreement it was a wrap.

I carried my dishes over to the sink and went upstairs to get ready for work. I was slipping into my new Vera Wang dress when Kaleb stepped into the room. He gave me a look then moved over to his dresser.

"What?" I said with attitude.

"Nothing."

"Then why did you just look at me that way?" I said

without skipping a beat.

He frowned as if I was the one who was being ridiculous. "What you talking about? I didn't look at you any kinda way."

I was starting to get frustrated. "Whatever. You're fucking retarded." Ain't no way in the world I'm gonna let this dude start making me think I'm crazy. I zipped my dress then slipped into my green pumps. The sooner I got up outta his house the better. I didn't have to put up with this shit. I had a restaurant to run and a million things to do.

I guess Kaleb sensed I was pissed because he walked over to me and took my hand.

"Babe, c'mere." He had that sexy grin on his face I loved so much. "Babe... Look, I'm sorry if I'm taking my frustrations out on you. I don't mean to," he added, with so much sincerity I suddenly felt guilty for planning an evening that didn't include him.

"It's okay," I said, then I tilted my head as his mouth met mine. Just the feel of his warm mouth made my nipples tingle for a quick romp in the sack.

"I just wanna marry you and share our lives," he said with a pout.

So that's what this was all about. Last night after we'd made love, Kaleb had suggested we run off to Las Vegas next weekend and get married. I didn't mean to laugh at him but I did, which obviously had pissed him off. Then we argued for the next hour, as to why I wasn't in a rush to get married.

I needed to see how I could benefit from this relationship before I decided to get married. After he received his inheritance, if I stilled loved him as much as I did now, then we could set a date. But even then, I needed at least a year to plan the event of the city. Of course, I didn't tell him that. Instead, I made up an excuse, and told him even though I loved him, I was scared and needed more time before we set a date. Kaleb said he understood.

Now I knew he had been lying.

"Boo, I want nothing more than to marry you when the time is right." I suggestively stroked his crotch, then gave him a long, deep kiss until I had him moaning and unbuckling his pants. I smiled triumphantly. One thing I knew how to do was turn him on, and I made sure Kaleb left the house completely satisfied.

By the time I finally made it to the restaurant, April was waiting in my office for me. "You're late," she said and swiveled away from the financial report she was working on.

"Yeah, yeah. It was one of those mornings," I replied with a playful eye-roll. "Men."

She grinned knowingly. She'd been happily married for twelve years. "Well, I've got some news that will cheer you up."

"What?"

April came around the desk and held up the morning paper. "You won!"

It took a moment for her words to register. "I won? Oh shit!" I snatched the paper and read the announcement and sure enough FoxTrot had been voted as Columbia's *Restaurant of the Year*. I started squealing with delight. "I won!" April draped an arm around me.

"Congratulations Jae!"

"*Ohmygod, ohmygod!*" I had tears running down my face. All those years I had poured into making my dream a reality had finally paid off. "I should be thanking you, April. You've had my back since the beginning." It's rare to have family who believed in your dream, but my cousin gave up her job as a shift supervisor at Hardee's to come and help me run FoxTrot and I've never regretted my decision.

"I've spoken to the mayor's office and he's schedule to be here on Friday at ten to personally present you with the award. I've already confirmed Channel 8 News and the *Columbia Daily Tribune*. Everyone is coming!" she exclaimed.

I was so overwhelmed with emotion I had to take a seat before I collapsed to the floor. "*Ohmygod!* I can't believe this!"

"Well believe it," April replied, her chocolate eyes were cloudy with tears. "You sit there and enjoy your moment. I've got a restaurant to run."

I grinned. "Thanks April."

"Anytime, girl." She squeezed my shoulder and exited my

office.

As soon as she left, I reached for my phone and called Kaleb. He answered on the first ring.

"Whassup?"

"Hey baby, guess what?" I said trying to contain my excitement.

"What?" he replied and I ignored how flat his voice sounded.

"I won! I won *Restaurant of the Year!*"

"Oh really? Congratulations," he replied yet his tone said something altogether different.

"What's wrong with you?" I was so disappointed by his response.

"Nothing, why?"

"Because I just shared with you the most exciting news of my life and you act like you don't care."

"I *said*, congratulations," he said and sounded just as flat and unenthusiastic as before.

"Yeah, but you don't sound excited."

Kaleb sighed loudly. "Listen... I've got a lot going on right now with my investors so I'm sorry if I sound distracted, but it can't always be about you Janelle," he hissed.

I closed my eyes, counted to ten then blew out a long breath. "What's going on at work?"

"White folks ain't never happy, no matter what I do and how I do it. I'm getting sick of their shit!" He rattled on and on, and I just pressed a finger to my temple and prayed for strength. He bitched and complained so much, I was starting to wonder if this man knew what being happy was. It was always everyone else's fault. He was always the victim. Oh my God! Enough is enough.

"Then quit."

"What?" he sputtered.

"You heard me. If you're that miserable, if everyone is always fucking with you then quit." I have never known a man who didn't know how to be happy. Misery loves company and I wasn't jumping onboard.

"Wow really?" His tone was laced with sarcasm. "I

thought you had my back?"

"I do, which is why you need to quit. You're miserable, yet you have the biggest portfolios and the largest number of clients. So start your own firm and take them with you. Whatever it takes to make you happy, then do it." I was just sick of listening to it.

The silence after my comment stretched so long I guess he realized he had struck a nerve because he said, "Jae, I'm sorry for complaining. You're right. I need to make some decisions. In the meantime my baby has been awarded *Restaurant of the Year*. I'm so proud of you." Now *that's* the tone I wanted to hear from my man.

"Thanks, sweetheart. It means so much coming from you. The mayor will be here on Friday to present my award."

"Then I'll be right there with you. We definitely need to celebrate this weekend. You still gonna come watch me play this evening?" he asked.

I looked at my calendar. "I have a meeting with a distributor at five so I'll try to get there after he leaves."

"That's fair enough. See you later babe. And hey?"

I released a tiny sigh. "Yeah?"

"I love you."

I grinned and purred, "I love you too."

* * *

I didn't make it home until close to nine. I was gossiping on the phone with Nyree about her wedding plans, when I spotted Kaleb. I already knew there was a problem.

"Ree, I better let you go. Kaleb is sitting on the porch staring me down my throat."

"Good luck with that shit."

"Right," I groaned, then quickly ended the call but not before Kaleb straightened up on the chair, looking over at me.

I pulled into the garage, climbed out, then reached for my briefcase from the back seat. I don't know what was up, so I was definitely tryna stall for time so I could prepare myself mentally for what was about to go down. I took so long, Kaleb came around the house to see what I was doing.

"You need some help?" he asked.

I answered with caution. "No, I got it." I walked over, smiling, and kissed him hard on the lips.

"You didn't have to get off the phone."

Here we go again. "I was just talking to Nyree."

He made some rude noise and I could tell he didn't believe me but I was too tired to care what he thought.

"Let's sit outside awhile," he suggested, and pulled me to him and gave me a big hug.

"Okay, let me take my bag inside and I'll be right down." I was trying to simmer whatever was stirring inside his head.

I went up to the master bedroom and gasped at what I saw sitting on the nightstand. A beautiful pink bouquet of roses, a congratulations balloon, and a card. As I read the loving words, I couldn't stop smiling. My man was really something else.

I put my bag away, slipped out of my heels then hurried back outside to join Kaleb on the porch where he was sitting and drinking a beer. "Baby, thank you so much!" I said and wrapped my arms around his neck and kissed him deeply. "That was so thoughtful."

He grinned. "What are you talking about?"

I laughed. "You know what I'm talking about. Thanks. I love you." I kissed him again and moved over to the other rocking chair.

"You're welcome babe. I *really* am proud of you."

Honey was still sniffing around the yard. I settled back and enjoyed the peace and quiet. The breeze was perfect for August. I was grinning when I caught Kaleb out the corner of my eye. The weird look in his eyes spelled trouble. Mr. Hyde had returned.

"Baby, look at me. What's wrong?" I took his hand in mine.

Something strange passed across his face, for a brief moment and then he shrugged. "Nothing's wrong."

I tried to sound casual although my frustrations were brimming at the surface. "Then why have you been so quiet and distant? You've been like that ever since you got up this morning."

I could tell he was struggling to keep his temper in check. Good because he wasn't the only one.

He drained the last of his beer and then his face grew serious again. "I'm not distant. It's just been a long week."

"What's going on at work?" I asked.

"Nothing," he retorted in a tone that said he didn't want to discuss it.

"Whatever." I wasn't going to let him spoil my mood. I watched Honey play in the yard and decided to change the subject. "What did y'all have for dinner?"

"We just made some sandwiches."

If he wanted me to feel sorry for them, that wasn't happening.

"What did *you* eat?"

My eyes shifted away from his. I didn't dare tell Kaleb me and Nyree went and had Thai food and celebrated. I would never have heard the end of it. "I had a salad at the restaurant. Sorry I couldn't make your game. How'd you do?"

"We lost." Kaleb sounded sad, then started staring off in space again, so I just heaved a huge sigh. He never was very talkative, but this was ridiculous. When Honey decided to run after a stray cat, I used it as an excuse to get away from his sour attitude.

"I better go get him." As soon as I was around the corner I rolled my eyes. I don't know why I had bothered rushing home tonight. Knowing him he was either mad because I didn't come to his game or that he came home and dinner wasn't ready. The dude was just too damn immature. The problem was he's rich and I loved him, and for selfish reasons I was willing to deal with just about anything. But even then, I had my limits. And Kaleb was taking me there quick, fast and in a hurry.

By the time I found Honey and brought him back to the house, Kaleb had already gone in the house. I just heaved another long sigh and went inside. CJ was sitting in the living room on my new white couch, watching television.

"Hey Ms. Jae," he said without looking away from the television.

"Hey CJ," I said. "How was summer camp?"

"Good." There was that annoying voice again.

As I started up the stairs, I spotted the bag of potato chips he was trying to hide.

"CJ, I thought I told you no greasy potato chips on my sofa." *That kid doesn't listen to shit.* The last time I caught him he had left crumbs and grease stains.

"Sorry," he said with a hint of sadness then he rose and carried the bag into the kitchen.

I was sick of telling Kaleb his son needed consistent reinforcement so I just shook my head and went on upstairs.

When I moved into the room Kaleb was lying across the bed, texting on his phone. I was so tempted to ask him who the fuck he was texting since he was always asking me, but instead I didn't say anything and took a seat beside him. "What's the score?" I asked trying to make small talk and take my mind off of our problems.

"Three to five Cubs." He didn't even bother to look up from the phone.

I went and changed into a pair of knit shorts and a t-shirt. He finally put his phone away and leaned back against the pillow.

I enjoyed baseball and was yelling at the screen every time the batter missed a pitch while Kaleb was back to not having shit to say. I slid over and rested my head on his chest then tilted my chin for a kiss. He smiled and kissed me then his phone started beeping indicating he had a text message.

I lifted my head. "You need to get that?"

He rolled over and reached down for his phone, then started texting again. Okay, this was getting ridiculous.

"What's up with all the texting?" I said trying to keep a smile on my face.

"You gotta lot of nerve. It's one of my clients," he hissed. His attention was focused on the cellphone screen.

Two can play that game.

I rolled over to my side of the bed and reached across the

bed for my phone in the side pocket of my purse and noticed I had a text from my brother. I gladly sat there, smiled and texted him back. The whole time Kaleb glared at me. I had to resist the urge to laugh. "My texts are to my family. You can't say the same."

His phone beeped again. As he reached for it, I guess he noticed me roll my eyes because he had the nerve to laugh and say, "I know you're not tripping the way you stay on your phone."

I cussed his ass under my breath and decided to surf the net for a few moments and noticed an email from Frankie.

> **Hey Jae, here's the directions to that Old School spot I was talking about. If you're man ain't acting right let me know and I'll take you. LOL.**

Last week Frankie and I met for breakfast and he had mentioned a new lounge that had opened in Jefferson City. Since there weren't too many places for black folks to go and have a good time, this was big news.

Something in my face must have caught Kaleb's attention because he was practically leaning across the bed all in my face.

"What? Your man sent you a message?"

I sighed, growing tired of this whole thing and put my phone back on the nightstand then started enjoying the second half of the game. After a while I noticed that he was getting into the game as well. We're both Cubs fans. But then his phone started beeping and again he was reading more of his so-called work related text messages. By then I was too through with his attitude. When the game ended, I climbed under the covers.

"Babe?"

"Yeah?" I said and I faked a yawn, so he would know I didn't feel like talking.

"What time do I need to be at the restaurant on Friday?"

I hesitated before answering, "What does it matter? I'm getting the award not you."

He actually laughed at me, which pissed me off. "Oh yeah,

I forgot. Friday is *all* about you."

I have never known a grown-ass man to be jealous about anything that didn't deal with him. Friday was a big day for me and I could already see he was going to try and ruin it for me.

I sat up on the bed and turned to him. "Do me a favor and don't come to my ceremony."

"*Are you fucking serious?*"

"Dead serious." I didn't even want to see his pathetic face. "I don't want you there stealing my shine."

"Stealing your shine?" he mocked and then he had the nerve to laugh. "You act like it's a big deal."

"To me it is a big deal and the fact you don't see that shows just how selfish you really are. I am sick of your negative attitude! And I'm tired of you always trying to control this relationship."

"You're not gonna be talking to me any kinda way!" he snarled.

I smirked. "See, that's what the damn problem is. You're so used to those minimum wage hoes that let you run them. But you can't run me! I worked too hard to get where I am to let someone like you bring me down." I gestured over to his phone. "So all them hoes who keep texting you that you're pretending is *work related*, keep on doing you because I'm definitely gonna do me."

Next thing I know Kaleb snapped. "Get your shit, and get out my house!"

"What?" I know he wasn't about to make me leave in the middle of the night.

"You heard me. Give me my ring then get your shit and go!"

I heard CJ's bedroom door open so I know he had to be listening. Thank goodness because he saved me from sticking my foot in his father's ass.

"Really?" I slipped off the ring and tossed it on the bed. "Fine," I said and started laughing.

"Good riddance," Kaleb barked then picked up his phone and started texting again.

I couldn't believe he had dismissed me like that. Of course, I had to have the last word.

"You can't fuck, so you did me the favor!" You should have seen his face. "Lying on your back like a bitch... with that stupid-ass smirk on your face. That ho can have your tired ass!"

Kaleb stood there looking stupid before he stormed downstairs. Probably went to look at his dick in the mirror.

I changed clothes then grabbed the small suitcase I had tucked away in the closet and quickly filled it with a few things. "I'll be back for the rest of my stuff," I said as I went downstairs. Kaleb was sitting on the couch, with his head in his hands. He rose and walked over towards me.

"Babe... wait...," he said but I brushed past him and kept on walking.

"C'mon Honey." I stormed out to my car. I couldn't believe he had treated me that way! But as I climbed into my vehicle, I couldn't resist a smirk.

I may have been stupid to have moved in with him, but at least I had sense enough to make that mothafucka put the title to the BMW in my name.

31

NYREE

I was just finished evaluating the first job vacancy when my office phone rang.

"Master Sergeant Dawson speaking."

"Whassup sexy."

I smiled as I twirled around in my chair. Man, Timmy always managed to sound so sexy on the phone. If he took it down just a notch he could have given Barry White a run for his money. "Hey you. How's the new job going?" I asked.

"I'm still tryna settle in this little country ass town."

"Where you living... Knob Noster?" I teased.

"Hell no. I found me a nice spot in Sedalia."

I gave a rude snort. "You know my father's from there. That's not saying much."

"No, I guess it ain't." He laughed. It was a deep robust sound that made me feel so relaxed and at ease. "So how have you been?"

I twirled the phone cord around my finger as I replied, "I've been good. Can't complain."

"Dude still treating you right?" It was obvious, Timmy was digging.

"Of course. You know I won't settle for any less."

"That's whassup." His voice trailed off and I could tell he wanted to say more but then decided against it. I was almost tempted to ask what was on his mind but decided I better keep it professional.

"So what can I do for you today?"

"Well... I hear you're doing some onsite training sessions on the new hiring process." He must of read my mind about keeping it professional, although I felt slightly disappointed.

"Yes, I have a few site visits scheduled over the next few weeks. I'm probably making a lotta work for myself but I decided it was easier to train right on each supervisor's system than trying to get all of you in one room."

"Can a brotha get some of that one-on-one training?"

There goes the sexual innuendos again. "Absolutely. I can schedule to come out to Knob Noster before my honeymoon."

There was a slight hesitation. "Honeymoon?" he said incredulously. "Damn! You about to tie the knot already?" Maybe I was feeling myself but I was sure I heard disappointment in his tone.

"Yep, we're taking the plunge." I suddenly felt the need to explain the rush and told him about Jeremy being offered a transfer to Hawaii.

"No joke? Hawaii? You're gonna love it there."

"I sure hope so," I replied and then there was another pregnant pause that I wish I could jump in Timmy's head and know what he was thinking.

"Yo, I really am happy for you," he finally said.

"Thanks, that means a lot coming from you."

After we ended the call, I sat back and I couldn't help thinking what if things had been different. With Timmy moving closer we would have had a chance to build on our relationship and there is no telling where it could have gone. But there was no point in thinking about what coulda-woulda-shoulda when I had an amazing fiancé.

At twelve I stepped outside the building just as Jeremy pulled up into the circle drive and climbed in his vehicle.

"Hey baby!" I sounded way too happy even to my own ears.

"Hi Angel." He leaned over and pressed a kiss to my cheek. "What are you so happy about?" His eyes were sparkling with interest.

"Everything." I was grinning like crazy as we pulled away

from headquarters.

"Care to share?" There was that worried look in Jeremy's eyes. I'll be so glad when he learns to lighten up.

"The wedding... moving to Hawaii, just everything. I just can't wait to start this new life with you." I was talking excitedly with my hands.

He brought one to his lips and kissed it. "Neither can I."

As Jeremy pulled onto the highway, I leaned back on the seat with the air conditioning cooling my skin. It was the middle of August and well over ninety degrees. I slid over on the seat and rested my head on his shoulder, which wasn't easy to do while driving in a Tahoe, but I do it all the time anyway. I can't help it. I loved being under my man.

"Where you wanna eat?"

I shrugged. "I don't care. Sonic's is cool."

Ever since our engagement had become official, Jeremy and I had been riding to work today. We figured since we both had to make the thirty minute commute to Jefferson City every morning why not make it together and save on gas. Saving money had always been a really big thing of mine. I expressed to Jeremy as soon as we were married we needed to open a joint saving's account. I was no fool. I think all women needed to have their own account to save for a rainy day, but a couple also needed to pay bills in a joint account.

"Angel we need to get the rest of your stuff moved into my place before my kids get here," Jeremy reminded me as he climbed off the highway.

"I know. I promise to finish packing my things this weekend."

"I'm going to hold you to it," he teased and gave me a corny smile.

We pulled into Sonic's drive-thru and I ordered a double burger and fries and he did the same. While we waited, I tilted my head and stared into his eyes. Have I mentioned how much I loved this man?

"I've been online looking at places to live in Hawaii. I even asked one of the guys in my unit about it. He was stationed there for a while."

For a moment we were both quiet.

"Let me ask you a question," Jeremy began then hesitated before saying, "Is that the only reason why you're marrying me is because we're going to Hawaii?"

I swung around on the seat and met his gaze head-on. He was dead serious. "What? Why you say that?"

"Because," he swallowed dryly. "That's all you talk about."

I shook my head. "That's because I'm getting ready to uproot my entire life to go there." What was wrong with him?

He dropped his head and stared down at his hands then back at me. "I'm sorry Angel I just feel that's the only reason why you're with me." Our eyes locked. "You hardly talk about the wedding, but Hawaii is always the first thing outta your mouth."

"That's because I am excited about the two of us starting a new life, but that's not the reason why I agreed to marry you. We could be going to Alaska somewhere and I would still marry you."

His brow rose and he looked surprised. "Would you really?"

"Yes, I would." I was getting a little testy. I couldn't believe he was questioning my reason for marrying him.

Jeremy breathed a sigh of relief, "That's good to know."

I was starting to wonder if there was more going on than he was saying. "Why, is there something you need to tell me?"

"No, why do you ask?" he said as our server arrived on roller skates with our order.

"I'm just asking," I mumbled and suddenly had a bad feeling.

<u>32</u>

JANELLE

I shook hands with Mayor Castle, turned toward the camera, and smiled while the photographer for the *Columbia Daily Tribune* took another round of photographs. As soon as he was done, the mayor turned to me and gave me another firm handshake.

"Congratulations, Ms. Fox."

"Thank you, sir."

As he stepped away, I glanced around my restaurant grinning my ass off. This was such a proud moment for me.

"Janelle, girl, I'm so proud of you!" Nyree sauntered her uniform-clad body in my direction and wrapped her arms around me.

"Thanks, girl," I began and then my eyes widened in amazement. "I can't believe how many people turned out for this event!" Everybody who was anybody was there sampling food and admiring my restaurant. My hostess wasted no time letting me know she had made so many dinner reservations, we were booked every weekend for the next three months. This was any restaurant owner's dream.

"Well it's happening and you deserve it." That's what I loved about Nyree. You would have thought it was her restaurant the way she was beaming. "Look, I gotta get to work, but I'll call you tonight." I nodded and blew her an air kiss as she walked out the building.

After she was gone, I walked around, shaking hands with patrons congratulating me on their way toward the door. I felt like I was on a cloud.

"Look at little Jae doing her thang!"

Grinning, I turned around as Frankie swept me into his arms and spun me around. "Put me down!" I was laughing and screaming at the same time.

Chuckling, he finally lowered me to my feet. "I'm so proud of you."

I had tears in my eyes as I took in how good he looked in Dockers and a yellow button down shirt. I know he couldn't wait to get back home to his wife-beater and jeans. I was just thankful he was willing to upgrade his wardrobe a few hours for little old me.

"Thanks for coming, Frankie." His support truly meant a lot. Especially since it was a shame my man couldn't share the same feelings for me. But just as I had instructed he hadn't even bothered to come although part of me had hoped Kaleb would have showed up anyway.

"Jae, how 'bout we go out tonight? We've gotta lot to celebrate."

My brow arched. "What are we celebrating?"

Frankie was standing in front of me showing off a pretty white smile. "You winning the award... and me getting my carwash."

"You got the carwash? I'm so happy for you!" I squealed.

His chest was stuck out with pride. "Yeah, it looks like I'll be able to finally get off the road." Since his return home, Frankie had been, doing deliveries for a local distributor that had him driving all across the state.

"We definitely need to celebrate. Where you wanna go tonight?"

He shrugged. "I don't know. How about some pool?"

I grinned. "I haven't played pool in a long time."

"No time like the present," he said with a wink.

* * *

When the lights came on, I wanted to scream. There was no way it was closing time even though I noticed several couples moving toward the door. Damn, and I was having a bomb ass time.

I tightened my arms around Frankie and continued to slow dance to Jodeci's "Forever my Lady." Jodeci did things to my body that I couldn't begin to imagine. In fact for the last two hours, I had been bumping and grinding, and creaming in my thong. Hell, if I had known it was going to be this kinda night, I would have worn a panty liner.

Even though we were the last two on the dance floor, I figured as long as the DJ was playing, I was dancing. I tightened my hold on Frankie, squeezing him across the back and savored the way it felt being held in his arms.

We had started the evening out shooting pool at this hole in the wall he found in Jefferson City near Lincoln University. They had pool tables in the far corner. A bar and a wooden dance floor. We spent hours shooting one round of pool after another while sipping Coronas. I think it was somewhere between bottles four and five that I realized the lights had dimmed and folks were gyrating all over the place. I looked over at Frankie and the moment we made eyes contact, he was putting our sticks away and leading me out onto the dance floor. And we had been there ever since.

"I think it's time for us to go," he whispered then pressed his lips against my forehead. Goodness them bad boys were warm, wet and once again had me wondering what they would feel like buried between my thighs.

"Okay," I said and I was sure he heard the disappointment before he drew back and stared down at me.

"You ready to go?" Frankie asked.

There was no way I was putting my feelings out there before I knew where this conversation was headed. "I guess," I said, nibbling my bottom lip.

"Quit lying. You're not ready to leave any more than I am." Frankie took my hand and led me off the dance floor. Neither of us spoke until we were outside and walking over to his Sequoia.

"What else is there to do at this time of night?" I asked. Well, I could think of a couple of things, but I wasn't about to go there.

"How about we go back to my place for waffles?" he suggested. "At least I'm close by." He had rented a two bedroom apartment in Jefferson City saying he was glad to be back, but didn't want to be in Columbia. Otherwise his mom, Ms. Lorraine would be dropping by every day. It was a good thing he didn't live in the area. I didn't have to worry about us running into Kaleb.

I laughed. "Waffles? You cook?"

"Anyone can cook using Aunt Jemima's Pancake Mix. All you do is add water."

I stuck a well-manicured finger into the air. "Don't say *anybody*? I met many who can't even boil an egg."

"Boiling an egg is hard work."

I looked over at him and grinned. "Okay, maybe I should have said water."

"Good answer." He playfully bumped my shoulder. "So how about it? I even have a floor we can dance on the rest of the night if you want."

I laughed and it truly felt good. Frankie always did have a sense of humor. "Sounds good."

He pulled away and headed to his apartment. I was impressed. It was located right near downtown but far enough away from the college crowd. I admired his simple decorations and unique pieces of art.

Frankie was reaching inside the refrigerator when he glanced over at me and said, "I got that while I was in Germany."

"Very nice." I put the unique paper weight back down on the shelf and padded into the kitchen with bare feet. As soon as we had arrived at his apartment, those puppies came off my feet. "I would love to live overseas," I said with a sigh, "but with the restaurant I don't know if that dream is ever gonna happen."

Shaking his head, he put a carton of eggs on the counter. "Quit doubting yourself. It will happen. Just like your dream of opening a restaurant. What you need to do is start taking time off for yourself. Your family is capable enough of running that place while you're gone."

I lowered onto a stool in front of a small island. "Yeah, you're right. I do need to start taking more time out for myself."

"Yo…, I'm just flattered you took time to hang out with little ole me." While grinning, he held his hands up in surrender.

I gave an exaggerated eye roll. "Whatever. I should be the one who feels special to be hanging out with such a gorgeous man."

His eyes narrowed as he smirked. "So you think I'm gorgeous?"

Damn, I put my foot in my mouth on that one. "You're a'ight," I murmured and yawned. Frankie took another look at me and we laughed.

While we waited for the waffle iron to heat, I scrambled six eggs and found a pack of breakfast sausages in the refrigerator. Frankie wasn't lying, he did have some skills. I watched as he mixed up the batter and added melted butter, then water and mixed it up.

"Now close your eyes," he said.

"Why is that?" I asked although I lowered my lids.

"Because I don't want you to see my secret recipe."

I laughed but kept my eyes closed as he reached into the cabinet for his secret ingredient, and added it to the batter before I could open my eyes again.

I moved back to the barstool, and took a seat. "I remember Mommy telling me you were engaged to this model. Why didn't you marry her?"

Frankie poured batter onto the griddle before speaking. "Excuse my French but Heaven was a ho. I'm serious. Anything that had three legs she was humping it." I giggled and he paused to laugh. "I'm serious. It wasn't even about money. It was about how many men she could screw in a year." He grinned. "But then I met Lynn while I was stationed in California and she threw me for a loop."

"You really loved her?"

"Yeah, my wife was my rock." He nodded and looked lost

in the memories before his smile returned again. Damn, I would give anything for a man to look like that while talking about me.

"So what's up this week with you and dude?"

I shrugged because to be honest even I didn't know for sure. "I don't know. I needed a break from him. I'm just not sure we're ready to get married."

"That's too bad." Yeah right. The smirk on his lips said he wasn't the least bit disappointed.

I blew out an exaggerated sigh and explained how Kaleb had flipped out. "I'm starting to think that everybody isn't meant to be married and maybe I'm one of those people."

The frown on Frankie's face said he didn't agree. "Maybe the problem is you keep picking the wrong men for the wrong reasons."

No he wasn't trying to analyze me. "Really? And what's your problem? You've been home for months. Why hasn't somebody snatched you up?"

He shrugged. "I don't want just anybody."

His words warmed my heart. "I guess I'm not the only one who's picky." We shared a smile.

While I scrambled eggs, I watched him remove one golden waffle after another. That man sure knew his way around his little kitchen.

Frankie had a folding table and chairs set up in the breakfast nook. I carried in the orange juice and the plate of bacon while he grabbed the eggs and waffles. I found a bottle of syrup in the pantry. Smiling we both took a seat, said grace, and dug in.

"Mmmm, now you have to admit this taste better than Waffle House," he managed between chews.

"*Ewww*! Anything is better than that dirty place."

He shook his head. "C'mon that used to be the joint after the club."

"Yeah when I was young and didn't know any better."

"And now you're a beast in the kitchen. I ain't mad at ya."

I smirked. "Thanks."

My cellphone vibrated but I didn't even bother to answer

it. I had the ringer off but chances were it was Kaleb calling to apologize like he always does after he flips out on me. My voice mail would be full by morning.

"You need to get that?" Frankie asked curiously.

I shook my head. "Nope. That part of my life is on hold."

After we cleaned up the kitchen we moved into the living room and he showed me his extensive music collection.

"Oh shit! You got Kurtis Blow?" I jumped up and pretended I was holding a mike. "Clap your hands, everybody... if you got what it takes... 'cause I'm Kurtis Blow and I want you to know... that these are the breaks," Frankie jumped up and joined in. We got maybe halfway through the song before we forgot the rest of the lyrics and started fumbling over our words like a couple of stuttering idiots.

I took another seat on the floor and started thumbing through his collection again and found Stacy Lattisaw. I had him put her album in and we started slow dancing again, and before I knew it he was staring down at me.

"If you don't want me to kiss you then you better say something," he whispered.

"Something," I teased and next thing I know I was tilting my chin and his lips were all over mine. His kiss was skillful, warm and wet and I was enjoying every second of it. His arms tightened around me and I didn't object when his tongue slipped inside. Frankie's strokes were steady and confident like we had all the time in the world. I guess we did because I didn't need to be anywhere until lunch tomorrow.

I felt my juices flowing and I knew I wanted Frankie to fuck me. I guess he wanted the same because his hand was under my dress and when he stroked my crotch, I moaned. My pussy dripped and ran down my inner thigh. Trust me, in the next few seconds I planned on having his dick inside me.

Frankie lowered his zipper, pushed my knees apart then slipped the head of his penis underneath my thong and across my wet slit.

"Please," I whimpered.

"Ask me to fuck you, Jae."

"Please fuck me, Frankie," I whispered. And before I could

catch a breath, he drove deeply inside of me. "Oooh!" I panted as he stretched me to accommodate every inch of him. Oh my, he was huge!

"Hell yeah," Frankie crooned then lifted me up at just the right angle for his thrust. "Jae, look at me."

Our eyes locked. Oh my God! This was so unreal.

"You like me fucking you?" he asked, pushing himself even deeper inside of me.

"Yes," I panted with broken breaths as he pumped faster. "Ooooh, yesss!"

He felt so good I knew it wouldn't last. I didn't want it to end so soon. I wanted to take our time, but I was too hot and wet, and Frankie felt too good to hold on for long.

"Fuck! I knew this pussy was good," he moaned.

"Aaaah, yeaaaah!" I cried. "Oooooh!"

I wrapped my legs around his waist and rested my hands at his shoulders as he drove into me hard again and again, slamming me against the wall. I screamed and with a curse, I exploded. His fingers bit into my ass and my back arched like a bow as we came together.

Frankie collapsed onto the floor with me on top of him. "You okay?" His voice was a soft caress.

"Yeah, I'm good." I nodded feeling better than I'd felt in months.

33

NYREE

"You okay?" I whispered.

Jeremy looked my way and even though he nodded his head, I could tell he was trying to hold it together.

We were in Memphis attending his father's sister's funeral. It wasn't the way I had planned to meet his family but I was enjoying spending time with them just the same. We had driven down and had arrived at his parent's house late last night. His mother Gail had greeted us at the door with a warm smile. She was short, dark, round and clearly the spitting image of Jeremy. His father was tall and light-brown and seemed almost as mean as Jeremy had mentioned he was growing up. I glanced over at his parents sitting in the front pews to the right. His father Jeremy, Sr. had a hard look on his face but that muscle ticking at his jaw hinted he wasn't as strong as he wanted everyone to think.

I squeezed Jeremy's hand and listened to the pastor give the eulogy. There wasn't a dry eye in the church. And when his Aunt Gerry got up and sang *His Eye Is On the Sparrow*, I started crying, and I didn't even know the lady.

After we left the cemetery we all headed back to Jeremy's parents' house for the Passover.

"Sorry we're meeting on such sad circumstances," Elijah Samuels said with a big hug and a smile. We were standing in the dining room that was filled with friends and family. Jeremy's older brother was tall and light-brown, like their father, with a head full of dark curly hair. The brothers were like day and night.

"It's a pleasure to meet you Eli," I said as he released me and pointed to the short woman beside him.

"This here is my wife, Amy."

She was a pretty brunette with a big smile who seemed nice enough.

"And that there is my baby sister Carrie and her husband Clark." He pointed to a dark-skinned woman wearing a short curly natural. Goodness her spouse wasn't black, either. Jeremy's other sister Chelsey was out on the deck with her Italian boyfriend. What's up with that? Although, as I walked over to greet the two, I noticed how much her fiancé resembled Brad Pitt. Now that's one yummy, white boy I'd take any day.

We all laughed and talked and I ended up in the kitchen where I met so many family members I lost count. But I had a good feeling about all of them, especially the ones who made me feel welcomed.

Jeremy was sitting out on the deck with his father and I was sitting at the kitchen table with Aunt Gerry and his mother, who started asking me all kind of questions.

"You think y'all might be getting married?" his aunt asked.

I gave her a weird look. "We're getting married in two weeks."

"Two weeks?" His mom mocked with surprise. "That's the first I've heard about that."

Now I was really confused. "Jeremy said he invited all of you."

She and her sister exchanged looks before she snorted. "He hasn't said a thing to me." It was easy to see her feelings were hurt.

I was blown away but decided I needed to smooth things over until I had a chance to speak to Jeremy. "It's just something small. Since it's both of our second marriages he probably didn't want to make a big fuss."

His cousin Hannah looked at her sister Karida before she

turned my way and blurted out. "You know this will be his fourth marriage, right?"

I cringed. There was no way I had heard her right. "Fourth?" I looked to his mother and auntie for verification, but his mother rose and walked over and busied herself with the potato salad, while Aunt Gerry stuffed her mouth with pound cake.

"That fool's always falling in love." Hannah laughed, until her mother waved at her to shut the hell up.

I just sat there in a daze because what they were telling me was my man had lied again. First the kids… now this.

Okay, wait a minute. I needed clarification. "Excuse me Mrs. Samuels? Did she just say your son has already been married three times?'

His mother waited until she pulled a ham out the oven before she looked in my direction. His cousins were leaning against the island smirking at her and then at me like they were watching a movie. The only thing missing was the buttered popcorn.

That sweet woman finally shook her head and replied, "I don't know why my son has started that lying again. Yes, he's had three wives. I know that's not something to be proud of, but it's the truth."

His cousin shook her head. "You sure you wanna marry him?"

"Karida, shut up." Her mother warned.

Yeah, shut up. I was sitting there feeling stupid enough as it was.

"You said y'all getting married in two weeks?"

I nodded and forced a smile. "Yes ma'am."

"Hmmm." Aunt Gerry sat there with crumb on her bosom wearing a thoughtful look. "Gail you going?"

His mother waved her hand in the air. I could tell she was getting agitated. "How can I come to something I knew nothing about?"

I shook my head, embarrassed beyond explaining. "He said he told you."

"Girl, my cousin be lying!" Hannah cackled and Karida

joined in on the fun.

"Don't pay them any mind. I don't know why he didn't bother to tell us." Aunt Gerry straightened her wig, then sighed. "I guess he had his reasons."

"Hell, is he even divorced from the last one?"

The two hyenas were at it again.

Jeremy's mother looked up at the ceiling like she was saying a silent prayer. Prayer wasn't going to help her son by the time I got done with him.

"I think his divorce has been final for a while." It was obvious his mother was trying to take up for him. I guess I would do the same if it were my son. Not that it was going to help him any.

Karida started chatting away. "You might wanna think twice about marrying him. There's no telling what other lies he's told you."

She did have a point but I wasn't about to let her know that.

Aunt Gerry waved her hand like she was shooing a fly. "Don't pay them no mind. My nephew has a good heart and good intentions I just think sometimes he just tries to impress people."

Karida mumbled something under her breath. I couldn't make it out, but Hannah had and she was cackling like a hyena again.

Aunt Gerry sucked her teeth. "I give you both my blessings, but you might wanna maybe take a little more time to get to know each other first."

I realized—with resignation—that she had a point. "I agree and I had every intention of taking things slow but..." I sighed. "He accepted a transfer to Hawaii and has to report there next month. He doesn't want to leave without me." Despite what I was feeling I smiled at the thought.

His cousins were laughing again.

"What's so funny?" I said with attitude. Those two were getting on my damn nerves.

Karida had the nerve to roll her eyes and suck her gold tooth. Hannah just shrugged and was about to say something when his mother came over and placed a comforting hand at my shoulder.

"Don't pay them no mind."

"Whatever Auntie. I'd be checking his behind," Hannah said in defense. "Giggles always be lying."

My brow rose. "Giggles?"

His aunt decided to explain. "When he was a kid, he used to laugh all the time, especially in church, so we all started calling him Giggles."

"Yeah and Giggles is full of crap," Karida huffed. "I don't know why you wanna marry him and take on all them kids?" She gave a look like she was trying to figure me out as if I was the one who was crazy.

"Karida behave," her mother warned. "This's that chile's business, not yours."

She rolled her eyes again. That chick was so disrespectful. If it had been my mama, she would have been sprawled out on the floor, knocked unconscious.

She finally slid off the stool and signaled for Hannah to follow her outside. *Thank goodness.*

Jeremy's mother was smiling as she came around and returned to her seat at the table. "Since you're gonna be my new daughter-in-law, tell me something about yourself."

At this point, marrying Jeremy was the furthest thing from my mind. If I hadn't road with him, I would have already jumped in my car, heading home. But a part of me really wanted them to like me. "Well, I'm in the United States Air Force."

"Really?" His aunt looked impressed. "What do you do?"

There were so many thoughts swirling around in my mind that it was hard to focus on what they were saying. "I'm in labor relations. I negotiate union contracts for our civilian employees."

"Impressive," his aunt said, then reached down to fix her thigh-high stockings that were now peeking out from beneath her polyester dress. "Any children?"

I shook my head. "No. None."

"None?" Aunt Gerry looked surprised. "How come?"

I couldn't believe the two were putting me through the third degree. "Because I have been focused on my career and I wanted to be married first."

They looked at each other.

I felt I was losing points with these two. "I love kids. Now that I'm marrying Jeremy, his kids can be my kids."

"Well you're definitely taking on a small baseball team," his aunt cackled.

I couldn't resist a laugh. "Yeah, I guess I am. I met the ones in Chicago when we attended Tiffany's graduation."

His mother released a long sigh. "I couldn't make it. Of course their mama dogged me and my husband out on Facebook."

My eyes widened. *Talk about childish.* "You're kidding."

I couldn't believe the way her head was rolling. "Now, *that's* an evil woman. I don't know how Giggles was married to her for so long."

And she was the only wife he claimed. What was up with that? He definitely had some explaining to do. *And no time like the present.* I looked up to see Jeremy stepping in to the kitchen, followed by his brother.

"We're ready for some of Aunt Gerry's apple pie." He had the nerve to have that stupid grin on his face.

I glared at him, trying to make eye contact. When he finally did, I rose from the chair. "Can I talk to you in private?"

Jeremy looked nervous. "About what?"

"About your *three* wives."

Where the hell did they come from? Once again his nosy cousin Karida was all up in our business. I wanted to snatch her tracks out of her head if I wasn't already anxious to get my fiancé alone.

"My three wives?" he repeated like he hadn't heard his cousin the first time. It was clear he was stalling for time. "What are you talking about?"

"I don't know why you lied to that girl like that?" his mother shook her head.

He must have glanced around and realized that everyone

was looking at him because he did something I never expected.

"Is that what you told my family?" he accused and had the nerve to look like I had betrayed him or something when he was the one who had betrayed me. "I don't know why you sitting there telling that lie. I *told* you I had three wives. Hell you met one of them while you were at Tiffany's graduation!"

No he didn't just embarrass me in front of his people. "But you didn't tell me you had two more."

"What you in here doing... fishing for information from my family? You wanna know anything then you need to ask me. All you're doing is looking for an excuse to end our engagement. Fine... you don't wanna marry me, then don't!" He then grabbed a chicken leg from the island and stormed out the kitchen.

34

JANELLE

I left Frankie's place and headed back to Columbia with a big shit-eating grin on my face. We had just spent a fabulous weekend together, and I was really feeling that dude.

Here was my homeboy from back during a time when he had a big crush on me and I was fucking older boys with jobs and cars. Now he was a man I was really feeling. Don't get me wrong there wasn't a day that passed I wasn't missing Kaleb. I missed his smile, his touch. I even missed that cripple-ass walk that was his own unique swagger. I couldn't get him off my mind. But as much as I wanted to be there when he received his next installment check, I'd be damned if I was going to continue to be disrespected. And to prove to him how serious I was, I waited until he was in Kansas City on business and had all of my things moved from his house and into a storage unit. He'd been calling and begging ever since. Like I told him before, Jae is not to be messed with.

I pulled into Columbia and felt this need to drop by and see my mother. I usually saw her on Mondays but for some reason I just wanted to talk to her and share what was going on in my life and hear what she had to say. I drove down Providence Road past the park. They were playing hoops so the park was packed with wall-to-wall brothas. Back in the day I couldn't wait to get my hot ass down the hill so I could be seen in the hood but that was before my father started sliding up and embarrassing me. Nothing worse than a cop snooping around. After that I started going places he never could find me.

I made a right at the light and a few seconds later I pulled in front of the house. That eerie feeling returned but I pushed it aside. Today I wasn't letting anything steal my shine!

I was surprised to find the door locked since Mama always wanted to make it easy for her nurse to get in without having to roll her wheelchair to the door. As much as I complained, she was too damn paranoid to give the healthcare agency a key.

A little annoyed, I reached for my keys and opened the door. As soon as I stepped inside, I gagged at the stench of stale cigarettes.

"Mommy!" I called between coughs. "Where you at?"

It wasn't until I had cleared my throat that I heard moaning coming for the rear of the house. I dropped my purse and raced toward her bedroom. The last time my mother had fallen it had taken two days for someone to discover her.

I pushed her bedroom door open and braced myself for the worse. "Mommy, you—" My breath stalled. I shook my head to make sure I wasn't seeing things but even when I opened them again the image was still there.

Mama in the bed getting busy with Uncle Todd.

He was in mid-stroke when I came barging in, and he leaped off my mother like a crusty old frog.

"You've gotta be fucking kidding me!" I sputtered, while still trying to process what I was witnessing.

Of course his fake ass was the first to speak. "Jae, it's—"

"Save it!" I screamed while I just stood there looking at the two of them in disgust. Here I was thinking Mommy's moans had been a result of another fall. Yeah, she had fallen alright. Right onto Uncle Todd's little-ass dick.

"Jae, I know you're upset," she managed to say.

I glared, while they tried to cover themselves up. "You couldn't begin to know how I feel. The two of you disgust me!" With that I turned and left the room.

Uncle Todd called after me just as I was turning the knob

to hurry out to my car.

"Jae, you hear me talking to you."

Like a child who had been raised to respect her elder, I stopped, blew out a long breath then slowly turned around. There wasn't shit he could say to explain what I had just seen, but I did as I was told, even though I felt two seconds away from throwing up.

"We need to talk."

At least he had taken the time to put on a t-shirt and his pants.

"How can you betray my father like that?" All I could do was shake my head in disbelief.

"Your father has been dead for almost twenty years. He was my best friends. Don't you think he woulda like to see me and your mother happy, even if it's with each other?"

I gave him a look that said he knew better than that. As selfish as my father was he would rather we all be miserable as he was.

"But you're my godfather. Why couldn't you have picked someone other than my mother?"

He stuck his hands in his pocket and moved closer. "Claudette is a good woman. I'm not going to make excuses for loving her because I do. But we should have told you. I'm sorry."

I brought a hand to my waist. "And how long has this been going on?"

Uncle Todd couldn't even look me in the eyes, which meant it had been going on longer than I wanted to know. Maybe even while my father was still alive. I shook my head and this time he didn't stop me from leaving.

I left the neighborhood, angry and frustrated. My perfect morning had been ruined. *So much for not letting someone steal my shine.*

I pulled up at the hotel where I had been staying, ready for a hot shower. As soon as I climbed out my car, I spotted Kaleb's Range Rover rolling up beside me. I couldn't get out the car fast enough before he dashed across the parking lot towards me. I swung around so fast, I saw him flinch.

"What do you want?" I asked through gritted teeth.

He smiled. "Babe, before you go off, hear me out."

I dragged my purse over my shoulder and rolled my eyes. I'd been blowing off his calls for days, but I'd be lying if I said I wasn't curious to hear what he had to say. "What do you want?"

"I miss you."

I tried not to get excited by his confession yet damn this man did things to me. But then there was that crazy side...

I glanced around to see if anyone was watching. Just in case Kaleb decided to go off again at least I would have witnesses. Sadly there were none.

"You gonna stand there and act like you don't miss me."

At his words I felt the area between my thighs spring to life, but I quickly shook it off. "Yes, I miss you but that doesn't change anything."

Kaleb looked at me with this knowing smile. "Yes it does. I know you love me and I love you, and as long as we have that we can work through anything."

I stifled a laugh. "Work through what? You being controlling? That's never going to change."

"Yes, it will. Just give me time baby and I'll work on it. I'll even see a therapist if that will help."

I was speechless. Maybe he was trying to change. "You'd do that for me?" I asked although I was still suspicious.

"Anything to have you back. I feel like someone has chopped off my right arm." He leaned in to kiss me, but I drew back and he caught my ear instead. There was no way I could think straight with his hands all over my body. One touch and it's a wrap. I had gone through his bullshit enough times to know that it was going to take me not putting up with his bullshit for things to finally change in our relationship.

"I'm willing to do whatever it takes. Just come back home." He was practically pleading.

"I *am* home," I snapped and didn't mean to sound upset but I was. He was trying to play mind games with me again. Have me move all my shit over so he could get mad and send me packing again. I just wasn't sure if I wanted to go through that again.

"Babe, please. I love you too much to lose you."

Kaleb then got down on his knee, pleading in the middle of the hotel parking lot. "Babe, I love you." He took my hand in his and then reached inside his pocket. I spotted the engagement ring as he attempted to slip it back on but as good as it looked on my finger, I yanked my hand away. "Stop it!"

"Stop what?" he persisted. "Loving you? Wanting my fiancée back?" he sighed. "I messed up. Babe… I admit I scooped the poop, but it's nothing we can't fix."

That was easy for him to say. I wasn't the one who was crazy and wishy-washy.

I took a step back, putting a little space between us. He was wearing that new Armani cologne I bought him and it made me wanna bury my face at his neck and inhale.

He rose and signaled with his hand, "C'mon. Let's go inside and talk." As usual, Kaleb was trying to run things.

"How about we don't." I was getting a little annoyed at the way he was acting as if this was so simple. "I'm not ready yet to hear what you have to say. You said you're willing to get help then do it, and when I see you're trying to change, then I'll be willing to listen!"

He was trying to maintain his composure but I knew he was ready to go off or so I thought. "Janelle, I will do whatever it takes to get you back in my life." He tossed his hands up in surrender. "All this instability… I'm fucking up my son's life."

Now that was one thing I couldn't argue. "Then get yourself together for your son's sake, not mine." At least I tried to sound sympathetic.

Kaleb shook his head. "There's no me without you. Don't you love me?"

There he goes with that Jedi mind-trick shit again. "Of course I love you. But love just isn't enough.'

"Don't say that. Love is what's holding us together," he insisted and I noticed him rocking on the balls of his feet the way CJ does when he's nervous.

"But I need more than that to come back to you and for me

to wear your ring again."

"I'm going to get you back," he said with a smirk. "That much I'm confident about. I love you and we're good for each other. I don't know why you can't see that."

"All I see is a man who wants to control me and every aspect of our relationship and I'm tired of living like that."

"No, you just don't like to listen!" Kaleb snapped.

See, I told you it was just a matter of time.

"Listen to what?" I was all up in his face now. "You ain't my daddy. Nobody tells me what I can and cannot do. And until you get that in your thick skull we'll never have a chance!"

Suddenly he was scared and we stared at each other silently.

"You're right. I gotta let you be your own woman. And I'm gonna work on that and with the help of a good therapist, I know I can do it. I just ask that you don't give up on us just yet. Give your man time to get his head on right. Please... I can't lose you." He sounded desperate I had yet to respond. "I'm getting ready to get this money and I need you. Babe I can't lose you."

At the mention of money I wanted to throw my arms around him and tell him all was forgiven but that's what he wanted me to do and then I would be back under his roof with him cracking the whip again.

However, the heart wants what the heart wants.

"Get it together then come back and talk to me." I kissed his lips then went inside the hotel and didn't bother to look back.

<u>35</u>

NYREE

"You need to leave that lying mothafucka alone! First, he lied about his kids, now you find out he's been married three damn times! Girl..., I told you, you need to run the fuck away while you still can."

I asked Janelle to come over because I needed someone to talk to. Ever since we had gotten back from Memphis on Sunday, I had been miserable. The ride home was long. While Jeremy pleaded his case, I completely tuned him out. Today he showed up at my job but I just didn't want to hear shit he had to say. Thank goodness my realtor hadn't sold my house yet.

However, as angry as I was, I hated myself because I was missing him like crazy. Jeremy had been sending me bible scriptures and texting me discussion topics from *Our Daily Bread* and I just couldn't resist responding. I had never had a man who I connected with on a spiritual level before, so it was just hard. But I wasn't no fool. He had not only embarrassed me but he did it in front of his family. Hell, they hadn't even known we were engaged. I felt betrayed and used and I wasn't sure if I was ever going to forgive him.

"Have you called and canceled the catering?"

I dragged my legs up to my chest and groaned. Damn. I had forgotten all about the wedding plans. Hell, I was supposed to pick up my wedding dress from the cleaners tomorrow. "No, I haven't done anything."

Janelle blew out a long breath. I knew she was getting tired of me. Hell, I was tired of sitting around all day feeling sorry for myself.

"Nyree, you need to figure out what you're gonna do."

"I know," I spat and was frustrated at her for even bringing it up.

"I wouldn't be a friend if I didn't say I think you're rushing things. Obvious after this incident you don't know enough about him."

"You gotta lot of nerve," I snarled and glared over at her. How the hell she gonna talk about me when her ass was engaged as well?

"I gave Kaleb his ring back but even before that I wasn't talking about marrying that crazy mothafucka." Janelle shrugged. "I'm well aware Kaleb's fucked up in the head. I make no excuses."

"And that makes it right?" Sometimes she has the most ridiculous shit coming out of her mouth. Janelle crossed her legs and rolled her eyes. She hates hearing the truth.

"Whatever. We're talking about you, not me. You have a wedding next weekend and almost two hundred guests coming. Are you marrying this dude or not?" Janelle sat there swinging her leg showing off her pink pumps.

"I don't know."

"Well then you better figure it out." Rising, she moved toward my kitchen. "You want something to drink?"

I shook my head. Ever since our falling out I couldn't eat or drink. All I could do was think about how much I missed him. No matter what he had done or said, he was still my soul mate. I could feel it in my bones. What I couldn't understand was why he felt compelled to lie to me about stuff that I would eventually find out the truth about anyway. "I don't know what to do."

She sauntered back into the living room holding a Pepsi can in her hand. "Well, the only other option is to go talk to the fool and find out why he be lying like that."

Janelle was right. We needed to talk but I just wasn't sure yet if I was ready.

"What's his family say?" Janelle asked between sips.

I blew out a breath and replied, "I spoke to his mama. She said she understands if I decide not to marry him. No one deserves to be treated that way."

Janelle gave a rude snort. "Ain't that the truth."

I decided to ignore her response. "She said Jeremy has self-esteem issues. Always has. Feels like he has to try and be better than everyone else. He'll do anything to make himself look good for attention. I don't get it and neither does she."

"Did he seem like someone with self-esteem issues when you first met him?"

I took a moment to think about that question. "Not at first, but since his daughter and the weekend at his parents, he's been stuttering like crazy and putting himself down."

Of course at any sign of weakness, Janelle turned up her nose. "Girl, he sounds too pathetic. I don't know how you deal with all that."

"Probably the same way you deal with that crazy man of yours, going off every other week."

She gave me a silly smirk but I could tell my comment bothered her. "It adds excitement to the relationship."

"We're way too old for that kinda of excitement. That's shit we do in our twenties." I added with an eye-roll.

"Anyway…" Janelle dismissed my comment by a flick of her wrist. It kills that girl for me to be right.

"And what about Frankie? You can't keep playing with him like that. You know he's feeling you." A few days ago I had run into Frankie in Walmart looking gorgeous as ever and all he could talk about was this heifer here. Hopefully, Janelle will wake up and realize what she has before it's too late. "Trust me, someone as fine as him is not going to be single for long." I could tell my comment really bothered Janelle. What the hell she expect Frankie to do? Continue to be her side-dick? "You really need to decide."

Like I said she is quick to flip the script if we're talking about her.

"Uh-huh. Don't you worry about Frankie. Now… what I need to know if we're gonna have a wedding or not. I just bought a dress. I got an appointment for both of us next Saturday to get our hair done and the girls and I have planned a bachelorette party for Friday. Time is money, baby," she added with a two-finger snap.

Before I could answer I heard the doorbell and my heart started pounding like crazy.

Janelle jumped up from the couch before I could. "Let me get that for you."

I didn't object and waited as she swung open the door. As soon as I heard her suck her teeth, I knew who it was.

"Hey Jae."

"Jeremy... what can I do for you?" She blocked the door.

"Jae, go ahead and let him in," I said because I just wasn't in the mood for anymore drama.

"I guess," she mumbled and stepped aside for him to enter. As soon as I saw him my mouth went dry and I hated the way I was feeling, yet I couldn't deny how much I missed him.

"Hey Angel," he said and I tried to ignore the look of remorse on his face. "Can I please talk to you... in private?" Janelle was still standing by the door with her arms crossed looking like she was ready to knock him upside his head.

"Jae, can you give us some privacy?"

"Whateva," she mumbled then sauntered to her purse and swung the strap over her shoulder. "I expect you to call me tonight with an answer."

As soon as she was gone, Jeremy walked around and took a seat on the couch. The same place he was sitting the last time we were dealing with his bullshit.

Finally, he looked at me. "Angel, I'm sorry."

"You're *always* fucking sorry!" I snapped.

"I know and I don't know why I didn't just tell you the truth."

"Ya think? Especially since the truth was gonna come out eventually."

"I know, I should have been honest. And I'm sorry," he stammered, struggling for the right words. "I guess I wanted so badly to impress you that I was afraid you wouldn't be interested in me if you knew the truth."

"And like I said before you need a woman who accepts you for you."

"Does that mean you no longer wanna be with me?"

"No, what it means is that I'm tired of the lies. I have tried to be nothing but honest with you since the beginning yet all I keep hearing is lies and more lies. I just don't get it."

He shrugged his shoulders. "I know Angel. And it hurts my heart every time I think about the lies I have told you."

I surprised myself by laughing. Hell, it was either that or cry. "And then you embarrassed me in front of your family! How could you have treated me that way?"

He looked like he was on the verge of tears. "I'm so sorry. I just was embarrassed that my family put my business out there and I didn't know how to react."

"Why didn't your mama know we were getting married?"

He leaned forward with his elbow resting on his knees as he spoke. "I told her on the phone I wanted to get married again but when she started telling me it was too soon, I backed off. I was planning on announcing it before we left Memphis. You just beat me to it."

"Because I *thought* they knew," I said defensively. He wasn't going to blame this on me.

"And I apologize for that. I didn't want to worry you about my family being against the idea so I lied and told you I had told my parents about our wedding. I know now that was wrong, but I knew they wouldn't believe how much I loved you until they had a chance to meet you. Now, they think you're the best thing to have ever happened to me."

I smirked a little. Knowing his parents liked me really meant a lot. Especially since my ex-mother-in-law couldn't stand me for no reason at all.

"I should have told you the truth. I knew they would judge because this would make my third marriage and I just didn't want anyone trying to talk me out of it. As you can see my cousins had a field day."

"This is your *fourth* marriage." I wasted no time correcting him.

He shook his head. "I wasn't ever married to Jasmine's mother. I just told my mother that. She and my dad had been getting on me and I just decided to tell them we had gotten married so they would leave me alone. But Angel, she was never my wife."

I looked at the defeated look on his face and all I wanted to do was believe him, but I just wasn't sure yet.

"You embarrassed me in front of your family. Not to mention you have lied to me so many times before that I just don't know what to believe anymore." Tears started to stream down my face. Nothing made any sense.

Jeremy turned on the seat and reached for my hand. "Nyree, I have lied. I have mistreated you, and taken your love for granted and for that I am so sorry." He took a deep breath. "All my life I desired to meet a woman like you and then when I find you I let my insecurities get in the way. But I swear to you that from this day forward I'm going to treat you like a queen." He waited calmly, even smiling ever so often. There were tears in his eyes and I could see he was trying to hold it together yet a voice in my head kept reminding me that this wasn't the first time he had lied.

And I had a sinking feeling it also wouldn't be the last.

36

JANELLE

"Janelle, did I tell you what happened to Crystal?"

I looked up from the *Essence* magazine I was browsing through to look over at Veronica. "No, what happened?"

She shifted on the chair and smacked her lips. She did that whenever she was about to say something juicy. "Her man wiped out her bank account."

"What?"

While she went into details about this trifling chick we had gone to school with, I leaned back in the massage chair. We were at Lucky Nails doing some female pampering. Lord knows I needed an hour of relaxation. Because my man was enough to make you think you were losing your mind. And then there was that situation with my mother and Uncle Todd that I refused to think about. Mama had been blowing up my phone but I just wasn't ready yet to talk to either of them. Fucking in my daddy's bed was wrong on so many levels. I was so embarrassed I couldn't even call my brother and tell him what I had seen.

With all the unnecessary stress in my life, I had decided to schedule a pamper day with my girls. Nyree needed it. She had been going through some bullshit with that lame-ass fiancé of her. I hadn't seen her in three days and when I texted and asked her if she was still planning to get married. She had texted back, *I don't know.*

"I thought Nyree was coming?" Veronica asked.

I looked down at my cellphone. It was after seven. "She was, but I guess she got tied up. She and her mom were supposed to meet with the caterer this evening." Although, I think she wasn't planning on being there. I hated seeing her going through all the drama. I could handle shit like that but for Nyree it was just too much. She did everything she could to try and please everybody else all the time. That why I hoped for once she would do what she wanted to do.

Veronica beamed. "Isn't it exciting she's getting married?"

It took everything I had to keep a straight face. "Yeah, it's great. I'm happy for her."

Really, I'm not a hater. I was happy for her. I just felt she was rushing things. Marrying Jeremy was like me being stupid enough to marry Kaleb when I knew we couldn't go a day without arguing over something as silly as dripping water on the floor after a shower. Don't get me wrong. I loved him and the drama, but I'll admit at times, it could be a bit too much.

The nail technician was painting French tips on my toes when I spotted Nyree coming through the door.

"Heifer, where you been?"

She gave me a look like I didn't want to know. Wrong. I wanna know.

"I need a pedicure — bad!" she mumbled and took a seat in the chair beside me. "Hey Ronnie!"

"Hey girl! One week until your big day!" Veronica looked more excited than we did.

"Yep... it's right around the corner." Her words didn't quite meet her eyes.

I waited until Nyree put her feet in the water and relaxed in the chair before I said, "You okay?"

She didn't even bother opening her eyes. "Yeah, I'm good."

"How was the catering appointment with your mother?"

"I didn't go." She turned to look at me.

"What?"

Nyree shook her head. "I told my mother I was having second thoughts and then blocked her number so she couldn't call me."

"Are you serious?" I gave her a weird look. Where was Nyree? And who was this imposter because my best friend never stood up to her parents.

I had been around the Dawsons for years and although they tried to act like a Huxtable family they had issues just like everyone else. Well, not like mine but what I'm trying to say is they weren't perfect. One thing I immediately noticed was how her parents always tried to control her. Nothing Nyree decided on her own was good enough. She wanted to be an engineer but her father insisted she join the military. When she married Shane without their approval they stopped speaking to her for over a year. After that Nyree tried to do everything she could to make them happy and I found it so sickening the way her mother would turn her nose up at her. Ms. Mabeline needed to look at herself with that hairy double chin she was sporting. That chick was no better than anyone else. Okay, let me quit.

"What did your mother say?"

She didn't even look over at me. "I didn't even give her a chance to speak. I just hung the phone up before she could get a word in."

"Gurrrl! Mabeline was probably so pissed she threw that tired wig of hers across the room!" I joked.

Her eyes widened. "Oooh, you know you're wrong for that!"

I started laughing and despite the way Nyree was feeling, she joined right in.

"What's so funny?" Veronica asked. She had been on her phone gossiping.

I shook my head. "It's an inside joke."

As soon as our pedicures were done, Veronica had to hurry home to her boo. For once I didn't have anywhere I needed to be. As usual Kaleb was blowing me up with text messages, but I just didn't rush to respond anymore. He was supposed to be working on getting himself together. And I'll admit he seemed to be acting a lot better on the phone but as many problems as that man had, I knew it would be weeks before I saw any significant changes. In the meantime, I was keeping my hotel suite.

"You got time to run to Starbuck's?" There was something on Nyree's face that said she needed to talk.

I nodded. "Sure girl. I'm not doing anything but going back to my hotel."

Nyree shook her head. "I don't know why you won't just come and stay with me."

"Because I like my privacy and you get up too damn early for me."

She gave me one of those playful eye-rolls.

I hopped in my BMW and headed toward the coffee shop and noticed I had a missed call that I needed to return.

"Hey CJ, whassup?"

"Hi Ms. Jae. Can I stay at my friend Jordan's house?" he asked

Why the hell was he calling me? "What did your dad say?"

"He's got a game and he's in Kansas City until tomorrow. I tried to reach him but he isn't answering."

My eyebrow flew up. "Gone until tomorrow?" *What the fuck?* The mothafucka had been texting me all afternoon but not once had he mentioned anything about being in Kansas City. I made a right at the light and asked, "Who's watching you?"

"Nobody."

See…, niggas ain't shit. Who leaves their thirteen-year-old home alone without letting another adult know they were leaving town? I could feel my blood pressure rising. Those two were definitely stressing me the fuck out.

"Yeah, go ahead and make sure you come back in the morning and let Midnight out."

"Okay," he replied in that irritating voice.

"Oh CJ!" I yelled before he hung up. "Make sure you leave your phone on. Matter of fact, text me when you get there so I'll know you made it." Jordan only lived around the block but in this crazy world anything could happen.

I ended the call and was prepared to call Kaleb and cuss his ass out for leaving his son alone. Sure, CJ was responsible and used to taking care of himself, but that didn't make it right. Besides, I already knew he wanted me to call him and that shit wasn't happening. I'd just drop by in the morning and check on CJ and Midnight.

By the time I made it to Starbuck's, Nyree was sitting at a table in the corner of the shop. "Let me order me something," I said and put my purse down on the table. "You want anything?" She quickly shook her head.

Whatever was bothering my girl had her looking worried as hell. Nyree was probably afraid her mother was going to show up at her house tonight.

I ordered a hazelnut macchiato, then walked back over and took a seat.

"Ree, you look like you just lost your best friend and I know that isn't the case because I'm right here."

"No..., it's worse." She had poured herself a glass of ice water and brought it to her lips.

"Worse? What in the world did you do?" I asked and then leaned forward, elbows on the table and waited to hear what she had to say.

"I had sex with Timmy," she confessed.

"What? Whoa!," I held up my hands. "Time out." I needed a moment to clear my head and make sure I had heard her right. "You fucked Timmy again?"

"Damn, why you gotta say it like that?" Nyree had the nerve to suck her teeth and try to look disgusted.

"It is what it is," I said with a dismissive wave. "And when did this shit happen?"

She took a moment to form her words. "Yesterday." She then shook her head. "I told you I would be down at Knob Noster for a few days doing some training, right? Well, I was working with Timmy and his team. Anyway he and I had dinner yesterday and one thing led to another, and we were sexing it up at his place."

"Hell nah!" This was just too juicy.

Nyree shook her head and looked like she as on the verge of tears. "I've been feeling guilty ever since."

Her comment threw me. "Guilty for what? You ain't

married."

"But I'm engaged to be married! Engaged people don't sleep with other people." Panic was written all over her face.

"You do when you know something ain't right about the person you're engaged to."

Nyree looked like she was ready to defend that lame-ass fiancé of hers. Thank goodness the barista called out my order. I walked over and retrieved my drink, then grabbed a few napkins before I lowered back on my seat. I decided I needed to wear kid gloves with her.

I took a sip then asked, "So what's Timmy saying?"

She blew out a long breath. "He wants a relationship. He's made that clear from day one he wants to be with me."

I wanted her to be with Timmy too. I've never met him but Nyree's talked about him so much, over the years, I liked everything I'd heard. But I had to remind myself it wasn't about me. "And what do you want?"

"I just want to be happy." There were the tears and I quickly passed her a napkin so she could wipe her eyes. "Thanks girl." She managed between sniffles. "I have never loved a man like I love him."

"Who Timmy?" I knew who she was talking about but I love to play dumb.

She swallowed hard. "No, Jeremy."

That was the last thing I wanted to hear but like I said, it wasn't about me. "Then what are you doing to do?" I asked between sips.

She paused, glancing up at the ceiling as if the answer was written on the tiles above. "I don't know. Part of me feels that once we're married everything is going to be a'ight. That all Jeremy needs is the love of a good woman. But, then there is that part of me that keeps saying he's still hiding something."

Probably two or three more kids, but I wasn't even going there.

"And then there's all that money that's been spent. My dress is bought, the banquet hall reserved, invitations have been sent out."

I sucked my teeth. "Forget all that. Fuck that money and

your parents because I know that's what's really bothering you. For once do you boo."

"That's easy for you to say." Nyree paused and took a sip of water then cleared her throat. "I'm not like you."

I brought my coffee to my lips then shook my head and said, "That's where you are wrong. You're more like me than you think. You just have to start believing it."

There was a long silence and I could tell she wasn't completely convinced.

"Try putting together a list of pros and cons. Reasons for marrying Jeremy and reasons for not." She may not see it but I already saw a long list of reasons why she needed to stay the fuck away from him.

There was this sad distant look on her face. "Together Jeremy and I have been on this spiritual roller coaster ride and I don't want to get off. I love having a man who I can pray and fellowship with. Men like him are rare."

"But liars come a dime a dozen," I murmured.

Nyree cringed at the mention of his dishonesty but she had known me long enough to know I don't hold punches for anyone.

"If Timmy was the one, we would have already been together yet something has always kept us apart."

"How about miles?" I answered without missing a beat. "He's now within a ninety-minute commute. You've known him long enough to know what you're getting yourself into." I took another sip then leaned in closer. "Look, I'm not saying break up with Jeremy. Hell. If you love it—I like it. What I'm saying is maybe you just need to take a little more time to get to know him… and his kids before you decide this is the man you want to spend the rest of your life with."

She stared at me for a moment, then nodded. "Maybe you're right."

Of course I am. I grinned and brought the cup to my lips.

37

NYREE

We had just gotten done with our Monday morning staffing meeting and I was heading back to my office when I saw something that made me duck behind a chair in the conference room.

"Girl, what's wrong with you?" Jenna said and laughed. I guess I did look ridiculous trying to hide. What I really wanted to do was slide under the table.

"I think I just saw my mother go by," I whispered.

"Why in the world would you be hiding from your mother?"

"It's a long story." My heart was pounding like crazy. I prayed to God I was just seeing things. "Can you please go tell her I'm not here?" I know I was being a coward but what choice did I have?

"Are you serious?" Jenna had this incredulous look of disbelief on her face.

"Yes!" I snapped then waved my hand. "Go—now—before she comes and find me."

"Okay, I—" As soon as I heard her voice trail off I already knew even before I heard my mother's voice that Mabeline had stepped into the room.

"Where's Nyree?"

"Sorry, but I can't lie to your mother." Jenna whispered and before she scurried out the room I caught her pointing down at me.

Traitor.

"Nyree Gail Dawson, get from under that table."

Oh my goodness. I peeked out over the edge of the table. "Hey Mama."

"Don't, hey Mama me! You have a lot of explaining to do."

I guess I could pretend I had no idea what she was talking about but Lord know I'd been avoiding her calls all weekend, and for obvious reasons. I needed to figure out what I wanted to do about my wedding to Jeremy that was five days away.

I rose to my feet and watched as my mother closed the door to the room. I swallowed hard and hoped there were no meetings scheduled because Mabeline wasn't going to tolerate any interruptions. Regardless of who it was.

"Sit down," she ordered and I quickly dropped onto the nearest chair. "What's going on with you?"

I counted to five, drew a deep breath then replied, "I'm not sure if I want to get married." I leaned across the table and told her about the last few months. All the lies... Jeremy's wives and children.

So imagine my surprise when she snorted rudely and said, "Is that all?"

Okay, so maybe she hadn't heard me correctly. "Mama, he's been lying to me!"

"So what? If anything you should feel flattered that a man wants to be with you so bad he pretends to be everything you are looking for in a man."

I never thought of it that way.

Mama was smiling. "Chile, that man loves you. You'll be a fool to let him go."

The look she gave me told me she definitely didn't understand where I was coming from and never would.

"Listen, Jeremy came to see me and he told me everything, but the only thing I heard was how much he loved you."

I stared at her for a moment. "He came to see you?"

"Yes he did." She nodded. "Nyree, see, what you don't understand is you and Jeremy didn't put this together. God did!"

God?

I felt myself sitting up straight on the chair.

"What you fail to realize is… this isn't about what you want or what Jeremy wants, it's what the Lord wants."

I took a moment to let her words process and what she said made sense on so many levels, and yet all it did was make me feel even more confused than before.

"Mom I understand what you're saying, but I just don't know. Jeremy and I are so different. If he had been honest in the first place, he and I would have never gotten together."

"Exactly! That's how we know you didn't put this together." She smiled. "God has a plan for the both of you."

I drew out a long breath. As much as I wanted to believe what my mother said was right, I just couldn't help but think about the way Jeremy had gone off and embarrassed me in front of his family. Was that God's plan as well?

"Mama, I just need some time to think about all this."

What in the world did I say that for? The smile slipped away from her lips and she glared across the table as she sneered, "Then you should have thought about that before you announced your engagement at church."

What? Was she serious? "Mama, people change their mind all the time."

"Not my daughter." She spat then pointed her finger over at me. "We told you to marry Charlie and you went off and married that fool Shane, and what he do? Dog you out and bring you down! Since then all you've done is make a mess of your life, and your father and I are tired of it. Jeremy is a good man and he loves you."

"But love isn't enough." I was pleading for her to understand.

"Well, you should have thought about that." She reached up and scratched her chin. You have no idea how many times I've been tempted to grab a pair of tweezers.

Mama shook her head. "Your father and I have shelled out thousands for this wedding on Saturday and I advise you to be there."

I lost my composure. How dare she tell me what to do?

"Mama, I'm not a child anymore! I don't have to do anything I don't want to do."

She gave this loud obnoxious laugh that sent chills down my spine. "Like I said God is in control, not you, not me."

I swallowed and didn't know what else to say.

Her expression softened as she reached over and patted my hand. "Marriage isn't easy. But you'll learn that soon enough. It takes hard work on both your parts but Jeremy is a good man... a God-fearing man."

"If he feared God then he wouldn't lie to me all the time."

She waved her hand. "Like I said before, he loves you and people in love do stupid stuff. I'm sure you've done a few in your lifetime."

Sure, like dating a married man even though I knew he had a wife.

"You have a lot to learn but there will be plenty of time for that later. Right now you need to get your head on right and whatever you've been doing, needs to stop, now!"

I tried not to flinch. How was it she always knew?

"Call your fiancé and apologize," she ordered, then patted my hand again. "We'll see you on Saturday." She started for the door then swung around and narrowed her gaze at me. "And if you embarrass your father and I..., I swear you'll live to regret it."

With that she left the conference room with me sitting in the chair for the longest time trying to figure out how I got myself in such a mess.

38
JANELLE

I woke up in Frankie's bed, and his arms wrapped around me. I smiled and tried to remember what happened the night before and grinned. It was one of those rare moments when you can lie beside someone and not have sex and I enjoyed it more than I had imagined.

I stuck around long enough for him to make us breakfast, then I went into work. We had several dinner reservations tonight, including the mayor and a few of his colleagues. People can say what they want, but white folks like soul food just as much if not more than us. Once the mayor got a taste of my baked macaroni and ribs, he's been sending one of his aides over to pick him up a special order.

I parked my BMW on the street and was walking along the sidewalk when I passed Frontline, Alphonso's store. I stopped, and did a double-take. In the display window was a slamming jeans jumpsuit with a wide belt and a plunging neckline. As much as I hated Alphonso there was one thing he offered his customer, original pieces. Meaning, if I bought something from him I didn't have to worry about some other bitch buying the same outfit at least not anywhere else in Columbia. And that outfit had my name written all over it.

I went inside the restaurant and walked to the rear where April was sitting at a round table working on the employee schedule for the next pay period. She was better at that than I was.

"April," I called and I strutted over to her in white pencil skirt and a yellow halter top. On my feet were neon green sandals.

"Yeah?" she answered and didn't even bother to look up. Anyone else I would have felt some type of way.

"I need you to do me a favor."

"What kinda favor?" April finally glanced my way with her brow pointed toward the ceiling like she was expecting me to ask her to do something crazy.

"I need you to go next door and buy that jean jumpsuit in the window." I took a seat across from her.

"You mean from that *tacky* store next door?" Her voice was dripping with sarcasm.

"Okay, whatever," I commented with a playful roll of the eyes that sent her giggling.

"Why don't you go and get it yourself?" she teased.

"You know why." I rose and headed back to my office.

Fifteen minutes later April appeared at my door. "Al says if you want it then you need to come and get it yourself."

I gasped. "*What*? You told him it was for me?"

She had the nerve to try and look offended. "*Really?*"

I shrugged. "I'm just saying…"

"You know me better than that. Al said he saw you salivating when you walked by his window."

I blew out along breath and muttered, "Bastard."

"If you want it then you better go get it before someone else does." With that she left me to figure out what I wanted to do.

I sat at my desk until lunch time thinking about how good that outfit would look on me before I finally sprung from my chair. "Fuck it."

I strutted over to the shop and stepped inside. Damn! He really had upgraded the place. I tried to pretend I wasn't impressed by how upscale the store actually looked but I was. It was nothing like that little hole-in-the-wall he had on Vandiver Road.

His skinny little sales associate came over to assist me. "Can I help you?"

I nodded. "I would like to see that jumpsuit in the window." I turned around to point at what I was talking about and gasped. It was gone.

"Oh I'm sorry. I took that down a few minutes ago. Alphonso said it was no longer for sale. But I have a few other styles on the rack near the right of the store," she said trying to ease the disappointment.

I glared at her and without another word I headed toward the back. There was only one outfit I was interested in and Al knew it.

His door was shut but I didn't even bother knocking. But what I stepped inside and saw, I wasn't prepared for. He was sitting behind his desk whacking his dick to a porno that was playing on a flat screen mounted in the corner.

"Oh shit!" he hollered, jumping up from his chair.

I shook my head with disgust. "By all, means don't let me interrupt. I just came for my outfit."

He stood there, smiling while I watched him put his small package away. Sex with him would have truly been a waste of time. "Jae, I was just thinking about you."

"I bet you were," I murmured and glanced up at the actress on the screen. If her ass was bigger she and I could have been twins.

Reaching for a remote he pressed the big red button and flicked off the television. "What can I do for you?"

I stared at him. "I want to buy that jumpsuit. You know it's perfect for me." I kept my voice soft and even.

Alphonso was quiet for a long time as he settled back onto his chair, smiling. "Of course it is. I was wondering how long it was gonna take you to come and ask about it."

I leaned over the desk, making sure the tops of my breasts were on full display. "Well, I'm asking about it now. How much is it?"

There was that coy smile of his. "For you it's free." His eyes traveled all over my body. "Damn you got some sexy legs. What time do they open?"

I couldn't stop myself from laughing. I wasn't interested in his sexual favors, especially now that I've seen what he's working with. "The last shot you had of getting any of this pussy was when you decided to move in next door to me. Now it's strictly business."

The smile slipped from his lips. "That's too bad. I was hoping we could work something out." He rose and walked around his desk with his jeans unzipped.

"The only thing we can do is negotiate a deal, otherwise you can find another buyer," I said with enough attitude I hoped he knew I was serious.

He walked up to me, crowding my personal space, and had the nerve to run the pad of his thumb across my lip. "Give me a hundred dollars and the outfit's yours." Alphonso was staring at me with those big eyes of his and I got so caught up in looking at him that I didn't hear those familiar footsteps until it was too late.

"I knew yo ass was fucking around!"

I jerked around to find Kaleb standing in the doorway, chest heaving, hands balled at his side. "Oh shit!" I'm sure things looked suspicious. "Kaleb it's not what—"

"Don't!" he barked as he stood in the doorframe glaring from me back to Alphonso. "Don't lie! I can see what's going on here. This is that same mothafucka who bumped into me at the restaurant!"

This didn't look good at all. "Baby, it's not what you think," I said as calmly as I could manage, although I was starting to get nervous at the crazed look in his eye.

"Who's this punk-ass nigga?" Kaleb said and was trying to get past me so he could step up to Alphonso. But I wasn't having it.

"Nobody," I said hoping I could diffuse the situation with a smile and the purr of my voice. But that fool wasn't listening.

"You don't want none of this," Alphonso taunted and tossed his hands in the air. I jumped between them.

"I was just leaving. Kaleb let's go back to the restaurant." I moved toward the door hoping he would follow, but the second I stepped away from Alphonso, Kaleb lunged forward and landed a blow at the side of Alphonso's head. I screamed and jumped in just as Al got Kaleb with a jab in the stomach.

"Stop it!" I cried and tried to pull Kaleb away.

"I'm tired of this dude disrespecting me!" Kaleb cried as I tried to drag him toward the door.

Alphonso had the nerve to start laughing. "I don't know what the fuck you talking about. Nigga I was getting that pussy long before you caught your first whiff."

"Excuse me?" I said, eyes wide with outrage, and just because of his slick-ass remark, I released Kaleb's arm. He lunged forward and grabbed Alphonso in a head lock and the two landed onto his desk and then down with a loud crash onto the floor.

"Why you gonna sit there and tell that damn lie? I ain't never let you smell my goodies and you know it!" I yelled and kicked Alphonso in the leg with my right heel for lying.

I heard running feet and his sales clerk came rushing into the office to see what was going on. Alphonso and Kaleb both jumped to their feet. And the two of us watched in horror. Kaleb was landing punches but then Alphonso got the advantage and punched Kaleb right in the jaw so hard, I practically felt the pain.

"You bitch-ass nigga! You need to stay the fuck away from my fiancée," Kaleb hissed and rushed Alphonso so fast he rammed him hard into the wall knocking the television off the stand and onto the floor with a crash.

"You want me to call the police?" The sales clerk looked scared to death as we both jumped out the way.

I shook my head. "No, these two will get tired eventually," I said. "Go on back to work," I instructed then took a seat in the chair near the window and crossed my arms. The two of them were now rolling around on the floor, like idiots.

"Do you have any idea how stupid the two of you look?" I said.

They stopped, got up from the floor, then went back to throwing punches at the sides and stomachs. *Idiots.*

"Enough!" I screamed and got between the two of them. Kaleb had his arms around Alphonso's neck. I pried his fingers loose. "Stop it I said!" I guess my screaming finally got their attention.

Kaleb backed up, breathing heavy. "Why you lie to me?"

I glared at him. "I wasn't lying. There ain't shit going on between me and this knucklehead except that he stole my space and opened this got-damn store!" It was then I noticed the jumpsuit folded on a shelf in the corner. I walked over, picked it up and examined it to make sure it looked as good as it had in the window then I reached inside my purse and tossed a hundred dollar bill on the desk. "It was a pleasure doing business with you." Alphonso was sitting in his chair, nose all bloody. Men can be so stupid.

I turned and stormed out of his office and had just stepped out onto the sidewalk when Kaleb came limping beside me.

"You don't have anything to say?" he asked with this incredulous look on his face. Not to mention his lip was busted and he was holding his side. He looked more pathetic than ever.

"Nope, nothing. I was in the shop buying a jumpsuit and you just *assumed* there was more going on. I need a man in my life who trusts me."

"*Are you fucking serious?*" he said like I needed to lie.

I stopped and swung around. "Kaleb, I thought you were supposed to be taking medication?"

"I am," he replied defensively.

"Then the shit ain't working. So until it does, stay the fuck away from me!" I snapped, then walked inside the restaurant.

<u>39</u>
NYREE

"Good morning, Mrs. Samuels."

I rolled over with a smile on my lips. "Good morning."

It's been two weeks since we were married and I hadn't regretted a moment of it. The church had been filled to capacity and my parents were quite pleased. None of the Samuels's attended. Jeremy said it didn't matter but I could tell it bothered him. Mama made sure to fill the pews on the groom's side with church members. We had yet to have any of them call to congratulate us. But Jeremy said, as long and he and I made it to the church, then that's all that mattered.

"You want some breakfast?" I asked even though I already knew he did. He loved my cooking.

"If you feel like cooking," he said and kissed me once, twice then drew back and stared into my eyes. Have I mentioned how much I loved this man?

I felt his dick harden against my thigh and being the gentleman he is, he waited for some kinda hint that I wanted to make love. I fought back a groan and reminded myself I needed to continue to be patient because the more confident he became the better our relationship would be in the end. I just needed to continue showing my love with words of affirmation.

With a moan I reached down and squeezed his erection and instantly Jeremy sprang into action. I smiled and allowed him to ease my nightgown off my body and closed my eyes. Lord forgive me, but as he kissed his way down to my kitty-kat, I started thinking about Timmy pounding his dick deep inside of me. There had been nothing gentle about our lovemaking at his apartment like the stuff Jeremy was doing right now. Hell no, it had been rough, hard, and so fucking arousing! Often I found my mind drifting off. I keep remembering how good the sex had always been between us and I have even been comparing the two men. Lord, I know it's wrong on so many levels only I couldn't help it no matter how much I tried. Sometimes a girl just wants to be fucked. But as Jeremy slipped his dick inside and started stroking, I moaned and reminded myself this was my husband and the Lord put this together, not us. Mama had been right. Jeremy was the man God had sent to me.

I locked my legs around him and started gyrating my hips and tightened my vaginal muscles so I could feel everything he was pounding me with. Don't get me wrong. Sex was good with my husband. I just made the mistake of experiencing something far better.

That evening I had been drinking but I remembered Timmy fucking me all over his apartment—starting at the front door and working our way back to his kitchen counter.

"I'm about to come," I heard Jeremy hiss, breaking into my thoughts. But it was the memories of Timmy pounding me in the shower with my legs up around his waist that had me crying out this morning.

"Yesss, yesss, baby!"

When Jeremy was finished, he rolled over looking quite proud of his performance. I felt so guilty I couldn't even look him in the eyes—so I closed mine.

"I love you, Mrs. Samuels."

I smiled and whispered, "I love you too."

I got up, showered, and threw on a cute white robe Jeremy had bought me at Victoria's Secrets then went down the hall into the kitchen and started the bacon. By the time I was scrambling eggs, Jeremy entered the kitchen.

"I brought the fellowship." He held up the bible and *Our*

Daily Bread in his hand.

"Oh good," I replied as I poured eggs onto a plate. After the thoughts I was having this morning, bible scriptures were exactly what I needed. I had every intention of being a good and faithful wife no matter what obstacles came our way.

We sat down, said grace, and started eating our food. Fellowship was always saved for the end of our meal.

"Baby, we need to finish clearing out my house today so I can have it cleaned before the open house next Saturday."

"We'll get it done," he reassured me.

"I hope so," I said with a sigh and then reached for my coffee. "I didn't realize just how much crap I had until I started moving everything over here."

"How long have you been in that place?" he asked between chews.

I took another sip of my coffee while I tried to remember. "Wow! I think almost five years. I was planning on buying a bigger house this fall but I guess that wasn't in God's plan," I said with a sigh and a smirk. "I'm just excited about the life ahead for us in Hawaii."

"Yeah," he mumbled and then I noticed the way Jeremy's eyes shifted down to his plate.

"What's wrong?" I asked and had a feeling I wasn't going to like what he was about to say.

"Angel, I don't know how to tell you this but... we won't be going to Hawaii."

"What?" There was no way I had heard him right. But his eyes were shifting everywhere but at me and I knew what he said had to be true. "Why aren't we going?"

"Political bull crap. Someone internal applied for the administrator position and when I got it he filed an appeal. Apparently it was reviewed by personnel and he was awarded the position."

I'd worked in human resources long enough to understand the appeals process. I didn't like it but who in their right mind would fight federal regulations? "And what happens with you?"

"I have been encouraged to apply for other positions

within the Department of Transportation." He shrugged. "Well, at least I still have my current job."

I suddenly lost my appetite. There was no way in hell this was happening. I had been looking forward to moving away and starting a new life with my husband.

"Are you mad that we're not going?"

My eyes shifted to him. "Of course I'm mad but there's nothing we can do about it now, is there?" I rose and carried my plate over to the trash and scraped it then moved to the sink and started washing dishes.

"I knew you were going to be mad!"

I swung around so fast I noticed Jeremy flinch. "Of course I'm mad. I thought we were moving to Hawaii in a few weeks!"

Now he was shaking his head with this look of disbelief. "That's the only reason why you married me."

No, that wasn't completely true. But maybe just a little. "I married you because I love you. But I'm not gonna lie, if I had known you weren't going anywhere then I wouldn't have rushed to marry you."

"So then it *is* the only reason why." He was actually whining like a big ass baby.

"Call it whatever you want. I just said I was still going to marry you I just would have waited until the spring." I swung around and started washing dishes. Jeremy got all quiet while he finished eating his food. Let him pout! I don't care.

I continued washing dishes and didn't bother to turn around as I said, "What you fail to understand is this isn't *just* about you. I've been busting my ass, trying to pack up my house and move over here. And let's not forget that I initiated a transfer with my National Guard unit. Hell, I even turned in my resignation for my full-time job! So, like I said… this isn't *just* about you Jeremy." I could just see going back to work on Monday and telling my boss I wasn't leaving and asking for my job back. I already hated his ass enough as it was.

"Angel, I'm sorry. What is it that you want me to do?" There was a sadness in his voice that made me put the plate down and return to my seat.

"Nothing." I blew out a breath. "I know it's not your fault you didn't get the position."

Jeremy nodded then looked up at me and I could tell whatever he was about to say was difficult. "Does that mean you want a divorce?"

My eyes widened. "Divorce? Of course not!" I reached over and took his hand and noticed he'd been biting his fingernails again. "I married you Jeremy Lee Samuels because I love you and for no other reason."

"You're sure?" There was that insecurity again.

"I'm positive." Leaning forward, I kissed his lips. And finally the light returned to his eyes. "But if we're going be staying in Missouri then we definitely need to either move into my house or find a bigger place."

"Anything you want Angel," he replied, then rose and carried his plate to the sink. As he turned I noticed a weird smirk on Jeremy's face and I couldn't help but wonder if we were ever really moving to Hawaii.

40

JANELLE

Kaleb was crazy in so many ways. He was selfish and controlling and had absolutely no respect for me or our relationship yet I thought about him all damn day.

I couldn't understand it and was starting to think that maybe I needed to see a shrink. Because no one should have that much control over you. Maybe that's what made him such a master manipulator. And then there were the daily texts from him, expressing his love and asking for a second chance. According to the three dozen voice messages, he had learned his lesson and was going to be good to me from now on. Every time I heard his voice, I felt myself softening up to him, especially when I heard his son in the background.

Speaking of CJ....

He had called my phone to ask if I could take him to see his therapist because Kaleb was in a meeting. Lord knows I wanted to say no but I knew someone had to take the poor kid, otherwise, he would stop getting help. I don't know why I felt like I needed to save those two. They weren't my problem. But yet I felt somewhat responsible.

I left the restaurant around two and drove over to West Junior High.

"Hey," CJ said and climbed into my car.

"Hey you," I said, reached over and squeezed his hand. "How was school?"

"Fine."

"Good." And then the conversation ended. Even though I

knew it annoyed him, I turned up the music and sang along with Beyoncé. Anything was better than the awkward moment. That feeling of sorrow was back and I just couldn't shake it no matter how loud I sang.

I parked the car then walked inside with him and took a seat in the waiting room. CJ started rocking on the seat. I blew out a long breath then started surfing the net on my cellphone.

"Are you coming back home?"

I looked up and noticed that the others sitting in the waiting room were looking at me out the corners of their eyes. "I'm not sure," I said low enough so that everyone wasn't in our business.

"How come?" he whined.

"Because your dad and I are having problems. But what's going on between me and your father has nothing to do with you." I felt compelled to say that because it wasn't CJ's fault his dad was crazy, although it was his father's fault that CJ was.

"Christopher Kerrington!"

He rose and looked like he had been called to the principal's office. I blew out a long breath. His father should be here with him. Not me.

CJ was walking out the waiting room when he stopped and looked over his shoulder. "Ms. Jae, are you gonna be here when I get back?"

As much as I didn't want to, I nodded. "I'll be right here."

With a nod, he followed the nurse back to the therapist's office. I crossed my legs and shifted through my emails while I waited. Of course Kaleb showed up while I was texting. He glared down at my phone but I ignored him and finished my message before I acknowledged him.

"CJ's been in there for about fifteen minutes," I commented with a phony smile.

He nodded and looked like he wanted to say something but thought better of it. Good decision. Kaleb was standing there looking fine as ever in navy blue slacks, a striped shirt, burgundy tie, and designer wingtip shoes. It was a shame the mothafucka was crazy.

"I'm going back. You gonna still be here when he gets out?"

I nodded. "Yes. I promised CJ I'd wait."

He bobbed his head again then walked on back.

I sat there thinking how dysfunctional the three of us would be as a family. And I thought the Foxes were a hot mess.

I was playing *Words with Friends* when Kaleb came out looking more upset than when he walked in.

"Where's CJ?"

He pointed toward the rear. "He'll be out in a minute. But before he does I wanted to tell you what he said in his session today."

Finally, a breakthrough! I was all ears. I followed him outside the building and around to the side. The entire time I was dying of anticipation. "Okay, so what's up?" I asked.

Kaleb's gaze met me head-on. "He told his therapist when I'm not at home, you mistreat him."

There was no way in hell I was hearing him right. "*Excuse me?*"

He shrugged. "Don't get mad I'm just telling you what he had said."

"You know that isn't true." I searched his eyes to see if Kaleb believed me but his expression was hard to read.

He glanced over his shoulder as if he was concerned CJ might show up at any moment. "He told her when I'm not around you call him stupid and talk about him."

I can't even begin to tell you how much that pissed me off. Everything I tried to do for that kid, clothes, toys, allowances, and this is the way he treated me!

I sucked my teeth and replied as politely as I could manage. "And what did you say?"

He hesitated. "I told the counselor that didn't sound like you but I would talk to you about it."

"*Doesn't sound like me?*" I was appalled. Thank goodness no one else was standing outside but us. "You should have told them, hell no! You know I wouldn't do that." I didn't like kids, but I have never mistreated one in my life. I didn't appreciate that.

"Why are you getting all upset?" he snarled toward me.

I couldn't take it any longer. *"Really*? Your son has the therapist thinking I'm beating him when you're not around!"

"Okay, then we'll fix it when we get home." He tossed his hands in the air like it was that simple. I just stood there sulking and didn't respond.

"Are you fucking serious? Now you mad! Jae, it's not always about you. My son has an issue with lying and we'll take care of it." He shook his head as if I was the one being ridiculous. "You're *so* damn worried about what other people think about you."

"Hell yeah I care what other people think, especially when I didn't even wanna be bothered with somebody else's kid in the first place!"

"Oh, so you're saying my son is a bother?" He now had a nasty scowl on his face.

"I'm saying this is what I get for doing something I shouldna been doing in the first damn place."

"So what are you saying? Huh Jae? You ready to end this?" He was definitely agitated.

"See that's the problem with you. Every single argument ends with splitting up. And I'm sick of it!"

"I don't care about what you're sick of," he mumbled. "You didn't wanna be with me and my son in the first damn place."

"Then why the hell am I here? It wasn't like you put a gun to my head or had something that I wanted." I lied. "Hell no! I'm with you because I want to be with you not because I have to be, but you're too stupid to see that."

"So what do you wanna do, Jae?" He was edging me on.

I swallowed and watched my chances of getting my hands on all that money go up in smoke. "I'm saying... It's time for me to get off this roller coaster ride."

Kaleb suddenly looked like a crazed lunatic. "Then go tell CJ that!" He pointed toward the door. "Tell him you don't wanna be with us anymore!"

"Whatever. You fucking tell him!" I hissed. "I told you

about always getting him involved in what's going on between us. That's why the kid is fucked up in the head."

"Okay, now you're talking about my son!"

I pointed a finger in his face. "Face it. The boy has problems. He's thirteen and walks around carrying little men in his pocket!"

Kaleb shook his head and stuffed his hands in his own pockets like he was afraid he might do something else. *Good decision.* "Yeah you're right. It's time for us to go our separate ways," he muttered.

I don't know why but I started laughing like a crazy woman. Maybe because I was so fucking mad, my head was spinning. "Well about damn time! I'm glad we can finally agree on something!" I tossed my hand over my head and stormed across the parking lot to my car.

41

NYREE

I got up on Saturday and spent the better part of the morning paying bills. Jeremy and I had finally opened joint accounts and I was staring down at the checks with both of our names on them, grinning.

Last week we had sat down and put together a monthly budget and then determined just how much we needed to deposit in both our checking and savings. I loved the way my husband and I were able to work together as a team. One of the fellowship books we had studied talked about finances and marriage, and we followed the guide inside to the letter. According to the book, money, sex and kids were the three main reasons for divorce. I didn't want any to be a problem in our marriage.

As soon as I paid the last bill online, I walked into the living room where Jeremy was sitting on the couch, watching a baseball game and lowered beside him.

"Baby, you wanna start moving stuff back into my house today?" Once I discovered we weren't moving to Hawaii, I had taken my house off the market.

"Sure, Angel, whatever you want to do." I loved the way he was always so agreeable. It made being married to him so easy.

"I was thinking... after we get the house situated, how

about we go down and pick up Jasmine and let her stay with us for a week. I'm sure Mama wouldn't mind watching her while we're at work?" Instead of answering, Jeremy started biting his nails and then went back to watching television. "Baby did you hear me?"

He sighed. "Yes, I heard you. I'll have to ask her mother and see what she says."

"*What she says?*" I mocked with an incredulous look. "Adopted or not, that's your daughter."

Jeremy shook his head and I could see he was trying to keep his temper in check. "Yeah that's what I thought but apparently that isn't the case."

I gave a rude snort. "Mia doesn't have a problem cashing that child support check from you every month." I write the checks and the amount he was paying was enough to make his rent payment.

"That's because it's always been about the money with Mia."

"Well I want to spend time getting to know my stepdaughter." I figured I had a better chance of making an impression in the younger child's life than I did the older ones. Teenagers were usually already set in their ways. I was disappointed we never got to spend any time with his other children during the summer. They either had summer jobs or were involved in sports. Personally, I think those were just excuses. "Call her."

Jeremy took a deep breath and nodded like a little boy. "Yes, ma'am. I'll call her during the next commercial break."

During the break, I went and made some nachos while he grabbed his phone and went into the other room to call. I didn't trip because I knew he needed his privacy and, personally, I didn't want to hear what the two of them had to talk about.

Jeremy was coming from the bedroom by the time I was walking into the living room. "What did she say?"

Jeremy grinned. "She said I can have her for two weeks."

"Cool."

I could tell there was something else he wanted to say, but

I waited until we were curled back up on the couch together to see if he'd share what was on his mind.

"I wanna talk about something." See, I knew it.

I rested my head on his chest and said, "Sure, what's up?"

There was hesitation which is never a good sign. "Jasmine has a friend... a little playmate."

"Uh-huh." I had no idea where this was going.

"Mia's been raising her for years." Okay, now he was procrastinating. It was probably a good idea to urge him to get straight to the point but I had one question first.

I raised up so he could see me. "Where's her mother?"

Jeremy frowned. "Around... sometimes, but she doesn't like being around her."

What kinda woman doesn't like being around her own child unless... "Was her mother raped or something?"

He swallowed and then slowly wagged his head. "Mia's never said but I think she was. Anyway, ummm, the girls are always together and she wants to know if Caitlyn could come to?"

What the fuck? I already had five stepchildren. Now I had to be a stepmother to another. "Hell no."

"No?" Don't you know my husband had the nerve to look offended?

"No. I want a chance to get to know Jazzy, *not* babysit. Mia ain't dumping her excess baggage off on us!"

Apparently Jeremy didn't get it because he clearly looked confused. "What difference does it make? She'll be good company for Jazz."

"It makes a big difference!" Clearly he wasn't hearing me. "The way you're acting you must have already told Mia it's okay."

He sat there looking like he'd been scolded again.

"Dammit Jeremy! I wanna spend a week getting to know my new daughter. That's it. Nobody else. So you make sure you call her back."

I was so sick and tired of his shit! I got up from the couch and went to our bedroom to watch TBS. I was through dealing with the drama of his kids. It was enough I didn't know he had four only to find out he has another.

It was almost at the end of the movie when I heard Jeremy coming down the hall. I looked up to see him standing in the doorway.

"Angel, you're right. I'll tell her we're just getting Jazzy."

I nodded, even though I had a feeling this conversation was far from over.

<u>42</u>

JANELLE

"Please let her be a'ight."

I was driving like a crazy woman trying to get to the University Hospital and Clinics. I had gotten a call Mommy's sugar had dropped so low she was delirious.

Ever since I caught her in bed with Uncle Todd I hadn't been around anymore than needed, and now I was praying for a chance to talk to my mother again.

By the time I made it to the emergency room I was frantic. The nurse directed me to her room and I hurried down the long hall. The moment I stepped inside, I released a sigh of relief. Mommy was sitting up in bed watching television.

"Mommy, you scared me!" I said as I came around to the side of the bed and pressed my lips to her cheek. It felt so good to be able to do that again.

She waved her hand dismissively. "I don't know why they're making such a fuss. I'm fine."

I lowered onto one of those hard plastic chairs. "Mommy you couldn't have been okay, otherwise your nurse wouldna called the ambulance."

"All she had to do was give me some orange juice," she explained with a scowl.

"She wasn't risking her license fooling with your mess." She just scowled, which pissed me off even more. "Mommy you really need to start listening to your doctor before you lose more than a leg."

For once she actually looked scared.

A nurse came in and checked her vital signs and explained they were waiting for her blood work to come back before she could be released. I figured we'd be there at least another hour or two so I clicked on the evening news and eased back on the chair. It was my Saturday off, so I had nothing but time.

We were sitting there talking when I heard a soft knock and the curtain was pulled back. As soon as I saw who was standing there, I frowned. "What are you doing here?"

"I just found out your mother had been brought in," he said, ignoring my tone.

As much as I wanted to be angry at Uncle Todd's sorry behind for showing up, there was no denying the concern in his eyes.

"Sweetie, how are you feeling?"

Mommy waved an impatient hand. "I'm fine, really. It was a little scare. I just need to remember I can't be skipping lunch."

"No, you can't," he scolded and anyone could see he cared about my mother. However, that didn't stop me from mumbling under my breath.

She patted his hand. "Todd... can you give me and Jae a few minutes alone, please?"

He hesitated but finally nodded, kissed her cheek, and stepped back out of the room. I leaned back in the chair and waited.

"I owe you an apology," she finally said.

"Yes, you do," I said and crossed my arms. I know I was acting like a spoiled brat but I didn't care. "How could you do that to Daddy?"

"*Do that to him?* What about what he did to me all those years!" she cried and I flinched. Never and I mean never in the twenty years he's been dead had she ever mentioned the way he'd treated her. "I was nothing but a good wife to him. Cooking, cleaning and raising his children yet nothing I did was ever good enough."

She was right. It never was.

"So why didn't you leave him?"

Mommy sighed. "I tried."

"You did?" That was news to me. "When?" I pressed on, hoping to get her to continue.

Mommy nodded and suddenly had this distant look in her eyes. "Chile, I tried to leave him so many times I lost count! But each and every time he would make me feel so sorry for him I took him back."

The same way he used to do to me. Daddy would play on my sympathy, beg me to forgive him.

The same way Kaleb does.

"But after a while I got tired of the mood-swings. One afternoon I packed you and Brice up and left."

I wanted to ask her how old I was but I was afraid if I asked too many questions she'd stop talking so I just sat there and waited for her to continue.

She shifted on the bed. "I went to live with my sister, but Bradley used to come over and act a damn fool all the time. He had your auntie so scared I decided to leave."

"Why didn't you get your own place?" I blurted out.

"With what?" she snorted. "My good looks? I didn't have money like that. I wasn't working. So I went back to your father and once he knew I had nowhere else to turn, that's when he got crazy. Nan couldn't even control her own son." She paused long enough to scratch her stomach through the hospital gown. "Once he started beating me again, I knew I would never be able to get away from that man. I tried going to the police but that was a waste of time. He was a cop! They were all Bradley's buddies and they never did anything except tell me they'd talk to him. Yet it didn't matter how many black eyes or busted lips, they still wouldn't charge him. And he knew it."

My stomach flipped when I spotted a tear running down her cheek she didn't even bother wiping away. "When he started beating you and Brice, I realized just how helpless I was to do anything to help us."

I was lost in thought as I remembered the way Mommy used to try and protect us the best way she knew how. One time Brice was playing baseball in the yard and had broken the window in the kitchen. Mommy lied and said she didn't know what happened just to save us from a beating—Brice for breaking it, and me for failing to keep my brother out of trouble.

"By the time Todd had returned to Columbia and had rejoined the police force, things had gotten so bad I was just trying to keep the entire neighborhood from knowing what was going on in our house."

We all were. But according to Frankie, they had known our dirty secret.

Mommy looked at me with a sad smile. "Right off the bat, Todd could tell something wasn't right at the house, so he asked me about it. I denied it and when he confronted your father, Bradley came storming home." She paused and drew a shaky breath. "That was the first time I was actually afraid he was going to kill one of us."

A shivered raced up my spine at the memory. *The dungeon.* It was our nickname for the basement where he used to lock us when we were bad. After Uncle Todd had questioned him, my father had locked all three of us in the basement for the weekend. The dungeon was damp and full of mice. He used to unscrew all the light bulbs so the room was dark. At night, we used to climb to the top step and pray the mice didn't come up there.

"Right after that last weekend in the dungeon, Todd came over while your father was at the range, and told me you told him about the beatings."

"That was because he had touched my shoulder and I flinched!" I cried in a panic and realized I was still afraid of Daddy finding out I had told.

"It doesn't matter. By that time, I just lost it and told Todd everything."

I was afraid to ask but I did. "What happened?"

"I confronted him."

At the boom of Uncle Todd's voice, the color drained from my face. I watched him step back into the room and lower on the edge of the bed. This time I didn't ask him to leave because I wanted—correction—I needed to know. "What happened?" I dared to ask and noticed I was whispering.

"I told Brad I was giving him to the end of the week to pack his shit and get out of that house. After that I was going down to the precinct with your mother to file charges that I was going to make sure stuck." Uncle Todd turned, gazed at my mother then reached for her small hand. As soon as I saw the way the two of them looked at each other, there was no denying the love.

"Did you kill Daddy?" I asked suspiciously.

He looked at Mommy, meeting her watery eyes. "Go ahead and tell her," she whispered.

I felt the hairs at the back of my neck stand up. "Tell me what?" I asked although I was afraid at what he was about to say.

Uncle Todd finally looked my way and said, "I didn't kill Brad. Your father killed himself."

<u>43</u>

NYREE

I was sitting at my kitchen table reading the newspaper when the phone on the wall rang. Frowning, I went to retrieve the call. The only people who had the number to the apartment were doctor's offices and telemarketers. Neither Jeremy nor I had an appointment so I was all prepared to cuss someone out for disturbing my Sunday morning. "Hello?"

"Is Jeremy there?"

This didn't sound like any telemarketer I knew. *Not with all that attitude.* "Who's asking?"

"This is Mia." She said pronouncing every single syllable slowly like I was illiterate or something. I wasn't about to let her know she had ticked me off.

Somehow I managed to respond without a touch of attitude, "Hello Mia, this is Jeremy's wife, Nyree."

She made a tsk sound. "Hello Nyree. You tell that mothafucka I want my child support!"

"We sent you your child support." Like I said before, I pay all the bills.

"No, I've only been getting *half* my child support. I'm still waiting on the other half."

Half? What the fuck! "I don't know anything about that so I'll have to have my husband call you when he gets back from the gym," I said innocently. "But while I have you on the phone, I wanna thank you for allowing us to have Jasmine come down."

"Excuse me, Nyree, but I didn't even know Giggles was married. And now that I do, I understand why he suddenly has an interest in being a daddy. He must be trying to impress you."

"*Impress?* I'm the one who told him to call and get Jasmine. My husband wants to be a father to his daughter. I mean come on, Mia, you conned the man into adopting your daughter, then you want child support, but yet he has to beg you to spend time with her."

"First off, I didn't con him into doing shit!" This wench truly had a lot of nerve barking at me.

"*Oh really?* He's paying for a child that isn't even his and then you have the *audacity* to ask us to keep her little friend Caitlyn as well. So tell me what do you call it?"

"I call it a mothafucka who's got you fooled." That bitch had the nerve to start laughing. "Now believe it or not because I really don't give a fuck either way, but Jasmine isn't adopted. That's Jeremy's *biological* daughter."

Her words sent chills down to my toes. "What?"

"You heard me. And since you *know* so much, Caitlyn ain't nobody's *little friend*. She's that mothafucka's daughter, too."

I felt a wave of panic and stumbled back over to the table and practically fell on the chair.

"Hell, I'll even email you their fucking birth certificates if you don't believe me."

I wasted no time in giving her my email address. Because before I tore into my husband's ass I needed proof.

"You tell him I better have my money wired in the morning or I'm calling my lawyer." And then there was a click.

I paced back and forth waiting for the email. An hour later, still nothing. It took everything I had to keep it together when he came home from the gym. While Jeremy showered, I checked my email on my phone for the twentieth time feeling hopeful that Mia had been simply messing with me, but sure enough there was an email with an attachment waiting. I went over to the computer we kept in the back bedroom and took a seat. As I clicked Download, my heart raced like crazy. *Please let it be a lie.* I prayed over and over again and when the file finally opened my heart sank.

Jeremy's name was on both birth certificates. And just in case I still thought Jasmine was adopted, Mia also included a copy of Jasmine's footprints, taking the day she was born. *Baby Girl Samuels.* So much for being adopted.

I printed off a copy and gazed down at the evidence. Either Mia was good or they were both Jeremy's daughters.

I was lying across the bed when he stepped out of the bathroom wrapped in a towel.

"How was your workout?" I asked, trying to remain calm.

Jeremy had the nerve to be smiling. "It was good. You really need to come and join the gym with me," he urged and walked over to his dresser.

"We might have to do that," I mumbled then watched as he rubbed baby oil all over his hairless body. *Lying bastard.* "Did you get a chance to talk to Mia about Jasmine?"

He shook his head. "Nah, she hasn't returned my call but I'm definitely going to tell her what my wife and I decided."

I rolled over to the edge of the bed and said, "Oh well, then you might want to give her a ring. She called while you were out running. We had a pretty interesting conversation."

He shot me a look. "What?"

Nodding, I slipped my feet into my sandals. "Oh yeah, she said to tell you the other half of her child support was late."

At first he tried to play as if he had no idea what I was talking about but I guess he figured that move wasn't going to work so he tried that dry laughter of his. "Oh yeah. I'll send that to her in the morning."

I think my puzzled expression frightened him. "Now I'm confused. I thought we paid your child support for the month?"

He gave a nervous head shake and replied casually, "No baby, you must have confused what I said. That was only half. We have to pay that same amount again in two weeks. But I guess she changed her mind and wants it all at once."

He had some damn nerve trying to act like I was the one who was confused. "Hmmm, so I guess I'm stupid now, right?" I said and noticed the way his big shiny bald head was sweating as I reached down on the side of the bed for my purse. "So tell me... is Jasmine really adopted?"

He blew out his breath the way he always does when he doesn't want to answer the question. "Angel, what difference does it make?" he asked suspiciously.

I looked at him with sheer disgust because that's exactly what I was feeling at this point. "Oh it makes a difference, so I'm going to ask you again, is Jasmine adopted?" I paused, then added, "Oh and once you get done answering, let's discuss Caitlyn too." The color drained from his face. I was hoping he would just confess everything. Instead, he took forever to speak again. That was all the proof I needed to confirm what I already knew—I was married to a liar.

Jeremy was slipping into a pair of boxers as he said softly, "Nyree, I wish I could answer that, but I honestly don't know if they're really my daughters."

My eyes nearly popped from their sockets. "Oh my God! Here we go again! When are you gonna stop with the lies?"

He turned to me. "I'm not lying."

What hurt most was that my husband really thought I was an idiot. He managed to fool me before and he really thought he could fool me again. *Sorry, not this time.* "From the word go, you've lied to me. You've lied about kids, jobs, moving to Hawaii, degrees you didn't have and now a three and a four-year-old I had no idea you had. I am sick of it. You hear me! Sick of it!"

"Angel... I just—"

"Save it!" I screamed, wishing I had followed my mind and not my heart with this man. "I've had it with the lies and I've definitely had it with you!" I left the apartment before the first tear had fallen. There was no way I was giving Jeremy the satisfaction of knowing just how devastated I was over this entire situation.

44

JANELLE

We had just finished the lunch rush and I was showing a contractor a small leak in the ceiling when the door to the restaurant opened. I looked over and spotted CJ heading my way. There were still several customers talking and eating so I waited until he was close enough before I said, "Why aren't you at school?"

"I left early." CJ shuffled his feet slowly toward me. "Can I talk to you?"

"Where's your father?" I asked and looked toward the door expecting Kaleb to step through the door at any moment.

He shook his head. "He doesn't know I'm here. I caught the bus."

I stood there with a hand at my hip gazing at him with so much resentment, CJ suddenly started rocking on the ball of his feet.

"Come, let's go to my office." I turned and headed toward the back and didn't bother to check and see if he had followed me until I had reached my chair and took a seat. As soon as CJ moved inside, I pointed toward the door. "Close it and have a seat."

"Yes ma'am." He looked so afraid I almost expected him to bolt out the room. Instead he closed the door with a *click* then slipped onto the chair across from me.

"What can I do for you?" I sat there with my arms crossed waiting for him to find the courage to talk. Under normal circumstances, I might have taken pity on the kid and helped eased his mind. But I don't forget that damn easy.

"I-I wanted to tell you... I'm sorry," he stammered nervously.

"Sorry for what?" I asked, while tapping an impatient fingernail onto the table.

"Sorry for lying on you." There was that damn rocking again.

"Help me to understand why you would tell your counselor those lies."

Rock. Rock. "Because I was mad."

"Mad? Mad about what?" I didn't mean to snap, but I did.

"I..." He swallowed. "I was mad because you left me. You promised to be my stepmother." *Rock. Rock. Rock.*

Damn, I did promise. My voice softened. "I know and I am sorry. Sometimes things don't work out the way we want. But, it has nothing to do with you."

His lips quivered. "But I-I was hurt."

"And you think I wasn't hurt when you said those mean things about me to your counselor?" CJ pushed his glasses onto his face and looked on the verge of tears. "All I have tried to do was provide a little normalcy to your life. Lord knows I never had any in my life but I thought you and I understood each other."

"I do—I mean—we do. I was just angry."

"You can't be blurting out and doing things just because you're angry because one of these days you're going to do or say something you can't take back and there..." my throat caught and it took me a second to pull it together, "there can be consequences."

"Yes ma'am," he said with a nod.

"And quit all that rocking. What did your counselor tell you? You have to start being aware of what you're doing."

"Yes ma'am." And then a tear rolled down his cheek. Ugh! The whole situation had me so damn frustrated. Why did I have such a soft spot for this kid? Yet even though I'd rather not be bothered, part of me wanted to do whatever I could to help him.

"I forgive you, but next time, I'm going to be the one popping you upside your head. You understand?" I said bluntly.

He nodded. "Yes ma'am."

A small smile curled my lips. "Now come and give me a hug." I rose and he came around my desk and I wrapped my arms around him and squeezed him almost as tightly as he was holding me. "Just because I'm no longer with your dad that doesn't mean I can't still be a part of your life."

"Okay."

I rubbed his back and kissed his cheek the same way Uncle Todd had the day he found out Daddy had used my right shoulder as an ashtray.

For years I had felt guilty believing it was my fault that my father had been killed. That just my mentioning our family secret it had come back to bite me in the ass. Until a few days ago, Uncle Todd had never mentioned that day and neither had I. Now I knew; I did have a hand in my father's death.

According to Uncle Todd, they had been called to investigate a possible burglary at a warehouse. The intruder fled the scene and dropped his gun onto the floor. Once they found the building all clear, Uncle Todd confronted my father. When he told him he was going to bring him down, revealing what Daddy was doing in front of the entire city, Daddy snatched the gun and shot himself.

He was more of a coward than I had ever imagined.

Uncle Todd covered it up so Daddy died with honor and Mommy could collect his pension. He had also hidden the gun, making sure no one was ever arrested for murdering a cop.

It was going to take a while for me to get used to the two of them being together but since Mommy was home and looked happier than ever, I was willing to try.

I released CJ, then gave him a stern look. "Now just because I've forgiven you that doesn't mean you're off the hook. For the next few weeks, you will be working here in the restaurant a few hours a week, after school."

"Oh cool!" he said and I couldn't believe the way his eyes lit up.

I smiled. "My cousin is leaving, and we need to teach

someone else how to make the cornbread. You think you can handle that?"

CJ nodded his head eagerly. "Yes ma'am."

"C'mon let me show you the kitchen." I draped an arm across his shoulders and led him down the hall.

"Ms. Jae, I think counseling is really helping me," he said as we were walking.

"Really?" I didn't see any real improvement but maybe I was missing something, "Good for you. I was hoping it would."

"Can I tell you something?" he said then stopped.

I turned to face him. "Sure, what do you want to tell me?"

"I think...," he started slowly, "I remember my mother getting killed."

* * *

"Thanks for letting me know he was here."

"No problem." I was standing behind the counter taking a delivery order when Kaleb stepped into the restaurant. Every woman in there was staring at him but the only woman he seemed to have eyes for was me. Not that I was surprised. "I figure this will give him something to do until you get off work."

"I agree." He looked at me as if he was trying to figure me out, which I don't understand. I was the best thing to ever happen to that man. But like so many before him, he was just too stupid to realize it.

"Can I talk to you for a moment?"

"I need to grab some paper towels so you can follow me to the storage room." I turned and walked back and was glad I had worn a yellow sundress with high heel black Jimmy Choos. As soon as I reached the door, I punched in the passcode and waited for him to step inside before shutting the door behind us. "Before you get started, I wanna talk to you about something."

He nodded. "Sure."

"A while back CJ mentioned he remembered his mother."

Kaleb laughed like what I said was ridiculous. "He was too young to remember her."

"That's not true. I remember my father tossing candy into my crib when I was two."

"Yeah, but CJ has always been a little..." he cringed like it was hard to say. "a little slow, and he's never mentioned his mother to me."

"Maybe because you're too busy yelling at the kid that you rarely listen." My voice was laced with sarcasm. "He's mentioned her to me. And today he told me he remembers seeing his mother's murder."

He laughed. "That's impossible."

"Why?"

"Because CJ was with me." He dragged a hand across his hair. "Listen, I think my son just wants attention. He misses you."

"I think it's something he needs to start exploring with his therapist. Maybe there's something hidden that is the cause of all his pain. He still has the little men his mother bought him and that might mean something."

He shrugged and didn't look the slightest bit convinced. "Maybe. I'll have his therapist talk to him and see what she can uncover." He said then cleared his throat and changed the subject. "Speaking of therapy, I want you to know I've started counseling." Leave it to Kaleb to always make things about him and his needs. It was apparent his son would always come second. I guess that's why I felt so sorry for CJ.

"Good for you. What are they treating you for?"

"Bipolar disorder."

Hell, I coulda told him that and saved him a few hundred dollars.

"She's started me on a medication. She said my mind was racing all over the place with negative thoughts."

"Good for you," I replied and was really happy for him.

"I can already feel a difference. I don't know how I was living with that hell in my head for so long."

Neither could I.

He reached for my hand. "All I want to say is don't give

up on us just yet. Please, just give me a chance to get myself together before you find yourself an apartment."

I stared up at Kaleb wanting desperately for things to be different between us but then I thought about my father and all the years my mother used to listen to the same pleas. "I don't know," I started and shook my head.

"Babe, please. I'm going to be a changed man. I promise," he said softly.

He reached for my other hand. And when I stepped away I felt something in my hand. It was my engagement ring.

"Kaleb I told you—"

He backed away out of my reach. "Keep it. That ring belongs to you and when you're ready you can either wear it or mail it back to me."

Without another word, I reached for a roll of paper towels for the bathroom. I was stepping out of the storage room when I ran right smack into someone. "Sorry, I—" my voice stalled when I realized that person was Frankie.

"Hey, I was just in your office looking for you." He was grinning until he saw Kaleb come out of the storage room behind me. Of course men can be so territorial.

"Babe," Kaleb asked eyes narrowed with curiosity, "who is this?"

"I was getting ready to ask her the same thing." Frankie stepped forward and placed his hand at the small of my back.

I looked from one to the other. "Kaleb this is an old friend. Frankie this is Kaleb."

Frankie instantly knew who he was but Kaleb was clueless. I could see him struggling to stay calm and the last thing I wanted was a repeat of what happened at Alphonso's shop. Kaleb was probably two seconds away from going off when CJ picked the perfect time to come out.

"Dad, come see! I made the cornbread for dinner." He signaled with his hand for him to come to the kitchen.

"Here I come, son." Kaleb then turned back to me. "Babe, I'll call you later." He leaned down and kissed my cheek.

As soon as they disappeared I knew it was only for a few minutes and then Kaleb would be back so I needed to get

Frankie out of there.

"So that's your fiancé, huh?"

I squeezed the ring inside the palm of my hand. "Yeah, that's him."

"Are the two of you getting back together?" I was getting ready to say no but something in my eyes must have said something else. He held up his hands in surrender. "Hey, do you."

His comment provoked nothing but attitude. "What the hell does that mean?"

Frankie looked at me, clearly disappointed. "It means you need to figure it out because you can't have it both ways."

I rolled my eyes. Frankie knows how I feel about ultimatums. I get enough from Kaleb. "Who says I'm tryna have it both ways?" I was just feeling overwhelmed right now. That's all. I felt as if I was being pulled in two different directions.

He shook his head. "It's no secret how I feel about you but I'm not gonna sit around forever waiting for you to figure it out. Either you want me or you're gonna be with dude. You need to decide." He pressed his lips to mine, letting his tongue explore my mouth. And then without another word, Frankie turned and walked out the restaurant.

45

NYREE

I woke up on Sunday and it took a few moments for me to realize I was staying back at my house, with Janelle sleeping across the hall.

Is this what my life has become?

I still couldn't believe what Jeremy had done to me after all the promises to come clean and no more lies — only to find out he had lied to me again.

I curled into a fetal position and laid there crying the way I had for the last week. I don't know why I was wasting tears on a man who was truly not worthy of my love but I guess we can't control who we fall in love with.

What I can't understand is how could one man lie so much? It just didn't make any sense to me, especially when I had proven time and time again I was willing to accept him and all his kids despite the lies. Yet he still couldn't just be a man and be honest with me. But why?

"Please Lord. Please take the pain away," I prayed. I just wished I could fast forward my life six months from now. By then, I would be over Jeremy and my life would be back to what it was before.

By the time I made it to the kitchen, Janelle was sitting at the island drinking coffee and Honey was eating from his bowl.

"Hey girl, you going to church this morning?" she asked.

I nodded. "Yes, I can't hide from my mother forever."

She gave me a look like she'll believe it when she sees it

but I ignored her and headed over to the coffee pot.

"You doing the Sunday brunch this morning?"

Janelle nodded. "April took the day off to spend it with her husband's family. So I'm gonna hold it down today." She usually had the day off but every now and again Janelle covered for her. I filled a cup with coffee then reached for the creamer and headed over and slid onto a barstool at the island.

"Have you spoken to Frankie?"

She shook her head and for the first time I saw something on her face that was so unusual for Janelle—frustration.

"Girl, just call him," I urged her.

Janelle took a sip for her mug then looked over at me. "Frankie's not having it. I either come correct, or don't come at all."

"Okay so what's stopping you?"

She tried to look like she had no idea what I meant. Then her expression softened. "I don't know. It wasn't until Frankie gave me that damn ultimatum that I realized how much he really means to me. And that's what really scares me. I thought I was in love with Kaleb, but now I think I feel sorry for him and CJ more than anything else. I just don't know anymore."

I leaned forward. "So what does your heart say?"

Janelle gave me a sad smile. "That's the problem. I don't trust my heart. I've always operated on what I wanted, not what I needed. Now I just don't know which way to turn." She sounded exasperated.

"That's easy. Crazy or sanity?"

Janelle gave me one of her Kool-Aid grins. "You know I like them crazy."

I blew out a long breath as I stirred my coffee. "I know and that's the problem. At some point you need some stability in your life."

"That's what you thought you had with Jeremy and you see how that turned out."

I turned my head, avoiding her gaze and took a sip. "True."

"The beautiful thing is I don't have to make any decisions

about my life. You married your crazy mothafucka, I didn't," she replied with a hand at her hip.

She was right again.

Between sips, she looked at me with skepticism. "I'll be honest. I am really feeling Frankie and I don't want to lose him but at the same time I feel like Kaleb, especially CJ needs me. There is something more going on with that boy. Kaleb said he was too young when his mother died but CJ says he remembers his mother reading and singing to him. I really think his problems…, all that rocking shit, has something to do with her."

My brow rose. "And you wanna save the day?"

She looked like she was trying to digest the idea. "Yeah, actually I do. I went through a lot growing up. More than I've ever shared with you. Frankie knows my pain but not too many others. I know the scars a past can bring. For some of us those wounds never heal."

My eyes shot open wide. "You really do have a heart."

She pointed a finger at me. "Yes and you do too. So do you, bitch, and follow your heart. Nothing worse than living a life of regret. I've been regretting shit for the last twenty years."

There was something sad in her eyes. "Is it something you wanna talk about?"

"Girl, no. That's a closed chapter in my life," she said and waved her hand like she was dismissing me even though something distant in her eyes said her demons were far from gone. Whatever it was I hoped someday she would share with me. "If Jeremy is where your heart is then take his crazy ass back and work through your problems, but he's gotta quit all that lying! Damn! Ain't nothing worse than a liar."

Her eyes met mine and I nodded. Janelle was right but I was starting to think that Jeremy had been lying for so long he didn't know what the truth was anymore. And that was a damn shame. "I don't know anymore. Like Mama always said just turn it over to the Lord and that's what I'm planning on doing."

Janelle nodded. "I better get out of here." She put her mug

in the sink then grabbed her Prada purse off the counter and left the house.

I arrived at church a little earlier than usual. Daddy was up on the front row with all of the deacons but Mama was sitting in her usual spot fanning herself. Knowing her, she had been shouting this morning and worked up a sweat. I decided to seat on the end of the pew near Ms. Chapman. I knew my mother wouldn't dare say anything about Jeremy in front of her friends.

"Good morning, Ms. Chapman," I said, with a wide grin, as I scooted past her and took a seat on the other side.

"Good morning, Nyree," she said softly.

I waited until I was seated to look over at my mother. She just smiled like everything was right in the world. *Maybe Jeremy hadn't called her.* Or maybe she was putting on a good front. Either way I was sure to find out by the end of service.

I waved and lowered my purse to the floor in front of me and got ready for the choir to perform. Within minutes they had the entire congregation off their feet and rocking to the rhythm of the music; I was listening to every word of Kirk Franklin's, *Imagine Me.* By the end of the song, I looked over at the door and gasped as I saw Jeremy walk into the church, holding hands with two beautiful little girls. Anyone could see they were his. They had the same chocolate complexion and big brown eyes. I couldn't move as I watched him point in my direction and then the girls came over.

"Hi, Ms. Nyree," they both said, and had members close by laughing and smiling.

"Hi sweethearts," I answered and patted the spaces beside me. Jeremy took a seat on the other side of Caitlyn. I refused to look at him and focused on the minister as he spoke. Halfway through service Jasmine fell asleep. She was resting her head on me and I draped an arm around her. I truly didn't think I had room in my heart to fall in love with two little girls but I already felt protective of them.

While praying, Jeremy reached over and took my hand in his, and instantly I felt that electrical charge. I turned my head and our eyes met.

"I'm sorry," he mouthed, with tears streaming down his cheeks.

I squeezed his hand and bowed my head, and prayed to the Lord for guidance.

After church I stayed long enough to talk to the girls and Jeremy, as he introduced them to my parents. Of course my mother was already in love. Jeremy promised to bring them by later.

"You have time to go with the girls and I to McDonald's?" he asked, searching my eyes, trying to get a sense of what I was feeling. I nodded then climbed in my car, and waited until he had already pulled off before I texted him and told him I couldn't join them. I know it was the cowardly thing to do but I didn't know how else to handle the situation.

I got back to the house, let Honey out and then took a shower. Once I was under the spray of water, I started crying until I couldn't cry anymore. My heart hurt on so many levels. I loved that man so much and his girls were so adorable I wanted nothing more than to be a part of their lives. But—not if I had to live a life of lies.

While I was lying across the couch I must have dozed off because I woke up hours later when I heard Honey barking. Someone was at the door.

I pulled the door open and there was Jeremy.

"Can I help you?"

He extended his hand and I looked down at it with curiosity before meeting his eyes again. And gasped. There was something there I had never seen before.

Determination.

"Hi, my name is Jeremy Anthony Lee Samuels, Jr. I'm broke, I have six kids, three ex-wives, and I only have an associate's degree. I'm intimidated by my fourth wife and have insecurity issues, but I have so much love to give, but if she'll give me another chance I promise to stop trying to be someone I'm not." His lips trembled and his eyes were so full of remorse; I was so choked up I could barely speak as I shook

306   *Daniels/Campbell*

his hand.

"Hello. My name is Nyree Gail Dawson and it's a pleasure to finally meet you." I was laughing and crying at the same time. I then threw myself into his arms and kissed him.

<u>46</u>

JANELLE

I saw a crowd gathering right outside FoxTrot. I tried to see what was going on without drawing too much attention to my guests, but then I couldn't take it anymore and I had to go out and see.

I pushed out the door and noticed the police cars up and down the street. *What the hell?* My eye scanned the crowd and I spotted Uncle Todd standing off to the side. I made my way over to him.

"Uncle Todd!" I cried.

He turned and his expression softened at the sight of me. We had yet to speak since I'd seen him at the hospital. I figured we'd have to talk eventually, especially since Mommy mentioned the two were talking about moving in together.

"Hey Jae."

As I moved toward him, a cop brushed past me and headed inside Frontline. I looked to my godfather for answers. "What's going on?"

He shook his head. "It's a sad sad day. Things like this just don't happen in our small town."

"Things like what?" I said ready to hear the juicy details.

"Suicide."

"What? Suicide? Where?" I asked and then followed the direction of his nod to the clothing store beside my restaurant. "Who? Alphonso?" I asked although I was suddenly afraid of where this conversation was going.

"Yes. The owner," he said and drew another breath. "They found him hung in his office."

"Alphonso?" I know I kept asking the same thing, but I guess if I kept asking eventually he'll say someone else's name.

"Yes, Alphonso Rucker."

I couldn't respond because my mouth was hanging opening. Alphonso was dead. I couldn't believe it. Just yesterday, I had cussed him out for stealing my parking space out back.

As Uncle Todd explained how a sales clerk found him swinging from the ceiling in his office, I stood there trying to wrap my mind around the fact that Alphonso was dead. It just felt unreal yet I couldn't tear myself away from the scene that had unfolded out front. The police were trying to get the crowd back out of the way, then seconds later I watched in shock as they wheeled his body out of the store in a black bag. I felt myself stumble and luckily someone was there to catch me.

"Whoa, you okay?"

I swung around to find Frankie's hand at my waist. "No, I'm not," I mumbled still in a daze.

"Here, why don't I help you inside," he suggested and I nodded. Sweeping the area, I spotted Uncle Todd talking to one of the officers. I would call him later.

Frankie helped me inside the restaurant and I ignored the curious stares. It was so unreal. Visions of Alphonso hanging from the ceiling danced before my eyes. I don't even remember walking to my office or Frankie helping me into my seat.

"You okay?" he asked again as he leaned against the edge of my desk.

I couldn't get the image out of my head of the medical examiner's office wheeling him out of the shop. "The guy next door committed suicide."

"Damn. No shit?"

Frankie listened as I told him what I knew which wasn't much.

"Are you going to be okay?" he finally asked.

I flinched slightly then reached for a bottle of water I had next to my desktop and took a long swallow. I would have preferred something stronger but it would have to do for now. "I'm fine. Really. It's just a shock to hear that someone I know killed himself."

"I can understand that." He then reached for my hand. "C'mere.'

He pulled me up from the chair and I fell into his open arms and closed my eyes. It felt so good being able to lean on someone.

"I care so much about you," he whispered against my ear. "I don't know what I would do if anything ever happened to you."

I pulled back stunned and gazed into his eyes. "Do you really mean that?" I asked.

He shook his head. "Ain't you figured it out yet? I love you, Jae. I always have." He gave a wicked smile, confirming what he said was true.

I tilted my head and met his lips in a kiss that was so hot I felt the flaming heat all the way down to my toes. When he finally released me I felt better. For a moment, I almost forgot about the suicide.

"What are you doing here?" I asked.

"You've been avoiding my calls, so I thought I'd come down here and claim what's mine."

"Oh really?" I laughed but when Frankie didn't join in I realized he was dead serious. "I've been doing a lot of soul searching about my life, my father's death, my ex-fiancé." I noticed the way his eyes lit up at the word ex. "And I just need time to sort through some things."

Frankie nodded. "I understand, but know this. I got your back, boo."

"Thanks," I said then glanced down at my wrist. "I gotta get in the kitchen. We're short staff this evening and I need to help out."

"Then let's go," he replied and swatted me on the ass. "Give me an apron because I'm here to help."

"Can you make cornbread?" I teased.

"Gurrrl, my cornbread's so good, it'll make you hurt your Mama. I've got a secret recipe I picked up from a sweet old lady years ago."

"Uh-huh. Her name wouldn't be Granby by chance?"

Frankie winked, then took my hand and led me to the kitchen.

<u>47</u>

NYREE

"Congratulations Mrs. Samuels, in about six and a half more months you're going to be a new mommy!"

I looked at my nurse, too stunned to respond. Was she serious?

Apparently she was, because she wrote out a script for prenatal vitamins, then told me to make an appointment to see an obstetrician after the Christmas holiday. I was in a daze as I left the clinic and moved out to my car. Once inside, I just sat there staring out the windshield.

I'm going to have a baby.

I was speechless. Lately I had been under the weather and thought maybe I had caught a cold. Sure, I've missed a few periods, but I thought it was because of the stress of the past few months; but never had I suspected I was pregnant. Maybe it was because I had been preoccupied. Jeremy and I had moved into my house and spent Thanksgiving with our children. All six of them.

I placed a protective hand to my stomach and then took a long shaky breathe. This would be my first child... our first child together and I was so excited. That is... before I remembered something that made me flinch.

Quickly, I pulled my calendar out of my purse and tried to calculate about when conception may have been.

Before my wedding day.

I picked up my phone and dialed a number. It was answered on the second ring.

"Janelle..., I think I'm pregnant with Timmy's baby."

<u>48</u>

JANELLE

I left my office and stared at the space that used to be Alphonso's store, and felt my heart flutter. As much as I hated the way things went down, the place now belonged to me. In the weeks following Alphonso's suspicious suicide, I discovered he had only been leasing the space. *All that tripping for nothing.*

I quickly contacted the property manager, negotiated a price and took out a loan. In the coming weeks the demolition would begin for my expanded restaurant. I was so excited.

I climbed into my car and headed over anxious to see the man who had made all this possible for me. It's amazing that in the midst of sadness and chaos you can sometimes find joy and maybe even your purpose in life.

Yep, I had finally found mine.

Mommy and I were back speaking and closer than ever. She was giving the house to Brice which I thought was a good thing. It appeared she really was planning on moving in with Uncle Todd. She mentioned the two might get married later but not right now and that was okay. All that mattered was that she was happy. Uncle Todd and I were rebuilding our relationship. I told him about me wanting to buy Alphonso's space. That's when he mentioned the police suspected foul play. Personally that scenario made more sense. The Alphonso I had known loved himself far too much to commit suicide. It would be interesting to see how all that played out. Some people even suspected it was drug-related. Others said a girlfriend scorned. Only time would tell... or maybe we'd never know.

As I drove down Broadway, I cranked up the music while I listened to Pharrell's *Happy*. Yes, Lawd! In the last few weeks I had found my own happiness with one man. The decision wasn't easy, but I had to remind myself I was living for the moment and what felt right.

As soon as I reached his place, I climbed out my car, and there he was, waiting for me.

"What took you so long?" he teased with a wide grin.

"Sorry, but I brought wine," I purred in my defense then held up the bottle as I leaned down for his kiss.

"C'mon, the movie's already started," he said, and together we walked inside.

Other books you might also like by Sasha Campbell:
Confessions
Suspicions
Scandals
Consequences

Other books you might also like by Angie Daniels:
In the Company of My Sistahs
Trouble Loves Company
Careful of the Company You Keep

ABOUT THE AUTHORS

Angie Daniels is a free spirit who isn't afraid to say what's on her mind or even better, write about it. Since strutting onto the literary scene in five-inch heels, she's been capturing her audience's attention with her wild imagination and style for keeping it real. This vivacious woman knows exactly what her readers want and is always ready to deliver. The award winning author has written over twenty-five novels for imprints such as BET Arabesque, Harlequin/ Kimani Romance and Kensington/ Dafina Books. For more information about upcoming releases, and to connect with Angie on facebook, please visit her at www.angiedaniels.com.

Sasha Campbell is the author ego of author Angie Daniels. Visit her at www.sasha-campbell.com.

CPSIA information can be obtained
at www.ICGtesting.com
Printed in the USA
LVOW07s1606231116
514274LV00001B/108/P